D1063982

HALF LIFE

G. P. Putnam's Sons
New York

Published by G. P. Putnam's Sons
200 Madison Avenue, New York, NY 10016.
Published simultaneously in Canada by
General Publishing Co. Limited, Toronto

The text of this book is set in 11 point Janson.

Library of Congress Cataloging in Publication Data

Scherer, Priscilla, date.
Half life.

I. Title.
PS3569.C4843H34 1985 813'.54 84-24790
ISBN 0-399-12994-4

Printed in the United States of America
1 2 3 4 5 6 7 8 9 10

For Alma and Herman Scherer, with love

HALF LIFE

Lydia shoved her glasses up on the bridge of her nose. She leaned close to the old woman's ear, "Irma!" she screamed. "Irma Heller!" not an inch from her ear. But Irma slept.

Lydia yelled, "Irma!" and shook the woman too, and then watched for some sign of waking, a spare flutter of eyelash, but there was no response. Lydia checked off the box labeled EYE OPENING—NONE, barely glancing at the form she marked on.

She tickled the woman's nostril with the cotton tip of an applicator. She poked higher, she jabbed, but nothing. The respirator wheezed air in and out of Irma's lungs, lifting, sinking, lifting. Lydia pressed the side of a pen into the woman's thumbnail. Not much. A flicker of movement, not positive, not negative, but something. She took the opposite thumb and pressed into it. A slight drawing away, inconclusive. She did it again with greater attention. A slight drawing away again. Not exactly voluntary but not exactly primitive. Lydia pushed up her glasses and immediately felt them slipping down. Now the feet.

The feet drew back to her bothering. A small scratch on the sole, back and back and back. The same, one time to the next, both feet, back as if leaping away from glass or a bee sting. Reflex. Nothing thoughtful about it, just reflex. Monkeys and small infants did the same. Cats too. She pulled out her reflex hammer, thumped on knees, ankles, elbows, and Irma slept on.

When she examined the comatose patients, Lydia felt like a robot programed to inflict pain and general discomfort, without compassion or bias, as mindless as her patients. There had been a time when she flinched watching the doctors dig their magical fingers into eye sockets and chest bones, but now she did the digging herself, unflinching, no magic about it. Younger nurses looked at her the way she used to look at doctors, like she was the Big Meanie. It's stimulation I'm giving them, she said sometimes to the sweet new nurses, discomfort, not pain, not really, the patient's not aware, she explained. "It's like turning an ignition key. Sometimes it catches, sometimes not, but there's always that mechanical whirr, at least until the battery's dead. You see what I mean?" Although she wasn't completely convinced herself.

"Unclassifiable movement of both upper extremities, reflex flexion of both lower extremities, bilateral Babinskis." She checked off the last boxes on the examination form and wrote "thirty-six-hour exam" across the top of the sheet.

Once she had been awestruck, a long time ago, by the jargon that was hers now: reflex posturing, primitive response, decorticate, bilateral Babinskis, she now said them all with a straight face. Once she had hardly been able to use any of the lingo without long hesitations to get it straight in her own mind, to be sure she was saying it exactly right. Once, the most coherent phrase she could come up with was "I hate neurology," right after she came to New York, when they first assigned her there.

She had been new then, a sweet new nurse like her charges now, believing most of all in tenderness and compassion, believing in her calling. They had used that word, "sweet," back when "girl" was only just beginning to sound patronizing. "Such a sweet girl," Lydia had overheard one supervisor telling another. She thought it was probably the Southern manner she had brought with her, which had more to do with regional style than with personality or disposition.

"I hate neurology," she repeated softly, meaning every word. "Not to be disrespectful or anything, I hope you won't take offense, but I have always felt uncomfortable with neurology. I honestly hate it. Truly." She thought they would respect her honesty.

"Try it out." The supervisor smiled gently, benignly. Hadn't she heard Lydia say "hate"? "There's an intensive care unit on neuro," Mrs. Rogers continued. "Best in the country." She was a black woman with short gray hair and a cute Anglo-Saxon nose. She still starched her uniforms, she still wore her cap. "Neurology and neurosurgery, you get both together. It can be very exciting, believe me." Her speech was careful with hard consonants, correct and practiced. Lydia had never heard a black person sound so Episcopalian, no jive. They never talked like that in Tennessee.

"I don't know anything about neuro, Mrs. Rogers. Not hardly anything. I know strokes and train wrecks, but nothing subtle at all." She knew there could be perfectly normal-looking people with bad backs, or with headaches or seizures, or even with nothing wrong except clogged-up arteries waiting to be reamed out. But it was too chancy. Things changed in a minute and mostly for the worse. "I'd feel very out of place there. Very inadequate." Perfectly normal-looking people with time bombs ticking off in their heads, hear the timers tick? She had hated neuro.

Lydia glanced over the exam form, filling in blood pressure and pulse readings, temperature, respirations, with five minutes to spare before admissions conference at seven-fifteen a.m.

"Be back soon," she called to Diana, the night nurse.

Diana hunched behind a stack of charts on the desk, writing her night-shift notes. "Not soon enough!" she called back, without interrupting herself.

Lydia took the long way, stopping in the medicine room for some coffee to take with her, then down the hall, around two supply carts and the emergency EKG machine, the defibrillator, a stretcher scale, past wheelchairs and IV poles and a few patients roused early for breakfast and set out in the corridor. Next to the linen cart and facing the solarium, old Max Fish hung to the left over his tray table, snoring. Lydia patted down one of his cowlicks. He acknowledged her with a sharp, stuttering snort.

Just short of the solarium, Lydia made a right turn, leaving East Wing and the Good Samaritan Hospital proper, and entering North Wing, the medical college, cooler and more subdued than the hospital, quiet, organized. She walked the empty hall to the conference room, holding her coffee cup up and out, away from her, and humming a waltz which, according to her mother, would keep your hands steady when you were carrying something spillable. She reached the far end of the hall and opened the door.

The conference room was a square around a large circular table. There was a set seating arrangement for the important participants. Harry Bristol, Chairman of Neurology and Neurosurgeon-in-Chief, had a place with a view of the door so he could watch latecomers slink in. Directly across from him sat two chief residents, neurologist and neurosurgeon, Christine Burke and Casper Culpepper this year, ready to present cases, X rays, scans, life stories, the secrets of each person admitted to the ward.

Between Chief and chief residents was room to seat six, three on each side, fanning out from Dr. Bristol, assorted professors of neurology on the left hand, neurosurgery on the right. Lining the walls in straight-backed chairs were the junior residents, fellows and Lydia.

She scanned the early-morning faces, some of them still puff-eyed from sleep. It was July, the beginning of the medical year, so the residents and interns were all new to what they were doing. Men and women in their late twenties, some with families of their own, reduced to freshman year, ears sticking out from hair cut too short, necks scrubbed raw. A universal warning—Lydia had heard it in East Ridge, Tennessee, way back when, and yearly in New York—was don't get sick in July unless you have a death wish, a warning spoken with a wry smile and maybe a laugh, but it was true. All of them, from the most junior through to the chief residents and fellows, had never before done exactly what they were about to do. The junior residents, especially, laughed too quickly, with a smile lingering even through a reprimand, they were that eager to be agreeable, to fit in.

Lydia took her usual spot, behind the place where Dr. Bristol would sit when he came in. She felt invisible back there, but also she faced the one window in the room, so she could escape if she wanted, by peeping into apartments across the street.

She attended these meetings as a liaison between doctors and nurses, to encourage continuity, they said, and communication, for better patient care, they said, so she was not expected to participate. One time she offered something, and a silence followed, as if she had made a great social gaffe, like speaking to the Queen before being spoken to. Bristol didn't even turn around, he sat stock-still in front of her, with his neck hairs bristling. That was her lesson. She wasn't there to contribute, she was simply meant to take information and complaints back to the ward.

Sometimes Dr. Bristol used up the entire forty-five minutes musing on the various social and political issues of the day. And the whole room sat rapt, all heads nodding in his direction, small smiles up and down nodding, everyone agreeing with the Chief at that moment.

Sometimes they spent many minutes playing a sort of "Can You Top This?": a case was presented, and then each professor in turn would reminisce about one of his own cases with a slight variation, which made the diagnosis or treatment exceptionally difficult. The females didn't really compete like the males, who took every opportunity, a natural extension of locker-room camaraderie—"Mine's bigger," "No mine," "Yeah, but look at mine now."

Now everyone but Bristol was in place. They all drank coffee and chatted. Christine posted a series of brain scans on the view box. Casper dug wax out of his right ear.

"Hey, C.C.," someone yelled, one of the second-year guys. "You took Jackson back to the O.R. last night?"

"Had to," Casper answered. "Clot reaccumulated. Had to suck that bugger out of there." He studied his fingernails, pushed the cuticles back one by one. "He's okay now, back to baseline."

"Moves all fours?"

"As of six-fifty-five, he did."

"Awake?"

"As awake as you were twenty minutes ago."

Regular banter, back and forth, mixed with slurps of coffee, the running hostility between neurology and neurosurgery, like sibling rivalry. Who was better, who was smarter, who cured more, who killed more.

Lydia watched the first-year residents getting ready, sitting forward, clean-shaven anticipation on their faces, waiting to jump into the game, as into double-dutch jump rope, waiting their turn. She wanted to warn them not to get too excited, not to get carried away, warn them not to be fooled or else the letdown would be so great later on.

Bristol arrived, and all activity in the room stopped cold. He walked in, checking his watch, making excuses. "What time do you have?" he asked, and sat down as everyone else compared minute hands. He leaned on his forearms, propping himself on the conference table. He smiled at the silence.

Harry Bristol had a thick nose and pale, see-through eyes. Waves of white-blond hair and a close-cropped beard drew some attention away from his ugliness. But intelligence shot out from him, and confidence, and an aura of electric power. When she first saw him, Lydia was reminded of one of the Judges from her old *Old Testament in Pictures*. Not a Prophet, but a Judge.

"We're late," he said. "You'd better begin."

"Sophie Glass," Christine recited, "is an eighty-three-year-old white female admitted emergently for fever and dehydration. I think some of us know Mrs. Glass."

Sophie Glass, the white tornado. Who could forget her. She

stood well under five feet tall, with poofs of creamy curls to add height. She wore heavy mukluks regardless of the temperature, and padded through the ward looking to houseclean, to cook dinner, to stick her nose into somebody's business.

It had all started with a stroke on her eightieth birthday. In the years before that, Sophie had probably suffered five or six strokes. Not so anybody noticed, least of all Sophie, just little inconvenient ones that laid her up for a week with a clumsy hand or a numbish foot. Nothing paralyzing or anything like that. She probably even had a few she didn't know about, thought they were a virus. But the one on her birthday tipped the balance. Her CAT scan was shot full of holes, little holes of dead brain, shrunken brain, and the topmost cut resembled a walnut, the folds and creases were so pronounced.

They labeled her "multi-infarct dementia, compounded by cortical atrophy not inconsistent with the patient's age."

Not a bad life, multi-infarct dementia. It drove everyone around her crazy, but Sophie herself was quite content. She kept busy advising contestants on *Family Feud* and advising a succession of roommates, whether they liked it or not. Between conversations, Sophie fidgeted and she ate.

"Fever and dehydration!" Bristol snapped. "I do know the woman. You only recently sent her home, am I right?"

"Yes sir, last week."

"Well?"

"She's had the fever since discharge, according to her daughter. And she won't eat, which is unusual for Mrs. Glass," Christine explained.

"I'm sorry. Fever and dehydration are not commonly noted neurological disorders. Why didn't she go to medicine?" he demanded.

"Yes sir, well, she's ours, we know her. We were afraid of the possibility of meningitis. We thought we might have missed it last admission."

Bristol tapped all ten fingertips on the table. "Go on."

"We initiated a complete fever work-up, including a spinal tap last night—"

"So now she can have a headache, too. Continue."

"Everything within normal limits, sir. We also got a repeat CAT scan, to rule out abscess. She has a history of endocarditis."

Bristol shook his head. "You people have got to learn"—he pulled half-glasses out of his shirt pocket, a handkerchief from his pants pocket, and he massaged the one with the other—"to learn to be less soft-hearted. You're not doing anyone any favors with admissions like this. You think it's kind." He held the lenses up to the light, squinting. "It's not. Suppose a young woman with a real meningitis needed that bed. What would you say? I'm sorry, but an old lady with a urinary-tract infection, the likeliest diagnosis, you know, she took the last available bed, which incidentally we are all paying for, including the girl with meningitis, through Medicare. This old lady took the last bed because we didn't have the guts to turn her away. To send her home to the care of a loving family and a few days of antibiotics and cranberry juice. It is not kind. Someone else might have come to us, needing the bed desperately." He rose and walked to the view box, to scan Sophie's scan. He placed the glasses in front of his eyes and shook his head. He laughed, forced a laugh like "huh, huh, huh," staccato and all smiles, and shook his head some more. Then he began to stroke his beard with his hand, the thumb to one cheek, fingers to the other, massaging in a circular motion with the palm half hiding his mouth.

In a world of experts and specialists, Bristol had become an expert in two specialties, neurology and neurosurgery. No one denied this was quite an achievement. He claimed he was a neurologist by choice, a neurosurgeon only by necessity, for quality assurance.

"When I retire," he was saying, "I'm going to set up a stand on the boardwalk in Atlantic City, huh, huh, huh, and I'm going to guess ages by CAT scans, like those guys who guess your weight, huh, huh, huh. This is an old lady's shrunken brain. That's all." He removed his glasses and returned to his chair. "Nothing to do for it. Send her home with a prescription for Gantrisin, free up a bed. Today. Next patient."

"Florence Worrell," Casper started.

The door opened. A tall, gawky man walked in and looked around for an empty chair, started across to it.

"Florence Worrell is a fifty-six-year-old woman," Casper continued, but Bristol waved him to silence. He was on a roll.

"We start on time here," he said to the stranger, who stopped halfway into his stride.

"Yes sir. I got lost finding the room."

"Seven-fifteen. I expect you to be here. No one comes late. I hope I won't have to start locking the door." He waited and watched while the man slid himself awkwardly into a chair under the window. "Sorry for the interruption, Dr. Culpepper. Next patient."

"Florence Worrell, a fifty-six-year-old woman with—"

"Try to speed things up, Culpepper."

"Brain tumor discovered following a seizure. Probably glioma, nondominant hemisphere, not good but operable." Casper spoke confidently, rapidly, precisely—"not good but operable"—to make H.B. proud of him.

A window went up across the street and a fat woman leaned out into the warm morning. She looked down at the sidewalk, then yelled something and waved, and Lydia wondered who she was waving to. She guessed it was the woman's husband, or maybe her child.

Casper was pointing to a new brain on the view box, the younger, fifty-six-year-old brain, with some mottling in the right half of the second cut, close to the surface, infiltrating down.

They all got up to study the X ray, all the senior men and then all the residents, craning their necks forward and frowning. Lydia stayed put, as did the stranger. She smiled at him once but he glanced away quickly, keeping his expression steady, inoffensive, neutral. He folded his arms in front of him, wristbones poking out from his sleeves. He crossed his legs, uncrossed them and recrossed them like an adolescent not yet comfortable with his growing limbs. He even cracked his knuckles once, waiting for the others to return to their seats. He folded his hands and worked each knobby knuckle until one finally gave a louder crack, and he looked around to see who heard it. Finally he smiled at Lydia.

"Who's operating?" Bristol asked.

"I am, sir," Casper said. "She's on the O.R. schedule for tomorrow."

"Good. Who's next?"

Christine's turn. "John McNulty, forty-nine-year-old male with sudden onset right hand and arm weakness. Resolved over five minutes, recurred one hour later and again in our emergency room, lasted half an hour this time and included some slight word-finding difficulty, mild dysnomia."

"Risk factors?"

"No prior medical history. Blood pressure in the E.R. was one-eighty over a hundred, though, and has leveled off to one-sixty over ninety-five with diuresis. Family history of stroke, and he's a smoker."

"Plan?"

"We started him on heparin anticoagulation last night, in view of the recurrence of symptoms. He's been stable since then. No deficits, CAT scan is negative." She pointed to the last of the three X rays. "He's scheduled for an echo and a twenty-four-hour tape. If his heart checks out, we'll probably have a look at his neck vessels, see if the problem is there. Long-term treatment depends on what we come up with. If his arteries look bad enough he may be a candidate for surgery, if we decide to consider surgery."

Bristol stroked his beard. "You hesitate, Dr. Burke?"

She smiled at him, a good-natured smile, all gums and square teeth.

"You don't believe in endarterectomy?" he asked.

"Well, I'm just not so sure it works. Or that the benefits are worth the risks. Has anyone got any consistent data? What's the consensus here on endarterectomy? No one seems to agree."

Bristol looked from one face to the next around his table. "Mitchell? Opinion?"

Mike Mitchell shrugged. He was already dressed in his greens and clearly impatient to get to surgery and do some real work. "The consensus is there is no consensus. Depends on whose series you look at. Our experience at the Samaritan is good, as you know, sir. We have a high success rate."

"Success rate, meaning what?" Christine asked.

"Meaning we clean out the artery and the symptoms stop. No new symptoms for up to ten years."

"Complications?"

"Practically no one strokes out intra- or postoperatively, if that's what you mean, practically no one reoccludes his vessel. Only four deaths out of almost two hundred in three years."

"That's what I mean," Christine persisted. "A two-percent death rate is too high, for me."

"They weren't all related to the brain or the artery, though," Casper answered. "A couple or so had myocardial infarcts, I think, and one had a pulmonary embolus. It wasn't the procedure, per se. Just bad protoplasm on the part of the patient."

"In my experience," one of the older professors began, ". . . very useful in cases of . . ." Senior attending, hardly ever did surgery anymore. "But I do recall one particular patient . . ." And the massaging began, the bellowing.

They tossed the question back and forth across the table, each in turn adding clauses and modifiers, retrieving it when possible, endless volleys taking up time, bouncing high across the room.

The fat woman across the street leaned out of her window again, looked up and down the block and fanned herself, a whole day ahead of her to make into what she wanted. Lydia envied her that. She could do nothing or anything. She could shop or clean house or read a book if she wanted to, she could entertain strange men for large sums of money, or she could watch television and pretend to be a nurse saving lives at General Hospital.

"Dr. Wheeler," Bristol was saying. "We haven't heard from you yet."

The new man, the stranger, unfolded his arms and uncrossed his legs. He coughed.

"What's your feeling about the question? And the European position? You've been over there recently, what treatment do they prefer?"

Dr. Wheeler took a moment before speaking. "There is as much disagreement in Europe as here." He wasn't European, he had no accent, except maybe East Coast. "But they tend to treat more conditions medically instead of surgically. For instance, antithrombotic agents are popular, with direct injection into the artery, streptokinase, a few other synthetic compounds, also laser therapy, more so than actual surgery."

"Can you compare the medical to the surgical experience?"

"Same as here. Any treatment depends on who does it, where it's done, who it's done on, who you talk to. There's no consensus there, either."

"Well, that's a relief," Bristol said, without a trace of sarcasm. "Thank you, Sam. Before everyone leaves, let me introduce Dr. Wheeler, the newest member of our faculty." He stretched his left arm out, opened his hand in welcome. "I knew Sam when he was a tabula rasa in medical school. Since his residency at Columbia he's been around the world studying brain chemistry, electrophysiology and coma. I'm sure you know his papers." The arm came back to his side. He pushed himself to a standing position, a signal. The rest of the room stirred, and Casper scraped his chair back from the table. "He'll be the junior coma expert here. Together," Bristol droned, "we plan to do some significant work in that area." More scrapings of chairs and mumblings.

"Class dismissed," Mitchell said under his breath.

Christine pulled X rays from the view box while the others filed out. Dr. Bristol waited for Dr. Wheeler to greet him.

Lydia started off down the hall alone, walking quickly. This conference always made her late. The leisurely discussions of lives and deaths, academic speculations on worthiness and suitability, were isolated from the real world of mucus and blood, falling pulses, rising blood pressures. They could talk all they wanted, Lydia was late.

"Hey, Legs! Wait up!"

Mitch would set her way behind if she stopped. She didn't.

"Legs!"

He caught up with her, he and Casper, one on each side. "Welcome to the Good Samaritan Hospital," Mitch mimicked. "Together—take note: I said together—we plan to do significant work in that area. Read: you do the work, I get the prize. Another lamb to the slaughter."

"Don't hold me up," she said. "I'm late. Regina'll kill me." Sometimes when she walked between Mitch and Casper, Lydia felt protected. Today she felt dwarfed. "Anyway, you'll ruin my reputation. Surgeons aren't nearly intellectual enough."

Casper snorted and smiled.

"So what did you think of the new man, Legs?" Mitch asked.

"I think you're jealous."

"First of all, I'm not. I'm glad to be out of the spotlight for a while."

"Why don't I believe you?"

"Besides, the pendulum swings back and forth. It'll swing back to surgery again."

"H.B. loves surgery," Casper offered. "In his heart of hearts, he does." He went for his nose with his left pinky.

C.C., she almost said, have you ever considered the aesthetics of a surgeon with boogers under his nails? Almost, but not quite. Sometime she would.

"Now I can do more of my own surgery," Mitch continued, "without him interfering so much."

"Bull." She opened the door to the 4 East corridor. The two men walked in ahead of her. "You loved his attention. You all love it."

"For a while, yes, I did, I admit," Mitch said. "But, Lydia, precious Lydia, a guy gets tired of being controlled. Of working his balls off for the greater glory of Harry Bristol."

Max Fish struggled with a soft-boiled egg and his pepper. He was shaking the sealed thimble for all he was worth but without reward. Lydia stripped off the cover, sprinkled pepper onto the egg and handed it back to him. She saw the day staff already assembled in the solarium, waiting for the night crew to come down. Diana sauntered out of intensive care, all hips and frowns. She stopped at the nurses' station to pick up Carole, the other night nurse. Lydia leaned against the wall and let the two men surround her.

"I still don't believe you, Mitch."

Mitchell took a fat cigar from his lab-coat pocket. "You're too smart for me, Legs." He peeled off the wrapping, rolled the end of the cigar against his tongue. "How about a movie Friday?"

"Uh-uh, but thanks for trying."

"I've been trying for years, literally years, C.C." His mouth made an O around the cigar. He clamped his teeth on it and grinned. "She keeps rejecting me."

"It's not years, and anyway, you'd be scared stiff if I said yes. I told you a long time ago, quit medicine and then I'll think about it."

Casper snorted.

"Lydia!" Regina's voice cut through from the solarium. "We're ready for report!"

Diana and Carole trailed down the hall toward her.

"Coming," Lydia answered.

As Lydia reached the solarium, Regina got up and scurried out past her. Regina never just plain walked, and she never ran. She strutted or scurried or plodded or schlepped or sometimes she ambled, all performance, Lydia thought, for effect, body language. Regina Baker, head nurse, was always so busy.

"Forgot something," she said. "Two seconds, don't start without me."

Lydia headed for the sofa. She sat down, the rattan crackled, adjusting itself to her weight. The solarium had faded over time, parts of it bleached by the sun, but it remained as incongruous as she had found it eight years before, on her first day at the Samaritan.

"Wait'll you see the solarium," Mrs. Rogers had said. "One of the glamour spots of the entire institution. It was just redecorated, as a gift from a patient. His lover's a window designer for Macy's, and he did the whole room over."

They stepped into a tropical fantasy: rattan garden furniture, matchstick window shades, bamboo coffee tables, huge shopping-mall trees. The carpet was a deep burnt orange, the walls a pale peach, and everything else ranged from apricot to kumquat to tangerine to pink grapefruit.

"Nice, right?" Mrs. Rogers asked. "You almost forget you're in a hospital."

"I don't think so." Lydia eyed the patients clustered off to the right. You couldn't just gloss over sickness and dying. Trying only made it worse. And the contrast between the *Hawaii Five-O* set and those devastated patients came up ghastly. "This rug washable?" Stupid question, make talk. She had noticed a brown stain and several small splotches near the door, that's all.

"Ummm. Oh, I'm sure it must be. Of course it is. Good question, though. I'm sure it must be washable. It would have to be, right?" She winked.

It was a late August afternoon. Most of the patients had been set in a grouping around the one air conditioner that rattled and dripped in the corner. Lydia kept telling herself that it would be better if she knew the patients, knew them personally, but they were awful that first time, all plumped and fluffed and balanced out with pillows stuffed into their armpits and underneath legs and shoulders as if to disguise the one-sidedness.

One guy stared pop-eyed straight ahead and unchanging, gradually slumping forward and to the right. He was ageless, head shaved and a neutral stubble growing back evenly, except not along the surgery scar above his left ear. An older man, similarly propped but distinguished, leonine, jumped through a range of emotions for no apparent reason. He chuckled then cried tears then swung a left hook at the air, pounded his specially extendable armrest, ripped at it, stopped, mused, chuckled, wept and swung, enraged again.

A young black woman sat primly upright in her wheelchair. She smiled at Lydia, met her eyes with alert intelligence, and with understanding. She had some wasting disease, maybe multiple sclerosis. Her shriveled, shapeless calves betrayed her and imprisoned her in the group. Her apologetic smile embarrassed Lydia. Near the window, a middle-aged lady with bluish-gray hair and foam-rubber hospital scuffies watered the trees, cutting long farts behind her.

The trees had been replaced a number of times since Lydia had come. Nothing grew very well back there. No time to work with plants, to nurture them. So the leaves fell off, which caused housekeeping to complain constantly, the branches browned and shrank and every so often somebody donated new trees. This year it was rubber trees and one ficus.

The rattan sofas had faded, the cushions worn nearly to gray by thousands of imprinted bottoms, and now Lydia was sitting on one of them, next to a new orientee. Opposite, on the other sofa, three junior staff nurses held pads of paper and pens. Two of them lit cigarettes. The night nurses lounged in bent bamboo easy chairs at the head of the coffee table. From there they could look straight down the hall, directly through the 4 East corridor, right to the automatic doors to the intensive care unit. If anything untoward happened, they could see it right away.

Change of shift was a precarious time, unsettled. Most of the nurses were in report, but the nurses' aides were out there, filling up water pitchers and answering lights, and one nurse covered in intensive care. Usually that was plenty. Except that half the patients got the urge to pee just then, and a lot of them, if they didn't go bad at three a.m., waited until change of shift. Most of the time this wasn't intentional, it simply worked out that way.

Sometimes there were patients who went bad intentionally. They studied the patterns, the timing. They knew most of the staff was tied up for half an hour at eight in the morning, four in the afternoon, and midnight. They knew. And if a patient was the slightest bit off, that's when he would hang himself, or jump out the window. Right during change of shift.

Diana was filing her nails. "Anything good in conference, Lydia?" She was a large black woman, with bright red Cupid's-bow lips that could change from pleased to disgusted with one twitch of her lower lip. She pulled a heavy beige sweater around her bulky body, even though it was already eighty degrees at eight a.m. The night-shift chills, she said. Everybody felt cold after working all night. That was a fact. "They say anything?"

"The usual," Lydia answered. "Nothing monumental. H.B. has a new coma expert. Dr. Wheeler."

The orientee looked up, and the three junior staff nurses stopped talking.

"Don't get excited, now," she said. "He's at least forty, I think, and probably married."

"Gonna shed some new light on dying, right?" Diana sniffed. "Anything else?"

"Not really. Neurosurgery is in favor of operating, neurology is against. That's about it." And they all laughed, even the new ones got the joke.

Regina returned, holding up a big gum eraser and a pencil, like prizes from the Sunday-school picnic. She closed the glass door so patients wouldn't wander in, then she turned on the air conditioner and squeezed between Lydia and the new nurse. "Suffocating," she said. "Let's get started."

Diana tugged her sweater tighter and looked at Regina sideways, as she might regard a rotten head of cauliflower. She heaved a sigh. "Mr. Maurice Jackson is a fifty-year-old patient of Dr. Kennedy's, in with a subdural hematoma, evacuated yesterday."

Lydia jotted everything down, blood pressure, pulse rate and rhythm, temperature, Tylenol dose, respirations, and oxygen concentration. "IV rate?" she asked, and wrote that down too, out of interest, out of habit, to keep from dozing off. The newest nurse wrote furiously at her end of the couch, shaking Regina and Lydia both with her effort.

". . . Stable until about three," Diana continued. "Then I'm over there getting his output and for some reason I decided to check his pupils again. Maybe I didn't like the sound of his breathing. He had blown his right pupil and I couldn't get him awake. We called the intern, gave Mannitol and Decadron, hyperventilated him, and sent him back to the O.R. for another evacuation." She stopped. "That intern took forever to come. I almost went and did everything myself, without an order, it took him so long. We could have lost the man, waiting for that intern."

"I know, I know," Regina said. "But what can you do?" She had been erasing the patient-care cards, updating them. She brushed eraser bits onto the floor. "Give me his name. I'll report him to Chris Burke."

"What earthly good's that?" Diana said. "It's not just him, it happens all the time. Sometimes they're busy out on the floor, sometimes they can't come right away, sometimes they slow up 'cause they don't know what to do. It's July."

Regina dropped the eraser onto her lap. She looked up empty-handed at the night nurse. "So what are you telling me? You can't give those drugs without a doctor's order. It's policy." If nothing else, Regina knew all about policies, procedures, and hospital protocol, not to mention proper channels. She kept her hair precisely at chin length, and above the collar.

"Diana has a point," Lydia said. "Especially nights and evenings."

The other night nurse, Carole, nodded. "In coronary care, the nurses bolus people right and left for arrhythmias. We should be allowed to administer a few emergency meds up here. At least the senior people should. Especially on nights."

The air conditioner hum turned into a buzz, and Lydia watched beads of moisture drip onto the orange rug. The carpet had turned out to be washable but not stainproof. Regina picked up her eraser and started on the next Kardex. Her lips were squeezed shut, and they twitched and twisted as she rubbed out the old words.

"The best I can do," she finally said, "is to get permission for verbal orders. In an emergency. That's the best I can do. It's policy."

"It's ridiculous," Lydia said.

"It's policy."

"Change policy."

"The hospital would never back you up if anything happened. Never."

Diana said, "Oh brother," and Carole shook her head. Regina kept her nose in the Kardex, her mouth working into a snarl. "Please continue report."

"Irma Heller is a . . ."

The door swung open and Jane Clarke came in, tying a red bandanna around her neck. She brought a slight breeze through the door.

"You're late," Regina snapped.

"First Avenue bus, God, it's the pits. Even the Express bus." She fell into a plain upright chair next to a rubber tree. "I think it's the Fifty-ninth Street Bridge traffic."

"Get an earlier bus."

"I'm sorry, okay?" Jane rummaged through her purse until she found a pen and a scrap of paper. "Okay?"

"Irma Heller . . ." Diana repeated, smiling.

Jane used her lap as a desk. She shook her pen, scribbled, licked the tip of the ballpoint and tried again, failed again, sighed. Lydia found an extra pencil and tossed it to Jane, over a few heads. Regina pursed her lips, lowering her head farther into the Kardex.

Lydia had been instantly appalled by Jane when they met, and then, as instantly, Lydia became infatuated with her.

When Mrs. Rogers had told Regina that Lydia had some reservations about neuro, the head nurse had grabbed Lydia's elbow and propelled her up the hall. They stopped at the nurses' station for "two seconds," which turned into ten minutes before Regina was back holding her elbow.

"Did you see Jane at all?" she asked.

"I don't know Jane at all," Lydia answered.

"Oh. Right. Tall blonde. Stockings wrinkled at the ankles? No?" Then she released Lydia and took the lead, peering into room after room until they reached the last one on the left. "Here you are."

Lydia looked past the head nurse and into a tiny space that somehow contained two beds, two lockers, a sink, two patients, and one nurse, feeding syringe in her left hand level with the patient's mouth, rectal thermometer in the right farther down and about to be inserted.

Regina turned clear around and looked into Lydia's face. "Lydia Weber, right?" and then pivoted back to the nurse in the room. "Jane, this is Lydia Weber. Lydia, Jane Clarke. The two of you should have a lot in common, Jane is from North Carolina." Again, she looked at Lydia. "You're from somewhere down there, right? Lydia has lots of questions and I'm very busy so I thought you'd be the perfect person for her." She started out the door. "Your technique is disgusting, Jane."

"Saves time, R.B. You're not the only one who's busy around here, you know. What the hell? I ask you? I'm not touching anything, and I think I can tell which end is which. I won't get them mixed up." She didn't sound Southern.

"It's the idea."

The digital thermometer registered, beeped, all done. Jane pulled the probe out with her gloved hand, read off the numbers, and ejected the probe cover and the glove into the wastebasket. Regina was long gone.

"Hi, Lydia. You from North Carolina?" She talked like Archie Bunker.

"No, and neither are you, right?"

"Nah. I just went to school down there, UNC, so these bozos all say I'm from the South, great joke, right? I'm really from Queens. Astoria. Started here about six months ago."

"I'm from Tennessee. East Ridge?"

"Never heard of it. So you have questions, so shoot."

"Well, I don't actually have any questions. I just don't want to be assigned up here. I hate neuro."

Jane smiled. "Me too." She laughed. "I should say, I did hate it. It grows on you. At least you're honest about it. Lots aren't, and lots hate it."

She was taller than Lydia, and lanky. All arms reaching every which way, and fingers ready to slamdunk, she loped from place to place. And her hair—she should have been a Breck girl, making three times the pay—her hair was golden blond and wavy all the way to her waist, but trained back into a braid that first day Lydia met her. Gorgeous, except for the way she talked.

"I don't really hate it that much. I did, but I don't so much anymore. What can you do anyway, once they've made up their minds? Nothing. You have to get through three months before you can even request a transfer. So relax. That's all you can do."

She poured the last of the beige formula into the syringe, watching it empty into the tube that was threaded through the woman's nose, down her throat and into her stomach. The woman belched.

"Damn. This takes so long." Jane dropped the syringe three inches to slow the feeding down some. "You work before?"

"In Tennessee. About a year and a half. Intensive care." It seemed important to say that, "intensive care." It spoke of experience and pressure and knowledge. Action and thought joined so you couldn't tell which came first.

"Yeah, me too. Out in Queens. Can you get a pressure on this woman? I'll take her pulse." As the last of the feeding dripped in, they finished Jane's work and straightened up the bedside.

"Come on," Jane said. "Let's go chart and then we can get out of here. We'll have a beer someplace, and talk on the outside."

Lydia completely missed the last two patients, for all her daydreaming. Diana was sitting back, relaxed in the easy chair, her arms on her wide stomach. "Questions?"

Lydia reached for the patients' clipboards and scanned them for information. A mess of dots and Xs and lines blinked up at her. She shook her head, cursing herself silently for drifting off. She checked over the graphs and numbers once more and said, "No, no questions."

"Okay, let's move along."

The neurology service combined intensive, subacute and, reluctantly, some chronic care, on one long floor. They had thirty beds, six of them ICU, with the rest for preop, treatment, and early rehabilitation. The nursing staff moved back and forth, week to week, from the ward to intensive care, back to the ward again, because one provided respite from the other. At first Lydia thought it was a terrible idea, now she liked it a lot. Sometimes she loved the emergencies, the action, but sometimes she just wanted to sit down and feed farina to a patient, and talk, and listen.

Carole took over with a report for the ward. She was as skinny as Diana was fat. She kept a quart of Diet Pepsi by her side, chugging it down.

"Sophie Glass is an eighty-three-year-old—"

"Sophie's back?" someone exclaimed.

"And in fine form—eighty-three-year-old patient of Dr. Feldman's in for rule-out meningitis."

"Not meningitis," Lydia interrupted.

"It's what they said, it's written down right here in front of me."

"Urinary tract infection. They said meningitis so they could admit her to neuro. But the scan is negative, the LP is normal. Bristol says a UTI."

"LT?" the new nurse asked.

"LP. Lumbar puncture," Jane explained. "Spinal tap."

Carole humphed. "I wish they would tell us these things about our own patients." She swigged the Diet Pepsi aggressively, like whiskey. "Make a fool of myself."

"Bristol wants her out," Lydia added.

Regina had stopped erasing but was taking her turn writing down details from Carole's report. "Fat chance," she said.

"He wants her discharged today. That's what he said this morning."

"He's never had Sophie's daughter to deal with. Let him talk to her, if he wants Sophie out so much. Mrs. Goldfarb could never handle her by herself now, even if she wanted to." Regina attacked as if it had been Lydia's idea to discharge Sophie. "She can't take her home yet. She needs a few days, she has to make arrangements, get help in. Sophie's a handful now."

"I'm telling you what he said, just reporting back, the way I'm supposed to."

"It won't happen. That's all I'm saying. Sylvia brought her to the hospital because she couldn't handle her at home. How much you want to bet? It'll never happen."

"Fine."

Jane winked at Lydia. Gave her a thumbs-up.

"You have a blood pressure on her, Carole? Do you have anything?" Regina asked.

"A hundred over seventy-two." Carole continued on down the list. Three surgeries, two arteriograms, a myelogram and four discharges.

"John McNulty is a forty-nine-year-old staff patient in with transient ischemic attacks. Right arm went out on him twice, the third time was here. He's back to normal now. On a heparin drip, twenty thousand units in five hundred five-percent dextrose at twenty-five drops a minute, a thousand units an hour."

"Blood pressure?" Regina asked, fixated on blood pressures.

"One-fifty to one-sixty over about ninety. He's on nitropaste and Lasix."

"Pulse?"

"Eighty-two, regular."

"Pupils?"

"Equal and reactive. I was going to tell you, Regina, but you didn't give me time."

"Moving all extremities?"

"Yes, he's back to normal, I said."

"Not necessarily the same thing. Okay, go on. Who's next? We're running behind."

"I want to mention something else about McNulty."

"Yes?"

"He's a big, strong-looking guy. He plays that up."

"So?"

"But I think he's really scared. He kept asking me all about if I ever saw anyone with symptoms like these before and what happened to them and what can you do for them, things like that. He doesn't want surgery. He's really scared of it."

"He said that?"

"No. What he said was, how many people die under anesthesia, could I give him an estimate. How many people turn into vegetables, he asked me. I'd say that means he's afraid of surgery."

Regina nodded. She looked at each of the three junior staff nurses and back over them again. "Who wants to talk to Mr. McNulty? We don't even know if he'll need surgery, but it sounds like he could use someone to sit down with him and talk."

Jane volunteered. "I'll do it."

"You're in the unit with Lydia today," Regina said. She waited twenty seconds. No volunteers.

Jane picked two shriveled leaves off the bottom of the rubber tree trunk. She tore them into bits and poured them out onto the dirt.

"The unit's quiet, I'll have time," she said. "Maybe I can get someone who's been through it to talk to him. Mrs. Hardy, maybe."

"Okay," Regina agreed. "You can come out for a while this afternoon. But nothing mystical, understand? Stick with a few basic facts. And if you have any problems, you'll tell me."

Jane smiled. "Absolutely."

Lydia knew she wouldn't, either have problems or tell Regina. It wasn't part of Jane's nature. Strong opinions and strong language, those were her nature, and action and impulse. These had drawn Lydia to Jane from the beginning. She never had figured out what it was that attracted Jane to her, though.

"You're very grounded," Jane had told her, which Lydia took to be a polite way of saying boring and overly earnest. But Jane enjoyed instructing and guiding, and Lydia needed both just then. She had known right away that first night that New York was a bigger bite than she could chew.

The evening they met, Jane and Lydia worked their way down Second Avenue, stopping at bars, drinking beer and making a meal of free appetizers, like old ladies on fixed incomes. They talked their way through Lydia's family—her father was possibly the most eloquent preacher in east Tennessee—and on to Edgar Cayce, whom Jane considered to be a great prophet and wise man, to feminism and nurses' rights—Jane was militant—to potholes and public transportation. Lydia ate up everything Jane said. Looking back, she pictured herself glowing clean, and hungry, ready to gorge on experience. More than anything, that night she had wanted to be sophisticated and ready with a comeback.

By ten-thirty and still in their uniforms, they were skipping across the graveled rooftop of the Americana Hotel, high over midtown Manhattan, sure they would be locked out by some security guard and not really caring if they were.

Lydia thought she would fall off, there was barely a wall, only knee-high, to keep her from stepping off the edge. She stayed back, nearer the middle. But Jane went clear to the ledge, and shouted messages to the people of New Jersey, Staten Island, Brooklyn, Queens, the Bronx. She hit all four corners, and then shouted to the streets below—nothing messages, traffic reports, weather forecasts, and a short tirade on terror in the subways, and hospital farina.

Jane left the north corner and rejoined Lydia in the middle. "It's a crime, the food they serve there," she said, wheezy after calling out to the masses. "Even in the towers they get watered-down farina. Taste it sometime for yourself."

They sat down cross-legged, facing each other. Jane hitched her skirt up, all knees, and began unbraiding her hair. "The soup is another matter. They make good soups, but that's about it. Place is too big, too many meals, too many requests, you know how it is. They eat better in the towers, they should eat better, they pay for it, right? But still, it's not great. Only the soup. God, my hair is all knots." She tugged into the tangles, using her fingers and a brush to work through all of it.

Lydia watched her easing out the knots. A sliver of new moon hung just above Jane's head. "It looks like a cathedral," Lydia said. "The hospital. With those two towers pointing up to heaven. It put me in mind of a great cathedral when I saw it. The place where I came from is like a factory from the outside. Just a big old yellow brick box with a huge parking lot and little shrubs lining the walls."

A gust of wind caught a piece of Jane's hair and twirled it out of her hands. She grabbed at the stray and smoothed it down with the rest.

"But that neuro ward," Lydia continued. "There's nothing to prepare you for that. How can the outside be so beautiful and the inside so grotesque?" She picked up a piece of gravel from the roof and flung it hard into the wind. "I don't like it there," she said. "I mean, thank you for trying to make me, I don't know, feel at home and all, but I don't like it. It's so depressing, just to look at that ward gets you down, don't you think?"

"Sometimes. Like I said, it grows on you."

Lydia sifted gravel dust through her fingers. She tossed some of the smaller stones straight up or over her shoulder, bounced them in her palm. "I can't stand neuro patients, to be perfectly honest."

"They grow on you, that's all I can say."

Jane tugged at the last of the tangles and then brushed through the waves with long strokes. She threw her hair over her head and came at it backward, then started braiding it again.

"My mother did this twice a day. Only her hair was even longer than mine. Morning and evening. She said you had to work through the knots twice a day or they'd never come out. I used to do it with her. Only missed once, and she was right about the knots."

"She's in Queens?"

"She's dead. Henny's alive, though. My pop, in Queens. But Ma died, oh, almost ten years ago. I was fifteen."

"I'm sorry."

"Nah. It's a long time ago." Her head was still down, with the braid hanging forward. She finished it with a rubber band and flipped it behind her. "There's irony for you. Intracerebral hemorrhage. I had to watch her die in steps. Pop kept telling them, 'Do everything you can.' He didn't know any better, me either. She died by halves. I thought she'd go on forever. God. Like an isotope.

"Pop wouldn't let her go. He didn't know. He thought maybe a miracle. A miracle. I just wanted her to die sooner." She stood and shook out her uniform. "The Fates put me on Four East as penance. My chance to make up for being glad when she died."

"You couldn't help but feel that way. It's hard."

"Oh, yeah, I know. I just hope I never put anyone through that when I die. I just hope I go quick." She reached her arms out and stretched, trembling. "Oh, God. Let's get out of here. Can we change the subject? Let's move on. Let's do something."

"What I want to know is, can she hear us?" The new nurse, Eileen, squinted sincerely and nodded a lot. "Do you think she can hear us?" in a low-pitched voice. She stood on one side of Irma's bed, her fists pressing into the mattress, as she watched Lydia struggle with the ambu bag and the endotracheal tube.

"I have no idea," Lydia said. "Do you think you could bag her a few breaths while I suction?" She handed the ambu over to Eileen, connected the adapter and squeezed the bag once to get her started.

"Reason I ask is that I had a friend in a coma once. She was in a terrible car wreck, everyone else was killed except the driver. Isn't that funny? Do you know why that happens so much, that everyone in the car gets killed and the driver walks away without a scratch. Is there a reason for that?"

"Breathe her, Eileen. She's not breathing unless you do it for her. Bag her." Lydia reached the bag with her free hand and squeezed. "Go on. A couple more." She turned the respirator alarm off, removed the ambu bag, squirted saline down the ET tube and replaced the bag over it. She squeezed it once to get Eileen started again. "It's the steering wheel, I imagine. It protects the driver more. Give her another breath and I'll suction."

"So anyway, this friend of mine was in a coma and sometimes, when a few of us were there with her, sometimes we'd get to talking about the accident."

"Hook the bag back onto the tube, then squeeze. Three times. Good. When we're suctioning, we suck out oxygen along with the secretions, so she needs a little more of it than usual. Again."

Eileen squeezed, and she squeezed again, the squint took over her face for a time. "So anyway, we'd talk about the wreck and about the people in it and about Bill coming away without a scratch and then one day I said, 'Wait a minute, I don't think we should be talking like this in front of Debbie,' that was my friend's name. I said, 'What if she can hear us?' That's why I was asking about it. Don't you think I was right?"

Lydia sucked gray mucus out of the patient's lungs. She turned the respirator oxygen up to a hundred percent and gave her a few sighs, and then turned it back to the original setting. She stopped to look at Irma. Can she hear? Lydia wondered. The MA1 respirator delivered deep, heaving breaths, like sleep breathing. Her eyelids were closed, as in sleep. Was it sleep or was it death?

She flipped the pillow over, fixed a fresh linen-saver under Irma's head to catch the saliva that would inevitably drip from her mouth, wiped sweat beads from the patient's forehead. "On some level, I think they can hear."

"Do you?" Eileen's eyebrows narrowed earnestly. She nodded. "Debbie finally died, so we never found out."

"Don't forget, I said on some level. Which level, I don't know. And you probably couldn't find any doctors around here who'd agree with me. There's no evidence or anything."

"But that's what you think."

"Maybe only me. Let's get her vital signs, and get her turned, and then we can go over procedures." Lydia handed the thermometer to Eileen and took the stethoscope from around her own neck. She pumped up the cuff. Through the window, in the periphery of Lydia's vision, a helicopter hovered over traffic on the FDR Drive.

The intensive care unit sat in the eastern tip of East Wing, one more step and you would drop into the river. It was directly opposite the solarium at the other end of the hall. Cool, functional and overbright in daylight, its concerns were with immediate matters of life and death—action, not talk. Looking straight out from the automatic doors, through the cluttered hallway, past the nurses' station, the medicine room and on down, you could see the white trash bins standing sentry outside the solarium, and on into the peachy warm space. Sometimes you could see grieving family members, waiting their turn to come into the unit.

Inside intensive care, large-paned picture windows dominated the three outside walls. They could be opened only from way up on top, and then only ten inches, so nobody could jump out. That had actually happened some years ago, and once it had been a nurse who jumped.

In the wall space between windows and on countertops around the entire perimeter of the room were evidences of modern medical technology. Monitors for the heart, blood pressure, pulmonary pressure and intracranial pressure stacked up one on top of the other by each bedside, in addition to two oxygen outlets, suction, an ophthalmoscope, otoscope, manual blood pressure manometers, five light switches, seven or eight electrical outlets, including two for emergency backup in case of a blackout, and a color TV hookup for good measure. Respirators had to be ordered separately from respiratory therapy.

There was space for six patients, two to a window, arranged in a horseshoe around a central desk area. All the monitors in the room fed into a master scope on this desk, so you could keep an eye on things all around without making a move, except to flip a few switches to focus on whatever bodily function you were specifically interested in.

Behind the desk was the only wall without windows. It was all shelves, top to bottom, crammed with supplies and equipment, including at least six different kinds of catheters for every imaginable orifice in the human body plus a dozen more to fit the man-made holes, a small stock pharmacy, and a cubbyhole for the defibrillator, plus the only door, which swung open by electric eyes and was made of glass with Wedgwood-blue trim.

Curtains hung from tracks between the beds, to separate patients from each other, for privacy and to hide dead bodies, as if patients clear across the room couldn't sense death when it stopped by, couldn't smell it all over. The curtains were striped with Wedgwood blue and a green apple green dizzying in early morning light, but generally rather pleasant.

Whatever extra time there was, quick silences snatched between routines and crises, Lydia spent watching out the windows. Musing, daydreaming, gazing without thought, staring at the motion out there. For her the windows were a special attraction. For the patients, though, they seemed to be a kind of mean joke.

On the other side, life moved along, fast or slow, mocking the inside. Cars on the FDR, planes up from LaGuardia, gulls in the wind swooping down to peck at garbage and waste floating side by side with tugboats and barges on the river. Perpetual motion. In counterpoint to the stasis inside. Static, balanced, stable, unchanged inside. Movement confined to EKG tracings bouncing a line within ten-inch gray screens propped high over each bed, urine confined to a tube, silently trickling down to collect in a plastic pouch, and air forced into baggy lungs and returned through a closed system of synthetic aqua hoses.

The brightness through the windows disguised much of the intensity of intensive care. In the evenings, the jewel-box lights strung on the bridges and the subdued, indirect lighting of the unit made it resemble the Stouffer's Starlight Room in downtown Chattanooga. Overhead spotlights on each bed, lit for times of direct patient care, added the impression of a salad bar, dessert tables, the hors d'oeuvres buffet.

Today Jane had three patients, with a nurse technician to help her. Lydia and Eileen took two, plus the empty bed, which would probably be filled by the end of the shift. A relaxing day, paced and instructive, time to help Eileen figure out the rationale for some of the procedures.

Eileen held Irma on her side while Lydia pushed a pillow in tight behind her back.

"You think what we said had a bad effect on Debbie's mental state?" Eileen persisted. "I mean, maybe she just gave up when she heard about the others. We shouldn't have been speaking right there in front of her. But I guess we'll never know, right?"

"Could you hand me the other pillow? Thanks." Lydia bent the woman's knees slightly, so her legs looked as if they were running, and then she put a pillow under the top knee. The monitor alarm rang, like old-time department store bells.

Eileen sprang back from the bed, her eyes wide, horrified. "Oh, my God!" Lydia groped in the sheets until she came up with two chest leads which had unsnapped during the turn. She pressed them back on Irma's body and the monitor picked up where it had left off, lub-dub, lub-dub.

"Geezo, I thought her heart stopped," Eileen gasped.

"Not the patient's, just the machine's."

Eileen shook her head and squinted at the monitor.

"I'm not really as blasé as I seem," Lydia explained. "Really. It'll only take a few times for you to recognize when a lead's come loose compared to real trouble. Believe me. By this afternoon, tomorrow at the latest, you'll be an expert on loose leads."

"Believe her," Jane called from the desk. "You should have seen us when we first started up here."

"Hey, speak for yourself."

"It's true. You could have come in with an ingrown toenail and we still would have checked your pupils, your grips, everything, believe me, everything, just in case. We didn't want any surprises. We were so careful. Middle of the night and there we'd be with our flashlight on some poor soul's chest, everyone's chest no matter what, we were watching, waiting for them to move, to breathe, any sign of life. We'd turn to leave and turn back quick, just be sure they hadn't died in that split second."

"That lasted about a month," Lydia added. "Too nerve-racking."

"Also, they never went bad when we expected it. They always surprised us anyway, somehow." Jane got up to take Maurice Jackson's urinal from him. "Good work," she said to the man, raising the urinal high.

Lydia turned to Eileen. "Did you understand what we were talking about this morning in report? The Mannitol business?"

"Could you explain it to me again?"

"Well," Lydia started, "you know what herniation is."

"When the brain pushes down on the brainstem."

"And knocks out function from the top down. Because of swelling or pressure from an expanding mass, a brain tumor or subdural hematoma, sometimes after a big stroke. If you don't reverse it quickly, the patient will die, more or less. Any ideas on how to reverse it?"

"I guess surgery."

"Good. Sometimes. But before you get to surgery, what?"

"Um. Mannitol, I guess."

"Why?"

Eileen stared, blank. Lydia couldn't tell if she was even trying to think of an answer. "It's a diuretic. I know that much."

"What kind?"

Nothing.

"Osmotic," Lydia offered. "It pulls fluid from brain tissue, pulls it into the bloodstream and out through the kidneys. Literally shrinks the brain and buys time. Steroids, like Decadron, are anti-inflammatory. They work on the swelling brought on locally by the mass or damaged tissue pressing on brain. Look them both up and know the effects and side effects by tomorrow. The third thing is hyperventilation. Carbon dioxide is a vasodilator, and dilated blood vessels carry more fluid in. When you hyperventilate you blow off C-O-Two, the blood vessels constrict and the engorgement decreases. It's the fastest of the three. Okay, so someone starts to herniate, what might you see?"

"The pupils blow."

"Or one pupil blows, on the same side as the pressure. But before that, sometimes they're restless, then sleepier, maybe a headache, vomiting, then the pupil goes, from pressure on the third nerve, blood pressure shoots up, pulse goes down to fifty or so, breathing may become irregular. I've made it sound neat, it hardly ever is. Mostly it's fast and disorganized. For now, what you should remember is that any drastic change in any of the above should be checked out by the doctor. Immediately. Know what to have ready in the meantime. Call the doctor. Be sure the patient has an airway, put one in if you have to. Get the Mannitol and Decadron ready to go, and hyperventilate him. Fifty to a hundred grams of Mannitol, and up to a hundred milligrams of Decadron."

"And give it if I have to, if the doctor takes too long. Like they said in report this morning." Eileen frowned the intense frown, but it couldn't hide her excitement. This was life-and-death stuff, the real thing.

"No. Do not. Just have it ready and wait for the doctor to give it. You don't have the experience or the background. You can't order treatments or medications. Some conditions get worse after Mannitol, sometimes even the hyperventilation can be bad for them."

"But Diana said this morning—"

"Diana's been around for fifteen years. Diana knows the possibilities, she knows the ailments and emergency treatments backward and forward and still she would hesitate, and wait. It's only when she thought she'd lost someone that she wanted to go on ahead and do something. Also, she knows enough to know what she doesn't know. You just get the drugs ready, understand?"

Eileen looked disappointed. "Mannitol, Decadron, hyperventilation."

"First call the doctor."

"Right. The doctor." She shrugged.

Lydia spread out lines and needles and stopcocks on the empty bed. "Let's go over the arterial line setup." She hung a bag of intravenous saline on one of the IV hooks suspended from the ceiling, and pushed her glasses back up. "I'll show you once, then you show me." Lydia could have done it with her eyes closed.

She was about to explain the four-way stopcock when the smell of a cigar and the sound of a golden oldie floated through the automatic doors. The aroma was from a dead butt cupped in Mike Mitchell's hand. The song came from the new man, Wheeler, who whistled softly.

Mitch approached first. He checked out Eileen and the IV bag, picked up one of the needles. Wheeler came up behind him and extended his hand to Lydia, then to Eileen. "Sam Wheeler," he said.

"I'm Lydia Weber and this is Eileen Caffrey."

"Eileen, nice name," Mitch said.

Lydia screwed one last male into one last female connection and handed it all to the new nurse to look over. Wheeler shoved his hands into his pants pockets, looked around, whistled a line of some song.

"Who is Mrs. Heller?" he asked.

"Over there." Lydia pointed across the empty bed to Irma.

Dr. Wheeler looked at the patient's chest passively heaving up and down with the respirator's cycle. "Family wants to stop everything. She breathe at all on her own?"

"Nope." Lydia took the setup again. She pulled it apart and lay the sections on the bedspread for Eileen to put back together. Mitch dangled one of the tubings in the air in front of her.

"Blood pressure's maintained with a dopamine drip, urine output's practically nil. Cool it, Mitch. You're making her nervous."

"No, he's not. I'm not nervous."

Wheeler turned to Lydia. "Uh, could you help me?" Brown eyes. Clear, golden brown, like tiger's eye. "I'm just not familiar with the routine here, or the equipment."

"I can take charge of the A-line," Mitch offered. He winked.

"I bet you can," Lydia answered. "Eileen, you go on and put it together and don't listen to him. I'll be back in a few minutes."

She left Eileen and the arterial line, with Mitch leering at both, picked up Irma's chart and walked with Dr. Wheeler to her bedside.

"To make a long story short," Lydia offered, "she was found unresponsive with agonal respirations two days ago, after her maid heard her cry out and fall." Lydia leaned close to the woman's ear. "Irma!" Same as before. "CAT scan showed big-time blood," she continued. "Left hemisphere, with rupture into the ventricles."

Wheeler rested his hands on the side rail. Two fat veins ran the length of his forearms, crossing and parting, meeting again at the crook of the elbow, disappearing under shirt sleeves. His fingers were long but squared at the tips. His nails were trimmed to the quick, by clippers or teeth, she couldn't be sure.

"You talk like a doctor," he said.

"Curb your tongue," she teased.

"Sure you do."

"I've been working on a hemorrhage study, that's all, and cardiac arrest. You learn the lingo pretty fast, it's not a big deal."

"Maybe not."

He hesitated, staring at the patient, stepping back from examining her, as if she were Lydia's property and he was an intruder, a trespasser, aware that he would be judged, perhaps shot on sight.

Wheeler lifted Irma's eyelids and shined a light into first the left eye, then the right. They stared inward, sightless. Even the pupils didn't react.

"She doesn't have anything but a few reflexes," Lydia added. "Spinal cord, nothing above that."

He brushed the patient's corneas with cotton. "I believe you. I'm just going to go through it for myself. I'm a little rusty. Been working with rats." He turned Irma's head side to side, then jerked it rapidly side to side and up and down, to force the eyeballs, but they didn't budge. He went through the whole exam, quick but thorough. Lydia noticed he held the woman's head firmly in both hands, her feet, her fingers, her legs, held them as if she was a human being and not only a body.

"Okay," he said. "I guess that's it." He patted Irma's shoulder gently. "A study, you said. For nurses?"

"For Bristol. Don't look so surprised. I'm just throwing everything into a hat, past history, hemorrhage history, course, treatment, outcome, complications, all of it into a hat and we'll shake it up later." Lydia put the side rail down on her side. "Could you help me turn her back again?"

Wheeler held Irma on her side as Lydia stuffed the pillow in behind.

"Why you?" he asked.

"What?"

"Why are you doing the study?"

"You mean why not a resident?" Lydia shook the sheet up in the air and let if fall softly. They straightened it out together.

"Sure," he admitted.

"Residents are too busy. I've done some research before. Nurses aren't morons. We're capable."

"I didn't mean it that way. Not at all." He folded his arms in front of him and rocked on his feet. "Uh, okay. I'll go speak with the family again and then I guess we can turn off the dopamine." Then he left, out the door. He looked like someone who would be more comfortable on a farm than in a hospital. Lydia imagined him steering a tractor, the sun burning his long, naked back.

Out in the hall, Sophie Glass shuffled between the hall sink and the main nurses' station. She walked like a toddler. She was using a wet washcloth and elbow grease on the stained white Formica countertops.

Irma Heller died with considerable slowness. They removed her IVs and stopped the medications at quarter to eleven. The respirator stayed on, the family couldn't bring themselves to cut that off, pull the plug, it seemed too deliberate. They had said their goodbyes after speaking with Dr. Wheeler and then gone home, to wait for the phone call. It was inevitable, only a matter of time.

Lydia set Eileen to studying the brown procedure manual, and Jane left for lunch.

On some level, Lydia had said, *I think they can hear.* On what level, she wondered? How many levels were there? What did Mrs. Irma Heller know of being let go, of letting go? She lay there with her heart pumping uselessly. Did she know? To let go? Had she heard and would she comply?

Her heart paused, the department-store bells bonged. Lydia shut off the alarm, returned to the desk. Another long pause, longer, while the heartbeat widened to a clumsy shape, unwieldy and large. Lydia's heart leaped, her own reflex response, a call to action by the stimulus of death. It was hard to keep still. Hard to watch it all happen and not do something quickly, effectively. Lydia guessed there was no agony in the dying, though, only in the watching.

The pauses were longer than the heartbeats now, and these were stunted into dwarf beats, simple two-wave blips instead of the normal, complex PQRST waves. And where were the doctors at a time like this? Off being pompous, off saving lives.

"Let's get her cleaned up," Lydia said to Eileen. "Get it done before visitors come."

"But she's not dead yet."

"She will be soon. Any second. Let's get her cleaned up. We won't say a word around her."

They wiped her off and even powdered her armpits, and by the time they were finished, she had died.

Lydia checked her watch. "Call Wheeler to pronounce her."

The MA1 worked air in and out, and nothing seemed changed except that the cardiac monitor showed a lifeless, irregular line with the gradual slope up and down of the air in and out. No rest for the weary, the machines kept up the pretense. They had to, by law.

The nurses worked around, checking vital signs on the other four patients. "Is she gone?" one of them asked softly, gesturing toward the drawn curtains. "I'm afraid so," Lydia answered, just as softly. They collected lunch trays and recorded liquid intakes, rolled the beds down and fluffed pillows. Lydia joined Wheeler when he came to pronounce death.

"What time?" he asked.

"Fifteen minutes ago, six or seven past one."

He took the ritual blood pressure and felt for a carotid pulse. "Okay," he said.

"The death certificate is on the desk. And the son's phone number."

She unplugged the respirator. A vacant silence followed, something hollow, missing, not pleasing to the ear for several moments until she got used to it. She started pulling out tubes and peeling off tape. Eileen scooted in behind the drawn curtain and watched at the foot of the bed.

"Is this your first death?" Lydia asked her. *This is your first death, I think.*

The young woman nodded.

"Maybe you'd like to finish preparing her, then. And be alone for a while?"

Eileen shrugged. She curled her fingers around the top foot rail and squeezed.

"There's time," Lydia continued. "It's a good thing for you to do. Clean off her face and everything and then we'll wrap her together."

After the first five or so bodies, they stopped being so wondrous. But Lydia remembered the first few vividly, and she knew these were important. Irma would be important to Eileen eventually, and ten years from now maybe Eileen would leave a new nurse alone, to tend to the dead, and she herself would go off somewhere and remember Irma.

Wheeler had already finished the paperwork and left. Lydia sat at the desk, pushed aside the death certificate and lay her head facedown on her hands.

The first dead person Lydia had ever seen was a rhythm-and-blues singer from Nashville, who was down in East Ridge for a one-night stand. He sang some Dylan and some Sweet Baby James Taylor, and stared a little too hard at one farmboy's girlfriend, which landed him his final gig for one week in the Hamilton County Memorial intensive care unit. A stunning blow to his left eye that snapped his neck and took his breath away. He painted his toenails, a hot sparkly pink shade that caught Lydia's eyes and held them when she walked in to wrap the body. Not that she hadn't seen his toenails before. A man wasn't admitted to Hamilton Memorial wearing hot-pink toenail polish without everyone being called in to have a look.

If he had been a woman, they would have cleaned off the polish without two thoughts, but because he was a man, his toes were treated as something sacred and magical. His feet may never have been washed that whole week. And the aides wouldn't go near him after he was dead.

"I ain't touching that queer man's body, not me. I'm taking my break. It's time for my break."

"Bad enough he's dead, but them toenails besides. You go on ahead, Lydia. Just go ahead and bother that body and see if something bad don't happen to you."

While they fought it out over who would have to come help wrap him, Lydia went into his cubicle to have a look. She had never seen anyone dead before and she wanted some time to herself.

It was three a.m., the place was pretty dark except for some muted yellow lighting overhead. She parted the cream-colored curtains, stepped into a space glaring white from a surgical lamp, a spotlight on the blues man for the last time, and the first thing she looked at, on the first dead body she ever saw, were his painted toenails. She stared and couldn't stop. She would look away, up to his hands, his face, but something kept pulling her eyes back to his feet, the way most people's eyes keep grabbing at a dwarf or a mongoloid, even though they know the fascination's not polite. It wasn't the oddness that held her, but the beauty. God had taken those dead dirty feet and matched them up in fine contrast to the toenails. The purply mottle really set off that hot-pink shade.

She dragged her stare up from his feet to his face, the one bruised eye was swollen shut and caked with dried black blood, too thick and hard to have washed completely away. His eye had oozed the whole time they kept him alive and even now there was a trickle seeping out of the corner. People who had heard him sing said he didn't sound authentic, he was too young, hadn't suffered enough. What Lydia wondered was, had he regretted dying now that he had suffered enough? Had everything always come just a minute too late for him? She glanced back at his toes.

"Your eyes are round and black as two caves in Rock City."

She started at the voice close behind her, her spine flushed. She turned to face the voice, a man's voice. It was an intern in green scrub pajamas. He smiled, broad and dark, and she felt the flush again in her spine, a tingling response to his hazel-eyed stare. She knew him only in the way a new nurse knows doctors, from the corner of her eye, and she was half afraid he would guess how new she was. An Egyptian named Ali, black-haired and fierce in an exciting-looking way, not sinister.

"This is your first death, I think," he said gently.

"You kidding? Heavens, no. I've seen loads of dead people before." A flutter in her throat betrayed the lie.

He chuckled. "I see," spreading two large hands out to her, an offering of service. "The ladies outside, they refuse. They dared me to help you."

"Oh. Well."

He tried not to laugh, his eyes bounced back bits of the spotlight.

"Well. Well, did they give you the morgue pack? You know, the shroud?"

He stepped out to fetch the kit. She turned back to study the body a while longer.

Somebody forgot to turn the respirator off. It trembled, lively behind the bed, whirring and wheezing, pumping air through green plastic hoses swaying with the breeze shooting into two baggy lungs. A breathing corpse. She shut him off, pulling out the rubber tube that connected his body to animation. Lydia half expected him to go whizzing around the room, spewing gases until they were all gone, but he just deflated, the flesh hung on him, flaccid.

She disconnected the tubes, the lines, the life supports infusing the façade. Now the only thing left was a shape, the outer structure of somebody's old home, all the people moved out, furniture, curtains, plumbing gone, not a sliver of soap on the bathroom floor, dry wall gutted, emptied. A vacant house.

"I think this is your first death." Ali handed her the shroud and tied an identification tag around the right big toe. He hummed while Lydia smoothed out the sheet, a curious tune, something in a mourning key, but turned jolly by a fast syncopated rhythm. An old Islamic funeral song, he said, to celebrate death with the dead man's spirit, who watched from somewhere above the cardiac monitor at that very moment. She knew he was playing with her, but she looked toward the ceiling several times before they finished, she couldn't help it. Afterward they drank strong coffee and smoked one Chesterfield between them, in the utility room, to the strains of a grinding autoclave.

"So, your first dead man."

"What of it?" She sat on the counter by the stainless steel sink, her restless legs dangled over the edge, wanting to swing, but she forced them to hold still. "Just what of it? You think it's funny? Right, hilarious."

He grinned, his teeth catching red and white beams from the signal lights of the blanket warmer clicking on, off, heat, cool, heat cool heat, keeping a constant temperature.

"I only think it's funny that you're embarrassed. Each of us learns in small pieces, one in its time. You aren't expected to have seen or done everything in the beginning. Nobody expects that."

"Well, I guess I do. I expect it."

He handed her the last of the butt, watching.

She was not beautiful, she knew that, but there were some things of beauty about her, and those things Ali treasured. Her long thighs for one, and her deep auburn hair. In the desert, red hair came in one color, dyed, with a synthetic bluish cast to it. She was virgin ripe, a persimmon heavy with juice and hanging low at the tip of a slender shoot, waiting to fall, waiting.

Her father, the Pastor, was suspicious of Ali. Her mother thought he was breathtakingly handsome. Her sisters said Lydia was using him to get back at her folks, the only way she could rebel anymore at her age, short of turning Catholic, which would have been extreme. Lydia herself thought that if it was rebellion, it was a rebellion against her sisters. They had both followed their mother's footsteps, both marrying preachers and settling in to the Ladies Aide and choir practice and Women's Missionary League potlucks until they reeked of baked beans and potato salad and ham.

Lydia felt sophisticated going out with an Egyptian, sophisticated and also sort of biblical. She thought at the time that she would convert him from Islam to the One True Faith, just by being herself.

When Ali smiled, he looked like Charlton Heston in *Ben-Hur*, but with a laugh to him, as if he knew all the jokes playing underneath the whole of life. At first Lydia thought he laughed at her, and then she thought he delighted in her, but finally she realized it was just his way and it didn't have anything to do with her at all. If she pleased him or infuriated him, no matter, the twinkle stayed the same. He smelled of sandalwood and cumin seed and tasted like patchouli. He kept her on her toes with ancient one-liners like "Hot words of love in the dark of night melt as butter in the morning sunlight." She took him on, intending to make those hot words stick through the morning and the afternoon and back into the dark of the night again.

They spent most of their time outside, in the beginning. Riding bicycles, riding horses, down by Moccasin Bend on the Tennessee River, walking around Missionary Ridge through Civil War battlefields. He knew about American history, much more than Lydia. He admired Ulysses S. Grant above all the usual men people generally admire, claimed he was the victim of bad press. Ali taught her about Grant and Mohammed, and about bird calls and nests and migration patterns. He would point out a jay or cock his head to hear a woodpecker way up in the hills, while she would focus on the angles of his neck, choosing a spot to kiss, or wonder how his thick fingers would feel rubbing along the small of her back.

For weeks they rode and walked and talked and listened, and Lydia imagined and wondered, wondered how and where and when, wondered finally if, and then wondered what in blazes was wrong with him—or with her—that he never tried much of anything. She expected at least some little bit of a skirmish with this dark and hairy big man. She longed to say no to him.

There was snow on the ground by the time he finally made a real move, nearly four months since that first night with the body. They had spent a lazy Saturday afternoon at his place, eating dried apricots and goat cheese. They listened to Beethoven and the Johnny Cash "Folsom Prison Blues" album over and over, and finally Ali kissed her, hot and wet and very long. He held her tight, so tight she could hardly breathe, but she didn't want to tell him for fear he'd stop.

He rolled them off the sofa to the floor, all the while holding on so breathlessly tight and then he pinned her arms down over her head and locked her legs apart with one of his great thighs.

By then Lydia was a little scared and thrilled and she wanted to say no, no, but was afraid if she said anything he would quit, so she struggled some with her arms and squirmed her legs only enough to harden his grip. His lips slid down her chin and caught onto her neck, and she heard these small gaspy high whimpers coming up from her throat. And then he stopped, grinned, she thought tenderly, but with a wink in it. That was all.

He stretched out, flushed and sweating. "I could have."

"Probably. I'm not fighting much."

"No matter, I could have anyway, right? Even if you fought me."

"I guess so."

"Yes. I could have. I could have done it."

"So why didn't you?" She curled herself around his rib cage, flushed and sweating, aroused, impatient. She rolled on top of him, surprising even herself, and kissed him aggressively, persuasively. He caught her heat and carried her along, pressing her flesh against him, finally pressing himself into her, the first one, the only one, forever and ever.

She felt like a full sorority sister and she walked around with what she imagined was a knowing, womanly look about her, a new grace. There weren't many more secrets left, she thought.

His idea fell out of the blue in the early spring, one day when they were back to riding and walking up on Lookout Mountain.

"I'm thinking of taking a residency in New York." He said "thinking," but he already knew. She could tell.

"New York City?" Her heart beat up to her throat and then slipped and fell to her stomach. "New York City? How come?"

"I like it there. I don't know exactly. It's a good opportunity." He walked a pace ahead of her, staring up at the buds just now popping out in knobs on the branches overhead. "It's time. It's time for me to leave here."

She walked one pace behind, eyes on the damp rotting mulch underfoot. A few early grass blades poked up through the compost. Her stomach rumbled. She would be hungry soon. "You've already decided, right?"

"I think I am supposed to go." He gazed off into nowhere, a long distance off. She hated this particular look. It reminded her of the way the Pastor looked when he prepared his sermons on Saturday nights. As if he had drifted into the Outer Limits. She couldn't reach him.

Her stomach growled. "I'm starving."

She left him alone about it, for weeks she let it go, all the time wanting to grasp and cling, to hold onto him, but making herself look cool and strong. She had never had any desire to live in New York, hardly any desire to live in Nashville even. Still, she bought the Sunday *New York Times*, circled want ad listings and wrote to a few of the hospitals there. The idea began to appeal.

She tried it out.

"Tell me about New York," she said, or, "I've never thought about living in New York," and, by May, "What if I moved up there, too?"

"How would you feel if I came up to New York, too? Is that a bad idea?" Because she wasn't sure if he was moving to somewhere, or away from her.

"It's a good idea," he said.

"Don't count on me," he said another time.

And another, "It must be for yourself, don't take me into account. You must want the move. You."

"You'll lose him," Pastor told her. "You know that, don't you? It's not right, running halfway up the East Coast after a man. It doesn't look right." His eyes were blue flames burning straight into Lydia. They were talking across the kitchen table after dinner. She had told him and Mama about moving to New York. "You'll lose him, you're bound to," Pastor said again.

They had always called him Pastor. All of them, always, except for Mama, who called him Honey, but never in public. They started it way before Lydia was born, so as not to confuse or irritate the church members, and also because it fit. The most they ever saw of him, the most he ever said to any of them in one sitting, was when he preached in his white robes, up in the pulpit Sunday mornings.

"It's one thing if you married him, heaven forbid," Pastor said. "I think you have more sense than that, but to go chasing after this man. He's not even—. He's not suitable."

It was hot for a May night, almost like summer, and the chiggers had already started. One of them kept sticking to a sweat bead on Lydia's forehead. She shooed him, but he came back time and again. She swiped hard, missed. "I'm not exactly running after him, you know. He's moving to New York, and he's asked me if I wouldn't like to go there too." Sort of. "It doesn't seem like anybody's running after anybody to me. Besides, I've always been kind of partial to New York. I've always wanted to see it."

Mama dried her hands and dried them, and dried them, on the corner of her dinner apron. She stood next to the sink, drying her hands, not saying a word. But she understood.

She and Pastor had taken an ink-blot test together years ago, for fun, after Dinah but before Marie. At some convention or for the benefit of a visiting evangelist trying to be innovative, something like that. Of the three girls she had told only Lydia, and then with some embarrassment, but also with a kindred heart, she had brought it out once when Lydia was feeling especially different from her sisters, abnormal. Mama and Pastor had sat side by side, looking at the same splotches at the same time. He saw praying hands, she saw a womb; he saw the Luther Rose, she saw a young budding breast; he saw Jesus Christ our Savior ascending into heaven and she saw a mons pubis, hung high and sweet. She and Lydia understood each other.

Pastor continued staring through her. He knew, Lydia could tell. There was knowledge in him. She had fallen off, overripe, married or not. He blinked once but he wouldn't look away. She wondered how long he had known.

She slapped at another chigger lighting on her cheek, thinking to hide the blush coming up from her neck, feeling stripped bare in front of her own father. She slapped high to make her eyes water over, and looked away, looked back at him.

"Daddy, I'm going and it'll be all right. I'm not any different from yesterday or tomorrow. I'm still Lydia and will be always, no matter what."

"Up and at 'em, old lady!"

Jane's voice.

Lydia lifted her head off the desk. "I wasn't asleep."

"I know, just resting your eyeballs." Jane was rewrapping her braid into a coil at the nape of her neck. "Mrs. Heller finally bought it, huh?"

"Yeah, finally. Eileen's back there with her." Lydia looked around. Everyone was snoozing before visiting hours. She smiled at her friend. "Remember Ali?"

"Oh God. What got you started on him?" Jane shoved a clip through the fat coil and fastened it. She made a face.

"Nothing. I was just thinking about him. He wasn't that bad. Never mind."

Jane removed the red bandanna from around her neck, flattened it into a square, rolled it, and quickly tied it on again. "I'll help wrap the body. We'll discharge her before visitors come."

"Skoal," Jane said. "Drink up, you need it."

The bar was jammed with customers in white coats and uniforms, winding down after work.

"Why did we pick this place?" Lydia asked. "Might as well have stayed at the hospital."

"Because we needed someplace cheap, and because you needed it quick. I could see it in your eyes. So don't look at the others, that's all. They probably don't want to see you here either."

"Thanks."

"Come on. What am I going to do with you?"

Jane drained her mug and ordered another beer. Lydia played with the condensation on her glass. She ran a finger through the wet, drawing spirals on the tabletop, arrows, flowers, a face.

People in whites crammed in, squeezed up to the bar. Lydia always felt that men and women in white coats were physically more dense than regular people, as if the jacket gave them substance, weight, and they gave off more body heat. Most of them laughed and slapped or shoved each other, like players on the same team. "You see the grunge we pulled out of that gut?" "What about that last admission? I told the nurses I wouldn't even talk to him until they fumigated him." "You think she really fell or did he hit her a few good ones?" Jane waved at a red-haired anesthesiologist and called for more pretzels.

A rousing lot of Clancy Brothers songs came on the jukebox. Someone turned up the sound. Lydia pressed her fingertips to her temples. "I'm too old for this."

"Hey, what about that Sylvia Goldfarb?" Jane said, ignoring her. "Bristol never even knew what hit him. All his charm failed totally with her. Totally. She didn't even feel the breeze."

"So he didn't get Sophie out?" Lydia grinned. "I didn't know. Tell me."

"Sylvia just wouldn't listen to him. Also, her husband writes for the *Post.* H.B. didn't dare get on her bad side once he found that out. Rule number one: stay friendly with the press."

"Or you'll end up like Ulysses S. Grant," Lydia added.

Jane looked at her, puzzled. "Grant?"

"Bad press. That's what Ali used to say."

"Him again. What's with you today? That's ages ago."

"So what? Sometimes he comes to mind. Sometimes I remember him. So? If it hadn't been for him, I wouldn't be here now."

"So I knew it was doomed the first night I met you. So did you. You were too much for him. He would have confined you."

"Maybe."

"Absolutely. You want some fries?" She raised her arm to signal the waitress.

Lydia drew stars on the tabletop. "You're probably right. What made me think I could live in Egypt?" The stars evaporated without a trace so she drew more of them, and a half moon. "Why would I even want to?"

"Missionary complex." Jane took a cigarette and handed Lydia the pack.

"No thanks," Lydia said. "Trying to cut down."

The waitress set a basket of French fries smack on top of the invisible stars. The potatoes still sizzled, twice fried, nice and greasy. Jane set her cigarette aside to pick up the ketchup bottle. She pounded it with her palm until a glop fell into the basket.

"Something eating you?" she asked. "You just tired?"

"It's almost eight years, you know. And here we are."

Had she expected too much?

After Ali, Lydia swore off doctors, but two years later she found herself with fond memories of dates with at least one member of each medical specialty, not to mention a few surgeons. She went back to school part time and set her mind to a future alone, not with bitterness but for self-sufficiency, regardless. She earned fifteen credits toward her master's and started seeing a calculus instructor who sailed model boats in Central Park. As soon as he finished his dissertation, he left New York to teach windsurfing at a Club Med in Cancún. Always hopeful, she surged ahead, looking to share things with someone, to find her perfect match. The aides said she was too picky. Lydia insisted that all she wanted was to fall in love, simply that. She tried professional men—lawyers, stockbrokers, an architect—interesting, fun, not quite her fit. There were blind dates, second dates, a few third dates, and, for the better part of one whole year, she juggled a psychologist and a painter.

For about two years she did medical advising for a soap opera in her spare time, teaching daytime doctors how to handle blood tubes and how to pronounce "quadriplegia" with precise nonchalance. The day came when they ran out of extras, they needed her on camera. Now she knew why she had come to New York City. She was to play a nurse walking into an elevator; she did five takes before she got it right. Pastor rushed a sick call to get home in time to catch her on national TV. The stars were all nice to her, and quite serious about their medicine, compared to real-life doctors. They didn't tolerate less than total commitment to an emergency, none of the usual joking around.

Lydia went out with one of the television cardiologists for some months. He looked just the way he looked on the screen, only shorter. They saw every movie worth seeing, a lot not worth seeing, and he taught her to make sushi and sashimi. They still saw each other for poker now and then.

"Eight years in New York, and we're right back here in the same bar we started at."

"Shit, I know," Jane said. "Are we crazy? We are. I'm working on it, though. I've got some ideas, Lyd. Exciting ideas." Jane ate a few fries, ketchup clung to her lips. "N.Y.U.," she continued. "Dynamic energies." She licked the salt and oil off her fingers. "Amazing."

Lydia waited while Jane searched for appropriately magnificent ways to express her ideas. Her eyes roamed across the ceiling pipes above the crowd, outside, inside. She retrieved the cigarette and her matches. She stared into the flame as she drew in.

"Therapeutic Touch," she simply said.

"You mean faith healing."

"Call it what you want. It works. I've watched it being done, I've done it."

"Which faith?" Lydia asked, slightly sarcastic.

Jane paused, her eyes icing for an instant, and then you could see the light bulbs flashing on in her head. "Faith in the healer, faith in yourself. That's what it's all about." She took in quick drags of her cigarette and blew them out of her mouth sideways, toward the wall. The smoke ricocheted back over the table in swirls and streaks.

Jane herself was a mass of contradictions. For all her mysticism, she should have been a vegetarian nonsmoker, pure in thought, word and deed. Instead, she appropriated what suited her. She was a woman with powerful weaknesses, which she enjoyed. She was a believer in energies and thought, karma, mind over matter, in self-reliance and making the most of the here and now.

She did not believe in a life after death, in heaven or hell or a soul that outlasted a body. She did believe that at the moment of death the essence of a life diffused itself into the atmosphere, staying there until someone or several someones had the need and the receptivity for it. But more than that, no.

She and Lydia shouldn't have gotten along.

Lydia had a strong belief in the soul and the life everlasting. She couldn't be sure that thought didn't go on after everything else was gone, and that thought might in fact be the best thing of all, inner life, contemplation. But sometimes she wondered if Jane was really the true believer and she, Lydia, was the heathen. Because Jane was ready to live and then ready to die, but Lydia hoped for that bit of extra time to talk things out, to resolve and reiterate her self, as if she could never be prepared enough to give up earthly life, never prepared enough to face up to death, as if she would have to persuade God Almighty that she had always meant well.

"Listen to me, all kidding aside," Jane was saying.

The first wave of post-day-shift patrons had left, cutting the crowd by half, leaving the neighborhood regulars to serious drinking and the local TV news.

Jane leaned closer to Lydia and lowered her voice. "I'm going to become a healer." As if the words were a prize. "There's a program at N.Y.U. It works, Lyd. I've seen it."

"Give me a break."

It was the old laying on of hands, as far as she was concerned, but Jane said no, it had to do with energy, a calling forth of positive energies from yourself and from the cosmic supply all around, to work toward healing. Once you learned the techniques, you could direct these energies through very specific pathways and into the unhealthy person, part, or even thought, and promote healing and wholeness. You could also teach people how to heal themselves, how to avoid illness altogether, once they were set on the right track.

It sounded supernatural and absolutely ridiculous to Lydia. She was skeptical, maybe because of all the quack fundamentalist faith-healing liars she had seen in the Tennessee Valley, or because she didn't really warm up to cosmic energies shooting off all around, asking to be lassoed and leashed. What they were really talking about was God and belief and the whole mind-over-matter thing, all old stuff, so why didn't they just say so. Dynamic energies made her think of invisible zaps from ray guns, bionic bounds across giant ravines, X-ray vision, faster than a speeding bullet, superheroes, comic books.

"You want to try it?" Jane asked.

Lydia looked at the fat men and stringy-haired women at the bar, at the blue light glowing over everything from the television set, and the still-bright day through the front window. "Here?"

"Yeah. Now."

"No."

"It works anywhere. You could use some energy. Let me send you some."

"Not today. Another time, maybe." She would be embarrassed, everyone would stare at them. "What do you have to do?"

"Practically nothing. I'll take your hand across the table and we'll do it. It's easy." Jane reached for Lydia's hand.

"No. Sometime, I promise. Not today."

"Okay, whatever." Jane put her hand into the French fries instead. "So who's this Wheeler guy? He sure was giving you the third degree."

"No, he wasn't. I think he was trying to be friendly."

"Well, he's cute, you agree?"

"I thought he looked really straight. Conservative. And uncomfortable."

"He can still be cute. Incidentally, your charms weren't exactly lost on him either."

"Come on."

"No, really. Irma Heller wasn't the only one he was checking out."

"Right, Jane. In the middle of pronouncing the woman brain dead. I'm sure."

"Not anything obvious. The man has class. Just a few furtive glances at your ass and your windblown curls, the stubborn jaw, the moist pink lips, et cetera. He noticed, that's all."

"Please. You want one more for the road?"

"Just trying to make you feel better."

Lydia went for the beer. A woman on the news was saying that Fire Island property values were plunging because of the AIDS scare. Some people thought it was transmitted by ticks going house to house.

Jane swigged half her beer immediately. "Ah. Finally the cold stuff." She lit another cigarette. "So what's your story? Is it Irma Heller or you got the general blahs for no particular reason?"

"Irma has something to do with it, but not the way you're thinking. I felt so mechanical with her today, it means less and less to me each time. People die, people live, they all sort of melt into one big patient until it's hard to remember who died and who lived. Eight years. I just keep digging in deeper and deeper."

"What about all the research? At least you've had that."

"Right." Lydia sighed. "How many different abnormal responses to pain do you think there are? I could go on the road doing coma impersonations, with three or four vegetatives thrown in for a small fee. Lydia, the living textbook."

"Not a bad idea. We could get a booking on *Ed Sullivan*."

"Ed Sullivan's dead."

"That's my point."

The news anchor scowled at them, dead serious. She spoke of a rent strike on the Upper West Side, her voice hoarse and provocative, as if she herself were one of the strikers, as if she herself had been denied hot water for washing her face. She switched to a beached whale on Block Island, looking into a different camera with the same face.

"Want to go into practice with me?" Jane asked.

"Practice?"

"Yeah. I want to open a private practice eventually. You know, heal people. Not like these jokers." Jane looked around the room. Most of the doctors had left. "No way. We'll help people get control of their own power to heal themselves, so nobody'll need doctors or drugs, any of that shit. We won't charge too much either. And the end point is health, prevention."

"With laying on of hands."

"Well yeah, Therapeutic Touch. I believe in it. I tried it on someone last week. Constipation. It worked. I sent green energy running through her system. It did the trick."

Lydia shook her head, she smiled. "Thanks for the offer, but you'd have to be a true believer to make it work, and I'm not."

"Let me show you," Jane insisted. "Let me."

Lydia looked up at the bar, everyone was watching the sultry brunette introduce the weatherman. The bartender was wiping out glasses with a towel.

"Okay," Lydia said. "Just to get it over with, though."

They linked fingers across the table.

"You have to promise to try."

Lydia nodded.

"Send me a color," Jane instructed. "Any color you want."

Several people turned from the news and stared at them. Lydia hesitated, then closed her eyes and transmitted orange with all her might.

"Think of the color," Jane said quietly. "Think of nothing but that color, what it looks like."

An orange flame, a burst of orange flame, like the burning bush in the *Golden Book of Bible Stories.*

"Think of it. Think of it over your head. It's over your head. How does it feel? Concentrate on how it feels."

Pleasant warmth on the crown of her head. Shimmering halo.

"Now, bring it down through your brain, through your neck, let it flow along the brachial plexus, through your arm, bring it down your arm and your hand and let it out to my hand. Think it. Do it."

Lydia tried with all her might because she was a skeptic. So she could say, well, she tried.

The burst of warmth jolted into her head, she saw it pointing into her crown and felt her brain turn orange. She gathered it into a stream and just let it run down her neck and through her arm and on into Jane. The whole right side of her felt the orange flow. Forever. It was taking forever.

Lydia's concentration lagged.

"Don't quit, I'm getting something, okay? Not yellow. I get not yellow, but yellowish."

Lydia renewed the thought. The whole pathway.

"Orange."

"Oh wow."

"It is?" Jane herself was surprised. "Orange? Amazing. Orange. Why orange?"

"Because I'm not an orange person. I'm blue or purple or green maybe. So it wouldn't be an easy guess."

"It worked. Amazing."

Lydia nearly believed. She did believe. Something had happened, no denying that.

"Martin Hellwig is a sixty-eight-year-old paint manufacturer with a history of rheumatic heart disease, a lumbar disc with laminectomy three years prior to admission, and mild hypertension, who presents with three days of fever, malaise and confusion," Christine droned.

A gull flew past the window, lighting on the rooftop across the street. It always caught Lydia off guard, seeing gulls in the city. Not at the river, but in the city proper, where there was no sand, no fish to stab, no clams. The gull strutted across the low rooftop railing, looked around, flapped its wings and took off.

"Last night at approximately midnight, he hallucinated a dark man at the foot of his bed. Mr. Hellwig conversed with the man off and on for an hour, began to argue with him, and that's when Mrs. Hellwig brought him in."

Sam Wheeler nodded at Lydia and smiled, she glanced away quickly, then looked back to him and smiled too. Professional friendliness.

Christine flipped on the light behind the X rays and everyone oohed and aahed at the small abscess, a neat little cyst in the left temporal lobe.

The gull returned with a friend. They stood on the same railing for several seconds before jumping down onto the roof, out of sight.

"We started ampicillin, gentamycin and chloramphenicol for now, until the microbiology report comes back."

Bristol walked to the view box and bent down, his eyes close to the lesion and the man's temporal lobes. He blew lint off his glasses, slid them into place.

"Wheeler!" he barked. "Why wasn't Mr. Hellwig afraid of the dark man at the foot of the bed? Enlighten the new boys. Why didn't he try to throw the intruder out of his house?"

Wheeler shoved his long torso up from a slouch. "Idiosyncrasy of formed hallucinations."

"Exactly," Bristol interrupted. "People are rarely afraid of or belligerent toward them."

"Probably because they are drawn from the person's own memory," Wheeler added. "Although that's speculation. No proof behind it. That's all I know about them."

"All anyone knows. People speculate, as you said." He walked slowly back to his chair, wiping his glasses with a handkerchief, frowning, presumably about formed hallucinations. "Thank you, Wheeler," before he sat down.

Wheeler shrugged. He looked around to see who was looking and caught Lydia's eye.

In the medicine room, Lydia stared out the window at the street five stories down, at the ambulances screaming into the emergency room, and at the gray stone buildings attached as wings to the main hospital. Seven wings. The place would never get off the ground with seven wings and no tail. It would veer left, and wings number two, four and six would crash into the psychiatric institute for sure, and then all the crazy people would have something of substance to worry about. She stood staring out the window at two of the seven wings, at the street five stories straight down, and at the Iowa-blue sky above, ridiculous to have such a sky over New York City. The Manhattan sky should be a haze of indeterminate color, like the smoke of a million cigars. Certainly not that innocent, washed blue.

Lydia fixed her eyes on the sky, looking for a small oasis, five minutes' refreshment between the morning confusions and the afternoon assaults. Five minutes before stepping back into the ward. More than anything, she wanted to escape. Second, she wanted a cigarette, and a few minutes off her feet.

A puff of cumulus floated past and, without taking her eyes from it, Lydia lit a cigarette and sucked in a long, satisfying drag. This would be lunch. The cloud skimmed out of reach behind the children's wing. She searched for another and, finding none, looked again at the street. Ambulances darted into the E.R. entrance bringing a fresh crop for the new residents to practice on. There were times when she wanted to warn them all away. "If you're smart you'll turn around and go back. They'll wreck you here." Times when there seemed to be a glut of routine procedures gone wrong, big wrong or little wrong, no matter. You could have a reaction to anesthesia and wake up with a rash, or you could never wake up at all, with halitosis and B.O. and sleep in your eyes twenty-four hours a day.

She pulled at a strand of hair from the crown of her head, twirling it through her fingers and thinking of nothing for that moment except the comfort of skin and hair rubbing against each other, one arm crooked and suspended overhead with the hand casting spells at the vortex. She used to twirl the Pastor's hair exactly like that on long car trips. The act and the sensation transported her to pleasance. She did it involuntarily when she needed to get away from the real world for a little while.

"Go back," she whispered out the window and into the thin air.

Waiting for her on the ward were patients of assorted size, shape, age, sex, mental and physical deficit: a fresh laminectomy, a brain abscess, several tumors in a variety of locations, strokes, aneurysms, multiple sclerosis, plus three nameless neurologic conditions of undetermined etiology, one migraine and a new endarterectomy on his way back from the O.R., and yes, on days like this one, nonstop days on the merry-go-round, she felt that patients became their conditions. They weren't people, not individual human beings, but neurological disorders on index cards filed in her head. There were Lydia, another nurse, brand-new, and three aides for the twenty-four patients multiplied by three complications per equals seventy-two potential disasters, not to mention the twenty-four groups of Hispanic, Jewish, Korean, black, Greek, Italian, Irish and upper-middle-class Protestant loved ones who would pounce in at two o'clock. Waiting for her.

A knock. Two knocks, and a voice, "Lydia, come. Quickly." The knocks and the voice and the door swinging open at once. Sheila Maxwell, nurses' aide, bursting in and calling, "Quickly, Lydia. Mr. Jaffe's back's come undone. Split open, wide open." Sheila tended to exaggerate, for effect. It usually worked.

Lydia came to, stubbed out her cigarette, three and a half minutes left on that one, and she and Sheila walked out and down the hall together.

"It popped. Like that. We were walking him, you know, and it popped. I heard it and so did he. He knew something was up, asked me was everything okay? He felt it besides. So I looked behind and there it was, opening up, and so I got him to his room and had him lie down on his stomach. It's open. The incision is wide open." She spoke with elongated Jamaican vowels, overpronounced and so refined and unexpected that an American ear often didn't understand the first time.

Mr. Jaffe lay prone on his bed. Two sutures had come loose, leaving an inch-and-a-half oval at the bottom of his incision line. It put Lydia in mind of a straight young river emptying into a reservoir. The fluid was cloudy, collecting in the oval. A leak, and probably infected.

"Have Bette page Dr. Mitchell, and bring me a culture swab. Bring two. And if Mitchell's in the O.R. or something, page Ratanski." Spinal fluid or maybe pus. Lydia leaned down to Mr. Jaffe's sweaty flushed face.

"Feel okay, sir? Any pain?"

"Nah. Not back there. Funny, right? I can barely feel anything back there."

"So tell me what happened."

"We were walking along, slow because I was a little sore, but no more than the couple of times I walked before. So we were walking along and I start feeling something wet and kind of warm back there, know what I mean? And then I felt something give, like."

"Did it hurt?"

"Well, sort of. Not bad, you understand. But then, whammo! I felt this snap, real hard, like one of them big rubber bands, and like all my back muscles slipped down a couple inches."

"And then was there pain?"

"Nope. Funny, right? There was that twinge when it snapped, pretty bad, sort of on the inside, aiming out like, but that went quick, and then it was just the wet, and a kind of tingle. Twinges, but nothing unbearable."

He was a big man, muscular and fat both, being very brave and helpful. He would have been scared, shaking and maybe even crying a little if he hadn't kept busy relating precisely what happened and precisely how he felt. "I can move my legs okay. I been checking them. They got real weak on the way back here to my room. But I been checking them and touching them and I can move them okay. See?" He wiggled his toes and made circles with his ankles, lifted his calves up from the knee. "See?"

"You don't have to worry about that, about not moving your legs or anything like that. Two stitches came loose. Nothing happened to your spinal cord. Only the incision."

"My spine didn't snap? Everything felt like it pulled loose. Like it all slid down somewhere. Nothing else came loose, you're sure?"

"Sure."

Now he trembled. He had spoken his fear, that his back had snapped and worse, and now it was out in the open to look at. He trembled and his eyes watered just so slightly.

"Miss Clarke here today?"

"No, she's off. You're making me jealous." She rubbed his shoulders, massaging out the tension. "If she were here, what would you ask her? Maybe I can substitute."

"It's nothing. She showed me a spot to press for my spine, before I had the operation. For the pain. I thought maybe that would help now, just in general, you know? But I can't remember the place. She said to think of the color blue and press on that spot. Behind my ears or something. Maybe my eyes. You know the spot? I can't think of it."

"I don't," Lydia conceded. "You're absolutely right, we do need her."

"It helped some with the pain. It did." His fingers still shook and his shoulders. "Not entirely, you understand. But it helped some. Nice girl, Miss Clarke."

"Maybe if you just concentrate on the blue. Maybe that would do something."

"Good idea."

"You're sure it's okay?"

He would shake for an hour, decide he'd had a close call, and then he would laugh about it, but only in private. The snap, the ping, and him thinking his spine had broken in two.

He lay his head on his quivering hands and closed his eyes.

"Did you see the sky today?" Lydia asked. "That's the color, I bet. Think of the blue of the sky today."

Sheila arrived with the culture swabs, plus dressing tray, suture set, sterile drapes, sterile rubber gloves, two bottles of Betadine, and a high-intensity lamp. "I wasn't positive about what you'd need, so I brought everything I could think of."

"What about Mitchell? Did he answer?"

"He's coming right down." She began setting up the supplies and instruments on the bedside table. "I'll stay with Mr. Jaffe, you go check Mrs. Stone."

"Mrs. Stone? What about her?" Lydia swabbed up two samples of the fluid from the oval split. "Did you bring any syringes?"

Sheila handed her a five-cc syringe. "She's drowsy. Since lunch.

Nothing else has changed, I think. She's quite sleepy though."

Lydia sucked cloudy fluid into the trunk of the syringe and held it up to the light. Colorless except for diaphanous strings of cirrus clouds. "What's her pressure?"

"Cindy said ninety-six over sixty. She said to get you."

Dragnet. Anne Stone's aneurysm could be leaking again. Or all the big and little arteries around it might be dancing and twitching in nervous spasms from the lower blood pressure. Or Mrs. Stone was taking a simple afternoon nap to make up for a restless sleep last night. Pick one.

"Okay, Mr. Jaffe. Dr. Mitchell's on his way, and I'll be back in a few minutes to check you. Just stay put with Sheila here. Have her sing 'God Save the Queen' for you. And don't move around."

"I'm not going nowhere."

Lydia walked down the hall past the medicine room and into the small private room closest to the nurses' station. The patient was curled up sound asleep in the cool shade. Cindy held up a medicine bottle to Lydia as she came in.

"She took her husband's Valium. I found it in her bedside drawer."

"Great." Choice four. None of the above. She took her husband's Valium.

"How'd you find out? Is she coherent?"

"She keeps rolling over and going back to sleep. I got her to tell me that her husband brought the pills in last night. But that's about it."

"That's probably a lot, considering. Thanks, Cindy. Okay. Mrs. Stone? Shit. Mrs. Stone. Anne. Come on, wake up a little. I have to talk to you and you have to talk to me, and I have to look at your eyes. Anne. I'm sorry but I have to."

She took a minute to confirm what Cindy had told her and then attempted to lecture the patient on the hazards of sneaking medicines. Anne nodded her head and nodded off. Lydia woke her one last time, irritated that an adult woman would put her life in Lydia's hands. Stern Mommy time. She hated that role, but it came up a lot. That, and fifty other ways to be a mother. She was getting wrinkles at the corners of her mouth.

"Keep a close eye on her this afternoon. Wake her up every half hour or so to check her blood pressure and everything. You know. I don't think anything will happen, but with her pressure down and the Valium, she could stroke out and we wouldn't even know. She'll be pissed, but that's just tough. And send her husband to me when he gets here."

So. Two within fifteen minutes of each other and only just barely past noon. Nothing ever happened singly around there, her mind always had to be chewing on several things at once, each distasteful but each important in its own way.

Her days centered around completing a set group of tasks within an eight-hour frame, meanwhile dodging and diverting a variety of unexpected hazards and calamities, like the old Uncle Wiggly game, or Space Invaders. So the hazards and calamities had to be dealt with but, more important, the medicines and blood pressures had to be given and taken at the appropriate intervals in the eight-hour frame, don't forget the baths and beds and hauling everyone up and out or side to side and back again before lunch, and out and up again before visitors. A mill wheel, so routine that she just kept plodding against the current, the distractions, any independent thoughts, plodding to finish the morning routine so there would be time for the noon routine to leave time for the afternoon routine and on. Mill wheels. Three wheels, three rings per shift and squeeze in the extras, fine, but don't upset the routine.

Twelve-forty-five. Well, the twelves and twos would just be given out together at one or so. Heading back to Mr. Jaffe, she spotted Mitchell down the hall in the ICU.

She pushed through the automatic glass doors and into the cool technology of the unit. Mitchell had Regina laughing about some tantrum Bristol had thrown in the O.R. over the temperature of the rooms. Bristol claimed they were too warm.

"He was furious about it," Mitchell was saying. "And then he worked himself up because no one else agreed or even cared. 'All right,' he says. 'All right, we'll see if it matters when all these patients grow out staph and strep in their wounds. We'll just see what you have to say then.' I wouldn't put it past him to go around infecting a few wounds, just to prove a point."

"Is it?" Lydia asked.

He looked her over, top to bottom and back up again. "Is it what?"

"Too warm."

"Hell if I know. Feels fine to me. H.B. just had a bug up his ass and decided to scratch in the O.R." He paused, looking her over again, but stopping at her mouth, not her eyes. "You called me. What's the problem?"

"Mr. Jaffe."

Regina moved in a little closer to Mitch, putting herself almost between him and Lydia, but Mitch kept looking at Lydia's mouth. Regina finally heaved a sigh and returned to her patients.

"Jaffe?"

"Lumbar lam three days ago. Big guy. Works on a loading dock." She ran her tongue halfway across her lips before she realized she was doing it and stopped. Mitchell grinned.

"Okay, yeah. He's a people's case, but I remember him. Muscular limbs, fat torso, big disc. What's the problem?"

Lydia explained while he washed his hands and hunted around for size eight gloves. She left him off at Jaffe's room. Five after one.

Passing 419, she automatically glanced in to check on Sophie Glass, who was just untying the last knot in her vest restraint. She picked at the thick straps, patient, determined and never doubting she would succeed, it was only a matter of time. Sophie looked up at Lydia. She smiled a grandchild's smile and resumed her work.

Lydia stooped to the old woman's eye level and fed her an orange wedge from the supply of bite-sized foods kept on the bedside stand.

Sophie had always liked to eat, but now she loved to eat. She was obsessed with it. She took most things in one gulp, like a python, with great delight and little satisfaction, which prompted the need for another gulp. Since it kept her reasonably occupied, everyone fed her. Grapes, raisins, and M&Ms were ideal because of their size. If left unoccupied for more than a few minutes, Sophie would unfasten the restraining vest and clean house, or she'd explore the far reaches of the hospital. On Sunday they had found her showering with Mr. Gonzalez, the two of them splashing and happy as a couple of toddlers playing in the backyard sprinkler.

"You do nice work, Soph." Lydia undid the rest of the restraint and started to fasten it again.

"So do you, so does he. We all try our best."

"I know. But you are especially patient with all these knots. Thorough. You keep us on our toes."

"Better your toes than someplace else, if you know what I mean. Call Sylvia, sweetheart. Call her for me."

"Sylvia is on her way. Another half-hour and she'll be here."

"Call her. Loud. She's out back. Call Sylvia for me."

Mrs. Williams, nurses' aide, passed by and walked in. She snorted. "She got out already? I just tied her up real nice and tight before I went to lunch." Willie punctuated her speech with a supply of assorted snorts and wheezes. "Sophie, you are hot stuff."

"Hot stuff I am, but you shouldn't call me that. Not in front of all these people. Mrs. B., you know, she repeats everything you tell her. It's all over the block by the next day, what you tell her. Call Sylvia for me, honey." She started in on the new knots immediately. Lydia handed her a pair of pajama bottoms.

"Could you tie these up for me?"

"You crazy? I tie these up, they won't fit. You just want to distract me. You tie them up. I'll untie them. Where's my Sylvia?"

"On her way."

There were no more places left to fasten. The vest was locked and triple locked to Sophie and to the chair, and they were working on a loop to the bed frame, just to make sure. Sylvia invariably showed up just after her mother got loose and was sprawled on the floor hunting dust pussies under the sink. Today Sophie would not get out. Lydia handed her the box of raisins.

"Sophie, I'm real busy today so I'm putting you on your honor. Stay put just until Sylvia gets here. Half an hour. On your honor?"

The old woman nodded and picked, already through the first knot and working on the second. "You talk to me like this? How can you ask such a question, it breaks my heart. Have I ever caused you grief? Have I ever? And this is the thanks I get? Call Sylvia. We'll have a nice lunch. Sylvia!"

"Five minutes. I'll be back in five minutes with your pills and then it's no time before Sylvia comes."

"Call her. On your way to the kitchen just stick your head out the back door and call her to come in. If it's no trouble, of course."

"Sure, no trouble at all." Lydia tied in one last knot before she left. She paused to check Mrs. Stone and to tell Cindy where she would be and finally, peace. She closed the door behind her. The meds could wait three and a half minutes. She sat down. Lit up. Sighed.

The sanctity of the medicine room. With the door open, people ran in and out all day, all night: nurses, doctors, physical, occupational, respiratory and speech therapists, social workers, chaplains, even a few patients and family members sometimes. Something comforting about that room, all the supplies and the clutter. Like the kitchen of a family home, busy and warm, always open. But when the door closed, such an oddity, everyone knew that the closer required privacy, everyone knocked, apologized, spoke softly, tentatively, "sorry to disturb you" was understood.

Dr. Bristol slammed open the door. "See here, Miss—"

She did not get up, scarcely looked up, did not turn around. Before she heard his voice she thought, What a very rude person. "Yes?"

"See here, Lydia. Doesn't anyone know how to work that infusion pump? The alarm—"

"Everyone does. Who did you ask?"

"No one. I didn't see anyone." He glanced at her cigarette tolerantly. "Not busy, I see."

"Always busy. I was just taking a few minutes to—"

"Take care of that pump for me. Mr. Hellwig. Four-twenty-two." He pointed another open-minded glance at her cigarette and pulled the drawstring on his smile. Corner of eyes up, corners of mouth up, hold, turn, and relax. Ah. Out the door.

Out the door and smack into Willie rounding the corner excited and full of disaster. They hit and deflected in a bouncing backward dance step. And he laughed with all the muscles in his face screwed up together to prove it was not a fake laugh, to prove his ability to perceive humor in unlikely situations. Even he, Chief Over All, could laugh in between important considerations.

"Couldn't find anyone before. Now they're jumping out of the woodwork," he chuckled understandingly. "Don't be in too much of a hurry or you'll lose your train of thought." He chuckled benevolently. For three or four paces down the hall, he chuckled.

Willie was not actually rushed but only looked that way. "It's Sophie."

"She's out of her restraint."

"You can say that."

"And cleaning under the sink."

"Not exactly."

"Or something."

"Or something I don't know about."

"So let's go string her up again. It's almost visiting hours."

"No."

"Well why not? Come on."

One of Willie's worst habits, maybe her only really annoying habit, was her fondness for guessing games. She enjoyed the sensation of suspense rising between herself and her questioner. She loved the power of causing puzzlement in another, all the while holding the answer to herself.

"Please, Willie. Not Twenty Questions. Not today, please? Just tell me what's going on."

"She's not there."

"Sophie."

"Right. The restraint is still mostly tied up but she's nowhere. She must have wriggled her way out."

"Great. Sylvia's going to go crazy. You looked everywhere?"

"Didn't look nowhere yet. Came to tell you first."

"Okay. Get Sheila and start looking. She didn't have money anywhere, did she? Or a subway token?"

"I'm pretty sure she didn't. Shoot, she couldn't get that far."

"Don't be so sure. Remember Theresa Farillo? All the way home to Bensonhurst during rush hour in her hospital gown."

"Oh yeah. Crazy Theresa." She snorted and wheezed both. "I remember that, now you mention it."

"I'll call security. Did she have a sign on her back? A 'Return to Four East' sign?"

"Not as I know."

"Okay. Just go. And hit Mr. Hellwig's IV on your way, would you?"

Lydia called security and reluctantly she called Regina, and then she stepped fully onto the merry-go-round, energized again, handing out the medicines and checking under each bed and in each closet as she went, hoping to catch Sophie doing a little late spring cleaning, and hoping Sylvia might be late today, just a few minutes, please?

"So where's my mother?" Sylvia said. "She's in the shower again this time of day?" Sylvia was short, skinny and strawberry blond with gray undertones to her complexion, and green pearlescent eyeshadow. She considered it her responsibility to be devoted. "You took her to the shower this time of day?"

"No."

"Well then, where? She's not in her room. I looked. Empty bed, empty chair, she's not under the sink, you say she's not in the shower. So where?"

"Um, she took a walk."

Lydia knew she shouldn't have said it when she said it. She should have risked Sylvia's hysterics and simply told the truth:

Your mother is missing. Right. Sure. Be realistic. It was simpler to lie at two p.m. with the meds only half out.

"A walk? My mother took a walk? My mother?"

"Yeah." She never could sustain a lie. Black lie, white lie, no lie. Her left eyelid twitched when she tried, and her throat dried up and caught when she talked. Lydia cleared her throat. "No. Look. Sylvia. I was in with her about one-fifteen, redoing the restraint and feeding her some orange. Five minutes later Willie tells me she's gone. She squeezed out of the jacket and walked off, I guess."

"You guess? So what are you telling me, my mother is missing?" Her lip twisted into a snarl, quivering involuntarily. Her voice rose in volume, pitch and speed. "Where were you? Why wasn't somebody watching her?" Somewhere between a whine and a wail. "You people! You drive me crazy! It's visiting hours and my mother is missing. During visiting hours. What kind of a place is this?"

From the corner of her eye, Lydia saw Regina running down the hall toward them, coming to save the day. She looked important, her eyebrows furrowed into a forty-five-degree worry line. This whole thing would make her day, Lydia could just hear her. She always forgot that she had been in charge when the famous Theresa Farillo got out, or when Oswald Kaffman slipped into bed with old Joseph Cruz, thinking it was his wife.

"Look," Lydia said, "Willie and Sheila are out after her, and the security people. She can't get out of the building," oh don't let her get out of the building, "and in fact I bet they've already caught up with her and she's on her way back right now."

"You better hope so. You people! I can't believe what goes on here."

"Me neither," but Lydia only said that under her breath. Above her breath she said, "Really, Sylvia. You know how we all feel about Sophie. You're right. Absolutely. Someone should have been there with her until you got here. But we're only four today and a couple of emergencies came up. You're right. I take full responsibility." Regina came to stand by them now. "If you want, you can complain to Miss Baker."

Regina put her hands on Sylvia's arm, first thing. "Now, Sylvia, let's try to be calm and understand." She spoke with exaggerated singsongy reason. "Everything is being done to find your mother," calm, professionally lowered voice, irritating, agitatingly quiet. Sylvia shrugged out of Regina's hold and stood with her hands on her hips, looking everywhere, nodding at everything. And then there was Sophie scooting toward them, as if she had never been gone, trailed by a volunteer demanding payment for the three Milky Way bars and two boxes of raisins that Sophie had lifted from the gift shop.

A happy reunion. Sylvia cried at the sight of her mother. Then she scolded her for causing so much commotion. Then she confiscated the candy bars and broke them into bite-sized pieces. The raisins had been ingested on the way back from the gift shop. Finally, Sylvia embraced Lydia and cried again.

Sophie hadn't encountered Sheila or Willie or even one security guard during her excursion. They had staked out the stairwells and obscure exits, forgetting that Sophie was not a runaway, but was simply looking for Sylvia in the backyard and lunch in the kitchen.

"You got no meat in the pantry. Lotta dry goods but no meat, and no pickles." Mother led daughter down the hall. "We gotta go shopping later."

Lydia resumed the filling of medicine cups with the prescribed colors and spheres. Attractive little packages, all of them. Party favors. Maybe Regina would do the place cards and they could celebrate something around a big table in the solarium. Patient with the most radiation rads to date, patient with the worst prognosis, highest grade malignancy, longest lifespan after being declared brain dead. The possibilities for celebration were limitless.

Sam Wheeler wore a bright purple-and-blue plaid tie with a mauve-colored shirt, a striking departure from the usual Samaritan white or blue oxford.

Bristol was preaching on nuances in cases of acute overdose patients, harking back to another time—"my time," he kept saying—when he was a young doctor. Wheeler kept his eyes on the Chief, smiling at all the right times, frowning, shaking his head, but occasionally Lydia thought he looked at her, behind Bristol and to the left. She couldn't be absolutely positive about it, but she was pretty sure, and sometimes she looked back at him, sometimes she raised her eyebrows, sometimes she looked down quickly and studied her nails.

"I remember one particular senior resident," Bristol said. "Louie Baxter, who without fail inserted a nasogastric tube, an endotracheal tube, an IV and a Foley catheter into each and every overdose he was called to see. Didn't matter how awake they were, they got the full treatment." He chuckled. " 'Serves them right,' Louie used to say. 'Teach them a lesson.' Huh, huh, huh!" Bristol ran his hand through the wave of his hair, massaged his beard.

A roach made its way across the conference room floor, stopping, starting, antennae twitching.

Bristol carefully coaxed several stray white hairs off his forehead and back into line with the rest. Lydia remembered when Bristol's hair was more blond than white. Six or seven years ago, the yellow had begun to look dirty, oily, compared to the rest, it had begun to clash. That was when, according to Mitch, Bristol started using a rinse on it. Mitchell said Bristol went to a stylist now and got a body wave every six months, although how Mitch knew all this, Lydia was never able to figure out.

"What about the head injury?" the Chief was asking. "Is he brain dead yet?"

"Charles Osborne," Casper offered.

"Charles Osborne," Bristol agreed.

"He's not brain dead."

The roach was under Mitchell's raised heel. Lydia waited for Mitch to mash it underfoot while leaning back or changing position.

"Technically, he's got some brainstem left," Casper continued.

The roach scooted out from under Mitch's foot. It headed toward the table leg. "He maintains his own blood pressure and has a partial response to cold water caloric testing."

"Poor man, poor man." Bristol hung his head in great theatrical despair. He folded his hands, lowered his voice so that all the others leaned forward and turned their heads to hear him. "What's the family like?"

The roach scaled the chrome table leg easily. It stopped at the top. Wheeler stirred, leaned farther forward and squinted, spotting the insect at Mitch's elbow. It zigzagged across the table to Casper.

"Hopeful," Christine answered. "His mother believes he'll wake up soon." She stared suspiciously at the cockroach.

"She spends her time planning meals with him, for when he

comes home," Casper added. A snicker from the far corner, because of the meal plans, or else because of the roach inching its way in fits and starts. "I mean, she talks to him about fried chicken and vegetable soup. Then she answers for him, and then responds to the answers."

By now the bug was smack in front in Casper, and everyone but he had seen it, but no one made a move to kill it.

Bristol observed it as it moved its feelers in one direction, then the other, turning in circles. "Someone must speak to her. Wheeler?"

"Yes sir?" Wheeler looked up from the table.

"We'll do an apnea test on him. If he fails that, you'll talk to the mother."

At last, Casper noticed the roach. He didn't move. In fact, the whole table sat, watching. Didn't they kill roaches at home? Lydia was about to stand up and swat the thing, but Dr. White, an old neurosurgeon, beat her out. He imprisoned the pest beneath a decisively overturned Styrofoam cup. Pop. Still, he hadn't killed him, perhaps there was a fear of roach karma in the group.

Mitchell looked at White with admiration. Casper let out a long wheezy sigh. Wheeler slouched into his chair, the mauve-colored shirt made his cheeks look rosy.

Bristol rapped on the conference table with his knuckles. "If the man can't breathe on his own, she must be forced to consider letting him go."

Charles Osborne had started GI bleeding fifteen minutes ago and Lydia was washing out his stomach with ice water when the patient in the next bed decided to assert herself. She arched up, all four limbs tied tight to the bed frame. She roared, bellowed, cursed, pounded hard on the mattress and arched up stiff again.

"Margo!" Lydia yelled. "Cool it, Margo!" She couldn't leave Osborne just that second and Regina had her hands full across the room.

Lydia decided her best bet was to ignore the woman and the commotion. Charlie didn't mind, he slept through anything, eyes half open but visionless, blinkless, tearless. Landing his head against the corner of Seventy-sixth and First had left Charlie carefree, absolutely. She turned her back on Margo and concentrated.

From behind Lydia came the sound of the human bowstring released twang against the mattress and the springs. Margo screeched "Damn you all to hell!"—her voice as strained as her body.

Lydia pushed ice water in through the nasogastric tube, pulling it out red and clotted in the same circular motion. She repeated the routine, back and forth back and forth back and forth until the water came back clear, then she shoved iced Maalox through. Stress ulcers in Charlie's stomach, just like that, as if he didn't have enough wrong with him.

His brain seemed more or less dead, but his heart kept pounding to beat the band. His mother visited all day, every day, clear from Montclair, New Jersey. She called him Chuck-boy, brought him the news of the world of today, the baseball scores, neighborhood gossip, she stuck a Walkman on his ears even though he couldn't walk, and wanted no stone left unturned for her son.

Not that anybody blamed her, nobody did. None of them knew exactly how they would behave in the same circumstances. But it got to be hard facing her untiring optimism about Chuck-boy. Her smiles, encouraging them all.

"He can still hear me, can't he? I understand that's true. They can almost always hear, even though they don't seem to. Isn't that right?"

"Well," Lydia would say. "Well, we don't know exactly what's preserved. But I'm sure that when you're here and when you talk to him, I'm sure he has to know that it's his mama, I'm sure he senses that, whether he hears you or not." She didn't know what else she could say. It seemed to comfort Charles's mother to think that he was reachable. Lydia used to believe it firmly, but now sometimes she believed only in energy and exhaustion. Even if he finally woke up, he wouldn't be Charles now, but only some speechless pet that bore a family resemblance to himself, something to feed and wash and talk at.

Margo bent herself in two. She gnawed quietly at her right wrist restraint. Her hair was cruddy with three days of sweat and saliva and vomit. Her face was washed clean but still carried tracks from the adhesive that had secured her endotracheal tube. Her life had been saved ("Here you go, we saved this one just for you"), and she was pissed. The more they meant their suicides, the angrier they always were to be saved.

Margo gave up on the restraint but moved her arm to the IV tubing. Lydia watched, fascinated, unable to leave Charles and aware that yelling wouldn't help. She watched Margo nibble at the tube and then bite clean through it. The fluid squirted onto the floor and blood backed up and out the other free end and also dripped down to form its own puddle.

"Thanks a lot, Margo."

Lydia shoved one last bit of Maalox into Chuck's stomach, plugged off the tube, moved over to Margo and clamped both free ends of the IV, then ran to set up a new bottle before the needle had a chance to clot off. She didn't much like Margo. Overdoses were the toughest to take care of, they hated you. Some of the doctors called them underdoses.

Margo got the bottle end of the IV tube into her mouth and jerked it to swing the bottle off its metal hook. She snapped her head back, and side to side, the plastic through her teeth a parody of Carmen, and the bottle swayed, upside down, jumping, clanking.

"Margo, for Pete's sake. It won't work anyway. Stop wasting your energy." And my energy, stop wasting my energy. "Just cool it, Margo!"

"Don't you dare call me Margo, you slut."

"Well. Thank you a lot."

She spat a glob of mucus at Lydia, but it missed her and landed in the puddle with bloodied dextrose and water.

"You're all a bunch of lesbians. I know. I've seen you."

Lydia took the old bottle down.

"But especially you."

Hung the new one up.

"You dyke."

And Dr. Bristol walked in.

"I said, you dyke!" she screamed.

He stepped through the automatic doors, standing just inside them. Arms folded across his chest, he surveyed the room, one bed to the next, patient to patient, he smiled, settled on Lydia regulating the drip of the new IV bottle in the midst of the mess, and his whole face squeezed up into a smile.

"Some things don't change," he said. "In thirty years, some things stay the same." Chuckling.

Lydia wasn't sure what he meant and he didn't go any further with it. She figured it was something about overdoses though, because he looked at her and Margo when he said it. And she guessed a waking-up overdose probably did wake up about the same thirty years ago as now. They did it the same in East Ridge, although there seemed to be a little more embarrassment down there, the anger edged with a touch of fundamentalist contrition.

Dr. Bristol didn't dwell on her or her little scene, but went over to take a look at Charlie. "Any change?" he asked no one in particular.

Regina had been suctioning a patient across the room but she looked up at the sound of Bristol's voice. "No," she hollered. "No change."

"He started with some GI bleeding half an hour ago," Lydia said quietly. She braced Margo's left arm with her right elbow to hold it still, held the hand flat by leaning down on it with her right wrist, meanwhile working on changing the tape and the gauze to make a sturdier dressing.

"Dyke! Bastard!"

Bristol picked up the blood pressure graph, scanned the checks and numbers, shook his head. "No signs of waking up, no spontaneous movements?"

"No sir. He's no different than he's been, as far as that goes."

"You blond bastard big shot! Look at me!"

With everything reattached and fastened, Lydia opened the stopcock wide. The glucose dripped in, sluggish, but better than nothing at this point. Margo winked at her and smiled.

"I bet you've got a dick. You got your own, don't you? And I bet it's bigger than Blondie's over there." She winked again.

Bristol concentrated hard on getting a rise out of Charlie. He jabbed his thumb into the bone above the man's eye without response. He pressed the shaft of a ballpoint into Charlie's thumbnail. His ears went a dark hot red from putting on so much pressure, or else from what Margo was saying about his penis.

Regina had finished up quickly and joined H.B., standing across Charles Osborne's bed from him, her arms on the raised side rail, her breasts resting on her arms.

Bristol glanced at her briefly, then returned to his knockings and pinchings and twistings. "Unless you have something to offer, Miss Baker, I suggest you either assist your colleague or see to your patients over there. I do not require your help."

Regina stared at Bristol. Her mouth opened and then clenched down so her jaws stuck out, stunned. She pushed herself back from the bedside, twirled around and flounced across the room.

Bristol was interested only in Charles's reaction to pain. He moved quickly, an expert at work, applying each stimulus on the mark and observing at least two if not three responses at once. His eyes darted from limb to limb to face to limb to chest heaving mechanically, watching out for the tiniest independent flicker, the slightest asynchrony. "Nothing."

Everyone talked about Harry Bristol. Lydia sometimes thought nobody around there would have anything to say if not for him. He seemed to be the reference point of all thought, Bristol Mean Time.

Everyone agreed on his genius, they could see it aimed all over the place. He was a genius at manipulation, at charm, at sizing people up, at honoring and wounding them, a genius at pinpointing the questions and stimulating the answers, and grudgingly they all agreed he was a genius at science.

People said he had wound down, mellowed out in the last ten years, but Lydia didn't see it. In the time since she came to the Samaritan, Bristol had perfected a basilar artery bypass technique which had preserved thirteen independent lives, he had invented a particular double-jawed clamp for clipping aneurysms, had written one book on the diagnosis and treatment of movement disorders and another about his internship year, plus numerous papers on memory, on language, on a theory of the chemical basis of behavior, had served on federal commissions, presidential committees, international boards, and appeared several times on prime-time television, spouting his philosophies for Barbara Walters.

No one knew for sure about his background, but they talked about it plenty. They said he came from Utah, from Mormons, or they said he was the bastard son of a Vanderbilt, educated through scholarships from the Christian Brothers. All the stories had some romance to them, and not one of them made a bit of difference in the presence of the man. What he did for himself made the difference, long after his beginnings.

He first became a biochemist and then an M.D. with a Ph.D. in neuropharmacology, a neuroscientist, it was all part of the plan. As an assistant professor of neurology at the Good Samaritan Medical School, he had his turn of responsibility for the ward patients, overseeing the work of the residents from time to time. During one of these stints, he argued with a neurosurgeon over technique and approach and the advisability of even attempting neurosurgery on one young patient with a large glioblastoma in her head. The surgeon operated, the woman survived as a vegetable for the natural lifespan of her tumor, and Harry Bristol arranged a two-year sabbatical so he could master neurosurgery. He wanted it all and he took it, so he could prove how easy it really was, so he could eventually become Chief Over All. He considered himself to be a physician, a scientist, a poet, a philosopher, a connoisseur of fine art and fine women, married only to his work.

Lydia pumped the blood pressure cuff on Margo's arm. A ship named *Daphne* cut through the river outside. From the bed height, Margo could just catch the top of the cabin and the chimney stacks, but she held onto it until her neck couldn't bend back any farther.

"Yeah, I'd like to be out there, too," Lydia said, as much to herself as to Margo.

The patient turned back. She looked pitifully into Lydia's eyes, snot bubbling from one nostril, called forth from her rage. Lydia took a Kleenex and wiped it away.

"I can't untie you. But please, it's for your own good, believe me." She felt like the Gestapo, like Goldfinger, like Snidely Whiplash and the bad matron standing over her restrained prisoner, reassuring her even while delivering the torture. Plain torture of life. The ones who meant it the most were the worst in general. They took more drugs and more kinds of drugs so they were a little delirious when they woke up and that magnified everything else.

Lydia washed the woman's face again, washed off dried tears and smeared mascara, adhesive markings, and spittle caked around her mouth. Margo pressed her cheek into Lydia's hand, nuzzled it, and tried to bite the thumb, bit down so hard that she would have drawn blood if not for the washrag. She twisted sideways away from Lydia and shut her eyes.

Bristol had finished his evaluation of Charles Osborne and was writing a note in the man's chart, shaking his head, clicking his tongue. When the unit door opened he stopped long enough to watch Sam Wheeler walk in.

"I've finished by myself," Bristol said. "You're late," and returned his attention to the chart.

Wheeler examined the patient quickly, his long fingers pressing and squeezing as expertly as Bristol had done. He whistled "Twilight Time" under his breath and winked at Lydia. A friendly gesture. No more than that, no less. "Any spontaneous respirations?"

"Not anymore," Lydia answered. "Day before yesterday he did, if we really stimulated him, but not since then."

"Do the apnea test, and you can add it to my note," Bristol commanded. He flipped the chart closed, came to stand next to Wheeler, shook his head, sighed. "Get a baseline blood gas and give him no less than ten minutes off the ventilator on a hundred percent O-Two."

"Yes sir. At least ten minutes. And another gas."

"I'll be in my office."

Bristol left, Regina flounced back to Lydia.

"Boy, is he in a bad mood," she said loudly. "Wasn't he rude to me? Did you hear what he said? Boy. So will you be all right here? I'd like to go out and check on a few things on the ward, but if you can't handle it, I'll wait." A challenge, delivered with such a beautiful smile.

"Are your patients all settled over there?" Lydia asked. "If they are, I'll be fine. If not, I probably won't."

"They're okay. A few ten-o'clock meds if you have a spare minute, but I can give them when I get back. Don't worry."

"No problem." Lydia lay a sheet over Margo, who was now asleep, sweet-looking and peaceful.

Wheeler rummaged through the shelves for equipment, syringes, oxygen flowmeter, a cannula, heparin, for the apnea test. "You've done this before?" he asked Lydia.

"Sure," she answered. She pointed him toward the blood gas kits, then picked up a few of them and several Styrofoam cups. "We're writing Charlie off?"

"Not exactly. If he breathes, we can't. If he doesn't, well . . ." He set his tools in a row on the bedside table, preparing to draw a baseline blood gas. "Uh, it might be better if he doesn't. For himself, his family, everyone."

"So, you're the Angel of Death now?"

He whistled softly. "Huh?"

"The Angel of Death, pronouncing people brain dead or not brain dead, or soon to be brain dead." She wrapped the blood pressure cuff around Charles's free arm. "I thought when you came you were supposed to be raising them from the dead."

He hunched over the arterial line, screwing in the syringe. He looked up at her, gold-brown eyes more like mud, no give to them now.

"I didn't mean anything by it," she said quickly. "I just thought, Bristol said something about your using something to stimulate the comatose brain, but all I ever see you do is his dirty work, sort of."

Wheeler drew up on the syringe, half filled it with blood. He handed it to Lydia. "I guess it could look that way." He resumed his whistling.

Lydia took the syringe from him, shot out the air bubbles, corked it and immersed it in a cup of ice. The blood was bright rich red, puffed up with respirator oxygen. She called for a clerk to send the specimen to be analyzed.

Sam Wheeler set up the oxygen flowmeter, turned it on full blast and replaced the respirator connections with one skinny cannula which ran straight down the endotracheal tube. He shut off the respirator alarm.

"Now we wait," he said. "You keep an eye on the monitor, and if he starts having any arrhythmias, or if his blood pressure does anything strange, let me know and we'll hook him back up."

He picked up Charlie's chart from the foot of the bed, flipped through to Bristol's note, but he set it down without reading it. "I do a lot of my work at night. The procedures and studies. Less traffic at night, less interference. If I had my potion, I'd certainly use it on someone like Charles Osborne, try to raise him from the dead, as you say. For now, I'm collecting controls."

He stood watching Charlie's chest not move. "What about yourself, Miss Angel of Death?" he asked, still with his eyes on the patient. "You're doing the same thing."

She looked away from the monitor briefly, glanced at Wheeler keeping watch. "No, I'm not. My role is purely observational. I don't set values on what I see. I don't make judgments."

"Sure you do. Just not out loud."

He had a point. She did make judgments, but they changed from day to day, even hour to hour. Some patients would be better off dead—on the other hand, maybe not. Maybe they needed the time.

She took a blood pressure reading on Charlie. It always surprised her how well patients could do with only a passive flow of concentrated oxygen. The organism could be sustained that way for at least ten minutes.

No respiration, but nothing else changed much. Charlie stayed the same, same color, same temperature, same everything. His pulse picked up about ten beats a minute, but nothing major to speak of. She kept her eye on the monitor and on Charlie, willing him to breathe, three minutes, three and a half, why did she want him to breathe? So he would pass his test? So they couldn't write "failed apnea test" in his chart?

The carbon dioxide level would be rising, as if Charlie were holding his breath, and the oxygen sensors, if they weren't dead, would soon begin to feel deprived, and if they weren't dead, he would be forced to breathe.

Four minutes. He would be better off dead, she did know that, but she couldn't help but want him to show them all. To breathe for starters, to open his eyes and focus, to talk, to chew on a few French fries sometime, and walk out of there. Four minutes, ten seconds, he gasped, a long stuttering loud intake of air.

"What do you know." Wheeler rushed to get another gas, to catch the CO_2 as close to the level that kicked it off as possible before Charlie pulled in too much new oxygen.

"I'll be." Lydia smoothed Charles's hair to one side. "Good for you, Chuck-boy."

Wheeler looked at her. "Good? Look at him." He shook his head. "Not good. Expensive, for his family. He'll drain them dry, for what? So someday they can feel real guilty for wishing he'd died now? Not good."

Lydia took the syringe from him, dark wine-colored blood, not so bright as before. She prepared the gas and called for the clerk. Wheeler checked the blood pressure himself, not fully trusting the A-line and its digital readout; he checked the pulse. Lydia picked up bits of paper, packing, alcohol swabs, and leftover syringes that were scattered across the blanket, Wheeler helped, and Charles Osborne breathed.

"I know it's not good," Lydia said. "I know."

"We'll send another gas in ten minutes or so."

"Right."

Margo was still asleep. Seeing her quiet, Lydia couldn't help wondering why someone so pretty would want to die at twenty-eight. Lydia looked over at the three other patients, their monitors bouncing and beeping cheerily. One empty bed.

Wheeler picked up the chart and read Bristol's last note predicting that the patient wouldn't breathe, outlining the steps required to declare the man officially brain dead, suggestions for dealing with the family, for turning off the machines. "Charlie sure fooled Bristol," he said, mostly to himself and the chart, and he began his note describing the procedure and Charles's response to it. He started whistling "Twilight Time" again, between his teeth, low and easy. He must whistle all the time, Lydia thought.

Margo stirred, just a twist of the head to start, but it grew into a writhing and tugging at the restraints, for old time's sake. She opened her eyes and searched the room. Lydia stooped next to her bed, mopping up the sticky paste of five percent dextrose in water mixed with blood that had already dried some.

Margo leaned close to the side rail to watch. Her stringy hair kept sticking in her eyelashes so she had to shake it away.

"I'll brush your hair back as soon as I'm done here," Lydia said.

"You keep your hands away from me, dyke. Keep your filth to yourself." Then she noticed Sam Wheeler at the desk. "Hey, doc!" she yelled. "Don't waste your time with this bastard bitch. Don't waste your time, doc. She likes women, believe me. Don't waste your time."

He grinned at Lydia. "She was still out yesterday when I saw her. When did she wake up?"

"Early this morning. With a vengeance."

"She's got me tied up, doc. I'm helpless. God knows what they did to me when I was out of it. God knows. Look at me. Doc! Get me untied. I'll be good. Promise. Just untie me."

"Right. I'm really tired of this." Lydia dunked the washrag into antiseptic cleaner and wiped over the floor one more time.

"Let me sit up at least, so I can see something."

Lydia rolled her head up about forty-five degrees. "If I weren't so tired, this would be funny. You dizzy?"

"Nah." Margo lay back, her arms tied straight out from her sides. She stared at Lydia. "I hate you." If she narrowed her eyes or screamed again it would not have been as chilling as the flat blank staring words.

Lydia returned to Charles to take more blood. Margo kept her eyes trained on Lydia as she adjusted transducer stopcocks, discarded the first syringe of blood and carefully drew up a second syringeful. She watched her irrigate the line, watched her pack the specimen with ice and call for the clerk.

"I hate you," she repeated. "I hope you're on a rack like me someday. I'll come see you, brush your hair." She laughed. Then she banged herself against the side rails so that they shook, reverberated, loud enough to wake up old Jim Beecher across the room.

"Miss!" he called.

Margo grabbed the IV again with her teeth, only this time she pulled at the needle end, jerked it and rubbed with her wrist up and down under the restraint.

"Miss! I need to urinate! Quickly!"

Margo screamed, "Ha! Wet yourself!" And succeeded again, pulling out the needle and everything this time, with blood and sweet water streaming together all over. "Ha!"

Lydia didn't do anything, as if she were wound down and couldn't move a muscle or a joint, couldn't even think. Wheeler jumped up and found the urinal for Jim Beecher.

"Let him wet himself!" Some large splotches of blood, that's all, and it had nearly stopped. Only the stream of IV solution slowly soaking the sheets. "Wet yourself, like me!"

Wheeler drew the curtain around the man's bed and waited. Lydia had managed to stamp a blood gas requisition and was checking off boxes on it. She turned away from Margo and closed her eyes.

Wheeler emptied the urinal and recorded the amount on the intake and output sheet. He made Beecher comfortable and gave him some water to drink, and then he joined Lydia at the desk. "If you have the time right now, I'll help you change her bed," he said.

"That's a beautiful tie, Dr. Wheeler." Impossible to handle Margo, impossible to deal with her sheets. "And shirt. I noticed them this morning in conference."

"Thanks. Call me Sam?" He lifted his tie for a better look, he beamed. "My boys gave it to me for Father's Day this year. Picked it out themselves. I found the shirt to match it. My wife hates them both. Thinks they're too loud." Still beaming.

"No, they're great." If she didn't change Margo's bed, she would be like Louie Baxter, teaching a needful patient a mean, useless lesson.

"Surprised you noticed in the midst of all that tabletop drama. Where do you keep clean bed linens?" He had a really warm smile, one that gave outward, it had no private jokes. Lydia gestured toward the linen cart. Sam got the clean sheets and said, "I'll hold her still while you replace the bedclothes." He carefully tucked the precious tie through a space between two shirt buttons, out of reach of Margo's teeth. Lydia unfastened the wrist restraints. Then he bent close to her. "Margo. We're giving you a dry bed. Let me help you over to this side." Soft spoken.

Margo smiled, responsive. "Sure, doc. I'll do whatever you say." She slid way over to him and hugged his waist. He winked at Lydia, but his ears got red. Margo pulled her head back, facing his chest. "I like your tie too, doc." She spat at him. It missed the tie but landed on his shirt.

"That's exactly how my wife feels about it." He didn't pull away. He didn't aggressively force her immobile with his strength. He brushed the spit off with a dry corner of the sheet.

Margo snickered.

He ignored her. "I thought about killing the roach myself this morning. I had a pad of paper. I could have smashed it. What was everyone waiting for?"

Lydia had untangled IV lines from the sheets and the side rails and was pushing wet linen out of the way. "Got me." She dried the mattress with a towel. "I think they were maybe waiting for H.B. to give his permission." She unfolded dry sheets over half the bed, tucked them in. Margo lay silent, planning her strategy.

"It crossed my mind that they might all be afraid of some kind of roach revenge," Lydia continued. "You know, nightmares, visitations, if they did away with the critter." Sam laughed, and even Margo giggled. "Okay, this side's done. Roll over, Margo."

The woman did not roll over, she slid to the dry side of the bed, staying turned toward Sam, her back to Lydia. Sam pulled off the dirty linen and stuffed it into the laundry bag. He wiped off the wet mattress, smoothed the new sheets out, made square corners.

"Highly suspicious, Sam. Nice, and neat to boot. Why are you doing this?"

"Why not?"

Sure, why not? He snapped the sheet tails, tightened them, serious, determinedly showing his skill at making beds.

There were no formally assigned seats in morning conference, but Sam had established himself directly opposite Bristol. One morning he casually sat down next to Lydia, and set the balance off.

"Quite a view," he said. His elbow touched hers, the chairs were too close. "I didn't realize you could see so much through that window."

People noticed him when they walked in that morning. He was

sitting in the wrong place. They raised their eyebrows, some of them, some of them cleared their throats, most were uncharacteristically silent, Lydia thought, although it could have been her imagination. It did seem pretty ridiculous that anyone would be upset by it.

On a color television directly across the street from the conference room Jane Pauley appeared on the screen and then the Pope, disembarking from an airplane. He stooped to kiss soil somewhere where the soil had never been kissed or stepped on by any Pope before.

"Amazing," Sam whispered. "I can even make out his ring."

"Must be a big screen," Lydia answered. Their elbows brushed again.

"Cloudy day. No glare."

"Could we have only one conversation in the room, please?" Bristol was forced to turn completely around to scold them. He looked surprised to see Sam there, and Sam flushed.

"Next patient."

An old man knelt at the Pontiff's feet and wept with happiness.

Of the six patients in intensive care, three were unresponsive, one was confused, one was aphasic, and one was depressed and had her back to the room. Just another day. Jane and Lydia worked their way around the unit making occupied beds, while the third nurse gave out medications.

Jane and Lydia had a system between them for changing sheets, checking neuro status and cleaning out the lungs all at the same time. It was assembly-line nursing, something never taught in schools but often learned in practice. They moved from one body to the next, one set of mucus and drainage to another. It was the most efficient way.

Lydia held the first patient to his right side, she clapped on his back to loosen the congestion in his chest, Jane tucked clean linen against him and, just before turning, Lydia tickled his left nostril with cotton. He sneezed. Big deal. They rolled him flat and Lydia wiped the sneeze off his face. His eyes were open. He blinked without making eye contact, staring out to some distant point that no one else could see. Jane suctioned the loosened crud from his lungs, and then they turned him to his left side, exchanging duties.

Jane clapped on his back. "This is not my idea of a lifelong career for myself," she said. "End of this semester, I'm out of here. I want some power of my own."

Lydia unrolled the bottom sheet, the draw sheet, the pull sheet, and four blue Chux. She pulled them tight, each layer in turn, pulled out the wrinkles, and the man nearly bounced like a Marine's dime on top of the smooth, tight sheets.

"No more of Regina's whiny 'You gotta work nights, there's nobody else' shit," Jane continued. "If I'm going to feel guilty, it'll be my own fault, no one else's." She tickled the man's right nostril, without effect. "I'll get a pressure on him."

Lydia made square corners and neat edges, smiling to herself and not answering her friend. It never did any good to answer her back. She fitted an extra Chux under the patient's bottom and arranged his urinary catheter tube so the urine could flow freely. Then she started on limbering the man's right arm.

Jane stripped off the blood pressure cuff. "One-forty over seventy-eight. You should think about it, Lyd. You've got a good thing going for now, I admit it." She exercised the left arm through a full range of motion, in and out and around. "I was a little jealous to start with, I admit that too. But not anymore. Because you're not independent either. It's even worse for you, in a way, with your studies. You have to answer to both of them, Bristol as well as Regina." She moved down to the leg, bending and stretching each joint. "Because they'll screw you, you know. One or the other. In a nutshell, this system here sucks. Always will. Let's pull this guy up."

The monologue had started as dialogue and had gone on for weeks.

"What exactly would I do in private practice?" Lydia asked in the beginning. "People in a coma don't, as a rule, come for office visits."

"You could give massage," Jane insisted enthusiastically. "And learn shiatsu. We could do Primal Scream, Therapeutic Touch, and maybe meditation techniques too. A whole package. I'm not kidding."

"It wouldn't work for me," Lydia insisted back. "I'm too traditional, that's all."

But Jane wouldn't quit, and finally all Lydia could do was smile silently through the one-way discussion.

They pulled the top sheet up to the patient's chest, placing his arms over it, which supposedly looked more natural to families. Otherwise, patients looked like parcels in wrapping paper, or bodies in shrouds, somebody said.

"Hold it a minute, can we?" Jane asked. "This guy has a fever. I'll help him out with it." She positioned herself at the foot of his bed and took each of his big toes between a thumb and forefinger, setting up a circle of energy to flow through her into him. She drew a deep breath, closed her eyes and nobly lifted her head.

Lydia straightened up the bedside, throwing away extraneous cannulas and used tissues. Jane breathed deep, heavy breaths, she opened one eye to check the patient. Lydia checked the supply of souffle cups, sterile saline and suction catheters. Jane released the toes and patted the bottoms of the patient's feet.

"You just don't have enough confidence," she went on. "But that'll come. It will. Remind me to get another temp on him when we're done." They moved to the next patient. "Think about it, give it a chance." Closing remarks. Lydia made sure that all tubes and wires and paralyzed limbs were out of the way, then she rolled this patient to her right side, clapping her back.

The door opened with its thunk and mechanical hum. Dr. Bristol walked in first, Sam Wheeler followed. They paused to look around.

Lydia pounded the patient's back for a few seconds longer and then rolled her flat and suctioned her.

"What about windowsills?" she heard Bristol say. "Wasted storage space there. A shame." The two doctors walked to the east window and measured the sill. They turned around and leaned on it, looking at the one wall, stacked to the ceiling with supplies. Bristol shook his head.

Jane held the patient toward her and Lydia pulled the clean sheets through. She tucked the square corners and watched as Bristol pointed to areas between the beds where there might be extra room.

"What're they up to?" Jane whispered.

"Well, uh, uh . . ." the patient answered. "Uh, yes, uh, well, uh . . ."

"Beats me," Lydia said. "Let's face her toward the window."

They moved on to the next patient, one to the right of the two doctors. Bristol nodded at them and smiled his social smile and then gave them his back and continued murmuring to Wheeler.

The day Bristol had invited Lydia to do research, he couldn't remember her name. Of course.

"Excuse me," he had called to her, down the hall, but Lydia

thought he meant someone else, the intern in the medicine room maybe, so she walked on. "Excuse me," he called out again, and she realized then that he might want her, but she didn't turn around. Let him use her name. "Excuse me!" louder still, then a mumble toward the medicine room, then an answer, then, "That's right. Uh, excuse me, uh, Lydia!"

She felt somehow she had the upper hand. Dr. Harry Bristol had bent to her will. She turned, faced him, smiled. "Yes?"

"Yes." He smiled back. "I have a favor to ask you." He shoved his hands into his pants pockets, jiggling keys and change and tightening the fabric across his crotch. "Come to my office in twenty minutes." He fixed his smile, turned and strode off down the hall without waiting for an answer, white coat billowing importantly behind him.

In exactly nineteen minutes, Lydia strode off after him. She had gone through a list of favors in those minutes and, feeling slightly powerful about making him use her name, she settled on the most unlikely favor and pursued it down the hall.

She would enter his office, hearing the click of the door behind her. Wordlessly she would convey her understanding of his needs, and when he stammered an explanation, she would touch her forefinger to his lips, begging his silence.

"I know all about favors," she would say, looking him straight in the eye.

Holding his gaze in hers, she would move her finger from his lips, down his chin, his neck, his chest, across the belt buckle to his fly. Unfalteringly, she'd unzip it and reach inside and grope around. And grope around some more, wait a minute. Just a minute.

She strode down the hall on the way to Bristol's office imagining her hand slipping inside his pants, rummaging around a bit, searching, trying to do the man a favor. Ah, here we go. But no, only squash balls, two hard black rubber squash balls, and let's see, oh yes, a pile of reprints from his series of articles on memory—immediate, recent and remote—the hippocampus, the temporal lobes. That's it. Two balls but no racket. She opened the door to his office.

"Ah, come in," he said, meeting her eyes.

She heard the click of the door behind her.

"Have a seat, have a seat." He swiveled his chair to face away from her and spoke into a hand-held dictating machine.

The office was wall-to-wall books and professional journals organized in rows matched to subject and also to height as much as possible, the journals lined up by color, by year, by month. Squeezed between *Annals of Neurology* and *The New England Journal* stood a pedestal holding a plastic representation of the human brain. At the foot of the pedestal was a bronzed cat brain. Bristol's desk was bare except for one stack of operative notes on the right side, a stack of correspondence on the left, a cupful of pens and pencils at twelve o'clock, a red telephone at two, a digital clock at ten. His computer terminal sat on a shelf behind him, next to a bin labeled TO BE FILED, red like the phone.

Neat, empty, and the temperature felt a little coolish.

Lydia sat in a swivel chair directly across the desk from him. It had an uncomfortably deep seat so that her feet barely touched the floor. She wondered how long it had taken him to find just that sort of chair, that size.

The dictation took maybe thirty seconds extra in pauses and glances in her direction, such a busy man with such important, secret work. Finally he finished, turned back and looked at her over his glasses.

"Well?" he said.

"You asked me to come see you?"

Silence. As if weighing the wisdom of asking her to come here, of asking her a favor.

"I did."

He opened a right-hand drawer and lifted out several sheets of paper. "These are the chart reviews you worked on, some months ago." He held them up a farsighted distance away.

She felt nervous with him. Afraid to say something wrong, or something right but in the wrong way. After the years she spent ardently not awed by him, now she wanted his approval.

She had changed her mind some about Bristol. She still basically didn't like him, she thought him ruthless and manipulative. But somewhere along the way he made it clear that he appreciated her quiet style, he recognized her intelligence. And she appreciated his appreciation; she was only human, after all. She knew that he thought he could use her intelligence, and her pride, to his advantage. She knew that he underestimated her perceptions, and her will.

"Good work." He removed the paper clip from the first report.

"They were actually Dr. Bergman's projects, you know." Jonathan Bergman. She cleared a frog from her throat, a lump. "They were, um, his ideas."

"My ideas," Bristol corrected. "Your work. Bergman was an operator. I knew him. I know them all, better than they ever imagine." He said the last quietly, looking straight at Lydia. He thinks he knows me too, she thought.

He unbent the first turn in the paper clip, straightening each ripple like Uri Geller melting down a fork. Two hard rubber squash balls, she kept thinking, and no racket. Hold that image.

"The point is, Bergman's not here anymore, but you are and you did a fine job on these," massaging the wire with his fingers. "I believe in rewarding productivity." He started in on the second turn of the clip. "I'd like to see you take the arrest audit a step further."

"Me?" She flushed. Two balls, no cock, keep it in mind, keep your perspective. Squash balls. And a bunch of reprints from the old days. "Really?"

"Yes. But instead of a retrospective chart review, a prospective study. Ongoing. Cardiac arrest and twenty-four-hour outcome of patient's post-cardiac arrest. A few simple questions. Direct, to the point." He wrenched the last bend straight out to make the clip 7-shaped. He twirled the stem between his thumb and forefinger. "Very simple."

"A nurse?"

"I wouldn't suggest it if I didn't think you could do it. You've proven yourself. And this is not unprecedented. Remember Miss Fitz? I guess not. In any case, we've used nurses before."

She felt good. Honored. Recognized. For several minutes, listening to him, she felt these things.

"You're reliable, presumably honest, interested. And you are a less biased observer than a physician would be." He changed the 7 to a semicircle. "By this time my residents know too many answers, percentages. They're full of statistics from other studies. They often see what they expect to see on the basis of these percentages, and not what is actually there." Now a horseshoe, again massaging it smooth in his fingers. "The bias has nothing to do with intelligence, understand, but with training and opportunity. In time, you may achieve your own biases, and we'll have to deal with that when it comes."

This made some sense to her but not complete sense. A nurse in charge? She knew she was capable, that was not the problem. She knew, but certainly the medical establishment didn't know. There was too much arrogance in medicine to accept a study with a nurse in charge. Definitely there was too much arrogance for Bristol himself to request it. But he was requesting it, right here, requesting her to do it, she heard him just this minute.

"Let me get this straight. You mean a nursing audit? Has something been wrong?"

"No. A general cardiac-arrest study. To see if we are effective enough, to see if we compare."

"Who's we?"

"Our unit versus the CCU, I think. You know, I'm sure, that we are periodically accused of not knowing what to do in a general medical emergency. Compared to the other ICUs."

Okay, a settle-this-little-wager-for-us kind of thing. Lydia stared at the red telephone, thinking ahead. Recognition. And resentment. The residents wouldn't cooperate, not really. They would resent her.

"What about the residents? They won't appreciate this much."

"I've discussed this with both chief residents. They don't see it as a problem."

Oh. First he asked the residents, then they refused, and then they all recognized her native intelligence and absence of bias. Now she saw.

"Did you try all the residents already?"

He twisted the wire into tight knots and tossed it into the waste can. "Okay. I think I can be frank with you. I did ask some of the residents. Some of them I don't entirely trust yet. Most of them are too busy. Three of them suggested you. So I went back over the retrospective study and decided that you qualify."

Still, this was something, a plum. She would take it, and not only for herself.

"Neuro versus coronary care?"

"An interesting comparison, no?"

"Yes. Very interesting. Consistency of care. Medical and nursing care, I think. Within one hospital in response to one specific situation."

"You'll take it on?"

"I'll take it on, I'll organize it. But I'd like to bring in some more nurses." She wasn't the only reliable, honest, interested nurse. They should know that.

"That wasn't exactly—"

"Just a few of us. Jonathan Bergman was a mixed blessing, but I'm the one who got him, or who got some of the better part of the mix. It could have been any of a number of intelligent women around here." Without him, she would still have been in one of the slots Bristol assigned all nurses. The "smart girl, for a nurse," slot. "I think it'll turn out better if there are a few of us, and maybe a few of the residents too. Working together. It wouldn't take much from them, but a joint effort could work real well. It might be better."

They stared each other down for a long five or six seconds.

"Okay. You organize it, write up your ideas and bring them here. Then I'll decide." He reached for his microphone, turned to face away from her. Go in peace.

She knew she was cheap labor from the start, but she enjoyed it. By now she had moved on from cardiac arrest into the kingdom of hemorrhage. By now he remembered her name. But still he gave his back to her and hunched away to tell his secrets.

He slapped Wheeler's shoulder, he patted it and chuckled and left. On his way out, he waved to the room in general.

Jane and Lydia moved past Wheeler to the next patient.

"Looks like an assembly line," he remarked.

"Feels like one," Lydia answered.

"What're you two up to?" Jane demanded.

"Looking for space to park my gadgets. And for help." He looked at Lydia.

She pulled the patient toward her so Jane could get started on the bed. Jane jammed dirty linen in under the patient's side, and then laid out the clean sheets, halved and in order. "You're not using this room," she said. "You're not using the window space."

"No. H.B. thought there might be room, but there's not."

"Don't get sucked in by that man." Jane narrowed her eyes at Wheeler and nodded. "I can see, it's already happening. You're the only one who understands him, you're the only one smart enough, sensitive enough, you think. I can see it. You think you're his confidant."

Wheeler shrugged. "I don't think anyone's honest with him. He appreciates honesty."

"Because he's such an honest man himself," Lydia added.

The sarcasm was lost on Sam. "Maybe."

"You're a goner!" Jane exclaimed. "So soon, too. The halls are tiled with the likes of you. Cast aside for a new golden boy, according to whim. Okay, turn her to me." They rolled the patient across the mound of sheets. "Mark my words, Wheeler. The scales will fall from your eyes and you shall know the truth. And it shall make you miserable." She grinned. "I hope I'm here to see it, and to accept your apologies."

He laughed, bowed to her. He checked his watch. "Lydia, I'd like to talk to you about helping me," he said. "Maybe next week. I have a soccer game today."

Lydia tugged the linen out from under the patient. "You play soccer?"

"Not me, my boys. But I have to be there."

"How old?"

"Nine and eleven. Their first season in the States. They love it."

"Are they any good?" Jane asked.

"No. The older one, Andrew, will be good by the end of the season. Joel just has fun. He's not serious enough yet." He checked his watch again. "I'll talk to you next week then, Lydia?"

"I'll listen," she said. "Enjoy your weekend."

They worked in silence long after he had gone. Suctioning, wiping, measuring, prodding.

"Idealistic," Jane said, walking back to the first patient's bed. "Watch out for that one," as she inserted the thermometer. And finally, "You think you'll work with him?"

"Probably not."

Lydia had been thinking of Jonathan, remembering. She felt heat behind her ears and acid in the back of her throat. More than anything, she hated being fooled.

Jonathan Bergman was the right man at the right time, short and dark, a neurosurgical resident, second year. Her eyes were level with his, or slightly above when she wore shoes, but neither of them minded. He liked her legs, and her healthy haunches, he said. This didn't offend her, not in the least. She thought he was just more honest than most of them, and she thought his haunches were nice, too.

Jonathan walked her home for the first time after an especially awful Saturday night and Sunday morning. They had lost a guy who struggled so determinedly against his tracheostomy and respirator that as soon as he managed to squirm it out, his damaged windpipe swelled and closed off and he was as good as finished. Jonathan tried to find an agreeable alternative, up and down the man's throat. He slit frantically in the inch-long space nature had allotted, only to find angry red swollen cartilage and muscle all through. The whole thing took seconds, half a minute tops, but long enough for the man to turn gray then blue then purple from the neck up and the wrists and ankles down. Nothing anyone could do, nothing they could think of to be done. They spent a good hour and a half explaining to everyone, defending each other and feeling like murderers, and then they walked over to Jimmy's, the only place they could find to serve them a drink at eight-thirty on a Sunday morning.

They did not talk at all. Their eyes wouldn't even meet. They felt guilty and accusing at the same time—where were you when? . . . why didn't you try? . . . what else could we do?—and they both would have cried if their eyes had met. He drank beer and she drank Bloody Marys, staring at the black-and-white set on the bar, watching hundreds of preschoolers playing Mozart violin pieces by the Suzuki method on Channel 2.

He walked her home through Central Park, where the jonquils and dogwood and forsythia were bright and cheerful and promised a full spring soon. He took her hand at the Seventy-ninth Street entrance, put his arm around her crossing the Great Lawn at about Eighty-fourth, and pulled her to him on top of the hill next to the playground at Eighty-sixth and Central Park West.

"Jonathan, I'm so sorry."

"Me too."

They kissed to drown out the sobs with wide open agonal moans. Nothing like death as an aphrodisiac. In five minutes they were inside her apartment.

Remorse melded with tension with desire with fatigue and morning alcohol, turning them both into one appetite, wanting, needing, both of them together at the same time that first time.

"It's not as if I've never lost a patient before." He ran the flat of his hand along the outside of her bare thighs. "You have the longest thighs. Me oh my."

"I still don't know what happened. He should have been fine. To have to stand there and watch it. If he hadn't screwed up his trach, mmmmmm."

They kissed quietly, without the desperation, more giving than taking this time, more awareness of the other than the self. His lips followed her chin and neck and shoulder, down her collarbone to the center very spot where their patient had failed them. They moved against each other, they rubbed, therapeutic touch. He massaged round and round and round, playing her body like an accomplished Suzuki violinist.

"Come inside me," she sang. "Please, now. Inside me. Now."

Finally he filled her, moved slowly at first, in synchrony with her moving, filled her with pure mindless sensation, made solely to please her. He was her instrument now, moving faster, his thighs slapping hers, faster, arrhythmic, convulsive. A pulse flushed over her, the meter of the music, in four-four time, radiating heat and the beat. He shuddered.

They slept into evening. She woke with a hangover and he woke up cursing. He had slept through some commitment, some event. She tactfully showered while he made his phone call, feeling slightly responsible for not waking him up in time to do whatever he was supposed to have done, knowing it was silly for her to feel responsible but feeling it all the same. Thinking he would despise her forever for keeping him so long.

"Tough. I don't care, it's your own fault," she muttered, coming out dripping into the bedroom.

"What?"

"Nothing. You want some eggs?" Feeling embarrassed now. What was Bergman doing in her bedroom anyway? "I'm embarrassed, Dr. Bergman."

"Yeah, I know. You smell great."

"That's not comforting, you know." She carried her jeans and a shirt to the bathroom, to dress in privacy. "Look." She called out. "I took advantage of the situation. You didn't have to walk me home, though."

He came in as she finished buttoning her shirt. That compact furry body. He carried it comfortably, unashamed, even unaware of it. His penis bounced and swayed, teasing her. She knew this body, she liked it. She patted the belly.

"Why do you think I walked you home? Those legs, those legs. Drove me crazy all night. Can I take a shower?"

"Sure."

"You shouldn't be allowed to wear trousers at work, not you. Too distracting, your rump. You got any shampoo?"

"Here. But listen, I don't want you thinking, um, I mean, oh, never mind." She just didn't want him avoiding her, thinking she expected something from him now. "I don't believe in true love and all that. Can you hear me all right? So that should set your mind at ease." Very nonchalant. "Don't imagine I'll be falling in love with you or anything because I won't. I just like your hands. And your body. That's all."

"Towel!"

"Did you hear me?"

"I'm crazy about your body too." He unbuttoned her jeans, unzipped them, got hard again. Wrapped his soaking naked self around her clean covered one. Zipped her jeans back up and buttoned them. "I wish I could show you how crazy all over again . . ."

"You tease."

"That's me. Gotta go. Sorry." He dried off, dressed, and was gone, like that. "See you later?" he said on his way out the door. "At work?"

She made coffee for herself, and scrambled eggs. She sat on the windowsill to eat them, and watched the soft spring night and listened to dogs and children out in the first warmth, and to mating calls from men and women walking by in the dark.

"It's down a whole degree!" Jane was holding up the thermometer probe in a bizarre victory salute. "That was quick, my focus must be right on. I'll just give him another dose for good measure." She positioned herself at the foot of the patient's bed and took hold of his big toes to reestablish the healing circuit.

"Anything else?" Bristol asked. "Complications with any of the patients?" His hands were poised on the edge of the table, pushing off. Everyone in the room looked at everyone else in the room with the same silent questions: Complications? Problems? Catastrophes? Lydia glanced at the empty chair next to her. Wheeler had been absent for more than a week.

Mitchell coughed. He looked from Lydia to Bristol. "There is a potential problem." The room was restless, papers being shuffled, Casper bent down to tie his shoelace. "Only insofar as policy goes, no harm has actually been done. I don't expect there will be harm done."

Mitch looked to Lydia again. "Better to tell him before he finds out on his own," he had said yesterday. "Believe me, I know him.

All it'll be is some anecdote for him to relate at conferences. That's all, if I handle it right. If he hears from someone outside the department, he'll think they're laughing at him. And Jane's ass'll be slung for sure," he had insisted. "I know what I'm doing." Lydia dearly hoped he did.

Christine pulled X rays down off the view box. Three junior residents mumbled together by the door, and the social worker stood up to leave.

Bristol adjusted the watchband on his wrist. "You have four minutes. Is it a four-minute problem?"

"I'll try," Mitch answered. He glanced once more at Lydia. "Uh, one of the nurses is practicing laying on of hands." He smiled genially. Presenting a simple, slightly offbeat fact.

The group by the door stopped mumbling. The social worker sat down. Casper's head bobbed up, his nose wrinkled, he sniffed.

Bristol pulled his glasses from his pocket and began wiping them with his handkerchief. "Yes?" Unmoved.

"She's a very good nurse. Been around a long time. Patients like her."

Pain had become Jane's particular forte. Her techniques worked wonders with headache, cramps and muscle spasm, which made a lot of sense if you thought about it. The whole process required a mind cleared of everything except blue faith in success. The patient's energy focused away from the pain toward the absence of it. Fever also responded. Lydia had been quite impressed.

"I mean, it's not the revival-meeting stuff." Mitch had his hand on the back of his neck, rubbing self-consciously. "The technique is from a Master's-level course. A form of meditation. Therapeutic Touch."

"Does it interfere with patient care?"

"Not at all, so far. People are using it in a couple of hospice centers in the city."

Bristol slipped his glasses on, looked over the top of them at Mitch. "Does she force this business on anyone?"

"Matter of fact, they ask for her." Mitch's upper lip was moist. He wiped it with his thumb. "Matter of fact," he smiled, "my laminectomy refused his preop meds yesterday. Insisted on having her treatment instead. Required less anesthesia, too." A few of the men laughed.

"Unorthodox." Bristol massaged his beard. He stretched his

head back and stared at the ceiling. Mitch glanced at Lydia, she shrugged. The room held its breath, three of the four minutes were up.

"Quite unorthodox." Bristol stayed still for fifteen more seconds. "Let's keep it to ourselves." He sat up straight and turned to look at Lydia, at the social worker, at the miscellaneous no ones who might not have gotten his point. "Let's keep it to ourselves." He smiled. "I'll speak with the nursing director," massaging his beard. "We can't condone it, of course. And we don't want it all over the hospital, or the country." Back to Mitch. "Less anesthesia, you say? Huh, huh, huh. Too bad you didn't come up with it first."

Time. Five seconds to spare.

Bristol scraped his chair back across the floor. Three residents mumbled in the corner. The social worker stood, and Christine packed the X rays into their giant yellow envelopes. Mike Mitchell rose last, following Lydia out the door.

"What'd I tell you?" he whispered. "Piece of cake."

"I'm just glad he was in a good mood." They walked several doors behind Bristol, through the halls to the ward.

"You and me both, Legs. I'd hate to lose Jane over something harmless like this. But if he found out from, say, the Chief of Medicine . . ."

"He would have been embarrassed, that's all. He has no jurisdiction over nursing. He couldn't do a thing."

Mitch took her elbow and stopped her. "Don't kid yourself." He looked around. "If it's important to him, he can apply more pressure than anyone around here."

"You're all too awed by him."

"Yeah? Well, I don't see you speaking up. It's a healthy fear. It's realistic. He's in a position to break us. All he has to do is forget me for six months and I've had it. My practice dwindles, my research gets published by someone else before me, I'm finished."

Lydia pulled her arm away from him and started walking again. "If it helped Jane, thank you," she said.

"Anything for you. Or her." He picked a cigar from his lab coat pocket, smelling it through the wrapping.

"Where's Wheeler been?" Lydia asked. "I haven't seen him around." She meant it casually, but it came out so casually, she thought, that it sounded important.

"Beats me. I'm not privy to the inside dope right now. I think he's around." He unwrapped the cigar. Smelled it ecstatically. "You sure know how to cool my jets, old girl." He opened the door to the ward and they stepped through together.

"You're late again," Regina called.

Lydia walked Milton Bonner, an old Parkinsonian codger, marched him one two three four up to the medicine room and back, singing light and bouncy with him, counting out the beat and stepping to the count, to overcome his hesitant shuffle, to even it out. They did "Sgt. Pepper's Lonely Hearts Club Band," marching together laughing back to his room, slowing down the beat gradually, to a halt at his bedside. Then she moved straight into "Lucy in the Sky With Diamonds," it was next on the album, except she substituted Milton for Lucy.

She had finished the last chorus and lifted Milton's skinny knees to help him into bed when Sam Wheeler looked in.

"Hi."

"Oh, hi," she said. "Long time no see." Original. "I thought we'd lost you."

"I've been setting a few things up. Working nights. Writing grants." He stood in the doorway, watching her positioning the old man, padding his bones with blankets and pillows. "Are you always so happy?" he asked.

"Not hardly. I just like Mr. Bonner here."

He didn't offer to help her, she didn't need his help, but he didn't offer it. He just watched. And after about a minute he left.

Lydia wanted to talk to him, to ask him about his project. He hadn't mentioned anything more since that day weeks before. She thought of going out and stopping him, then decided against it. If he wanted her, he could find her. She tucked Milton in tight and warm, gave him a drink of water and forgot about Sam Wheeler. He came around once more—she didn't see him but she heard his whistle: "Sgt. Pepper."

She heard him without seeing him for almost two weeks, walking his machines down the hall toward the unit and, a few hours later, walking back the other way. She always seemed to be in the middle of something. Altogether, he and his gadgets made a distinctive rumble, with one squealing wheel and Sam whistling something as he went. Golden oldies, Beach Boys hits. Not loud, but persistent and unself-conscious. Sometimes she found herself humming the same song, out of the blue, later in the day. It taunted her, that whistle.

She finally caught up with him on nights. She had piggybacked her last four-a.m. antibiotic when she heard it, Paul Anka's "Diana" coming from the unit, through the open doors and into the early-morning quiet. He was whistling to Diana, the night nurse, and to Charlotte Wilson, a comatose, sixty-three-year-old woman who never woke up after coronary artery surgery.

Most of the lights were off except around the central monitor and desk, in the middle of the room. The unit looked nearly romantic in the glow, calmed except for an overhead spotlight freezing one patient's cubicle into a sharp tableau. Sam whistled in the center of the bright clean beam, leaning over Charlotte, asleep and rendered more sickly pale and yellowish by that white white light. He was testing a nerve stimulus in the woman's right calf, buzzing it until her leg twitched just enough but not too much, to the strains of Paul's pubescent passion. His Adam's apple jutted to a point and bobbed with each new note. Lydia had an urge to touch it.

"You always whistle oldies?" she asked.

"Huh? Oh, hi." The electrode slipped from his grip. He replaced it on the woman's calf, taped it securely. He smiled at Lydia.

"You never whistle anything current," she insisted. "Not that I've ever heard around here, anyway."

"So?" He shrugged, turned to his machine.

It looked fairly complicated. There were several rows of dials and buttons, black with white numbers, red with black, and a few green knobs. Wheeler didn't seem at ease with the delicate settings, his fingers too large for the small levers and dials.

"Oldies," he murmured. "I never thought about it." He fussed with two neck electrodes, then calibrated the averager, and finally relaxed into a swivel chair placed between Charlotte's bed and the two electrography consoles. "No one ever mentioned it to me." He worked on his dials and graphs and electric currents, worked studiously, closing her out. "Guess I'm stuck or something," he said after a while, but he didn't look up so Lydia wasn't positive he was speaking to her.

She watched the wave spikes on his green screen, watched them change from one electrode to the next and the next, and finally she left. An hour later he bopped into the medicine room whistling a medley of Bo Diddley and looking for a cup of coffee.

She glanced up from the order books and laughed. "You're mocking me."

"Maybe. But only a little." He poured himself coffee with milk, no sugar. He sat down with her.

"So what exactly is it that you're doing?" she asked him.

"Making myself immortal," he said. "Good coffee."

"Thanks. Seriously, what are you doing?"

"Seriously, making myself immortal." He stared at a box of donuts set in the middle of the cart next to the percolator. "Anything to eat around here?"

"Help yourself."

"Thanks. I'll buy tomorrow."

"I've heard that one before."

"No, really. I will." He picked up two Boston Creams. "I see you don't believe that I'm making myself immortal."

"I see that you don't want to talk about it."

"Sure I do. I'm honored even that you asked. You know, you can do an awful lot of things around here and people act like it's all part of the program. Nobody's even curious." He sat down at the head of the work table nearest the window. "There are five, maybe six, yeah six, intensive care units in this hospital. I go into all of them to see patients, mostly at night. So I walk in and say, 'I'm Dr. Wheeler and I've come to do EMGs, NCVs, SERs, BAERs, VERs, EEGs, ultrasound, da da dadatadatadatada, on patient so-and-so, his family signed,' and that's it. They give me the nod, no questions asked. Nobody asks. Isn't that unbelievable? As if they know exactly what I'm talking about and it's the most natural thing in the world for some strange guy to come skulking in at three a.m. with four large machines and a selection of multicolored probes and electrodes. Nurses are too busy and the docs think they should know already so they're too embarrassed to ask. You're the first person who's asked what it is, exactly, that I'm doing."

"So what is it, exactly, that you're doing?"

He finished one donut and moved the second one to the middle of his napkin, precisely to the middle. "Making myself immortal."

This was getting tiresome. "I see why no one asks."

"It's true, what I said, I'm not kidding." He rotated the donut once more and finally picked it up and took a bite. "I'm establishing a battery of tests which will, I hope, predict the prognoses of comatose patients. So a hundred years from now, after Mr. X has his cardiac arrest and I'm dead, they'll run the tests and say, 'According to the Wheeler Scale, Mr. X has a good chance for a full recovery,' or 'By the Wheeler Index, Mr. X has no chance for independent function.' Immortality. My tests are more scientific and less subject to examiner variability than all the clinical predictors they've come up with so far. And the machinery's very impressive. Physicians like machinery, gadgets, computers. They'll eat it right up." He licked frosting from his fingers. "My name will be on the lips of necrophiliacs from Maine to California."

She laughed despite herself, laughed hard, small mouth wide open and whole head tipped back. He joined her, his Adam's apple sliding down and up and down along his neck.

He came and went with his whistle for several more nights in a row, coming and going. He added a little Billy Joel to his repertoire, provided donuts or bagels on alternate nights, and finally asked if she was interested in working with him on his project.

"I don't know," she said, her mouth half full of pumpernickel.

"Chance of a lifetime." He was cleaning goo off the ultrasound head. Going into the corners with a paper clip end.

"I still have the other things. The arrest study, and the hemorrhage stuff."

"But the cardiac-arrest study doesn't have me. I can make you immortal. The Wheeler-Weber Scale."

"Wheeler-Dealer Scale. I don't know." She pulled at a strand of her hair, twirled it between her thumb and middle finger. "It would be interesting, though. Something new."

"And you can use a lot of what you already know from the other business. We'll see some of those patients. Anyone in coma. Seriously, you'd be a big help."

She believed she would. "Maybe it's time to expand, you think?"

"Could be."

She stood to get more coffee and noticed the beginning of a bald spot on the crown of Sam's head. She was thinking of Jonathan and all the work she had done for him, all the energy she invested, being the mule and dumbly accepting the role. "I did this once. Worked with a resident on chart reviews."

"Bristol told me."

"Well, it wasn't exactly the same, I was sort of involved with the man and that confused the issue." Working side by side had seemed incredibly exciting. Same goal, same interest, a shared task. "I imagined I was important, even essential." She had felt so enlightened at the time, so wise. "It was a lot like a French farce."

Looking back, she could laugh, as most people laugh when they look back. She wondered if Jonathan laughed too, probably he was laughing already back then.

No expectations, no illusions, not she, not anymore. She played it all rather convincingly, apparently so convincingly that Jonathan risked seeing her often at first, knowing they were two of a kind, he wouldn't have to worry about her feelings or anything.

She thought she was gaining ground, making herself beloved and indispensable. And she decided she did love him, pretty quickly she decided that, something left over from way before, fucking without love was a sin. She never let on that she loved him, oh no. And she gave him plenty of rope. The wise thing to do.

Later, she saw him erratically, but always with passion. They fit together well. She liked the compact size of him and he liked her sweet ass, that's what he said. He bounded up the stairs to her place two steps at a time, and she was there waiting. They would kiss and kiss again and be half-naked before she locked the door behind him. Then sometime halfway through everything, she wondered had she locked the door, and she would have to get up to go look, like as not she hadn't. It annoyed him, her too, but it prolonged the foreplay so neither actually minded at all.

Afterward they took about half an hour to talk. About the study, about people at work. She would go to the kitchen naked and put water on to boil, then she'd get dressed and drip the coffee, and by the time it was ready, he was all groomed and ready too. Every once in a while she made a yeast bread or a coffee cake to go along with it. He always remarked on her baked goods.

She promised herself to keep cool about him. She unplugged her phone for days at a time so she wouldn't be tempted to answer it, just in case he was calling, and also in case he wasn't calling. She wouldn't allow herself daydreams about him, only the here and the now. She ran through her class presentations when she drifted off to sleep, or thought about the last time she had seen him, never the next time.

Jonathan gave her a kitten several weeks after her twenty-eighth birthday, he found it in his laundry room. A scrawny gray and white with a full furry face. She named him Bozo. He was such a skinny screaming chewed-up-looking squirt in the beginning. He ate huge amounts, he complained, and didn't understand about the litter box, she had to train him for Pete's sake, it took more than a week. Later he thrived, filled out, shone in the sunlight, a real beauty. He slept at her feet so she couldn't move in the night without feeling him there.

She allowed herself one daydream.

About inviting Jonathan home to East Ridge. In it he was quite nervous but determined. There was elaborate kissing and Jonathan said something about marriage.

Their study was completed. She didn't hear from him for almost a month. Once, after he brought Bozo, then nothing over Christmas or New Year's. She had already had the one daydream, and she felt like such a fool, looking back.

"Look, I could really use your help," is what he said when she finally did see him. Not marriage, but research, and he sounded so sincere. "I trust you, doesn't that mean something? There aren't many people I trust. Maybe none besides you."

They weren't even alone. She was cleaning crud out of Mickey Pollack's dried-up toothless mouth, in the ICU, and here was Jonathan to ask a favor, as if she owed him.

"I don't have the time to do it myself. Bristol expects something by the end of next month. Please? I need you." He bit his upper lip.

"I don't have all that much time either, you know. You think you can just snap your fingers, right?"

"You're the only one I trust."

"Bull."

"No, it's true. Please, Lydia. It won't take that much time."

"Like the cardiac-arrest audit I did for you. Not much time, my eye. Not much for you maybe. If it's not much time, then do it yourself." She dug deeper into Mickey's mouth with the forceps. Pulled out a crust of caked saliva and tube-feeding from his palate.

Jonathan touched her elbow. She jerked it away, losing the crust on the floor somewhere.

"Okay. You're right. You did the whole arrest review yourself."

"Don't go overboard. But I did do most of it."

"Your name goes on the paper. This one too. And I'll do a lot more this time. Please?"

Something about the way his lips moved, the set of them.

"What's it on?"

He grinned. "Transient ischemia." The winner and still champion.

* * *

"French farce?" Sam was asking. Lydia stood up from the table to sharpen her pencil. He held out his coffee cup for her to refill while she was up, plus milk, no sugar.

"Never mind," she said. "It's not important."

She and Jonathan had started in on TIAs right away, some evenings, some weekends, down in medical records or the neurosurgery office, working together half of the time and Lydia doing the rest. It was interesting and, besides, she got her name on the paper. She was learning a lot.

They spent less and less time together except for sifting through notes and O.R. reports and discharge summaries. It got to be a drag. She felt asexual and slightly testy.

"Look," his eyes gleamed. "This is my work. The most important thing in my life." Noble. "The Samaritan is my mistress. My work, my patients, will always come first. That's the simple truth." Worthy of Gregory Peck.

"Pretty narcissistic, if you ask me." She acted very offhand. "*Your* work, *your* patients. What would happen if not for *you*?" She should have stayed with that first insight, but at the time he even sounded noble. Altruistic. She saw him drenched with fever in Somalia, sweating streaks of dirt from the dust everywhere. "To hell with the fever. I must operate. My patient will die if I don't save him."

"Take it or leave it," he said. "You can spend time working with me here, or I can do it myself. But the work, Lydia, is me." Absolutely believable.

Within a week Dr. Bristol spoke to her about the previous study she had helped with. He asked her opinion on night cardiac arrest procedure and she gave it. Then he said, "That's what I think. Good work, we're all pleased," which elated Lydia despite herself. Recognition. A beginning anyway. Helping Jonathan had paid off. Not in quite the way she'd imagined, but a payoff all the same.

The following day, she overslept and got to work in the middle of things, feeling rushed. She wanted clean hair more than anything, would have settled for coffee and one quiet cigarette before starting in, but no. Nearly every patient had to be somewhere by eight-thirty and there were no stretchers and only two wheelchairs to take them. Regina was busy on the phone to the pharmacy about missing a box of codeine, and the unit manager decided that finding stretchers was not her job that particular morning. That's how it began.

How it ended was with Mr. Morrison herniating and going back to the O.R. He'd been returned at three-thirty, change of shift, after a pituitary tumor resection. He woke up fine in recovery, everything stable as stable could be, the pulse a bit rapid—probably left-over anesthesia—he would be fine, give him time.

By four p.m. he was all over the bed, restless, crazy and screaming, "I can't see!" The surgery was supposed to take the pressure off his optic nerve when the tumor was removed, but his vision seemed worse than preop. In practically no time he ticked off his brainstem, eye movements, pupils, face, tongue, only moments, no kidding, then the arms and legs.

A bleed they were sure, where the tumor used to be and more. Mitchell barked out orders for Lydia to push 100 grams of Mannitol into his IV line, to diurese the brain, dry it up, make space for the blood, buy time. The patient's breathing went shallow, irregular, he puffed and snored, so they reintubated him and hyperventilated him with a black rubber bag on the return trip to surgery.

Lydia herself pumped the ambu bag, while Mitchell checked and rechecked the pupils, pressure, pulse, both of them running alongside the bed, like something out of *Ben Casey*. Invigorating, because they were doing exactly what they could and should do for the man with the clot pressing down on his brainstem. Exactly.

Her fingers and forearms ached from the pumping by the time they got upstairs. Mitch made one last check on the guy before he took off to scrub. Mr. Morrison was stable, they had held his own for him and made it just in time.

Lydia was beat. She had no desire to abstract charts so she called Jonathan to cancel out. He surprised her, she had expected an argument, but he seemed perfectly reasonable. He thought he might go up to see Mr. Morrison and then work on the project himself.

She put her feet up and caught her breath on a cigarette, and when she was done she decided maybe she could look at a few charts and then go home. She would surprise Jonathan.

Medical records knew her by now. A woman named Georgia decoded Lydia's charts, pulled them, stacked them, and mourned the loss of unretrieved records and microfilms as if they were her own. She and Lydia smiled at each other in the cafeteria and nodded in elevators.

When Lydia went down to pick up the charts, Georgia waved, as usual, but then pointed to the outside work tables, raised her eyebrows. Some woman sat hunched over a pile of bound charts, Lydia's charts, what was she doing?

Lydia recognized her, she worked in the operating room, a scrub nurse or physician's assistant or something. A small blonde from Texas, Joyce, no—maybe Judy or Joanne. Lydia strolled over to check things out.

They were Lydia's charts, ordered for Dr. Bergman, his name was right there in her handwriting. The blonde flipped through them rapidly; obviously she knew what to look for and how to look for it, she knew the questions, she had done this before. She filled in the answers on forms Lydia had designed.

"You doing this for Bergman?" Lydia asked.

"Oh hi, yeah. I just help him out sometimes when he's busy." She winked a cowgirl wink. "Did you need something?"

"No."

"Because Jon should be back any minute. He went to the machines for some peanuts for me. I got hungry."

Lydia wanted to scream. She saw herself screaming over the noise of all the computers in medical records, over all the phones and the gossip. She saw herself making a scene, ripping the neat data sheets into tiny fragments and then stabbing Judy or Joanne or whoever she was with her bandage scissors, stabbing the charts, stabbing most of all Jonathan, stabbing him eighteen times. She saw peanuts rolling all over the floor, and blood. Housekeeping would have a fit about cleaning it up.

Sam sipped his coffee, waiting for Lydia to recall why she might not want to work with him. She stared at a complete blood count someone had jotted onto the Formica tabletop months ago, a permanent record of a patient long gone.

"It had to do with lopsided collaboration," she finally said. Her eyes blurred on the blood count, Hct: 47, skewed it out of focus. "Forget the personal stuff, that died. He didn't contribute much at all to the work." She looked up. "I'd have to get something out of this too. I mean intellectually. I want to learn something. I'm a good mule, but I have to be interested."

Sam let her talk herself out, sat there looking as if he had the right answers. He tossed his empty cup into the trash bin. "No problem." All the right answers. "You'll learn a hell of a lot. And we'll do it together, all of it. The other thing is, it's not only observational. We stand a chance of intervening, making a difference for people. The compound from Denmark."

He said "we." He was very excited about it, tiger's eyes shining clear gold at her, enticing. "As soon as the drug gets here and gets approved, we can start that."

"I'll think about it," she said. "It's a lot of extra time."

"We'll arrange it, Bristol will. I promise, you won't be sorry."

Lydia started coming in on her own time, once or twice a week, at night. She watched Sam run the studies and she read papers and chapters and whole books about electrophysiology and the brain. Then Sam taught her how to do all the tests and she began to understand what each small component meant to the overall picture. Through the fall to early winter they sat in the dark, among graphs and consoles and screens and people who were for all intents and purposes mostly dead, measuring degrees of death and a rare, full-blooming life.

She wondered why he didn't go home, why he seemed not to mind the hours. She offered to do the work herself sometimes, so he wouldn't have to stay at the hospital, but he refused. She imagined that he didn't trust her capability enough yet, though she already trusted him enough to offer it.

All the sharp spikes and slopes, the jagged lines, the blacks and the whites became familiar as friends. They had started out a jumble of meaningful confusion, intimidating her. Looking at them now felt like driving the roads of East Ridge, going from point to point without thinking, without attention, until some unfamiliar construction came up, a shopping mall or some new road across the highway. Then she would take note of it, figure out what it meant and where it might lead.

Sam indulged her. He took her speculations seriously, giving them his attention, enlarging on them, saying excitedly, yes, you might be right, or no, that's off the wall, and explaining specifically why.

He always sat next to her now. At conference and at work, as if they belonged sitting together, like cousins in school, or best friends. It was their natural place.

"Any developments on the Index so far?" Bristol asked at the end of an uneventful morning meeting. "Anything to report?" He turned his chair around, giving honor to Sam, and his back to the rest of the room. He winked. "I hope you're doing more than just spending time with a pretty girl all these nights. I hope Lydia doesn't mind that I call her a pretty girl." He winked again.

"Hardly a girl," she answered. Her ears felt red-hot. She smiled at Bristol in spite of herself. Her mouth seemed to know what was required.

"We'll have statistics for you by the end of next week. Comparisons of chemical versus structural causes of coma, early predictive schemes." Sam moved subtly closer to Lydia. Without touching, she felt his warmth warmer along her right arm. "If I'd had to do it alone, I could never have seen as many patients. Or asked quite the same questions."

"Don't overdo it," she murmured, and the whole room laughed, including Bristol.

He winked. "Smart girl."

She and Sam sat between monitors and half-dead patients and talked about electrophysiology and themselves. He told her stories about his garden, his children, and rampant gypsy moths.

She talked about Tennessee. About the Pastor, about Mama, Dinah, Marie and the church, as if the church were another sibling, the favorite child who demanded the most time, and whom she ignored now that she was away from the family.

"I lost the habit of it," she told him. "And they gave up asking somewhere along the line, that's all."

Long-distance phone calls with Mama chattering questions at her about churches in the neighborhood, and her own silence, and Pastor's silence, equal to hers. Sometimes he cleared his throat or coughed, and Lydia made noncommittal noises. She didn't hate God, she loved Him. She just never got to church.

"The first Sunday I ever worked was real odd," she started. "Right after I graduated and had my first job. It felt strange to begin with, and then it felt good, exhilarating in a certain way."

She was out of the house before anyone else even woke up. The air was still damp and dark from the night, she wore her navy sweater to keep out the chill. She passed the six-thirty Mass letting out at Our Lady of Perpetual Help and then, for the first time, she remembered it was Sunday. It had seemed like any day.

Later, church broadcasts through the bedside radio hookups, snatches of the First Christian Church of North Chattanooga, thin voices singing out Gospel melodies. Lydia joined in while she bathed old Otis Spitzer, she joined right in automatically, and he smiled when she got to "oh, refresh us, oh, refresh us, traveling through this wilderness." That's when she realized she had been singing all along. She mentioned it to Pastor at dinner that night, thinking he might be pleased, and he was. He smiled, much as Mr. Spitzer had smiled.

What she didn't tell him about was the great burst of freedom she felt when she finished singing the song. Knowing she didn't have to sing another one, knowing she could walk away when she wanted to, knowing nobody was watching. She felt absolutely separated and free in that moment.

Despite that feeling, after she left home and through her first year in New York, the seasons of the church year clung to her as extra layers of clothes cling in the summer, collected from Sunday to Sunday. She thought of them more than if she'd been faithful: the Four Sundays in Advent, Christmas Eve, Christmas Day (a heavy cotton flannel shirt), Epiphany, all the Sundays After Epiphany through to Quinquagesima Sunday, the ninth, then Ash Wednesday and Lent, Palm Sunday, Maundy Thursday, Good Friday, Easter Sunday, a thicker and bulkier mantle as the church year progressed through Pentecost and a thousand Sundays After Pentecost until she finally had to say to her parents, Look, I don't know when I'll go back to church.

"You don't want to alienate them," Sam advised, years of Sundays later, way after the fact.

She resented this advice. It's over. I've handled it myself, she wanted to say. "Of course not," she said.

The truth was, she didn't think about it much anymore. Only sometimes, Sunday mornings when she passed a church and heard the music.

"Not alienate. They just had to realize I'm different. Exceptional to the family rule. I'm not a sheep, I won't simply follow, not anymore. I'll come by my own way, in my own good time."

They shared bits and pieces of each of their lives, and these linked onto the research, onto patients, so that a landmark wave, a characteristic blip, set off the memory of a Wheeler soccer match, or a picnic along Moccasin Bend, and would forever set these off. A specific patient with his own specific history brought up an East Ridge Christmas program when Lydia forgot her lines, or whatever she and Sam were talking about on the night they studied that patient.

Marty Jerome, the forty-three-year-old man they were looking at again, reminded her of Sam's second son, Joel, playing the clarinet—she saw a small boy with curly blond hair blowing a reedy *Minuet in G*—because Joel had played his first recital the night before the first time they had studied the man.

"Remind me never to have a bypass," Lydia had said that time.

"Why do we have to do him again?" she asked now, the second time. It wasn't the work, it was the collecting of the evidence of dying in a man who had barely started living that got her down. She didn't need to repeat it. "I hope we're not doing this twice for my benefit, as a learning experience." She adjusted the last electrode onto the patient's scalp.

Sam secured the earphones into the man's ears. He frowned without answering, whistled softly through his teeth. He sat down in front of the console and turned on the left earphone. It would produce a click sound in the patient's ear.

"They think he's waking up," he said. "Jane told me he sometimes seems to be tracking with his eyes, and sometimes he seems to be smiling."

Lydia stood behind Sam. She watched the progression of waves on the screen as the stimulus click produced responses through the primitive brainstem structures and on up into the hemispheres.

"Look. Sam!" She grabbed hold of Sam's shoulder. "He's got some cortical response. Look! A lot of it!"

The patient himself appeared unchanged, oblivious to the awakenings inside his head. Sam turned up the click volume and the cortical wave increased in amplitude and complexity, he turned it down but the blip stayed, strong and dramatic. Sam put his wide hand over Lydia's on his shoulder, and he smiled. A gesture of friends sharing success. They stayed for several minutes, watching the screen. She glanced at Sam's face once, the greenish glow illuminating his anticipation.

"Maybe it's nothing," he said later, in the medicine room. "I mean, Jane did say she thought he smiled once. That was a clue. It's not as if he hadn't changed at all on the outside."

"Stop putting us down. Want a cigarette?" Lydia took one for herself and handed him the pack. He pushed it back without taking one. She hesitated, then threw her cigarette away. "We picked it up clearly," she continued. "Nothing subtle about it. He didn't do anything measurably different to the eye, but we got strong electrical evidence. Your stuff is way more sensitive than anything they ever had before."

He laughed at her confidence. "I guess you're right."

Instead of smoking, she played with the pack, balancing it on end, flipping it across the table with her right forefinger, flipping it back with her left.

"What I wish is that we could measure thought," she said, still playing with the pack. Sam groaned. Lydia persisted.

"If you can induce an isoelectric—is that right? flat line?—isoelectric EEG with a drug overdose, in which case you know the brain is not dead, then you aren't, you can't be, measuring thought, dreams, the unconscious, which go on in an O.D. Not with what we've got now, anyway."

"Put that way, I agree. But we have other tools. We can see dead brain on a CAT or NMR scan, for instance. And in an O.D. we see live brain."

"I don't accept that. Find thought, devise a way to measure it, and then we can talk about brain death. I don't think you can really be sure otherwise."

"We have studies showing that a person who fills all our criteria for brain death cannot live as an organism without total support to lung and heart." Dr. Wheeler. Impatient with intuitions and metaphysics. He dealt in facts and clinical papers, statistics, tables. "And that those who show no evidence of intellect for a set period of time, a month after the initial insult, overwhelmingly will not recover intellect."

"I don't care," she insisted. "You still can't be sure that there isn't thought, some kind of unconscious. You can't be sure." She wasn't sure she was right either, but she knew he couldn't prove her wrong.

He tipped his chair back and watched out the window. There were a few lights on in rooms in the pediatric wing, and a rare lamp was lit in the apartment buildings two blocks distant. There were no stars to be seen, not from the medicine room. He eased his chair flat but continued to stare outside.

"Why did you never to go medical school, Lydia?" he asked.

"Why do doctors always think nurses want to be doctors?" She picked up the pack, took out a cigarette, looked at it and then returned it to the pack. "The answer is that I wanted to be a nurse. I wanted to help people in fundamental ways, with my hands on them, touching them, being with them and talking to them, not speculating about them in the abstract, at the foot of the bed. I wanted to get close to them."

Sam still stared out the window, so that she wasn't sure he heard her answer. "What about you?" she prodded, and shoved his hand with her hand, twice, until he looked at her. "What made you want to deal in abstracts? Why did you choose an intellectual exercise like neurology research?"

"Family tradition," he said simply, and returned his eyes to the night outside. Was he thinking about thought, the unconscious?

Lydia gave in and lit up after all. She puffed away to her heart's content and wondered why she didn't go home now to sleep, in the middle of the night, and why he didn't do the same.

"First I tried law school." He continued his answer as if he had never paused. "Rebellion. We had always been doctors, probably since Adam, so I decided to try law. Like you and church. I gave myself the freedom to decide, and I hated it. Really hated it. The law is too easily manipulated." He turned back to the room and to Lydia.

"So you picked the most powerless specialty in medicine," she said.

"You may have noticed, though, that I'm working on ways to control it. We are."

"You made your family happy?"

"Sure." He sighed. "My Dad was happy till the day he died. Lot of good the medical training did us that day."

Third year at medical school. Neuropathology elective. Sam was slicing sections of brain for slides when the call came. Mr. A. E. Brick's brain he had been working on, A. E.'s brain metastases. And then someone, some secretary, came to get him for a phone call, which was odd. "Tell them to call me back or else I'll get back to them later," he had said. "No, this is important," she said, and it was. And then he was at his father's office, it took no time to get there. No time at all before he was there ready to resuscitate his own father, save his life. But the body was gone, and his uncle was already collecting the personal effects.

Anyone would have done, but Bristol came along, as if somebody cued him on, younger, as all of them were younger, but still somehow a man to look up to when Sam had finally started feeling good or reasonably good again about being a doctor. Bristol beckoned Sam to follow him into the paths of neurology. Dr. Harry Bristol wanted him. An honor.

When he spoke of Bristol, Sam's voice quieted some, whether in awe or fear of being overheard, Lydia wasn't sure.

She still thought H.B. was an evil genius, he held such power over his department, keeping everyone off balance just enough to be grateful for his steadying hand. They hated the power but were drawn to it and basked in its light when they could. Even Sam.

Once, before conference, Lydia had sat in H.B.'s chair. It was five minutes early and she wanted to bring Mitchell up to date on a patient while everyone else chattered and gulped down coffee before the Chief came in. Lydia had barely balanced herself on the edge of his chair when the room went silent, they all looked at her. Two residents whispered something in the far corner and Casper actually giggled.

"You're not sitting there, are you?" Sam asked.

First Lydia thought that he felt she had snubbed him by not sitting in her usual place. She was flattered. Then she realized that everyone was upset because she was perched on Bristol's chair.

"Right now I am," she answered Sam, then turned back to Mitch. "Mr. Cole had a little trouble last night."

Sam glanced at his watch and at the door. Lydia and Mitch talked. Sam looked at his watch again. "You're not stayng there, are you?" he asked. And from sheer spite and stubbornness she answered, "I'd thought not, but I don't know, it's kind of comfortable. I can see everyone from here. It's a good seat."

Sam looked at the door. "Lydia."

She slid back fully into the chair, she had everyone's attention now. She pushed her glasses up against the bridge of her nose, scratched at her chin, sighed, and finally stood and walked to a place by the wall.

"That was like *Rebel Without a Cause*," Sam said later. "Like stepping on the school seal."

Now she asked, "You came here because of him?"

"Much to the dismay of my wife, yes. She expected a certain standing when she agreed to be a doctor's wife. A certain amount of comfort. But that's not the way research works. Bristol promised me space, freedom and patients, plus a full professorship in two or three years' time. And himself. He's a genius." Sam leaned his forearms on the table. He picked up a pencil and studied the point. "Connie can't stand him, but most especially, she can't stand me when I'm around him. My theory is she loses her leverage with me, loses it to him."

Probably more like shifting loyalties. They all turned into different people around that man. Sometimes Sam seemed to fade visibly.

"I don't blame her. She probably isn't sure who you'd pick if you were forced to choose between her and Bristol."

He didn't answer.

"Who would you send to the firing squad?"

He didn't laugh. "It wouldn't matter," he said. "Because I would feel equally guilty about both for the rest of my life."

Lydia identified with Connie in some ways, and fantasized what she was like. She imagined that Connie was very tall, with slender legs and dark, shiny long hair, an efficient housekeeper, active in community projects.

Sam didn't actually speak of her much, except to repeat her complaints about him occasionally. But Lydia pushed it, uncovering his secret life, a different Sam, one who lived in the suburbs. Who had azaleas in front of the house, and peonies, and an herb garden in the back. Sam did all the yard work, Connie had allergies.

Connie, Andrew, Joel and Tricia. Warm in their home in Mt. Kisco, New York. Out there was like anywhere else in the country, like East Ridge. Out there, Manhattan was an alien place to visit, not to know, a place in old movies and *Kojak* reruns.

"Connie loved the city, but she thought it would be better for the children to grow up in Westchester County." A gray frame house, with white windows and every comfort, with Connie in the kitchen baking cakes and cooking soup, or on the phone for the neighborhood association or the Friends of the New York City Opera.

"There is nothing equivocal about Connie. Everything is kept in sharp focus. Everything."

She had been a social work major, but had never worked. She knew how to make a perfect daiquiri and a near perfect chocolate soufflé.

Andrew and Joel were born, boom, boom, within two and a half years of the wedding. Five years later, Connie had her tubes tied and then they adopted Tricia. "She didn't want to risk having another boy," Sam explained. "She needed a girl to raise in her own image." An edge there. Lydia appreciated the edge. If she ever married anyone, she hoped they would retain their sarcasm. That they would know each other's faults and be as open about them as Sam and Connie seemed to be, and love each other all the more, through the faults, despite them, because of them. Like a *Good Housekeeping* short story.

Someday she would meet Connie. Maybe if Connie stopped off

at the hospital to bring something to Sam, maybe at a departmental function. Anyway, she would meet her and they would hit it off right away, and they would become friends. They would commiserate and laugh together about Sam's idiosyncrasies. Lydia would invite them over for dinner, the whole family. She'd cook something Middle Eastern, and borrow extra chairs from Jane.

Then they would invite her out to Mt. Kisco, maybe a barbecue in the summer. She would rave about the marinade Connie concocted. Lydia imagined a huge green yard with tall thick trees and a brick patio off the house. The six of them would play soccer together, with Tricia running back and forth to retrieve the out-of-bounds balls.

"We never play soccer together," Sam said. "Connie doesn't play sports."

He was picking his Styrofoam coffee cup apart, tearing pieces off the rim and working his way down. He discarded the fragments into his empty cup so that finally the fragments filled what was left of it.

"When am I going to get to meet her?" Lydia asked. "Do you have a picture? I'd like to know what she looks like."

He pulled a snapshot out of his wallet, not of Connie, but of the children. All blond. The boys were curly topped, the little girl straight. Isn't that the way it always is? Lydia thought.

"You probably won't ever meet. Connie doesn't like to come into the city," Sam was saying. "Traffic, dirt."

"I thought you said she loved it."

"I guess she used to. Sometimes she's here for the opera. Maybe then."

Within two weeks Marty Jerome woke up and not only smiled but actually laughed. Everyone felt proud, as if by discovering the evidence of life they had actually given it. Jane felt proud for seeing intelligence behind the roving eyes, Lydia and Sam felt proud for measuring the first possible sign of volition in the man's waking brain.

They were all closer to Marty than to the usual patient, old friends in less than three weeks, and it had to do with believing in him and having him justify the belief. He grinned widely whenever he heard them approach.

They discovered the cortical blindness by accident, even Marty himself hadn't known, he had adapted so well and so fast. He awakened to an altered world, but since he couldn't remember the past one clearly, he took it all in stride and learned new cues and signals as if this were the most natural thing to do. He tried to explain it to Lydia later on, after he understood.

He saw everything, in the purely physiological sense. He just couldn't interpret what he saw, couldn't react in the old way to the old associations he would have made to faces, hypodermic needles, bedpans, because the old associations were gone, forgotten, dead, stroked out in specific parts of both occipital lobes.

He cast his eyes toward the door when Sam and Lydia walked in, looking in their direction but not at them. He was sitting upright in bed for the first time. It hadn't been so obvious before.

"Hi, Marty."

"Well, hi." He focused at the shapes approaching him, at the speaker. He put out a social hand for a handshake and smiled to the left of Sam's face. He had mastered a few people, aided by posture and voice. "Hi, doc."

He didn't know his behavior was different from anyone else's, or different from his own, as it used to be. He set up the new cues automatically, as he went. He didn't know he was guessing, unless someone put him on the spot. Then he thought it was a trick, a practical joke, a parlor game, and he hid his irritation.

"What's this?" Sam asked him that day.

The color red. "Well, it's red," Marty answered, reaching for the object.

"Without touching." Sam pulled it back. The red shape moved, up, around, in a circular pattern, for him to examine.

What was red? Apples, he remembered. Ribbons, bow ties, books, candy wrappers, all of this in split seconds. "A piece of candy?"

Sam put the red in Marty's hand.

"Oh, a pen or a pencil." Marty pulled off the cap. "A pen."

"Okay," Sam pressed. "Who is standing to your right?"

Marty looked to his right. Lydia smiled but didn't speak.

"Do you know that person?"

Marty chuckled. "What kind of question is that? It's my, it's my good friend." He patted Lydia's arm.

"Is it a man or a woman? I know it sounds like a silly question, but humor me."

"Damn right." He saw glasses. Glasses he had learned, just as he had now learned red pen. So glasses, face, light blue shirt. "Well, it's a boy, of course. My favorite boy."

"I know I'm flat-chested, but—" Lydia said.

"Of course. Lydia. I was teasing you." They tricked him, but he stayed good-natured about it. "I knew it was you. Of course." Right then, though, he knew he hadn't known it, and they knew too. And he said, "Wait a minute. What's going on?"

Sam took a long time explaining it to him, and he understood it intellectually, but he didn't really believe it, and he often forgot that what he was seeing had a different meaning for him than for everyone else.

Later, Lydia was helping him out of bed for his first lunch of solid food when Jane exploded, they heard her clear down the hall.

"I don't believe this place," she said, not screaming or hysterical, but with volume. And then she stomped into Marty's room. "I don't believe this place," she repeated, with less, but not much less, volume.

Lydia had just swung Marty up to dangle on the side of the bed. She steadied him there and they both looked toward Jane. Marty beamed at her. "Upset?" he understated. His sense of humor had been preserved.

Lydia paused long enough to assess Jane's degree of agitation. It had been this high before, but never this close to the surface. "Help me with Marty?" she asked. "And tell us about it."

"I don't believe this place."

The two women draped Marty's arms over their shoulders and heaved him to his feet. He had weak biceps, shoulders and thighs, strong forearms, hands and feet. He moved his limbs with effort, flailing them like the scarecrow in *The Wizard of Oz*. Since he was alive, he didn't mind the flailing. They walked him two steps to the chair, pivoted, and plopped him gently down.

Jane wheeled the tray table in front of him. "I'm out of here." She lifted his feet over the bottom bar and pushed the entire apparatus closer to him. "I was going anyway. This just makes it sooner." She sat down on the bed.

Lydia took the lid off the soup and placed the bowl in the middle of the tray, rearranging entree and dessert and several cups and cartons to make room. "Tomato soup, Mart. Here's your spoon." She put it in his hand in exactly the way he would use it.

"You can talk in front of me," he said. He scooped from the grape-drink glass. Lydia repositioned his right hand and the soup. She put his left hand on the lip of the bowl.

"Please," he continued. "I want you to talk in front of me. A little drama around here would be a welcome change. They homogenize everything, and pasteurize it, they protect us too much. Please. Talk." Marty abandoned the spoon and sipped directly from the bowl. "Come on."

Lydia shrugged and sat down next to her friend. Jane sighed, blowing a great deal of air out through her mouth.

"She gave me an ultimatum. Our head nurse. Just now. No more Therapeutic Touch, or no more Samaritan." Another big sigh, to vent the steam. "I'm so pissed." Her hands were fists and pounded her knees. "I wanted to quit when I wanted to quit."

"Which is when?" Marty asked. He had finished his soup and set the bowl to his right, off the tray.

Jane lifted the cover from his plate and began cutting the chicken. "Boiled chicken, lima beans and rice. Who picked this stuff? Some anorexic dietician? Get your fork ready."

Lydia laughed. She placed the fork carefully in Marty's right hand, propped the plate against his left. He stabbed at the food.

"I was going to leave in about two months. After this semester. As soon as I found office space."

"More time to look for it, then," Marty said, his mouth full of lima beans and shreds of chicken.

"What exactly did she say?" Lydia asked. "Your napkin's in your lap, Mart."

"She said some doctors complained." She paced around the tiny room, behind the bed, to the door, behind and back again. "Patients complained. I can't figure that out. She said I forced my ideas on them. Said they humored me but it was all basically tiresome and could I please stop. I didn't force anyone to do anything. Most of them asked me to come back again. Then she says that Bristol thinks it's unsafe. He's getting ready to pump people full of experimental chemicals—all due respect, Lydia, but that's what they are—and he has the nerve to claim that my energy's unsafe."

Marty felt for his spoon and found it. He scooped rice and gravy into his mouth. "Let me tell you something. He's jealous."

"Sure," Jane snapped.

"Listen to me," he insisted. "Shhh. I had three roommates last week, right? Down in four-thirty-two. One of them was Carl Haas, a patient of Bristol's, and one of them was Bill Stevens. Remember him?"

Jane stopped pacing. She scratched her head. "Yeah, sure. I brought his fever down a couple of times."

"So Thursday Bristol comes in to talk to Haas. Haas is in with a back pain that won't quit. I don't know, he may be a crock. But Bristol's saying something about enzyme injections in Canada, last resort, stuff like that, and this Haas guy says, What about Miss Clarke? No kidding, he asked for you, kid."

"Oh, wow."

"Professional jealousy. Plain as the nose on your face. I think he couldn't stand it."

"You're a threat," Lydia put in. "How terrific."

Jane peeled plastic wrap off Marty's peach melba surprise and poured him a cup of coffee. "A threat, huh?" She grinned.

Christmas Brunch was the annual consolation prize for working Christmas Day, the usual breakfast plus Sheila's meat pies, Wilma's curried goat, and Diana's sweet potato tarts. A festive table. The crew looked lackluster and pale in comparison, leftovers from the night shift, including Lydia who nearly always worked nights on Christmas. The day staff was out seeing to patients while nights took care of the preparations. Diana stood by the window, a makeshift kitchen on the counter. She dropped butter into an electric frying pan and whipped the eggs. Lydia propped her head up on her fists, her eyes hollow, wanting sleep.

"Knew we'd get at least one O.D. over the holiday," Diana said. "And some kind of trauma case, and a stroke, of course. But four emergencies in one night plus that cardiac arrest—" She poured the eggs into the frying pan. "Toast these, girl," handed Lydia a twin-pack of English muffins. "You look dead."

Lydia nodded. She slid one tray of muffins out of the cellophane bag. "We've never been that busy. Thank God nobody else went bad while we weren't looking."

"So far as we know," Diana said. And she laughed, now it was over. Proud of herself. "Need a revolving door in that unit."

Lydia split one of the muffins and put the halves into the toaster. "How many are we?" She had toasted the muffins for eight, maybe it was nine, Christmas brunches, and Diana had made the eggs.

"Three from nights, seven on days, plus whoever else smells the cooking. Think I saw Dr. Wheeler sniffing around before, and Mitchell always shows up for food, and Casper. Toast the whole lot of them."

Lydia shoved the toaster lever down. "Hand me the sausage. I guess I'll do the sausage."

Jane always did the sausage, but this year, her last, this day, her last day, Regina had broken tradition and stuck Jane in the unit with six sick patients.

"Give me the other pan."

Diana passed the sausage down and handed over another frying pan.

"I'll do the sausage," the new night aide offered.

Lydia attempted to lean back far enough to plug the extension into the wall socket without getting out of her chair. "No, I'll do it." It seemed right for her to do the sausage in Jane's place. "You do the toast." She stood up finally and put the plug in. She studied the settings on the pan handle. "Wonder why Wheeler's here today."

"Put it on high," Diana instructed. "It's the only setting that works on that one."

"You actually saw Wheeler this morning?" Lydia slapped the sausage into the pan. Not breakfast sausage but Italian, both sweet and hot. "Where's the lid for this thing? You actually saw Wheeler or you just think he was going to be here today?"

"I saw him. Seven-thirty."

Odd, Sam coming in on Christmas Day. Maybe the whole family came. For church at St. Patrick's or something. Or maybe he came to wish her a Merry Christmas. That would be nice. The sausage popped, she stirred it around. "Too bad it has to be busy on Jane's last day," she said. She took the lid from Diana and covered the pan.

"Too bad that woman made her go in the unit." Diana sliced hunks of yellow cheese and dropped them in with the eggs. And more butter.

"You go see how they're doing out there, girl. I'll watch the meat. Tell them hurry up or we'll eat it all."

Lydia pushed herself from the table. She stretched. "I'm too old for this." But she felt not quite as tired as she had, getting her second wind. She propped the frying pan lid to let the steam escape.

The hall was empty, quiet, everyone was either dead or settled. The first person Lydia saw was Sam Wheeler.

"Soup's on," she told him. She probably looked awful. Red-eyed and pale. She rubbed her left eye, wondered if she had blusher in her purse.

"Smells great." He carried two packages. A large white bakery bag, and a small brightly wrapped gift.

"Why are you in on Christmas?" she asked, and, too fast out of nervousness, "It's Jane's last day."

"I know." He held up the bakery bag. "I brought her a treat."

Lydia took the bag from him and opened it to smell.

"Christmas stöllen from Glaser's," he explained. He handed her the smaller package, a little red box tied with a green ribbon. "Merry Christmas."

"Why are you here on Christmas Day?" she asked, thinking of what to say about the gift, and then, "But I don't have anything for you."

"I'm covering for Bristol today. That's why I'm here."

The red box looked so fine, small, good things come in small fine packages.

"It's nothing. Really nothing. I just saw it and thought of you." He stood quite close. His tie had tiny Christmas trees on it with tiny gifts under them.

She untied the ribbon, opened the lid. Inside, a small jukebox, it fit in the palm of her hand, tacky bright yellow and blue and red painted tin.

He wound it and put it to her ear. The song was a slow "Shake, Rattle and Roll," tinkling like jingle bells.

"This is so bad." She laughed.

"You like it?"

"It's great." She reached up and kissed his cheek.

Watch out for that one. Jane's voice echoed in her head.

From the corner of her eye she saw Jane, coming down the hall to join them. Lydia slid the jukebox into her sweater pocket.

Sometimes on nights and at a certain angle, Lydia could see herself reflected back from the windows of the ICU. Most of the time, though, there were only the machines in the glass, a disembodied heartbeat amputated from the primary image of the monitor scope, the green oxygen light on the respirator, constant, a white flashing alarm light flashing sometimes, not always, orange assist light infrequently, if the patient took a breath, the tops of the aqua corrugated hoses dancing in with the good air, out with the bad, a crystalline gleam through the IV fluid.

They had tested this very patient last night, she and Sam, tested her from one end to the other, and she was not going to make it. Lydia could read the signs pretty well now and could predict failure with a ninety-five percent success rate. She still had some trouble with the good outcomes, and the gray areas in between, but she was getting there.

She had also mastered for the most part the electrical evidence of, say, drug-induced coma versus a structural lesion. Usually, of course, the diagnosis was known ahead of time, but there had been Mr. Jacoby, an elderly gentleman who looked as if he had had a massive stroke.

"I don't think it's a stroke," she said halfway into the study. "The patterns look more like an O.D."

"He's hemiplegic," Sam answered. "It has to be focal. We simply haven't found the focus." He increased the machine amplitude, searching for subtleties.

"These spikes are too fast for a stroke that size. Look at them. And too organized for a seizure." She watched the green lines sweep across the scope, up, down and across, they disappeared off the right and returned on the left, chasing themselves, up, down and across. "How about an old stroke, with a new overdose exacerbating the symptoms?"

It was too late to send a decent blood for drug screen. The patient had been in the unit over twenty hours by then, and if there had been drugs they had been flushed out a long time ago. They sent a specimen anyway, but it came back negative.

The man woke up on day three and on day four he admitted the suicide attempt, in tears, grateful, if you can believe it, grateful to be alive. His medical records showed an old right hemisphere stroke, the deficits had flared in the aggravation of the drugs and they resolved over days.

She brought bagels in to celebrate her win. Sam brought cream cheese and lox. They shared them with their risen patient. He thought he would never eat lox again, ever. It was one of the last things he regretted after taking the pills. Never again lox.

"What would you miss?" she asked Sam.

"Nothing," he answered.

"Come on. Party pooper. What's the one food you'd miss if you dropped dead right now?"

Mr. Jacoby had clearly thought this all out. "I was gonna miss lox, and I was gonna miss the special honey cakes the two sister ladies from upstairs make for me. Ach. They drove me crazy with their cakes. But I thought of them at the end." A whisper. "I will tell them this. When I'm home again."

"I think I'd miss hot dogs and baked beans," Lydia said. "I never eat hot dogs and beans. I hated it when we used to have them at home, but that's what I thought of just now. And maybe Mama's corn on the cob, she does something different to it. There has to be one thing you'd miss, Wheeler. Some small, mundane thing?"

"I would miss never having—don't laugh, okay?—I would miss never having the hospital's split pea soup again, don't laugh." They had to laugh. "No kidding, talk about mundane, split pea with ham and a slab of corn bread, ever had it?"

"Seriously? From the cafeteria downstairs? That's pitiful."

Sam nodded, shrugged his shoulders. She saw him reflected back from the window, collecting their leftovers into the Bagel Nosh bag. He was outlined in light, the substance of him dark, a ghost of himself, a one-dimensional shadow.

"Yep." He crumpled their trash into one big ball and tossed it at the hamper marked PAPER GOODS ONLY. The ball bounced off the words and into the sink. "And I'd miss you." Exit line. He walked out the door.

Mr. Jacoby's eyebrows folded into his forehead. "My word. Smart man. And a doctor, young lady. Good for him."

"Don't pay any attention to him," she had said. "He just wanted to embarrass me. He wanted the last word. That's all."

Some nights she couldn't see herself in the window at all. Not the right lighting or mood or something.

She looked for the halo of sunspots steaming off her tonight but, nothing. She could see the sheet on top of the woman in the bed, she could see her machines. She could make out the rounds of two knees, bent in a physiologically functional position, but she couldn't see her own self. No reason to panic. Lydia lay her hand on the top knee, there it was, like a painted-on hand, flat, but she knew it was hers and it was there along with everything else. A freighter cut through her reflection and the East River. It had lights strung around its edges and looked quite festive, obliterating all of them, the heartbeat, the life supports, the patient and the nurse.

Lydia turned the woman to face the other side, wiped her forehead with a wet cloth and repositioned her body into another physiologically functional pose. The legs appeared to be running or walking fast, as on an ancient Grecian frieze.

She emptied the patient's urine, checked her pupils, and adjusted the IV rate to compensate for a lowered blood pressure. She lay the sheet loosely over the legs and saw white foothills grooved with wrinkles in the window. She shut off the reflection with the light, then sat up on the wide windowsill to chart and to stare outside at the river going by in the night.

It looked most of all black. Provocative. Thicker than regular water, coated with a dull sheen from the overcast night, no moonbeams to make it sparkle. Smooth dimples flowed south to lower Manhattan, low tide. The East River ran both ways, with the tides, so if the current carried her down to the harbor right now, she would float back up this way in plenty of time for morning report, no problem.

She used to think it looked like the Nile. Especially at sunrise. She had daydreamed it, slitting her eyes and looking exactly through the second window from the right, early, while the river was still tame, before the day churned it.

She had mentioned this to Ali. Opened it up and laid it all out for him, like a traveling salesman lining up goodies on his rug. She had felt high and breezy and full of herself that day, driving back to the city from visiting some Egyptians in West Hempstead.

She practiced rolling her abdomen in the front seat of Ali's Le Mans, like Leila, the belly dancer they had just left. They crossed over the East River on the Brooklyn Bridge and watched the buildings sparkling light and scraping the sunset sky.

"I love the East River," Lydia had said.

"It's a sewage canal," Ali answered. Period.

"Oh, but it's beautiful sometimes. Like early in the morning, at work? I just stare out at it and sometimes I feel like I could be anywhere looking across any river. You should see when the sun comes up over Roosevelt Island," she chattered, extending the closeness. "Sometimes on nights I imagine I'm by Moccasin Bend, or sometimes in Egypt, and the East River is the Nile."

She had never said much about Egypt before. About being there or going there or living happily ever after there. She told him her secret through the buzz of the Brooklyn Bridge, then felt herself sliding unsupported.

"It's nothing like the Nile." Ali waved his hand in dismissal, dismissed the whole East River and Lydia too, in that flick of his hand.

"I know it's probably not like it at all. I'm just saying that sometimes I imagine it is. I imagine I'm in Egypt and that's the Nile. No big deal. There's a whole patch of land over there that could be country if you don't look to either side of it."

"It's nothing like the Nile. You'll have to imagine another river. Something American. The Mississippi."

"That's ridiculous. It's not wide enough." She felt herself about to slide through the links of the bridge, through the buzz. Off the edge and into the water and down through the soft silty bottom, buried, dismissed.

"Just forget the Nile."

She felt as if he had tossed her onto a pile of all things not Egyptian, a pile ready to be dumped. She locked her door, checked her seat belt.

"The river look nice, it's so black. Black as me."

A tingle shimmied from Lydia's throat to her stomach. She looked at the voice, recognized it and relaxed. Carlisle Simms. "Blacker than you tonight, Mr. Simms."

A dull brown face, as if somebody had come by and dusted it with a powder of soot that collected in the crevices around his eyes and his smile, then sprinkled ash on his hair to blend everything together like camouflage. Dull. Until you got close enough to see the eyes inside his squint. Basic common sense there. He drove his doctors crazy last admission. "So you say I've got this percent chance of having a stroke if I don't have surgery, and about that percent chance of having a stroke because of the surgery, not to mention dying. And you're not a hundred percent sure that even if everything goes just fine that it would stop them attacks. So why should I have the surgery? Just asking, you understand. Just wondering," he had said.

"You scared me, coming out of the night like that. When did you get here?"

"Yesterday. And walkin' the halls as usual." He worked nights for the MTA. He never could adjust to a daytime schedule, so he woke up at about midnight or one a.m. At home there was TV or he could read a magazine, but in the hospital he roamed the halls. "I don't mind. I like it, to tell the truth. I see a lot at night. More than most men see in the daytime."

"So why're you back? Trouble?"

"Couple a more what you call TIAs."

The first time Simms was in, his right arm had gone limp while he was driving the Number 1, Broadway local.

"Imagine riding a train with the engineer having a stroke?" Lydia had said to Diana.

"Girl, I'll be thinking about that all the way home to Brooklyn on the B train. Believe me."

"Good thing I take the bus. Right, R.B.?" Jane had chimed in.

Lydia chuckled, remembering how Jane took every opportunity to needle Regina. "Is it your right arm again, Mr. Simms?"

"Afraid so," he answered, "and this time they want to operate for sure. Ream out the right side, then ream out the left. I guess it's okay, right?" Big man, now he looked scared.

"Absolutely. Who's operating?"

"Dr. Culpepper."

"He's the best."

"You don't say."

"And you'll have Dr. Mitchell there looking over his shoulder, so it's double protection."

"You staring at that river again. You ever stop?"

"Not much. I like it. Sometimes I'd like to be the river."

"Yeah. What you thinking about can swim around some in that river. It's so damn black though." They watched a tugboat pulling a long barge down toward the bay. "Wouldn't mind driving a tugboat instead of subway train."

"Probably gets to be just as routine once you're used to it."

"Never. Not with the water and the scenes. Same scenes, right, but different moons, different weather. Not so much all the same all the time like it is underground." The barge cleared the Fifty-ninth Street Bridge. "And there's all kind of goods they find in that river. Junk mostly, but sometimes bicycles and furniture, dead babies, a diamond tiara, I read that in the *News* last month. A diamond tiara, you see what I'm saying? Must be a thousand stories in that river. Where's your friend, anyway?"

"My friend?"

"The doc. The one you always settin' in here with. You and all them machines, that big TV screen? You know, the doc."

"Dr. Wheeler. He left already. Night after tomorrow we'll be back with all that again. But not tonight. He went home a long time ago."

"He was always whistling, right? That one."

"I didn't know you even knew him."

"I don't. I just seen him around you. Bet he was sorry he had to leave you alone."

"Of course he wanted to go home. He has this great family out there waiting to have dinner with him." A crown roast? With twice-baked potatoes. That's what she would cook for him. Or Crab Imperial, and spoon bread, yes. And rhubarb pie. "Anyway, I'm not alone." She pointed to her patients and their respirators and hypothermia machines, all the paraphernalia. "Plenty of company."

"Okay. I get the hint. Keep your mouth shut, Carlisle." He looked around the room, from bed to bed. Half the patients were asleep, the other half were in coma. "Place is hoppin'. Any of these people had that what you call endirectmy?"

"Endarterectomy. Endo, the inside lining; arter, artery, inside lining of the artery; and ectomy, removal of. Endarterectomy. Removal of the inside lining of the artery, and all the muck and plaques and other debris along with it."

"Whoooeee. Now that's enough to make anyone turn right around and go home."

"Nah. Mr. Cook over in the far corner, he had one today."

"He's comatosed?"

"Just asleep. Like the rest of the world, besides you and me. It's a pretty easy surgery most of the time. When are you having it?"

"Monday. If I give the okay. They have to get some X rays first."

"Well, I'll be here Monday night, with Dr. Wheeler, so I'll check up on you."

"Not with those machines you don't. Look like you zap them people with those little pins and they don't never wake up." He grinned.

"Guess it does look like that. Sometimes I'm not sure myself. But the truth is, we only zap the ones already in coma. Coma first, then the zap."

"Whatever you say. Just stay away from me with them gadgets."

"Okay. If you have any questions, feel free."

"Okay. You got a cigarette?"

"Sure. On the table in the med room. Ask Diana, she's having a break. You should quit, Carlisle. It's bad for your arteries."

"Bad for your arteries, too," he said on his way out the door.

Lydia slid off the windowsill and started in on one last round of activity with her second patient, Luis Cruz. She meant to clean up his mouth and his face one more time before days came on. He was a head trauma, out on Lexington Avenue on a bike in a hurry to get home, thinking a hundred thoughts, not paying attention and, slam boom, propelled to the NICU. Suddenly without a thought in the world.

She left the scrapes and scratches alone as much as possible, so they could plug and dry up and scab. But elastic gray mucus was strung from his left nostril and his mouth onto the blue Chux under his head, and some of the dried blood and Betadine around the sutures could be cleaned off. Nursing nowadays, she thought, was like what doctoring had been early on, before drugs and machines made them all lazy and dependent. It was intuition and observation and touching people, draining off the bad juices, forcing them out with claps and suction, replacing them with, okay, IV fluids and antibiotics and blood transfusions, but also with something close to Jane's invisible energies flowing from her hard-working heat into some kind of hungry healing pathways coursing right alongside the arteries and nerves. Nurses used their knowledge, and then they used their wits and care.

She sucked mucus from Luis's mouth with the small clear suction hose, moved to his nose and the stuff hanging onto his left cheek. She wiped his face with peroxide, the streaks of blood and dried snot foaming up and loosening from his skin.

"Luuuiiiis. Time to wake uuuuuuup." She rinsed with saline and dried him off, spanking clean. "What were you thinking about, on that bike? Big night ahead of you? Studying in front of the tube?" She dunked a giant cotton swab into the Cepacol-laced peroxide and rubbed it around his mouth, watching the foam rise like meringue. She sucked it out and swabbed again with plain water. "Somebody said you go to N.Y.U. Computer science, right? Computers. They totally escape me. Probably a piece of cake for you. Okay, let's flip you over."

Diana came through the unit doors but stopped there to listen, almost filling the doorway with her bulk. "You talking to yourself? Who you talking to?"

"Luis, here."

"Luis? He woke up?"

"Nah, you kidding? I think it may be the big sleep for Luis boy.

No, I was just sort of wondering out loud. Help me turn him? Wondering, you know, what he had on his mind when that van hit him."

They turned him to his right side. "You can watch the river now, if you feel like it, Luis."

Diana adjusted the respirator hoses, the lines and the tubes, while Lydia flipped the pillows, punched them up. "You'll feel like you're on cloud nine," and positioned them under, between and around him. Collected tears trickled from the corner of his right eye down his cheek into his right ear and finally onto the pillow.

Lydia sang "Tears on My Pillow" to Luis Cruz, and then "It's My Party and I'll Cry if I Want To." Without Sam's whistle, she had to provide her own entertainment.

"Girl, whatever it is, I hope it's not catching."

"What's not catching?"

"All this singing and dancing and whistling around. You and Sam Wheeler."

"What're you talking about? I always sang things. Before I even knew Sam."

Was he sleeping? Five-thirty. Was he sleeping or was he reaching for his lovely wife right exactly now? Lydia blinked hard on that thought, blinked it out. She had begun to crop Connie out of the picture. Like the shadow image in the window, Connie was becoming a blank black space.

Cool it, Lydia.

But she couldn't stop herself wondering about him, a lot sometimes without even realizing it, she would catch herself thinking all about him. In Mt. Kisco in his backyard, she was there, and she didn't even know where Mt. Kisco was. Did he wear pajamas to bed? Or just underwear? Boxer shorts?

Sam came back Monday night.

They had a new patient to study, Mrs. Elsie Zumbrun, who was transferred from surgery when she didn't wake up after a routine gallbladder excision that morning. Carlisle Simms slept in the bed next to Mrs. Z.; he was stable, status quo, he would walk his halls same as always tomorrow night.

Sam wheeled two consoles through the unit doors, the electroencephalograph in front and the electromyograph behind, with Lydia trailing him, scooting the portable ultrasound and Doppler scan alongside her. They arranged their machines around Mrs. Zumbrun's bed, offerings at a sacrificial altar, or maybe headstones.

Lydia pasted the EEG leads at strategic spots on the woman's scalp. The paste smelled like toothpaste but had the consistency of hardening plaster. Sam worked on setting up the console, calibrating each channel for each lobe. They did an abbreviated study, enough for their purposes, a baseline, for comparison with later, more sophisticated responses to stimuli.

They kept their voices low. Once everything was set up, Lydia would pull the curtain around to minimize disturbance to the other patients. They needed a procedure room for their studies, an isolated place where they could work, even during the day. But there wasn't space for it, and most of the patients were too sick to be moved anyway.

"You remember Mr. Simms?" Lydia nodded her head toward the next bed. "Carlisle Simms?"

"Familiar name. Sure. Used to come by in the middle of the night. Drives a subway train, right? TIAs. He's back?"

"Endarterectomy today. He finally agreed."

"Even though they couldn't prove it would improve his odds by at least ninety-nine percent?"

"Well, his criteria must have dropped. Or he got scared. Anyway, he had the surgery. That's the last electrode. Machine ready?"

Sam pushed several buttons and pulled a switch, nodded. Twelve pen-points scratched blue-green lines on the graph paper, squiggles, curves, a few sharp waves, generalized slowing, no seizure activity, not brain dead by a long shot.

No such thing as a flat EEG anyway. Unless you wanted to measure the electrical activity of, say, a glob of clay in a windowless, doorless, unoccupied, unventilated room, and even then you had to take the mechanical fluctuations of the printer itself into consideration. No such thing as a flat EEG. Even a cadaver could pick up artifact.

"He's doing fine?" Sam asked. "Simms. Everything okay post-op?"

"Great. No problem. A good thing, too. After all the persuasion and reassurance, he was a prime candidate for some kind of complication. Things always go wrong on the reluctant ones."

"Keeps us humble." He shut off the graph and Lydia started placing the myography electrodes, and the tiny needle stimulus. This would measure the rate and the magnitude of the response to an electrical zap as it traveled from the peripheral nerve sensor in the leg to the roots, through the spinal column up the brainstem to awareness by the cerebrum. Ideally, the stimulus would produce a more lively pattern than the baseline EEG. They expected Mrs. Z.'s to be slowed at the level of the brainstem and severely retarded in the cerebral hemispheres.

Sam turned on the stimulator until they could see minute twitches in the patient's foot. He turned it down slowly, just to when the twitching stopped. "I have a song for you." He adjusted the upper and lower thresholds. "You're always complaining about my oldies, so I have something current." He tapped a red knob to make a fine distinction on the averager. "Hold on. Hold on, I had it. I had it all day yesterday."

"Current. Um, Eurhythmics?"

"What? No, someone else."

"The Feelines."

"No. A person. One person, not a group. How could I forget that song?"

"Um. Boy George? Eddie Grant? Paul McCartney?"

"Don't help. I have to get it myself. I can't believe I forgot it. I spent the whole weekend humming it, whistling it, so I wouldn't forget it for you. Damn. Andrew said, 'Dad, you're driving me bananas. Absolutely bananas.' But I thought you'd be pleased, so I kept whistling it."

He spent the weekend saving a song for her.

"No use. I lost it. All I'm coming up with is 'In the Still of the Night.' Forget it." He slumped in his chair, shook his head several times, stared at the screen in front of him, shaking his head.

"Ry Cooder?" she asked.

The response waves were delayed and stunted. Lydia turned up the stimulus dial to a slightly higher buzz. Not much difference.

"Your Wheeler Scale," she said. "I've been thinking about it a lot." She removed the needle from Mrs. Zumbrun's leg while Sam placed the small earphone in the woman's ear.

Lydia turned on the click. "It's a huge responsibility. What if Mr. X needs to work out a few things before he dies? Suppose he's not ready to die, which is why he hasn't died, because his soul is still sorting something out before it can rest."

"So?"

"So if the Wheeler Index says thumbs down, or even mezzo mezzo, Mr. X's care could change, his treatment altered. A respirator might even be shut off, right?"

"If everyone agrees, next of kin and everyone, yeah. It could be shut off. But that's not much different from what we do now. It's just that now we have even less to go on."

"But you'll be responsible for what all this new evidence means, and Mr. X may be dead before he's ready, so indirectly you may be responsible for his soul's restlessness."

"Do you believe that?"

"I'm not sure, but why not? It could mean the difference between eternal peace and eternal confusion. It's a big responsibility, this Wheeler Index thing. You could go crazy thinking about the possibilities."

Both of them stared at the waves being marked off on the recorder. Tiny, barely existent waves from a barely existent brainstem. Sam shifted in his chair. Their shoulders touched and Lydia didn't move away.

"Well, it should bother you, I think."

He leaned forward to change channels on the averager. Her shoulder felt a draft. Could he please sit back in the exact same position now? Her shoulder felt chilly without his. He sat back in the exact same position, his shoulder against her shoulder. She looked at him and he smiled in the dark at the averager making wave patterns. It was exquisite.

They stood up together and simultaneously stretched before unhooking the leads and probes. He started cleaning the white goo off the woman's skin while Lydia readied the ultrasound machine. The last test in the package, a gross assessment of the carotid vasculator and, by implication, the state of the cerebral circulation.

"I was looking at it from a different viewpoint," he said finally.

"*Your* viewpoint."

"My viewpoint, right. Of course my viewpoint. Who else's? Do you remember, sometime in the summer, an old man, a stroke, looked dead and everyone thought he'd be better off if he were? Patient of Bristol's, old friend of the family, so they gave it their best shot. Gorked for three solid days and nights, taking up a bed, staff time, running up a big bill, for what? I won't bore you with details, but the guy woke up. And he wasn't an overdose. Bright and early on day four he's awake and talking and moving all fours, and everybody's sheepish because they'd all given up on him."

"I remember. A rabbi, right? Rabbit Fierstein. As soon as he woke up, he drove us all crazy. He washed his hands before and after everything, two basins of water each time, we couldn't wait for him to be out of the unit and unrestricted."

"There should have been a way to predict the man's recovery. Some way to differentiate between him and the man next to him, who was a rose to start with but died after two months in a vegetative state." He fiddled with the nearest electrode, screwing and unscrewing it. "The point is, I wasn't looking for an excuse to pull everyone's plug. I was looking for ways to predict a good outcome, so people won't give up on any more Fiersteins before their time really comes."

"But define 'their time,' that's the problem. Nowadays how can you be sure it's come? Or what it even is? What about the inner man's need to make peace with himself? And what about all the karma you're probably going to pick up from all these perpetually confused souls?"

He dropped the electrode from his fingers, stepping back in mock horror. "Good grief, you're right." He shook his arms out, wiped off years of accumulated karma, forcing her to laugh. He slung karma onto the floor. "You do get worked up about things, don't you?"

"I know. It's a curse. There are just so many possibilities. Except I really do wonder about the whole death thing. I mean, who are we to pronounce death on people? Nobody's ever found the soul. And if you can't find it, how can you measure it? Who knows what might still be going on, deep in the sub-subcortex? Who the hell knows? Not you, certainly not me. Not even Harry Bristol."

She sat down by the head of the bed and positioned the ultrasound imager against the old woman's neck. The probe looked like a transparent bionic fist with a spindly wrist for a handle. A disk vibrated deep in the center of the fist, sending sound waves out through water, skin and muscle to be bounced back and mirrored into a picture of the inside of the neck.

Sonar. Meant to search out enemy submarines during world wars, but later developed to search out debris and enemy plaque in hardening arteries. The image was a feature film in black and white, revealing all kinds of secret goings-on in the blood vessels. By the end of the study Lydia would know if Elsie's arteries were thin and graceful or broad and squat, if there were bright hard calcifications inside or gray, membranous sludge building up and blocking normal flow, or she would see vessels clean as a whistle and elastic and young.

"Irene Cara?" Lydia asked.

"Who?"

"She did *Flashdance*."

"No, it was a man."

Sam typed the patient's identification number across the top of the video screen. "You know, I do think about the responsibility. More than you believe I do, apparently. They're already asking for my prognosis on some cases. And you're right, a lot of things can't be measured. There aren't any rules yet. No limits, no standard moral obligations. My obligation to the patients increases."

Lydia flipped on the scanner and the videotape recorder with two taps of her foot, and she and Sam turned their eyes to the TV screen. Bubbles, streaks and splotches of blacks through grays to whites filled it, right to left, flesh, fats, muscles, an aerial view of a farmland, plowed and planted. Cutting through the property was a great black river, throbbing with the beat of the woman's heart. "Left common carotid artery," Lydia said.

They scanned the screen, looking for gold, for plaques, bright boulders diverting the flow.

"Left internal and, ah, external, back to the internal again," she announced, turning down the audio. "I guess you have to depend on your own best instincts." She changed the beam of sound to far field for a clearer background and flipped on the Doppler switch so they could listen to the woman's life blood whooshing by. "You have enough ego for that?"

"Probably not," he responded. "As I said, it was meant to salvage life. All that business about immortality was sort of a put-on. Of course I'd like to leave my name on something forever. The idea of being part of future medical history is heady stuff. But honestly, not what I set out to do in the first place. Scan down the neck a minute? I thought I saw a lot of wall thickening back in the bifurcation, yeah, there. Is that real or just my eyes?"

"Hard to tell. Look at the transverse." She repositioned the probe for a cross section of the artery and turned on the videotape. "It's real. Good eyes, Sam. Significant, it looks like." Lydia wiped the excess gel off Mrs. Zumbrun's neck. She rolled her chair behind the bed to reach the patient's right side, positioned the imager, turned up the audio, "Right common carotid," and turned it down again.

"The thing is," she continued, "every time you decide that one patient will achieve independence, if we work real hard and give him some time, there's another patient exactly opposite. You place a value, your value, the examiner's value, or the interpreter's, whoever, but it's an external value from an external person on an unrelated life. How dare you? Or he? Or I? Was it Billy Joel? 'Piano Man'?"

"Current, I said."

"Right common in transverse, moving up to the bulb, and the bifurcation. Internal, external, done." She wiped Elsie's neck and the imager's head. "I don't know how I feel about all of it either, and I sound like I'm condemning you. I get just as frustrated as anyone, using up time and energy on a hopeless, basically dead patient. But I can't help but think there must be a reason for the lingering."

She rewound the videotape, while he pulled electrode paste out of Elsie's hair.

The curtain separating Mr. Simms from Mrs. Zumbrun and her entourage flapped and skimmed back on the ceiling runner. Simms propped his dull brown face on the side rail and looked at Lydia with his wide-awake eyes. "You two sure get along. What was I telling you? What was I saying last week?" He turned to Sam. "Hello, doc. Carlisle Simms. I drive subway trains. I been watching you and her and them machines for going on months now."

"We wake you up?" Lydia asked. "I'm sorry. We try to keep it down, but sometimes . . ."

"You just get carried away. I know all about getting carried away. Didn't disturb me. You know. One o'clock is my waking time. You let me oversleep, girl."

"Nothing wrong with his speech," Sam said. "Looks like the surgery went well." He crossed to Simms's bedside and adjusted the neck dressing. A spot of dark dried blood showed at the bottom. "Raise both your arms straight out in front of you. Good. Now turn them over, palms up, close your eyes." Simms obeyed, like a child holding his hands out for inspection before dinner.

"Looks good, Mr. Simms. Glad you went ahead and let them do it?"

"Just glad it's over and that's all." He looked around the room and out the windows at the night. "I asked them to put me by one of them far windows. I said I won't go into that intensive care unless I can watch the ships and tugs, and they said they'd try, but look where I am." He shook his head. "I guess it's okay, though."

"You'll be out of here in the morning anyway. You're a rose," Lydia said.

Simms grinned at her, all teeth and the fat neck bandage. "I'd still like to see out."

Lydia disconnected wires from electrodes, removed leads, straightened up Elsie Zumbrun, who didn't care one way or the other. Sam checked Simms's blood pressure, murmured, "You got it, a rose," and returned to help Lydia. They worked silently, independent of but tuned to each other, while Carlisle Simms watched them both.

"You sure do look good together," he teased. "You work together so fine. We was missing you Saturday night, doc. And I bet you was missing her." Back to his chatter. "Right, doc? I see a lot with these eyes. I know a lot of things."

Lydia stared at him with all the muscle she could put behind two eyes. "You want to go over the tapes now?" she asked Sam. "Or wait until tomorrow or something?" All the while shaking her head at Simms, Stop, don't say any more.

"Okay, I'll quit. But hey, doc, don't forget what I been saying. You find something you like, you keep with it."

If she could have gagged him.

Sam kept rolling lead wires into tight bundles, rerolling them, rolling them, for storage purposes. Maybe he hadn't heard Simms, but something about the back of his neck extended far forward and his head hanging low down, something about his concentration on digging out the last bit of paste from the electrode screw, paste that had been there for probably years. Something about the way he wasn't joking about it.

Then, "You're right, Simms. She's a great helper. I'd miss her help a lot." He looked at her, finally. "We can read these tomorrow. Ready to go?"

"Sure." A great helper? She stopped at the foot of Simms's bed, smiled, grimaced at him, could have strangled him and totally ruined the Samaritan's endarterectomy statistics.

"Try to get some more sleep," she said, and led the way out, rolling the ultrasound in front of her. The wheels screamed the whole distance to the storage closet. Sam's wheels only rumbled.

He started a low whistle. She thought "In the Still of the

Night," but it was too low to really hear and he quit by the time they reached the coffeepot in the medicine room. Sam served.

"That Simms, he really likes to talk, doesn't he?" She spoke into her coffee cup. She leaned back, connected the dots in the acoustical ceiling tiles. "People romanticize hospitals, I used to too, before I worked in one. Doctors and nurses, all those TV shows. Simms got carried away, I guess, seeing us working together so much." Perfectly civilized.

"Right. I can see why he thinks what he thinks."

Sam refilled their cups. No food tonight, only coffee. Two-thirty in the morning. She still hadn't looked at him.

She guessed he would stay overnight, down the hall in the physical therapy room, on an exercise mat. He often slept in the P.T. room and she often wondered about it but never asked. By now Lydia could have done the studies herself, with Sam going over them in the morning. But he kept coming in and spending the night. She asked him again one time didn't he want to leave early and go home to sleep, but he said no. He would wake Connie if he went home and then she'd be up for the rest of the night, she had some trouble sleeping. Lydia thought if he were her husband she wouldn't mind having him wake her up.

She finally looked at him and found him looking at her.

"Why haven't you married?" he asked.

"No one ever asked me," she answered.

"No, really, why not?"

"I just told you. Nobody asked me. Ever. Don't rub it in."

"If nobody ever asked you, you must have made it very clear that you didn't want to be asked."

"No. I don't believe that. The simple truth is, anybody who wanted to marry me would ask. Obviously, then, no one does. I never found anyone who loved me enough. That's all. Period."

She played with the filter end of an unlit cigarette. She tamped it on the table, on her hand, she held it upright, balanced it straight up on the filter, watched it fall.

"You'd be easy to love," he said.

She balanced the cigarette on her right forefinger, chased the tip for seconds, watched it fall.

"Did you hear what I said?"

She put it into her mouth and lit up, eyes crossed, focusing on the tip.

"I said, you'd be easy to love."

And because she believed he meant it, she blushed. "Was it Stevie Wonder?"

"I'm sorry, I've embarrassed you."

"No, you haven't. I'm flattered."

"No, I shouldn't have said that. It just, I just, I just didn't think."

"But really, I'm not embarrassed."

"Michael Jackson. It was a Michael Jackson song."

" 'Thriller,' probably."

"Never heard of it."

" 'Billy Jean,' then."

He shook his head.

"You're sure it's Michael Jackson and not the Jackson Five? Because that wouldn't be current if it's the Jackson Five."

"Give me a minute. It's coming." He whistled a line, went back and rewhistled it with corrections, looking at Lydia expectantly.

"I've never heard that one. What is it?"

"I don't know the name, just the tune."

"Well, I never heard it before."

He whistled his heart out, the entire song, three verses plus the reprise.

"Nope," she said. "Never did."

"Does that mean it doesn't count if you haven't heard it?"

"Meaning what?"

"Meaning do I have to come up with a new current song to meet your qualifications?"

Smoke streaked into the shape of a funnel cloud from the cigarette to just above their eye level. Lydia still wasn't sure what he meant. "Qualifications?"

She looked through the funnel into his eyes, and was stopped short by the direct stare into hers. His pupils widened, overtaking the gold flecks in his irises so his eyes turned darker, all black and brown.

If she didn't look away, what would that mean to him?

She risked it, holding steady the line between their eyes, thinking, What is this meaning to him? Then she saw what it meant and lost her nerve. She looked down at the inch-long ash hanging onto the tip of the cigarette, growing longer by the second. She flicked it off and took a drag.

"What are you trying to qualify for?" she asked. "Most varied whistling repertoire in the age-forty-and-up category?" Smoke drifted out of her mouth as she spoke.

"I guess you're right," he said. "You'll have to take my word for it." He whistled the chorus one more time.

Lydia could have stopped everything at that point. She saw it coming. All of it. Standing on the sidelines and watching. She could have stopped everything. But it was so exciting, and they got along so well.

They didn't say anything about it, just continued the way they always had, parallel and watching from the corners of their eyes. Waiting, walking sideways, barely brushing against each other, barely but nevertheless brushing, touching, accidentally, nonchalantly. Her skin tingled warm wherever they accidentally brushed. They smoked together, in the glaring clinical medicine room or in the dark, reviewing videotapes, listening to the beat of a heart on its way to a mind, and sucking on cigarettes, keeping busy.

She watched his hands in morning conference, and anytime, she was drawn to his hands and his arms, his forearms, the curve of the muscle as it left his elbow, three prominent freckles at the top of the bulge, Sam always rolled up his shirt sleeves. And he rested his left arm on the arm of her chair.

"Wheeler!" Bristol commanded. "What's your prediction on this woman, based on your scale?"

"We expect her to wake up but to be severely debilitated."

Lydia blushed self-consciously when Sam answered the question, as if she were answering and the attention were focused on her. When everyone looked at him, she looked at the legs on Bristol's chair, in front of her.

"There's about a three percent chance that she can achieve a moderate amount of independent function." The deepness of Sam's speaking-in-conference voice always surprised her. Like what the Pastor called pulpit speech. It gave him authority. If he had been a singer instead of a whistler, he would have sung baritone.

* * *

Mrs. Zumbrun woke up as predicted. Woke up, more or less, it was all pretty relative. On day two her eyes started roving, still without purpose but movement just the same, and there was a stirring in her right thumb, a twitch that maybe was voluntary. By day five she opened and closed her eyes, she blinked and looked in the direction of noises, and Lydia had to wrap her right hand in a mitt to keep her from pulling out the Foley catheter. She breathed by herself but choked on egg custard so they fed her through a rubber tube, for the time being. On day seven she chuckled for no apparent reason, and she grabbed her son's hand and wouldn't let him go so that he chuckled too. She seemed to recognize him sometimes but she didn't speak yet.

Carlisle Simms went home good as new about a week after surgery. He promised to come back in a month, to have the other side fixed, but no one counted on it. He'd be back in his own good time.

"Keep your eye on that river for me," he said to Lydia, and he winked.

On March 30 Lydia brought an iris to Sam for his birthday. He hung it through his stethoscope. "Do I get a birthday kiss too?" he asked, but she pulled back and shook her head.

"You'd disappoint me on my birthday?"

They were in the medicine room in the daytime, both standing against an overloaded supply cart.

"Don't tease me," she said.

"Don't tease me," he answered.

"Anyway, I wouldn't kiss you here."

"Where then?"

"Nowhere. Don't tease me."

"I'm not." He grabbed her face between his hands, the long fingers almost meeting at the crown of her head, but she ducked and he ended up kissing the left lens of her glasses, and they both giggled like kids.

Mrs. Zumbrun was transferred out of the ICU to the neuro floor. She developed a urinary tract infection and then an aspiration pneumonia. She had all the makings of a permanent nester, Lydia guessed at least a six-month stay, it wasn't unheard of. They had one patient around for over two and a half years, rejected by nursing home after nursing home, developing fevers or rashes, and diarrhea in between.

Three weeks after she opened her eyes, Elsie spoke. The night aides were turning her on two-a.m. rounds. Right side to left side but first clean her bottom, wipe off the stool, give her fresh linens and then right to left. She lay flat on her back, washed and powdered, and the two nurses' aides went to hoist her up on the bed and over on her side.

"One, two, three," they said.

"Four, five, six, seven, eight, nine ten eleven twelve . . . ," Elsie whispered, and kept on going. From that night on, she wouldn't shut up, unless she fell asleep. She picked up on fragments of overheard conversation and took off from there, counting. Numbers forward and backward both, days of the week, months of the year, years since creation, she counted. Forever. A rasping, barely audible count, continuously, without rhythm or inflection and barely with pause to catch her breath. Or if you said something to her—"Today is a beautiful day," for instance — she would take up key words and repeat beautiful day beautiful day beautiful day in that same breathy mechanical rush until someone distracted her with another phrase. Her son was delighted to hear her talking. Lydia and Sam restudied her after the counting started and found everything to be pretty much the same as before. Elsie had realized her potential. Lucky woman.

When the front door buzzer buzzed, Lydia was on the phone with Jane. Since she wasn't expecting anyone, she didn't buzz back to open the door, but she did lean far out her window to look down five stories to see who it was when the person left. The buzzer sounded a second time.

"Let me call you back," she said to Jane. "I've got to see who this is." She hung up the phone, looked out again, and saw Sam on the stoop. He stood there looking uncomfortable, out of place.

She first ducked back in, out of his sight, then she leaned out. "Sam!"

He searched up the block, down the block, searched for the voice in the air.

What was he doing here? How did he know where she lived? Why did he come? And mixed in with the questions was a thrill. The thrill of knowing the answer, the power of it.

She leaned out the window again and called, "Sam! Sam, up here!" Bozo joined her on the windowsill so when Sam looked up he saw both their round faces. He waved.

"You have a cat," he called.

"Very perceptive," she called back.

"What?"

"Never mind. I'll be right down."

"Can't I come up?"

"No, I'll be right down."

She checked herself in the mirror and smiled, grabbed an apple for Sam, then ran down the stairs. She put her hand out to shake his when she met him on the stoop, but that felt silly. She pulled it back quickly.

"Nice surprise," she said.

"I know."

"You look different away from the hospital. More like a regular person." She gave him the apple.

"You too. You look better." They walked into the park at Eighty-eighth Street. People were playing softball in the field to the right of the path. "You don't mind, do you? That I came over?"

" 'Course not. Just surprised. Something up?"

Sam chomped his apple, watching the game. "No, nothing's up. I finished early, remembered where you said you lived."

They strolled past the playground and through the trees outside the edge of the Great Lawn. Sam started whistling "Twilight Time."

"That song," she said, "makes me think of Charles Osborne."

"Old boyfriend?"

"No, a patient. You saw him with H.B. We did an apnea test on him, you and I. Amazing. Charles Osborne started breathing and you started whistling 'Twilight Time.' I thought you were kind of callous."

"I don't remember Charles Osborne."

"Just as well. Actually, he's alive, somewhere in New Jersey. Regina hears from his mother. Progress reports. They take him home on a pass for holidays, hire an attendant for the weekend and take him home. His favorite TV show is *Rocky and His Friends*, the Fractured Fairytales part. Bullwinkle makes him laugh out loud."

"Lydia, what're we going to do?"

"He was a stockbroker in a previous life."

"Lydia."

They were within sight of the Delacorte Theater, but isolated on the lower walkway. No one to see them, it was safe. He kissed her, barely touching the first time.

"Oh," he said. He sounded surprised. His long arms wrapped

around her, warmed her back, he kissed her again and she, she got lost in his mouth his sweet mouth kissing her, warm arms wrapping her up.

They sat on a stone hill facing the park, facing a volleyball game and behind it baseball, and the sounds of people playing, yelling. He kissed her again, they kept kissing, holding tight.

"What're we going to do?" he repeated.

"Nothing. Nothing." They wouldn't even think. "You taste salty, did you know? Just a little."

"Is that good?"

"Umm, neutral."

She watched the volleyball lobbing high, back and forth, and he watched her face watching until it was too dark to distinguish anything. He checked the time. "I've got to go home." They walked as far as Eighty-sixth, where he had parked his car, then he left her.

Lydia sat in the dark of her apartment with the cat in her lap. She stared into nowhere and into herself. Once or twice she closed her eyes, kissing Sam again.

The phone rang. Jane. "You didn't call back. Everything okay? I was worried in case whoever buzzed you was some rapist or something. If I'm interrupting anything we can talk tomorrow but I was just a little worried."

"No problem," Lydia said. "I lost track of the time."

"So who was it?"

"Huh?"

"At the door."

"Oh. Just someone I know from the neighborhood." The first of the lies, beginning of hiding.

She sat a while longer, with the lights out and the window wide open. Two boys pitched a softball from one sidewalk across to the other, over parked cars and moving cars. The air smelled of new green growth. When she felt the chill of the April night in her limbs, she closed the window.

"It's all wrong for me." For me, she said. At that point she was still thinking of herself. "I'm not the type. We can't do this, I can't."

They were alone in his office in the evening. Sam had spread an EEG out on the countertop in front of them for appearances' sake, a diversional tactic, if necessary. They bowed close to the printout, concentrating on each other. She wanted to end everything before it went too far.

They kissed long and held each other for the last time, her eyelids half open so she could see his jaw working the kiss, his eyelids wide open but set on the door, looking out for enemies. The slightest sound sent him leaping back and fumbling for words about evoked potentials, in a master-of-ceremonies voice. (You have correctly matched up this delta wave with both frontal lobes. Now, for the cruise and ten thousand dollars, can you find the theta?) Ridiculous.

"This is ridiculous," she said. "All your attention's locked on that door. Don't kiss me anymore. I feel like I'm being serviced." She turned toward the counter. "What do you think about this guy, anyway? The EEG's not bad, the evoked potentials are even better, did you see them?"

She picked up the other graph and unrolled it on top of the EEG. "Look at this, and then here, too. He'll do okay, don't you think? Maybe?"

He kissed her again but this time with his eyes closed and swimming against his lids. "I think you're right."

"He looks so bad now, though."

"Day three he'll start waking up. Sometime between today and tomorrow."

His arm rested on her shoulders, her head rubbed against his chest. He just felt so good to her, she felt so good touching him, the smell of him close by becoming familiar to her. They touched when they worked together up here, alone. Held hands in secret. Around patients, the accidental connections, brushing against each other in close quarters, took on a provocative significance. She didn't want to call it off.

The doorknob clicked. Sam jumped back, his arm flew over Lydia's head and fell onto the papers in front of them.

"You're developing quite an expertise," he said. He glanced at the doorway. "Oh, Casper. I was just saying how Lydia's developing a real knack for these electrical studies. Look at this one. We think this guy Simpson will ultimately do well. Have a look. Come on in. Did you need something?"

No. He was just wandering around and saw the lights on so he thought he'd look in, see what was up. He leaned over the charts, surveyed them with a frown on his forehead and a pinky in his nostril, as if he knew what it all meant.

"You can read these?" He turned toward Lydia.

"Not as well as Sam." Leave, Casper. We don't want you here. "But probably better than you."

The doctors chuckled. Sam launched into a lengthy explanation concerning evoked response. Compensating for his own irritation and embarrassment, Lydia thought. It was driving her crazy. Casper hung on and on, asking questions, telling stories, gossiping about H.B.'s latest tantrum. Get out of here and leave us alone, we hardly have any time together as it is and we don't need you around now. Why are people so dense, can't he tell? Sam started in on another Bristol story. Lydia, about to explode, left the room. She was ready to call it off now.

The hiding got to her. And the limits. She hated to have to pretend disinterest when she wanted mostly to shout, This man and I are in love! If only she could do that.

Sam found her in the library. "I don't think he noticed anything about us. I think we covered it pretty well."

"Covered what? So we've kissed. And held hands in the dark reading ultrasound videotapes." She shook her head, picked up a pencil and underlined headings in the index of a neurology journal. "This is a good time to stop. Before anything's started. I'm not the other-woman type anyway. I can't share, I couldn't share you."

"Okay." Sam pulled three textbooks from the shelves and sat down across from Lydia. He scanned the index of the first book, slapped it closed, pushed it away and began going through the index of the second book.

Lydia got up from the table to replace her journal in its stack.

Sam slammed down the cover of the second book, pushed it away and turned to the third. "Maybe I could just come over to talk, though? I wouldn't kiss you." He opened to the middle of the third book and found a diagram of the basal ganglia. "Some Saturday afternoon? When I'm down here working anyway?"

"I don't know. Maybe not."

The following Saturday he was in the city working anyway. They walked west to Riverside Park this time, and sat on a bench overlooking the Hudson.

They watched the morning cross west into New Jersey, the sky lightening from cornflower to pale powdered blue. They walked up to Grant's Tomb and Lydia explained all the good things about Grant that Sam might not know, how he died of a broken heart. On the far side of the tomb, out of sight of the whole of Manhattan, he stopped her mid-sentence, with a kiss long and longing, pulling her so close she thought she might have disappeared into him. He kissed her mouth, her cheeks, her ears, her eyes, her mouth, pressing her head to his chest.

He led her out into the open and they headed south through the shade. When they hit a sunny spot, one small square yard of unfiltered light, he grabbed her again and kissed her and raised his face to the sun, tilting her face up too. "This is what I've wanted," he said. "For us to kiss in the sunlight, out in the open for anyone to see." He kissed her, and he kissed her. They walked back into the shade and they kissed, with him squaring himself directly against her so she could feel how excited he was, tempting her. She pushed him away but he insisted, even his grip tempted her.

"What're we going to do?" he kept saying. "What're we going to do?"

Three very sunny, very distinct Saturdays followed that first one. They walked, always somewhere safe from Samaritan people, generally uptown and west. She wouldn't let Sam into her apartment. That sustained the illusion that they weren't having an affair but were just real good friends, talking about things. What things? At first, they hashed out the whole neuro department and also the Sunday *Times.* Now they stuck to boring reassurances of how much they missed each other and how it could never work out. Connie barely existed, except as a sort of institution they owed some kind of perverse allegiance to. Someone vaguely remembered, certainly not by Lydia. And the holding back was luscious.

By the beginning of June, Lydia realized that it was just a matter of time, and that prolonging the wait made it all sweeter than it would probably turn out to be. For once she didn't think about what they would do with it once they had actually made love, she didn't think about after at all. She knew only that they would do it eventually, so why not now?

On Friday afternoon, by the glow of Sol Heinmetz's videotaped carotid artery, Sam took hold of Lydia's hand so tightly that she had to pull it away. He took it again, pressing more gently. "Soon," he said. "Soon." The poetry of their hunger growing unimaginably in front of Sol's hardening arteries made her laugh aloud, and Sam caught on, laughing too, until they laughed their way into each other's arms, laughing tears, and Sam said, "Soon, soon," again.

She made a pasta salad to serve with French bread, St. André cheese and strawberries for lunch. Since Connie and Tricia Wheeler were allergic to cats, Lydia vacuumed her place three times and bought brand-new sheets so that Sam wouldn't take even a trace of dander home with him. She pulled yellowish leaves off her ivies and then overwatered them, and she waited.

At eleven o'clock, he called.

"I can't do it."

"What?"

"I can't come. I can't do it. I have to put up screens today. I promised Connie two weeks ago and then I forgot. I'm sorry."

"You can't come over today because of some screens?"

Silence on the line. Long pause.

"I can't do it. I love you, I do love you but I just can't do this to the kids. Or to Connie. I was all ready to come, almost out the door and I started thinking about them and, I can't."

Lydia's nose burned, she started crying, silent tears, not sobbing.

"I'm sorry," he said.

"Why didn't you figure this out before?" Her voice wavered a little. "Bastard."

"Good-bye. I'm sorry."

On Monday he brought her a stone, volcanic rock.

She managed to avoid him most of the morning, but still kept a high visibility. Eat your heart out, she thought. He started toward her a few times and that's when she would go talk to a patient or to another physician. She even flirted with Mitch for a while.

At twelve-fifteen Sam finally intruded on her while she fed Elsie Zumbrun. He stood on the other side of the bed looking serious. "I have to talk to you."

"Tough," Lydia said. "I'm busy."

"Busy busy busy busy busy," Elsie murmured.

"When's your lunch?"

"Sam, please." He looked tired, around his eyes.

"I made a mistake. I want to talk to you."

She turned her back on him, mashing together the peas and puréed veal. "Half an hour. Twelve-forty-five."

"Forty-five, forty-six, forty-seven, forty-eight." A bit of saliva bubbled from the side of Elsie's mouth, "forty-nine, fifty, fifty-one, fifty-two . . ."

They spent lunch walking south along the river. It was warm but windy there and the water sparkled in the sunlight, clear and refreshing at a distance. They stopped to track a small motorboat making its way up the river against the current. When Lydia looked straight down into the green water she saw Manhattan's wastes pouring out of a huge spout directly below them. She looked away quickly, to the sparkling flow up by the hospital, and back again to the gush of slime and shit and nonbiodegradable waste.

They walked as far down as Sixty-third Street and turned around to go back. Sam reached into his pocket, held out his open hand to her, offering her a rock, dull, dusty, charcoal-colored. "Volcanic. It's for you. It's a geode."

He turned it over to show a polished surface and the inside of the stone. She took it and held it up to the sunlight. The rim looked like black marble, with a white feathery vein running through it, mostly along its inner edge. Inside the edge was a hollow, lined with clear, hard crystals, shimmering unevenly, one of them big as a piece of rock candy.

"Steam gets trapped inside the lava flow, and it makes a sort of bubble. The crystals form from the steam, after the fire cools off." He took her hand and curled his fingers around hers cupping the stone. "I almost came in on Saturday anyway, I realized that I'll never kill this thing we have. I can't kill it and it won't die and I wanted to come to you and tell you."

A gray-haired man in a red T-shirt jogged toward them and smiled at Lydia when he passed.

"But you didn't," she said to Sam.

"I thought you'd throw me out."

"I probably would have. But I would have felt better all weekend."

"Will you keep the rock?"

She cradled it in both hands, like some fragile bird's egg. "Of course."

* * *

That next Saturday Lydia peeled peaches for fruit salad, passing the time. She paced from the kitchen to the front window to the bedroom to the window to the kitchen with a dripping half-peeled peach in her hand. She sliced it. She pitted eleven cherries and peeled another peach, this time in one slow, perfect unbroken spiral that tore anyway, toward the end, plus grapes, an apple, a handful of cherries, another peach, a plum. The buzzer made her jump. She had convinced herself he wasn't coming, so she expected the phone, not the front door buzzer.

He was a long time getting up the stairs, but he rounded the banister smiling and she smiled back. They kissed in the open doorway. Once inside and behind the door, double locked and chained, they kissed again, their lips barely touching as if they were sunburned, sore, barely touching, barely open burning lips kissing.

"You're sure?" she asked.

He moved his fingertips down the line of her spine and up, and down, again barely, as if her back had burned along with her lips, and his hands too. He moved his hands like that all over her back and then over her rib cage and up to her breasts. Through her T-shirt she felt his hands searing her breasts, but then under her T-shirt against her bare skin they felt cool and pressed hard.

She pulled off the shirt and unzipped her jeans, no sense holding back, not anymore.

"Wait," he said, and held her quietly against him for moments.

"No." She started in on his shirt buttons.

They were just inside her door, between the kitchen and the bathroom. Someone flushed a toilet somewhere, with Lydia half naked and clawing at Sam's buttons and him breathing hard, saying, "Slow down," and "Baby, my baby." The woman from upstairs ran downstairs with her dog. "Come on, boy, come on, let's go out!" The dog paused to sniff at Lydia's door. "Come on, boy!"

Lydia tugged at the third button, the fourth, the fifth, with all of them stuck or catching in threads. Sam kissed her cheeks, her ear, her neck, and her hands, he got in the way of her work, but she persisted, pulled his shirt out of his trousers and finally his undershirt. She slipped her hands under it, feeling the skin of his chest. She pushed the shirt up and pressed her warm self against him, "Ahhh," between the kitchen and the bathroom by the front door.

"Bedroom?" he murmured.

She took his hand to lead him there but he held back, looking at her, at her naked torso. He ran his hands over her again, tracing her contours with his fingers and palms. They kissed and squeezed so tight, breaths coming as loud and deep as a comatose man's. Sam slid his hands inside her jeans, pushing them down.

In bed she wondered at the length of his undressed body, and at the grace of it, the balance. She opened herself to him, to his grace and balance. They studied the look and feel and taste of each other as if this were the only time, the last time, the definitive time, excruciating time. They rubbed against each other up and down and sideways, feeling, smelling, tasting, in and around each other, moving together, apart, in sync and out, their mouths kissing wide-open kisses as if to take the other one in to be swallowed whole.

Lydia felt them melting together, their boundaries blurred, stuck one on one into one larger and complete. They were pure white wax figures without a seam.

"I was afraid I wouldn't be any good," he said later. They were still locked, still damp. "I was so nervous when I got here."

She massaged his backbone until the weight of him crushed her so she couldn't breathe, and then she pushed him off.

The second time she rode him like a bronco and they spent themselves laughing, giggling at each other, surprised and familiar.

"H.B. says men lose the ability for multiple orgasm after thirty-five." Smiling to himself, smug. "I believed him."

"So he's wrong. Shall we tell him?" A high bright June noon lit the bedroom. A room full of glee and the sun. "I think you should tell him."

"Nah. It'll make him feel bad."

"He'll probably think you're perverted."

"He'll ask for your phone number."

Lydia heehawed at the image of Bristol in bed, with no racket. One sunbeam spotlighted Bozo on the rug, another reflected leaf shadows and dappled the wall.

"We're different now," she said. "We won't be the same with each other. Never again."

"I love you, Lydia." Sam lay back and stared at the star quilt on the wall. "Lydia. I love to say your name. Lydia. Lingual name, lots of tongue, Lydia. Who was Lydia?"

"From the Bible. We all got names from the Bible. Dinah Ruth, Marie Elizabeth, Lydia Rebecca."

"Who was she?"

"Lydia?" She turned and faced his profile, his straight long nose.

"A Corinthian. Businesswoman, seller of purple, whatever that was."

"Tyrenian Purple, a dye. Royal purple for kings and noblemen."

"How do you know that?"

"I'm different now," he teased. "Magic. You've given me powers, I know things."

She punched him in the belly button. He turned and kissed her, nuzzled her hair, his penis poking between them. When she pulled back she saw he was looking over her shoulder at the clock.

"You have to go, right?"

Wall-to-wall people lay out at the tide line, wall-to-wall gulls stood alert at the trash line. Lydia brushed sweat from above her lip and rolled onto her stomach.

Jane slathered baby oil over her legs and rubbed the excess onto her belly. She shook her head. "I knew it. I told you to watch out." She studied the gleam on her thighs, evened it out.

The gulls were at attention, in platoons, watching at the distant horizon, waiting for leftovers in the trash bins, steady, straight, their beaks lined up in formation. Jaded Jones Beach gulls who knew their rights.

Lydia wished she had kept her mouth shut.

Jane lay back carefully in order not to disturb the baby oil. "Geez, I saw it coming. Why didn't you listen to me from the beginning?"

"I shouldn't have told you."

A Frisbee landed in the midst of the gulls. One of them flapped back, the others merely turned, noted the toy, and resumed their watch.

"I thought you'd be different," Lydia continued. "I thought you'd understand."

"What understand? I understand that my friend has set herself up for a letdown. That's what I understand."

"First of all, I didn't plan this."

"I warned you. In the very beginning. I saw it, I told you."

"I didn't plan this. It happened. By the time it happened, it was already too late."

"Never. You can always back out."

"Just forget it. Forget I ever mentioned it."

"You're crazy."

Lydia turned her head away from Jane. She watched a troupe of teen-agers settle themselves to her right. The boys made a big deal out of lifting two large coolers from one place to another within their small parcel of sand. The girls lay back on beach chairs, bored and already dozing. "You're in my sun," one of them said to one of the boys. He turned his ass to her face, half-mooned her, and she giggled.

Lydia rolled over and sat up to watch with the gulls.

The first time she had seen the ocean was there on Jones Beach with Jane next to her. Jane had jumped in without a second thought while Lydia stayed still, the water teasing her bare toes. It had felt icy and the great waves had scared her some, but she couldn't take her eyes off all the quivering blue stretched out in front of her. She had her geography wrong. She imagined she was looking toward England.

The teen-agers turned up their radio and started a sand fight, a small plane flew through her line of vision with THIRSTY? GIN AND SCHWEPPES in a stream behind it. She shrugged and lay down, shut her eyes, a cacophony of radios and tapedecks and kids hawking frozen Milky Way bars blaring around her.

"Let me tell you something," Jane blasted through the din. "He won't leave his family. He's not the type, but even if he were the type, they don't do it. Very few men actually pick up and go."

Lydia nodded, not because she believed it or agreed, but because she didn't know one way or the other, and Jane seemed to. She hadn't expected him to leave them, hadn't actually thought about it yet except for once or twice glimpsing them magically in a future together, eating breakfast, taking a walk. Mostly she didn't let herself think about it. She wasn't interested in breaking up a marriage.

"They might be thrown out, or have a mutual split, but very few of them pick up and go. It's a simple fact."

Lydia didn't want to get into it. She didn't want to discuss it.

"I wish I hadn't brought it up," she said.

"If this is exactly what you want, if you're sure, then fine. I hope you're happy. Just don't expect a lot. Don't fool yourself."

Jane lay perfectly still except for the movement of her mouth, every square inch of skin on the front of her body was evenly exposed to the sun. Her eyes were closed. Lydia thought Jane must be the meanest person she knew. She thought she hated Jane.

"You're not helping me," she said. "This doesn't help. It's mean."

"I'm sorry you don't like it, but I've never held back with you so why should I start now? You have to prepare yourself. No expectations. They don't leave their families."

"So what? It's not doing me one bit of good to hear it. What do you want from me? To say you're right?" Lydia sat up and put her glasses on. There were sailboats skimming far out. "You obviously know all about married men," she grumbled. "Right now, five minutes ago anyway, I was ecstatic, and already you're warning me off. I don't need all this wisdom. It doesn't help. You can say 'I told you so' in six months or something, just don't tell me so now. Please."

A sailboat shifted around, its spinnaker full to the beach, green and blue, with a large white star.

Jane turned sideways toward Lydia. "I didn't mean to hurt you. I just got carried away. Who knows? Who knows about people, right? You never know anything for sure, everyone's different. Look, I can see how this could happen. He's a lovely person, really. Smart man, kind of attractive. You, certainly, were attractive to him. That much was crystal clear. And who knows? Right? I'm just preparing you for the worst."

"We're happy together. I had to tell someone."

"Please, I'm not making any judgments. Believe me." She sighed, stood up, wrapped her thick braid into a coil. "I'm going in. You want to come?"

Lydia shaded her eyes to look at her friend. She shook her head and smiled. "Go ahead."

That first time Lydia saw the ocean, Jane had jumped in and disappeared for what seemed like too long. Lydia looked out for her, it didn't help that she wasn't wearing her glasses and had to rely on an impression. She had visions of the ocean sucking Jane under, while she stood helpless on the beach afraid of waves. She scanned the water beyond the surf. No Jane, not even the impression of her, and it seemed like way too long for her to be under. Lydia looked toward the lifeguard, she looked at the ocean, she watched the waves crashing in, watched for a woman's body being tossed to the beach, she wondered what to do and wondered what was taking her so long to do something, and then she saw Jane, way out, swimming back and forth as if doing laps in a backyard pool. She ran for her glasses to make sure it was Jane, and it was.

"I was afraid for you," Lydia told her after she had come in. "Don't laugh."

"I'm like a fish," Jane replied, laughing. "Anyway, I can't think of a place I'd rather die than in the Atlantic Ocean."

The power of the ocean was peace to Jane, helplessness to Lydia. In Tennessee, nobody swam like a fish, nobody she knew, anyway. The whole family had signed up for group lessons at the Y once, but they all quit halfway through, for various reasons, except Lydia, who stuck it out but still couldn't swim like a fish. The older girls were afraid their hair would turn brittle and green from chlorine, swimming caps gave Mama a headache, and Pastor was always getting called away for a death or an illness or a congregational crisis on those nights. He never even got his feet wet.

Lydia could smell the bitter female smell of the damp beach under her. Her ear pressed on the smooth-packed sand, she heard the sounds of running feet and running water, gulls cried, radios blared, and the Atlantic rushed onto the beach, advancing and retreating, slapping itself.

She didn't know if Sam could swim. Probably the Wheelers belonged to a club with an Olympic-sized swimming pool, golf course and tennis courts. She didn't even know. She vaguely recalled something about Andrew and a swim team at the community center.

"Elmer Dodge is a sixty-two-year-old white male executive from St. Louis, in New York on business, admitted following a confusional episode in the lobby of a midtown hotel."

Scott Schroeder was beginning his year as chief resident, taking over for Christine Burke. The cycle repeated itself, all the residents looked gawky and wet behind the ears again. The conference table dwarfed Scott, his jacket seemed too white, too well ironed.

Had Sam been that way last year? She barely recalled that he had. Now he had filled out, smoothed over. Or maybe Lydia couldn't see him clearly anymore, since she knew what he looked like naked. She couldn't judge accurately now. She knew him when he was ecstatic, transformed, she knew how he looked as he transformed her.

Their shoulders brushed. He winked at her.

"Speed it up, Schroeder," Bristol cut in. "You have sixteen minutes for five more patients. Three minutes apiece plus twelve seconds leeway, which I am using up right now. Go on."

"We have very little to go on, sir. The patient has no memory for any events after approximately ten-thirty last evening when he was engaged in conversation with a young lady," Scott coughed, "at a bar downtown. The next historian is the evening clerk at the hotel who called nine-one-one after Mr. Dodge ran through the lobby wearing only his undershorts, shoes and socks, screaming obscenities at the doorman, the bellman and the elevator operator. The patient then appeared to fall backward and to the right, and he collapsed, unresponsive."

"Back and to the right, you say?"

"Yes sir?"

"Past history? Risk factors?"

"Greater than fifty-pack-year smoking history, partial gastrectomy for a duodenal ulcer ten years prior to admission, mild hypertension, no heart disease, no allergies, according to his wife. We spoke to her long distance."

"Scan?"

"Entirely negative. He is awake this morning, oriented, light-headed with a mild dysarthria and no memory, as I said, of last night's events. Physical and neurological exams are normal except for the slurred speech and memory loss."

"What do we think this is?" Bristol snapped. He rolled a pencil back and forth between his hands.

"An ischemic event of some sort," Scott offered. "That was our assumption. Posterior circulation TIA. We opted to put him on aspirin instead of heparin."

Bristol turned to Mitch. "Dr. Mitchell? Opinion?"

"No past history of seizures?" Mitch asked. "Or other episodes of aberrant behavior?"

The question took off around the table. More questions were asked, giving rise to still more questions, with Bristol smiling broadly as each physician failed to find an answer. He rose slowly and strolled to the brain scan on display.

Sam sat forward, as everyone else did, straining to see something on the CAT scan. "Did he return to his room at all during this time?" he asked. "Does anyone know?"

His eyes sloped downward slightly. Something Lydia had only noticed from beneath him in bed, but which she noticed again now. During orgasm, his whole face drew downward and his eyes, instead of closing, opened wide, pleaded, until he resembled the face in Munch's *The Scream*.

"Any valuables missing that he's noticed?" Sam was asking. "Where did Mr. Dodge leave his clothes?"

Bristol turned, interested. "Exactly. That's exactly my postulation." No one else appeared to understand. "Explain, Wheeler. Enlighten the innocents."

"Scopalomine," Sam said. "They were using it in Copenhagen a few years ago. Professional thieves. The victim meets an attractive woman at a bar. She slips the drug into his drink and *voilà!* Compliance. The woman gets him to his room, an accomplice follows. The victim passes out, they rob him and leave. The victim awakens, sometimes hallucinates, exhibits fairly bizarre behavior, but the only thing he can remember is going into the bar for a drink. Can't even identify the thieves. I thought it originated in New York. Surprised you didn't know about it."

Bristol nodded. "We had a number of cases some years back. Then it slackened off. They must have been going to Bellevue. This is the first one in some time. But the story fits. The story fits." He chuckled. "Now you have ten minutes for four patients, Schroeder. Try to speed things up." He returned to his chair slowly. "Thank you, Sam."

"So should I take him off the aspirin?" Scott asked.

"You may as well," Bristol answered. "Work him up first, to be sure. Check out his heart, look at his vasculature. I daresay everything will come up normal, but you don't want to take any chances. Then stop the aspirin and send him back to St. Louis."

Scott wrote a few earnest notes.

"Hurry up, man!" Bristol bellowed.

"Uh," Scott stammered. "Uh, Carol, uh, Carol Boyd is a twenty-four-year-old black female with—"

"Wheeler," Bristol interrupted. He swiveled clear around in his chair. Sam moved farther forward. Lydia looked down at the chair legs.

"Wheeler, from now on, sit here with me at the table. Beginning tomorrow."

Lydia glanced at Sam, a serious frown on his face and his eyes even with the Chief's. She looked up at Bristol, but he was already turning back to the table.

"Uh, Carol Boyd . . ."

Watching from her bed, Lydia waited for the man across the street to fall from his window ledge. He wiped the windows clean with white foam, a large yellow cloth and busy swipes. It took surprisingly little time, except for the last window, far to the left. He balanced on a lower ledge, held onto the middle window and stretched, reached precariously, sprayed, set down the aerosol can, and wiped. She waited to see him fall, but he handled himself gracefully, picked up the can, swung back into his apartment.

Sam lay behind her, his legs and arms wrapping her to him. It was the only lazy time they had together anymore. "Tricia insisted on planting all the tomato plants in the spring," he was saying. "Her hands broke out in a rash, but she wouldn't leave my side until we planted every last one of them. So now we're up to our ears in overripe tomatoes, giving them to anyone and everyone. You want tomatoes?"

Her stomach turned. "Anyone and everyone?"

He tightened his wrap. "You know what I mean." He kissed the crown of her head. "Seriously, you want some?"

He was including her in the family, reminding her of the family, filling her in, leaving her out. Was it better if he had no awareness of what he was doing? He had none. Was it worse? The thought of Wheeler-family tomatoes squeezed acid into her throat. "Look how full that guy's spider plant grew over the summer," she said.

"Voyeur."

"Observer. Absolutely."

The tree in front of Lydia's window had also grown, so much that it partly obscured the view of her neighbor across the street, making it more provocative. The woman above him kept bushy plants in her windows. The man next to her was never home, or else he could be seen at his window, staring into hers.

Sam rolled flat on his naked back. He stared at the quilt on the wall opposite them, searching out new patterns. He said it was like self-hypnosis or repeating a mantra into oblivion.

"My chemical arrived. Four small vials. Kay-oh-six-six-seven-one-eight-one." He said it offhandedly, less important than overripe tomatoes. Behind the control, he didn't want to jinx himself, she thought. "Casper's already using it on rats. Bristol worked out a protocol."

Lydia flipped over, fitting herself sideways against him, her belly under his rib cage, left leg curled over his abdomen and around him, left arm resting on his chest, she drew circles around his right nipple. The strong smell of sweat and their loving floated in the air. Later she would cover herself in that smell in the sheets and sleep with it all night. Sometimes, in the middle of sleep, she would catch a whiff of him in her pillowcase and she would smother herself in it.

"At last, right?" She propped her head on his shoulder and brushed his check with her nose. "The cure."

She had, over the past year, picked up bits dropped like cookie crumbs, about the chemical, the K compound, he called it, his compound. She had mashed the crumbs together into a whole that was exciting and dreadful at the same time.

The compound enhanced axoplasmic transport and flow. She looked up axoplasmic transport in several physiology texts. It seemed to be the way products of the nerve cell bodies—chemicals, proteins, enzymes—moved on to the axon terminals of the nerves. Going a step further, some people thought it was a process necessary to the formation of neurotransmitters, the triggers of brain activity. K0667181 increased all that, in rats anyway.

The whole idea thrilled her. It was positive, and more than that, active. Doing something, doing something good. Raising brain cells from the dead.

"More like waking them from sleep," Sam reminded her. "Bristol's come up with a combination of drugs he thinks will increase brain function during acute ischemic events, and presumably diminish tissue loss in the process." He twirled short strands of her hair between his fingertips, twirled around and around in rhythm with her finger on his chest. "Casper's rats like it."

"What drugs?"

His right hand followed the angle of her waist at the hip and then rubbed along her thigh and back up. "My compound, plus a vasodilator like nitroglycerine, and an opiate antagonist, probably naloxone." His long fingers kneaded her rump and then reached clear around to tease the inside of her thighs from behind.

She warmed with the touch, purred like Bozo. "He thinks naloxone will work?" Her legs went limp but her arms reached around him to hug him closer than ever. Sometimes she hung onto him for dear life, his touch was unbearably sweet.

"Along with the other drugs, I guess. He thinks they may potentiate each other."

Lydia remembered the big excitement over Narcan a few years back. She called it the Walt Disney hypothesis of stroke. Narcan, generically naloxone, had been used successfully to wake up barbiturate overdoses and to reverse some anesthesias. But two West Coast doctors, working on the assumption that brain ischemia stimulated local endorphin release, had tried to reverse signs and symptoms during cerebral ischemia using that same opiate antagonist, Narcan. The brain cells weren't dead, only sleeping, like Snow White. She could see all the little axons and nerve cell bodies receiving the kiss of the Narcan molecule, stretching and yawning and returning to work. Those two doctors had reported great success with the magic potion, but no one else anywhere had been able to duplicate their results. Not with gerbils or rats or human beings. The excitement died down, and that was that.

"You know," she told him, "H.B. said something to me once about needing a Prince Charming to kiss all our comas. You think he's found one?"

"He sure as hell wants to find one. Think what that would do for him. Maybe a Nobel, why not?" He rolled to his side and pulled her close against him.

"So you'll get one too, right?" She stroked the soft underside of his penis, felt it already stretched smooth.

"Get what?"

"A Nobel."

He pulled back. "Ah ha!" Jumped up. "I knew it was my power that first attracted you." He knelt on her bed, torso and arms raised like King Kong, about to pound his chest. "You don't love me. You love my position, my power, the Wheeler Index!" His penis rose, full and tight, a fat arrowhead. Her own muscles relaxed, warmed, opened for him.

She pulled him down on top of her, moving to the perfect place beneath him, around him. He poked into her, quick teasing strokes so she grabbed his hips to bring him deeper.

He smacked loud kisses into her neck and gnawed at it. Her breath caught on the kisses and short little noises escaped from her throat. "Those little noises you make," he said. "They break my heart."

He looked at her alarm clock.

"Don't say a word," she said. "I know."

Abrupt. No matter how long they lingered, the ending was always abrupt, intrinsically, she guessed. Had to take the bad with the good, she guessed.

Postcoital debriefing, a regular routine, she laughed when she said it, the first time. The shower, the snack, the regretted good-bye. They emerged into daylight and waved, blew kisses back and forth, sometimes once more with her leaning her head into the front window of his car, kissing the driver's lips, and he'd speed off.

First the shower. He almost always showered, in order to remove telltale cat fur and Lydia's scent. Decontamination phase, a painful truth in the joke. Into the shower to remove all evidence, visible and invisible, and anything that might prove bad for the wife. She must be protected at all costs. Sometimes Lydia stayed in her bed while Sam showered, and thought about Connie. Not that she wanted one of Bozo's hairs to shed its dander on Sam's underwear, from there to Connie's bronchioles, leading to anaphylaxis and eventual death. Not at all. But Lydia spent what felt like an awful lot of time vacuuming and washing and changing sheets for Connie's sake. She pictured a dark silent house bathed in gray. Allergies flaring in proportion to anger. She imagined it from the bits Sam told her. She elaborated enormously. Occasionally she had fantasies that his beeper went off and he rushed away contaminated, later to be found out and thrown out, an expression of horror on Connie's face, one thin cat whisker held upright between manicured, trembling fingers.

Today they took turns under the hot leaky shower spray. A skewed stream shot level with Sam's eyeballs no matter where he stood.

"You want some coffee?" she asked, drying his back. "I made raisin bread."

"Maybe one cup. Andrew's pitching this afternoon. Playoffs. I need to be there early. You know how nervous he gets." He assumed that she knew his children as well as he did. An honest mistake. She wished she did.

Her windows stood open, letting the outside in, an alternative to going out. A dog barked. Sounded as if he was in the apartment with them.

"So how dangerous is this stuff, anyway?"

"Not 'stuff.' It's a chemical compound. You have to start talking like a scientist."

"Perish the thought. Just tell me."

"Not dangerous so far. Not by itself. We used it in Denmark on patients with Alzheimer's. They've been trying it lately to treat M.S. Some uncomfortable side effects, no fatalities. By itself. So far here, the rats have fared pretty well on the combination. Casper's still titrating doses, so he's had a few accidents, but they don't count at this stage of the game. Good bread."

He sliced a second hunk for himself.

Insulated at her table, they sat and listened to the barks and squeals of the world. He nibbled on raisin bread. Although she didn't dwell on it, she occasionally felt choked by the insulation, as if rebreathing used air, air like that near the church altar, thick with old prayers and supplications, or the air by the hospital kitchen, layered over with soup fumes. Sometimes after he left, she took a long walk in the park, savoring the relief of being outside, sometimes she could hardly wait to get out there and walk.

She broke everything off once because she felt so pitiful. She added up the time they had spent alone together, not including work, but stopped when she realized it was only hours, not even a whole day. They would never wake up together, never have dinner out with friends, never browse their way through Columbus Avenue with no plan in mind except being together. She couldn't stand it, it wasn't her style, hadn't she said so? Good-bye.

For three days morning conference was too long and too short. Sam sat next to Bristol and responded correctly much of the time, laughed when he should have and even threw in a bit of his own ironic humor. She hated him for functioning so apparently well without her. All she wanted was to leave the room, too many people there anyway. But when she caught him glancing her way after he had made one of his comments, to catch her reaction maybe, to indicate an awareness of her, then she could have sat there forever until he glanced her way again.

She skipped conference on the fourth day and buried herself with four patients in a far room so she wouldn't have to be confronted with Sam, although she saw him from behind once, walking away from her toward the ICU. He slouched and moved slowly, looking into the rooms from time to time, she imagined he was looking to get a glimpse of her.

By the morning of the fifth day, she no longer felt that she would burst into tears if anyone looked at her cross-eyed or, worse, said something nice to her. Her eyes weren't puffy. She had almost slept the night straight through. She arrived at the meeting with her stomach feeling neutral for a change.

Sam was there waiting.

She sat in her usual place and looked out the window at the woman across the street.

Sam had moved his chair forty-five degrees and sat practically facing her. She didn't look toward him, but in her peripheral vision, she saw that he was staring at her, in front of everyone except Bristol, who hadn't arrived.

When Bristol came, Sam moved his chair back to face the table, although he turned toward her once more before conference actually started. His eyelids were swollen, with dark streaks above and below, and his complexion had a yellow cast. If she looked as bad as he did, everyone must have guessed about them.

Afterward, Sam stopped her on her way out the door. In his master-of-ceremonies voice, for everyone to hear, he said, "There's something I need to go over with you."

She followed him to his office. He shut the door behind them, an unusually bold and potentially risky thing to do. Then she caved in. He held her to him, stroked her hair.

"I miss you. Don't ever leave me again," he pleaded. "I have no one to talk to when I can't talk to you. No one. I stare at medical journals and daydream a conversation with you. Connie doesn't know about the research. We talk about dinner parties and what she's going to serve. I wither without you. I'll die if you ever turn your back on me again."

It was the quality that counted, she told herself, not the quantity. And she was back to an endless cycle of rebreathing stale air and cleaning up to keep Connie from dying or sneezing or finding out.

Sam tried to read his watch without being too obvious about it.

"Two-thirty," Lydia said. She stood up and went for her keys before he could go into his wish-I-could-stay routine, and then they left together.

"You don't whistle anymore, not hardly at all. Did you know that?"

"Sure I whistle."

"No. Anyway, not around me. Really."

He held the front door for her and they walked out into the sunlight.

"I didn't know I'd stopped."

"You have. Now you sing sometimes, a line of lyric under your breath, but you've quit whistling."

"I know I used to whistle on purpose around you, once you'd noticed it, and you made that crack about oldies." They crossed the street, walked to his car, holding hands. "I was ecstatic that you paid attention. So I did it more and more, deliberately. I thought you'd like it."

"I did." She leaned forward against the hood, he slid into the driver's seat. "One of the first things I liked about you. I even whistled sometimes when you weren't around, like at home, to conjure you up, I guess. To feel close." A mating call then. Whistled ardently at first, to get her attention, to keep it. And now that they were mated, he didn't need it anymore. Just a theory.

She had put on red running shorts and a sleeveless T-shirt, and he touched her bare shoulder, held his hand on it for several minutes, he seemed to want to stay. Lydia ran around to the front of his car and propped her right foot on the fender, hands on her hips like

Wonder Woman, bringing him to a halt. "Don't go." She stood strong for a good thirty seconds, smiling, then came to his window, kissed him. "Don't go."

He turned on the ignition. "Got to. Wish I didn't. Honest." He pulled out to the street. "See you Monday."

She held on to the door handle and ran alongside him to the end of the block.

Seemed like work was either so slow you felt foolish being there taking up space or, more likely, it was chaos. They had beds or they didn't, no beds anywhere in the whole institution, and people were put on hold in the emergency room until someone could be discharged. No such thing as a comfortable pace.

That week was chaos.

Regina took the outside, Lydia took the unit. In a fit of generosity, Regina gave her two other nurses plus two nurse technicians, but still it was chaos.

The six regular beds were full: an acute cord compression, a brain abscess, two postop craniotomies, and two brainstem strokes, one sleepy, one awake, plus a jungle of wires and cords and bottles and bags hanging around each bed. Full to the brim. Until eleven-forty-five, when they seemed to be catching up, but an emergency rolled in with a team of doctors looking stressed, looking concerned, looking puzzled and looking around for a slot to slide the bed into. Full to overflowing. The patient was seizing to beat the band, she couldn't stop.

"Status epilepticus," the junior resident said.

"I can see that," Lydia answered. "I have no beds."

"I can see that," he answered back. "Neither does anyone else. I need some IV pentobarb, we've tried everything else, and I need another bottle of half-NS, a blood pressure reading, an oxygen outlet."

"An ambu bag and an intubation tray. And I'll call for a respirator just in case. Wilma," she called to the nurse technician. "Get Carl on the phone and ask for another respirator, and maybe a spare oxygen tank, and tell him we're using the extra ambu bag and the flowmeter from the supply shelf."

The old woman continued her unbroken spasms and jerks, her doctor impatiently pounding the headboard with his outstretched arm, waiting for the pentobarb. It looked as if the seizure had extended to him too. Lydia gave him an IV bottle and a stethoscope on her way to the sedative cabinet. Keep him occupied.

The whole maneuver, start to finish, took less than forty-five seconds. She handed him the pentobarb syringe.

"Finally," he sighed.

Wilma stood at attention to the right of the patient; she had set up the intubation tray just in case. Lydia hooked the ambu to oxygen, coming in close and standing ready, on the balls of her feet. The resident—his name tag said Bartlett—shot barbiturate into the IV line and opened the flow wide. An intern leaned on the patient's left foot, useless, much like the pentobarb, which wasn't affecting the seizures one bit.

The old lady snorted and hiccupped between spasms coming like waves, gentle jerks swelling to noisy crashing blows against herself, subsiding into twitches only to rise again and again. Lydia handed Bartlett another pentobarb.

"Could someone get a gas?" she asked. Gently. As if they thought it themselves. "Wilma, could you bring some blood gas kits?"

"Good idea," Bartlett said. He pushed in half of the second syringe, waited, then half again, while the intern struggled to get into the femoral artery. The intensity of the seizures seemed to be evening out to a roll, and then to a ripple. The woman's muscles slackened, her head relaxed in a normal sleeping pose. She snored, but without that gaping unevenness, and pretty soon she didn't snore, pretty soon after that she stopped breathing altogether.

Lydia bagged her a few rich breaths before Bartlett put the endotracheal tube down. They attached her to the respirator somehow, plugging it into the wall socket with an extension cord Wilma had dug out of the back of a desk drawer.

Lydia looked around the room, could she move anyone out? Even if she could, Regina didn't have any empties either. It would be the first craniotomy. He had gotten his twenty-four hours' worth of intensive care, and he was stable, he'd have to be the one to go.

"She's ninety-two over forty." Bartlett handed back Lydia's stethoscope. "Thanks," he said. "Not too bad, considering. I'm Richard Bartlett, call me Bart." He extended his hand.

Lydia shook it. "Lydia Weber." Was he really a knockout, or was it the white jacket?

Her sisters jabbered in the back of Lydia's mind. "He seems like a nice enough boy," they said. "Why can't you at least make an effort? He's not wearing a ring, just make an effort." Dark brown hair, hazel eyes, blue oxford button-down shirt, typical Good Samaritan issue, definitely enhanced by the white coat. "You get the role of Paul Bunyan when we do the play," she said.

He smiled, not obnoxious. "May I present Sophie Glass?" He nodded toward his sleeping patient.

"Too late. We've already met. Several times."

"Old player? I didn't get much history between seizures downstairs. Except she's never had seizures before."

"Right. Just strokes. Sylvia can tell you. Her daughter. Did you meet her?"

"Sylvia Glass?" he rubbed his chin.

"I think she's Sylvia Goldfarb. Frosted green eyeshadow, bouffant blond hair."

"I did meet her. She specifically requested a bed on Four East—'Lovely girls up there,' she said. 'Lovely girls, and they all know Sophie Glass inside out. They take good care of her up there.' Now I remember. 'Please doctor, Four East.' " He grinned.

"Bristol tried to send her home last admission. Old lady, nothing to be done, free up a bed. That was more than a year ago."

"Well, status should be an acceptable excuse for admission this time." Sarcastic. Hadn't had the fear of Bristol knocked into him yet. He flattened the emergency room record against the mattress and wrote. A furious account, from the looks of him.

Lydia scanned the room, the ruins. "Has anyone gone home on the outside, that you know of? Find out, could you, when you leave? I can't keep seven patients in here. I need a male bed outside. Ask Regina, okay?"

Paul Bunyan frowned at his note but he nodded and mumbled something sounding friendly, at least not hostile.

To top everything off, it was pouring rain outside, with thunder and clouds enough to make it look like evening. She would have to turn up the salad-bar lights and find an umbrella before she went home.

It wasn't really that bad, once she collected herself and saw through the mess of equipment everywhere. No catastrophes, everyone was busy handling everything, and Wilma had already started straightening up Sophie Glass. Nothing like Wilma to set things straight.

"Lydia," she called. "I think we have to change this bed entirely. No, not you. Geraldine will help me." Wilma gestured toward the exiting Bartlett, always looking out for Lydia's prospects. Lydia shook her head and Wilma smiled, showing a gap between her two front teeth wide enough to slip a straw through. Wilma believed that the gap gave her powers, strong intuitions and also the ability to whistle through it.

"Not at all, I'll help you. Geraldine is busy enough."

Wilma shrugged, Well, I tried, and don't say I didn't. She arranged clean sheets and blue Chux, carefully folding the bulk into a smooth column, to be unrolled magically under Sophie, behind the soiled linen.

Everything under control. Still, it looked like a battlefield. Was there that much difference? Bloody bandages, crud on the sheets and on the patients, there would have been moans except these wounded were mostly comatose with respirators to drown out the screams. The unit was not as dingy as a M.A.S.H., not so drab, and certainly better equipped. But the decay was there, and the dying. Every bit as unnatural and unnecessary as death by fire, bullet or bomb. A tumor wasn't natural causes, no matter what anyone said, or a pocket of pus or blood invading the brain. Here the war was going on inside, that's all, return of the bodysnatchers, not quite as ugly as invasion from the outside but just as devastating or maybe worse, nothing so awful as being betrayed by your own self. She turned Sophie to her side and heard a thousand dead soldiers chuckling at her naiveté. Then she turned off thought and just worked for the rest of the afternoon.

At three-thirty Sam came around looking for potential study patients. The battlefield had been cleared in the meantime, to become General Hospital, wrapped and tidy. Lydia felt a thrill go through her when she saw him.

He had already heard about Sophie Glass. "Perfect candidate for us, and for Harry. He's very excited. Trying to arrange quick approval for a tryout of my drug. He'd like us to use it on her." He wore a blue shirt, blue striped, the same shirt he had worn on Saturday. She had remarked on it then, it complimented his coloring.

"So soon."

"Not at all. I've been working toward this for years."

He looked better naked though, she thought. He was fluid without clothes, relaxed.

"I guess I'm just afraid a little. It could be such a big thing."

"We worked out an entire protocol, Harry and I, last night, late."

"Harry?" She wasn't sure she heard him right.

"Bristol. He told me to call him Harry. We'll do electrical studies and physical exams before and after administering the drugs. The one giving the injections will have to know whether they're cocktail or placebo, but the examiner won't. He'll be blinded, unbiased. We'll monitor the patients equally, regardless of what they receive."

A flush came up from under his collar, a flush of excitement, Lydia knew it pretty well. His cheeks would be burning hot, not because of her now, but from anticipating the experiment.

"When?"

"He has to get the go-ahead from the FDA, he's working on informal approval, and from the IRB, the Institutional Review Board, but that's no problem either, not for him. The biggest hurdle, the way we see it, will be getting permission from the patient's family. But if it does what it's supposed to, or even provides us with more information on a patient, I think families will go along with it, no problem. How well do you know Mrs. Glass's daughter?"

"Sylvia? Ha. Not well enough. No one knows Sylvia well enough for this. I couldn't possibly persuade her."

"No, I know. I just wondered how we should approach her. H.B. can handle that end of things, at least."

"With all his charm and compassion. They'll never know what hit them." She felt unprepared, rushed. The drug had arrived only last week. "You're really excited about this. Why am I so apprehensive?"

He looked from the future back to her in the present for the first time that afternoon. "I don't know. Harry and I are both quite confident." He returned to scrutinize the record.

"You're possessed. You really are."

"Are you kidding? Of course I am."

"By the project or by Bristol? Both, I think." She had forgotten the power he had over his boys. Forever. It slapped her as if brand-new and soaked in cold water. Something about the cast in Sam's eyes, distant from her, away. She hated it, because it was directed toward Bristol. Or maybe because it didn't include her, not even in the background, there wasn't any room. She left Sam hunched over Sophie's chart, protecting it for himself.

The project was exciting. To intervene in a positive way, to actually shift the course of an illness and improve on improvement, or prevent decline, that was thrilling. Why did it scare her?

She studied the effects and side effects of nitroglycerine and naloxone, she explained to herself what would happen inside the patients: Well, first we're going to rouse the stunned brain tissue and then rush blood in to feed it, and then we're going to clean up the transmission, clear out the synapses. Too cute. She imagined herself explaining to Sylvia when she asked. Bristol wouldn't explain. He would make the suggestion, point out the positives and bulldoze permission. The unknown was Sam's compound, and she would ask him to go over it with her a few times.

In fact, Sylvia needed no persuasion at all, and no explanation. She was more bulldozer than bulldozed. As soon as she heard "new treatment" and "few, if any, side effects," she was ready to sign. She ignored the "as far as we know," and "first U.S. trial." Her mother seemed to be lost to her, that's all she knew, and here was something that could bring her back.

"No promises," Sam kept saying. "No guarantees. Please take a minute to listen to me."

"Has it worked? In Europe it works?"

"In a limited way, yes."

"Has anyone died from the drug?"

"Well, no . . ."

"Say no more," she insisted. "That's all I need to hear. Please. Try it on my mother." Her shimmering green eyelids closed on eyes welling with tears. A stream tracked through her blusher. "Bring her back to me," she pleaded.

Sophie was the perfect patient because she had a stroke and probably a big one. Sam's electrical studies predicted stroke outcome with a high degree of accuracy now, so they would know if the drugs really changed anything. And they figured, as bad as she was, they wouldn't hurt her, couldn't make her any worse. It was a practice run, but if Sophie benefited, all the better.

It took two days for the okay from the FDA, and the go-ahead from the IRB. Sophie obliged by not waking up and by not needing any more barbiturates to control her seizures. She snored, deep and even, without the ventilator or the endotracheal tube now. Occasionally she sighed. And if you pressed into her chest bone pretty hard, she frowned and turned her head away from you.

Underneath the outer layers of sleep, though, a lot was going on. More than expected. She had some disorganization, and some slowing through the frontal lobes, but all in all, a lot of action, approaching normal. Folded up inside were responses to Sam's buzz, responses hunting around for a way out.

They completed the first battery, the clean baseline run of the tests, and started setting up for the second set.

"Sophie!" Lydia called in the woman's ear. She spoke conversationally as she wrapped on the blood pressure cuff. It was habit, just in case, you never knew, and it humanized the activity. Sophie didn't answer.

Lydia hung the nitroglycerine drip while Sam pushed naloxone through another line. They waited. Since it was a trial run, both of them knew they were giving the cocktail and not a placebo. Sophie's blood pressure held, her pulse rose insignificantly and her brain waves continued on their merry way. No change. Now the K compound, K0667181. There should have been lightning, and Mahler on an organ in the background. Sam pushed it in slowly, in quarter-cc amounts.

A true miracle drug. In the past year, the Danes had tried it out on almost any chronic neurologic condition that came their way. It had accelerated improvement to some degree in most of them: various organic dementias, Parkinsonism, recovering encephalitics, and most recently they had begun trials of it in the treatment of certain schizophrenias. The chemists were working on a time-release form.

It seemed universally effective and relatively harmless when given in small daily doses. The side effects were mostly benign—increased sweating, salivating, watery eyes, diarrhea, sometimes vomiting, dizziness, occasional dysequilibriums, rare tachycardias and a precipitous drop in blood pressure had been reported, all easily and rapidly reversed by discontinuing the drug. Eliminated through the kidneys, peak effect at 10 minutes, falling off and gone for the most part within 45 minutes. Straightforward information.

No one had ever given quite as large a single dose as they were giving now, or combined it with other chemicals, so no one really knew what would happen when it interacted with other drugs, specifically nitro and naloxone. Sam said no problem, at least in the rats. The three drugs potentiated each other, but none of Casper's rats had suffered any catastrophic effects from the combination.

"Blood pressure's one-ten over eighty-five. An eight-point drop, not bad. Lydia, flip on the EEG. We'll just keep it going." Sam injected a second quarter cc.

"Sophie!" Lydia called. "Sophie Glass!"

Nothing. Not a flicker.

Lydia pressed her thumbnail into Sophie's thumbnail and got a drawing in of the hand, not stereotyped reflex, but not a voluntary movement either, unclassifiable, same as before. "Come on, Soph. Give us a break."

"One-oh-four over sixty, pulse a hundred. Uh. Let's just see if there's a change in the somatosensories." He left his K compound syringe neatly stuck into a rubber injection site, half used and hanging there, waiting another turn. "Okay," and he buzzed a low current into the skin below her knee. The screen lit up green with bright white waves bouncing across it. "We'll give it a minute." But, nothing new, status quo, no significant change from baseline, except—

Sophie moved. Slight spontaneous facial grimace, a frown and then a miraculous pounding restlessness in her right hand. Impatient. Something you did to take your mind off the pain. Not necessarily intelligent but an evoked response to that buzzing in the leg. No change on the screen, none in the EEG, Sophie's eyes shut tighter. Her bowels cut loose with liquid stool.

"One-forty over ninety-six," Sam said. "That's odd. Nitro going? Up it a little. One-fifty over a hundred. Pulse one-sixteen." He removed the syringe from the injection site.

"Should I give her anything? More nitro?"

Sam shook his head.

Respirations sixteen a minute, the frown relaxed, eyelids unclamped, pupils equal and reactive, the hand movement stopped. Lydia's thumbnail pressed again into Sophie's hand and got the old drawing-in. One-sixteen over seventy-four, and the waves across the screen bounced along, indifferent, as if nothing had happened at all.

"Let's try it again," Sam said. "With more nitro going in."

"Seriously?" Lydia wasn't so sure. Her own pulse had shot up as high as Sophie's back there.

"It's okay."

It was okay. Nothing happened the second time. There were

minor fluctuations in the vital signs, no changes otherwise, in the brain waves or her coma. Inconclusive trial.

They took forever to clean off the equipment. Sam stopped several times, lifting Sophie's eyelids, shaking his head.

"We did what we could," he said later. "We had to stop that first time, we could have lost her, her pressure was rising too fast." He sounded as if he was rehearsing what he would say to H.B. in the morning.

"She did lighten up some, though. Or she got more active anyway. You think it was the cocktail or the high blood pressure? Or both?"

"Or neither. No idea." He tapped his fingers on the tabletop and stared through the window in the medicine room. Nervous. "We've never used this large a dose on humans before now. The side effects of the drug may be more annoying than any nailbed pressure you've ever inflicted. Sweating, diarrhea. She might have been responding to the greater stimulus. Her blood pressure may have been part of the response. Who knows? Who the hell knows?"

"Don't be so disgusted. We did the right thing. Bristol can't crucify you for that. She could have died or gotten worse. Don't worry about it."

"I have to get everything straight before I try to explain it to Harry. Everything has to be clear."

H.B. wasn't too upset at all about Sophie and her blood pressure. He actually smiled and said he understood, he probably would have done the same thing in Sam's place, except he might have gone with the K compound just a bit longer.

Sam spread the data sheets on Bristol's desk. On each were marked the times and doses of drugs from the night before.

"I'm sure the problem is directly related to the size of the dose. That, and its interaction with the other chemicals, of course." Sam sat in the deep-seated swivel chair in Bristol's office. His legs were more than long enough for it, he looked at ease there.

Lydia rested against the side windowsill, above the other two, separate, observing. She watched Bristol stare out over Sam's head. He folded and unfolded his hands in front of him. "Perhaps we should consider giving it in smaller increments, then."

"Won't work."

"Or a dilute form by continuous drip administered over hours. Hmmm?" He dropped his eyes to Sam's face.

"I have my doubts. The border of penumbral tissue is resistant, it requires a huge jolt to break through the confusion. The necessary doses have been consistently tolerated by rats, cats, puppies, baboons. It must be the combination of drugs."

"But as you say, Casper has been uniformly successful with his animals."

Silent, watching, Lydia leaned back with her arms folded across her chest. "Casper's rats are young nonsmokers," she said completely in earnest. "Without risk factors, don't you see?" Also without risk, she thought. They could take the chance of proceeding merrily along with the rats, who'd miss a few fat whites anyway?

Bristol turned his face to her and then looked down, closed his eyes and chuckled. "Out of the mouths of babes."

Sophie woke up yelling for Sylvia to get Sol out of her bed.

"Get him off me! Sylvia!" she called. "That man. Too much isn't enough for him. Sylvia! Get him off me!"

"Who's Sol?" Lydia asked and got a look that could kill for her trouble.

"You think I'd be in bed with anyone but my husband? Don't get the wrong idea, he's a wonderful man and I've missed him terribly, but he can be an animal. Roll him off me, honey."

Lydia felt like one of the peasants in "The Emperor's New Clothes." "He's not on you, Soph."

Another look that could kill.

"Point to him, then."

Sophie was lying tipped to her right side with her left arm resting on her torso. Using her right forefinger, she pointed vaguely toward her left. "Give me a hand," and then, "tch, tch, tch." With the palm of her hand and great force for her years, she shoved awkwardly at her left breast, and shoved at it, and shoved until it rocked enough to push her flaccid arm off her side to the bed behind her. "Thank God. Later, Sol. Is he okay?"

Sol had been dead for fifteen years, but it was the only acceptable explanation for the strange, heavy arm and leg Sophie found in bed with her.

"Be patient with me, Soph, and answer one question." Lydia picked up Sophie's left arm and held it in front of the old woman's eyes. "Whose is this?" she asked her.

Sophie rolled her eyes. "I get no help from either one of you girls. No help, only riddles. Ask Sylvia, if it's so important for you to know. Ask your father." She cocked her head to the left without actually looking that way. "Sol? Answer the girl. Go on."

She couldn't even be persuaded intellectually that the limbs were possibly hers. She behaved as if everything was cause for suspicion, she answered questions expecting a trick.

"Look, honey. You say it's my arm, okay. I'll agree to make you happy. It's my arm, see? But believe me, it's not my arm and even if I say it is, remember I know it is not. Understand?"

She also believed she was home but somehow Sylvia had set up an entire hospital room complete with roommates and staff in her parlor, for a special surprise.

Sylvia was delighted to have her mother back. She lost no time in resuming her complaints—about the other patients, their families, meals and the lack of supervision in general. Whenever she saw Sam, she bombarded him with questions about her mother's recovery and the possibility of a drastically improved future because of the "special treatment" he had chosen to give to Sophie.

He ran out of answers and took to making rounds before visiting hours.

From late September through to November, they made four further attempts. One responded, but, like Sophie, might have come around spontaneously, and the other three they had to abort. Two of those were halted because of the blood pressure, a sharp rapid rise with an accelerated pulse both times, just as they were at the point of producing some alteration in the brain's transmissions, just at that threshold. Four other patients obviously got placebo and showed no change at all.

However well Casper's rats did with the three-drug cocktail, Sam and Lydia, in several further tries, couldn't duplicate his success, and they weren't entirely sure why. Lydia held to her theory that risk factors complicated the course and action of the drugs. Sam wondered if the compound's base was perhaps impure, a complication that became evident only in human-sized doses.

H.B. pulled at his beard and nodded all through each report. "I don't understand you, man." He aimed at Sam with gunmetal eyes. "This is your baby, show some courage. Leave your skittishness with the ladies." He glanced at Lydia, laughed a hearty, staccato laugh, glanced at Lydia again and stopped laughing. "Give the body time to adjust. Do I have to walk you through it? The blood pressure will go down. This is science, man. Behave as a scientist or I'll leave you behind." Unbelievers. Doubters.

They agreed to keep trying, Lydia reluctant, but agreeing nevertheless. Okay, she said. We'll stay with it a minute longer, two minutes tops. We'll have the emergency cart right there, ready. Next time we'll go with it.

But next time came their winner.

She arrived in the daytime, a twenty-two-year-old female victim of electrocution. She had plugged her curling iron into the socket above her kitchen sink and then suffered cardiac arrest. Her roommate, a premed, had pumped her and breathed her until the paramedics arrived. The E.R. resident called Sam, and he and Lydia rushed downstairs, rolling all their machines with them, urgently, important, excited. They studied her within two hours of resuscitation. She had sluggishly reactive pupils, depressed corneals, doll's eyes, erratic but independent respirations, and reflex posturing of all four limbs. Her electrical responses to stimulation were a jumble of spikes and quivering waves.

"She should wake up, eventually." Sam lined up the drugs in a row on top of the ultrasound console. "By tomorrow if she's lucky. Making sense by tomorrow afternoon. But maybe we can speed things along."

Lydia hung the nitroglycerine drip. She injected the other two drugs slowly. She watched and waited, waited for something awful, to lose the young woman for the sake of an ego. Sam checked the blood pressure, watched her heart rate accelerate slightly.

After the cocktail there was a dramatic increase in the speed, quality and organization of nerve conductions and responses from the brainstem and the cortex. The patient woke to a stupor at one point, mumbling and restless, grabbing onto Sam's arm, pushing him away, dislodging the stimulus from her right calf with her left foot; she pulled out the earphone and threw it across the room. Better than she had been, faster than expected. Blood pressure up proportionally to her increased activity and wakefulness, not alarming at all. The effect was gone for the most part within an hour, and she lapsed into a quieter state but could be roused with stimulation. They mixed a K compound drip, steady slow infusion. In three hours she woke up enough to mumble confusion to her roommate, in five hours she was complaining clearly about the IVs.

Lydia felt full of helium and nitrous oxide, powerful. Sam couldn't stop smiling. As if they had given birth to the woman, no, raised her from the dead. Impossible to remember that Bristol had come up with the combination of drugs, and before him some chemist in Denmark throwing ions together, and before him, and before him, and before him back to God. For Sam and Lydia the miracle was theirs. They left the patient gabbing nonstop and begging for something, anything, to eat.

"Come with me to pick up my coat," Sam said, "and we'll go somewhere to celebrate."

"Oh, yes!" Lydia grabbed his hand, it felt like Christmas. "Tell me again. The woman would never have woken up this soon without us. It's impossible that she could have recovered so quickly except for us and magic K. Tell me."

"Right. I think."

"Don't say think, say know. Say absolutely positively."

They stepped through the door to the deserted college wing, and Sam put his arm around Lydia's shoulder. "Absolutely, positively. We did it!" he shouted.

"Let's go someplace special, let me think of a really good place. And maybe you can come over for a while afterward? A little while? Lord, it does feel good. Like nothing ever before. No kidding."

They turned the dark corner toward the maze of offices and labs. Sam pulled her smack up against him and kissed her, almost in public, out in the open there in the dark corridor where anyone could walk by if it had been two hours earlier. They leaned against each other, smiling, full of themselves and the win.

"We'll go to a place in my neighborhood. And we can walk home like a normal couple walking home."

He released her. "Can you believe she wants something to eat? She doesn't even know what happened. To her it was just a series of zaps." They started toward his office door at the far end, the one light still lit, aside from Bristol's light. "Zap, she's asleep, zap, she's awake, zap, she's starving."

"I know," Lydia said. "It's great. Actually, that's probably the first thing I'd think of, too." She reached up to kiss him on the cheek. "Maybe the second thing. First I'd say, Send Wheeler in here to give me a kiss. Excuse me, may Dr. Wheeler join me in bed? And, Regina, could you please pull the curtain as you leave?"

They were laughing when he opened the door to his office. Sam stopped short, Lydia stepped into his back, bumped against him, accidentally kicked one of his heels.

"Connie," he said.

"What about her?" She was about to put her arms around his waist and then she saw there was someone at Sam's desk. A woman. Connie?

Her mind went like sixty, good thing I wasn't kissing him when we walked through the door, too bad I wasn't kissing him, did she hear anything when we came down the hall? Who cares? and how dare she be here now, how dare she be here at all?

"Did I know you were coming?" Sam was asking her.

The woman sighed. "Of course you did." She stood up and came to him, took his hands, kissed his mouth. She smiled at Lydia. "These scientists," she laughed. "The dinner party with the Dean."

"I did know. I forgot, I'm sorry. Oh, excuse me, Connie, this is Lydia Weber, a nurse who helps me with my studies. My wife, Connie."

His wife Connie extended her hand. She had a soft, cool handshake. It made Lydia's skin crawl. Connie smiled enthusiastically. "So happy to meet you."

Once, she had been eager to meet Connie, it was hard to remember that time. Lately she had tried not to think about it. If it ever did happen, Lydia figured she would have the upper hand since she knew what was going on and Connie didn't. She had felt a little sorry for Connie. Lydia decided she would be friendly, not especially warm but kind, pleased to meet her. She would smile and then she would move on. She imagined it would be at a party, with other people around. She might ask about the children.

She had expected a tall, severe woman with aristocratic cheekbones, no makeup, dressed simply with little or no jewelry besides the wedding band. This Connie was surprisingly small and bouncy, energetic, round but not fat. Her blond hair was short, straight, and flattering. She wore a trace of suburban makeup—pearly blusher, lipstick and mascara. A perfectly pleasant-looking woman. Shocking. She looked Lydia straight in the eye in a way that was used to meeting people and making them feel comfortable. She had probably been a cheerleader in college.

Lydia nodded and flunked smiling, the side of her lip quivered when she tried to curve it up.

Did Connie have any idea about them? Sam said no, she was too wrapped up in her own activities to pay much attention to how he looked or talked or smelled on a Saturday afternoon. Once she had remarked on his good humor, one Saturday night after he had been up thirty-six hours working on his project, but she had noticed with very little interest, he said, she had barely looked up from her needlepoint to mention it, and then only because he had been whistling and it interfered with her radio show.

Sam filled his briefcase with folders. He removed his lab coat. Connie's diamond sparkled outrageously. It was really too large.

"Well," Lydia said. "I guess I'll go."

"We had our first real success today," Sam said. He took his suitcoat from its hanger and put it on.

"Darling, that's wonderful. You two were probably going to celebrate and I spoiled it." Connie pursed her lips in mock exasperation. "We've had this dinner date for weeks," she confided to Lydia. "I reminded him this morning at breakfast. Doctors. Never marry a doctor, Lydia." She laughed. Maybe she did know. Sam loaded himself into his overcoat. "You can have your little drink another time, though. With my blessing." Several gold hoops slid up and down her arm each time she patted or touched him. "We really must be going, dear." She handled her husband quite a lot. "We're meeting trustees," she said to Lydia. "Stevens Hoskins, Buzz Simon, you know. Oh, I guess you wouldn't know." She smiled. Like Lydia was just anyone.

Lydia tried smiling back, managed a grimace. "Well." She coughed. "Nice to meet you." She looked Connie back in the eye, glancing at Sam who shuffled from one foot to the other behind her.

"Thanks for all your help," he said. He shrugged *I'm sorry* behind his wife's back.

"Sure."

"See you tomorrow."

"Yes."

Connie stepped back and fitted herself in next to her husband. She put her arm around his waist, a unified front. "One of these days we'll have to have you out to the house. We've been wanting to have all you people out, so maybe we'll do it soon?"

"Sure. Well, 'bye."

"See you tomorrow," Sam called after she was far out the door.

She walked fast, stiff, down the hallway, tears ready to come but not coming because of embarrassment. *We've been wanting to have all you people out.* You people.

"I honestly forgot."

"It doesn't matter."

"She surprised me as much as you."

"Okay. I believe you. Forget it."

You two were probably going to celebrate and I spoiled it. Then the smile, gracious and comfortable with Sam and with Lydia. And smug, that was there too.

"You look like you communicate just fine with your wife."

"She always makes it look that way."

"What I really hated is that she talked to me like I was just anyone. I'm important to her. She couldn't even tell. What kind of a wife can't see who her husband's in love with? She doesn't even care. She talked to me like I was anyone."

"I only have eyes for you," he insisted. "Believe me."

Sophie's progress was slow but steady, she surprised the lot of them. It hadn't been her usual sort of stroke this time but a hemorrhage, so as the blood dissolved she regained the lost half of her body, and gradually recovered the sense of a left side. Although she sometimes forgot and would have left it behind if it hadn't been hooked on, over time she admitted that it was hers.

"Whose arm is this, Soph?"

"What are you, crazy? If you spent less time asking foolish questions and more time on grooming, young lady, you could find yourself a nice husband."

"Give me a straight answer."

"Well, it must be mine. Unless it's yours." She winked. "Is it yours?"

She moved from place to place with a walker. It cut down her wandering considerably so she didn't need restraints, and when she tried to scrub the nurses' station with her right hand, it was difficult to lean that far across so much hardware, so Sylvia brought her a feather duster.

The Friday after Thanksgiving, Lydia realized she and Sam were out of sync. One pushed when the other pulled, guilt plus desire, maybe that was what actually kept them going, one would retreat, forcing the other to advance. You always want most the very thing beyond your reach. What would happen if they both reached enthusiastically at the same time? They would explode and die.

Sam had started reaching the week before. He said, "It would be great to have the whole night together, and all day Sunday. To go to a movie, have dinner out?" So Lydia made a dream of one whole night and all day Sunday, making love, getting the paper, making love, reading the paper, going out for brunch, making love, a honeymoon weekend. She made up the dream and got a sinking feeling, she knew he would back off from coming so close.

The Friday after Thanksgiving he drove all the way into the Samaritan, to call and tell her.

"I can't come over," he started. "Connie is pissed as hell."

"Where are you?"

"The hospital. My office."

"You're here, but you can't even come over?"

"The yard is full of leaves, the rainspouts are clogged, I'm never home. Connie's fed up."

"Hire someone to rake the leaves."

"Lydia."

"Okay."

"I have to be there today. Or everything will fall apart."

"So?"

"I have to at least try," he continued. "I'm going crazy with this. Believe me. I love you, I will always. I think of you when I'm with them, but I think of them when I'm with you."

Lydia had spent Thanksgiving thinking about him and his family around a perfectly browned turkey, fire in the fireplace off to the side, raising wine glasses with the in-laws and a smile pasted across Sam's face, Connie's face too.

"I'm torn," he was saying. "I hope you believe me. I am torn between you and them. I do love you."

"I believe you."

"I have to do this for them."

Humphrey Bogart in *Casablanca*, giving her up for the Republic or something. Except he was forcing her into the Bogart role with himself as Ingrid Bergman, who ended up with a mate. There they were sacrificing personal happiness for someone else's future.

I said I would never leave you.

And you never will. We'll always have Paris. Fade out. Cut. And print. She didn't care for the ending. Bunch of rot, she thought. Deceptions.

"What do you mean, 'do this for them'? Do what for whom?"

"You know. Keep the family together."

"Oh yeah, like *Father Knows Best.* I didn't ask you to tear it apart. I didn't ask you for anything."

"I'm torn," he repeated. "I'm torn apart." His voice cracked. Very convincing. "The children."

Now the clichés. Undisguised. Get them all out in the open, she thought. Come on, make me feel like a phase in a book about predictable crises. Just another country-and-western song.

The selflessness, she actually appreciated that. She also appreciated that selfishness was part of what kept him there in his sweet all-American household. It was comfortable, it was known, he had gotten used to Connie's cooking, neat rows of underwear, and heaven knows Lydia didn't take to the idea of ironing his shirts much, although she would have done it. At any rate, the disruption would have been great. And his image of himself as the dedicated doctor and family man would have suffered. Lydia had confronted him with this and he never denied it.

"So leave me alone then." Lydia interrupted Sam's excuses and explainings. "Completely."

He didn't answer her right away. She could see him leaning in toward the phone, characteristically hunched over it, she heard a few of his breaths. She hung up.

The Monday after Thanksgiving he raced into work all very urgent and full of regret. And Lydia felt such relief from his urgency and regret that she forgot the weekend spent cursing and asking God, Why me, Why me? Sam gave her an hour and a half that evening, before heading home to the family, and when he repeated, "I love you, I love you, I love you" with his whole body in and around her, she burst into tears.

He held her head, stroked her hair. "Doesn't say much for me as a lover. You suddenly crying like that." He smiled at her, kissed her softly. He thought he understood.

Lydia was cursed with believing they were a perfect match. She heard his commentary about everything, heard it in the background wherever she went. Hearing him in her background comforted her. Knowing him better than anyone, sharing the medical part of his life, and the sexual, and the academic. Really, she kept telling herself, I have more of him than anyone else. I just don't have him at home. Maybe I wouldn't even want him at home.

The euphoria of the one win and of being together propelled them. Lydia and Sam searched the hospital for candidates in need of their miracle. A woman with a hypertensive encephalopathy received placebo, changed not a bit, and a man in renal failure was rejected. Another patient fit the criteria but started having runs of multifocal premature heartbeats soon after getting the first shot of naloxone and so became their third abort. They waited, wound down, got lethargic, almost forgot their excitement.

They resorted to reexamining numbers, to making graphs of every possible variable and comparing them vertically and horizontally, sometimes even on a diagonal, it seemed. Finally on December twelfth, Bristol brought them the perfect candidate, he said.

"Sixty-year-old previously healthy white gentleman, no significant prior medical history. Yesterday while lunching with his business partner, he experienced the sudden onset of severe head and neck pain. Grabbed his head in both hands, his partner says, spoke a few unintelligible words and slumped onto his plate. At that point he was arousable with difficulty, agitated when aroused, and still in excruciating pain. They took him to New York Hospital, but his wife requested he be transferred up here, under my care. I agreed."

Bristol shoved the X rays onto the view box in his office and adjusted his glasses. "Subarachnoid blood, some ventricular enlargement." He rapped on the picture of the man's cerebellum absently, tap tap tap tap tap, with the end of a ballpoint pen. "Gradual increase in obtundation since yesterday. Unarousable now, with large nonreactive pupils but doll's bilaterally, absent left corneal, erratic breathing, he's on the ventilator, and reflex posturing of all four extremities."

"Less than twenty hours ago?" Sam asked.

H.B. discontinued his rapping but started slapping the ballpoint into the palm of one hand. "Yes. But rapidly failing."

"You tapped him?"

"We tapped him and he lightened up to minor withdrawal of his right side, flexion of the left, maybe a slight constriction of the right pupil. Depends on who's looking. Mannitol and Decadron around the clock. He's barely maintaining."

"So?"

"So. I want you to try the cocktail on him. He's not a candidate for surgery yet, if he ever will be. I think the drug would work. We could buy some time with serial taps, but I have a feeling about this man and I think the cocktail would do it for him."

"I don't know. An aneurysm. With the problems we've had with blood pressure?"

"The man has no risk factors."

"He's sixty."

"Works out regularly at the Y, no history of hypertension or heart disease. When was the last time you even had a pressure go up on you? A month?"

"Five weeks," Lydia said.

"Five weeks. Our electrocution victim showed no signs of it. I've told you, it's just an idiosyncratic transiency. I think it would level off if you once gave it a chance."

"His wife?"

"In complete agreement with me. I have carte blanche. Do whatever you can, she says. How about it, Sam?"

"And no heart disease."

"No heart disease."

He didn't need convincing, he was eager to work miracles again, Lydia too. They talked about it on several of the long quiet nights when they had no candidates. He didn't need convincing, but he wanted some. His questions were deliberate, careful. The elation after the miracle had felt too sweet. He was afraid of stumbling in his rush and pulling a patient down with him, he told her.

The man's name was Jameson Brewster. Rapidly failing. A young-looking sixty, strong defiant chin, he had not been the type to give up on anything. Ice-blue eyes, steel-gray hair. Mrs. Brewster also well preserved. Pale blond, tanned in December, she resembled him around the mouth and eyes.

She probably handled things exceptionally well before all this, and even now she was handling most of it, directing friends and business associates away, or to the solarium, being gracious, no faltering. She wore cocoa-colored trousers and a creamy silk blouse, perfect hospital visitor attire, sober not somber. But Lydia noticed a grease spot on the front of the blouse, and a few startling potato chip crumbs clinging to her pants legs.

Sam drew the woman aside to explain the protocol.

"Anything," Mrs. Brewster was saying. "If Dr. Bristol thinks this will help, please go ahead with it. Anything. I have complete confidence."

"But you should understand what we're doing here, and what you can and cannot expect from it."

"No, no problem. Anything is okay." She shook her head nonstop, a senile tremor, nerves. "Just go and do it. Must I sign something?"

Sam sighed. "Not until you listen to me."

Mrs. Brewster continued shaking her head through the whole explanation, not hearing, humoring Sam because she was a gracious woman. Lydia wanted to make her pay attention until she could repeat the whole thing back, word for word. But people preferred ignorance. In a way, she was glad, otherwise the woman might have withheld permission once she realized this wasn't a cure. Lydia was eager to work another miracle too.

At twenty-six hours post onset, Brewster's pupils were up to five millimeters around, nonreactive to light, pointing straight ahead. No spontaneous eye movements, no pursuit eye movements, they didn't budge no matter what. Sam tried ice water in the left ear, then the right, the strongest stimulus to force the eyes to move, but nothing. Absent corneals, maybe a flicker on the right, probably not. No independent respirations, but all four limbs twisted awkwardly into puppet dancing with each artificial breath or touch to the body. Rapid failure, nonstop express. Not dead but close. His brain waves and nerve conductions were likewise contorted and slowed.

"Doesn't have much, any way you look at it," Sam said. "Let me make sure Bristol doesn't want him tapped again."

Over the phone Bristol said stop fooling around and give him the cocktail. We'll tap him afterward. And, he said, I'll be right over.

Sam gave Lydia a thumbs-up.

"One-twenty-six over eighty-four, pulse seventy-six. Ready?" She hung the nitro and he pushed the naloxone. And they waited.

"One-twenty-four, eighty, pulse seventy-six. Pupils equal, nonreactive, status quo."

Sam drew up the K0667181, flicked air bubbles to the top and shot them out of the needle. He injected the first quarter cc and started whistling "Twilight Time." He winked at her.

Working together was a great turn-on. Watching his concern and his expertise. Moving through the sequence of exams, anticipating his next important question, his doubts, these were at least as intimate as knowing how to mix his nightcap. Lydia hummed with his whistle. He injected the second quarter cc.

The blood pressure jumped. One-fifty-two over eighty-eight, pulse ninety. Bristol strode in, strode over, a take-charge gait.

"How's he doing?"

"Pressure's just up now." Sam nodded toward the reading on the monitor.

"Stay with it."

Lydia flipped on the recorder, wrote 152/88–90 on the monitor tape, and concentrated on the video screen. No change. She checked his blood pressure manually and charted 160/96 on the printout.

"Stay with it," Bristol repeated.

"One-sixty-four, ninety-eight, pulse one-oh-two." The wave patterns reorganized into a more even cycle, uniform peaks and valleys. Their speed increased, barely. Jameson Brewster perspired. His right hand tightened, clenched into a fist that trembled with the effort.

"One-sixty over one-oh-six, pulse one-ten." The assist light flashed on the respirator, Brewster had taken a gasp of his own.

"You see?" Bristol said. His fist clenched and trembled as Brewster's did. He pounded the footboard of the bed. "You see? He's leveled off. Give him another fraction of the compound." Sam obeyed. Brewster farted, let loose a liquid stool.

"Pupils reacting, sluggishly. Left for sure, right maybe."

"You see?" He pounded.

"One-sixty-six, one-ten." The man's fist relaxed, spread itself flat. He rubbed the sheet with his thumb. The blips paced up, swift and graceful, regular. Until one spike introduced a syncopated rhythm, and another spike, sharp, unexpected, then another. The fist clenched. "One-sixty over one-eighteen."

"Okay, okay, hold off a minute," Bristol said. "Let him level out, okay, okay."

Sam withdrew the syringe entirely, watched the spikes going crazy on screen, incoherent, arrhythmic, fast then slow then fast. "Mannitol?" He looked at H.B.

"Pupils nonreactive, right is six and a half millimeters, left still five." Extremities stretching stiff, unrelenting, rigid. Sam turned the respiratory rate up to forty.

"Give a hundred of Mannitol. Now!" Bristol yelled.

Lydia pushed Mannitol into the IV line, pushed so hard that the end of the plunger imprinted itself on her palm.

"Pupils fixed, six millimeters bilaterally." Sam jerked Brewster's head side to side, going through the motions. "Absent doll's, absent corneals." The eyelids lay passive, not open, not closed, glazing, eyes of death.

"One-ten over sixty."

"You have the Mannitol?"

"I gave the Mannitol. A hundred grams."

"Okay. We're okay." Bristol patted the footboard. "He's about at his baseline, wouldn't you say?"

Sam wouldn't say, didn't say. He glanced at Lydia, met her eyes. The EEG and brainstem evoked potentials had deteriorated from baseline. Subtly but significantly. Disconnected spurts, short fits, with quivering feeble long intervals between. Ominous intervals.

"Ninety-six, sixty."

"Get some dopamine ready." Bristol looked from Sam to Lydia to Sam again. "He's about the same as when I saw him this morning. Before the tap. He was just about like this." Believing makes it so. "We haven't caused harm, he was deteriorating anyway. We did what we could." He shrugged his shoulders.

"Ninety over fifty-five."

Lydia went to mix a dopamine drip. Jameson Brewster's body relaxed.

"I'll go speak with his wife," Bristol said. "I don't think we need another scan." He retreated to the solarium.

The wife opted out of extraordinary measures and artificial means. They tried another spinal tap, without effect, and during the night Jameson Brewster died, body and mind, "With a little help from his friends," Lydia said when she heard.

Harry Bristol recovered nicely.

"We nearly did it! I'm convinced that it works, it does work. Brewster improved dramatically for a few minutes."

Define drama, Lydia thought. Define improvement.

Sam stayed silent. "We made him worse," he had said last night. "We shoved him around the wrong corner. I should have tapped him first. I should have stopped the drug sooner," he said last night.

But today, "Brewster would have died sooner or later. He was doomed," Sam finally said, a changed man. "With or without us, he was doomed."

"We'll work on the dose," Bristol continued. "Change the dilutions. We should have three separate IV lines, with the two support drugs entering continuously, and finally a bolus of our compound, full strength. I'm sure that would work."

Sam agreed. "I'll call Denmark for an update on their clinical trials." Caught by Bristol's enthusiasm, and his own, his eyes lit up. "They haven't used it in quite the same way we are, but they may have new information on side effects."

"That's fine. Meanwhile, we'll continue."

Lydia looked at her lap. She risked looking at Bristol, head-on. Nothing but sincerity, a master at his art, he convinced himself entirely, Sam too. A true believer.

"At what cost?" she asked, head-on. Her voice caught, she cleared it, her eyes pounded.

Bristol's eyes narrowed on her. "It worked. We all saw it, if only for a few minutes. We are bound to go forward now. If you wish, you can stay behind."

Sam offered nothing. He didn't speak. He lounged in the swivel chair, his hands folded loosely in his lap.

She had to doubt herself, maybe she was wrong. Both of them were so sure it was right. What kind of a life would Brewster have had to look forward to? What kind of a death? The same, only farther down the road, a few days, maybe a few hours. Was it so offensive to attempt to rescue a man when the only risk was of accelerating the inevitable?

Could he have broken through it? He improved, he moved his hand. He made a fist and pounded. Not precisely an intelligent thing, not necessarily human but also more than an automatic reflex. Perhaps that's all he would ever have succeeded in doing. Perhaps. A pounding clenched fist, into infinity. Maybe so. All the blood from the original hemorrhage probably fouled up too many neurons. Probably. He would have died anyway, probably.

"I can't figure why you've stood it for this long." Jane propped a twin mattress sideways against the wall and arranged foam cushions on the floor, wall to wall, mattress to mattress. She was setting up her new healing space. Fifth Street and Second Avenue, a bigger space than before, she shared it with two Primal Scream therapists and a social worker.

Lydia had brought three old contour sheets for the mattresses, a pastel stripe, pale blue flowers and one plain white one from the hospital. "Well, the independence helps. Really, I like it. I just think Bristol's rushing things."

"Now there's a case. He's certifiable if you ask me." Jane fitted six cushions into the striped sheet.

"Probably only impatient."

"No. Dangerous. Why are you defending him?"

"Was I?" Lydia gave up trying to even out the mattresses. She started tucking the white sheet around one of them. "Maybe I'm trying to justify doing this work with Sam."

"You can't. There is no justification. It's dangerous. You don't really know anything about that drug." She sat on the covered cushions and kicked against a mattress, she punched it. "Not bad. Look, Lyd, you're my friend, but I think what you're doing is wrong."

Lydia pulled the sheet tight around the upper left-hand corner. The mattress bent forward. The lower right-hand corner sprang like a rubber band and the sheet rolled up, loosening the upper right-hand corner.

"There is some justification. I don't know if I go along with it entirely, but think of breast cancer, think of Hodgkins." She yanked the sheet, lay the mattress down on the floor cushions and started over with everything flat. "While they were developing the treatments and juggling chemo, thousands of people got sicker, thousands maybe died of complications from the treatments. So that now we have the right combinations to cure some cancers."

"Sure. But you tell me, how many of those thousands that got sicker and died were doctors with cancer? They don't screw around with their fellow physicians. They don't experiment on themselves. They use the standard treatments on each other, the tried and true. You can't tell me they don't."

Lydia propped the covered mattress against the wall. She threw herself against it and fell to the cushions, looked at the padding that lined Jane's room. "This stuff you do isn't exactly guaranteed either, you know."

"Okay, okay. I'm just glad that man wasn't around when my mother was dying. Help me hang the blue sheet over the window and then we can go."

Traffic and the smell of curry and cooking lamb came up through the window. Jane opened it wide to bring the aromas in. "Ma used to make lamb at Christmas. Lamb and turkey. I'd say, Ma, why're you doing both? We never ate it all. She gave it away, she froze it, there were leftovers forever, but Pop liked both so she made both." She shut the window, pulled herself up on the sill with sheet in hand. "You working Christmas? Want to come to Queens?"

Lydia was working this year, as usual, but right then, when Jane asked, she thought she might like to go home. She'd been back several times since she moved to New York, but never for Christmas.

She arranged things, rearranged them. Switched time with someone and then with someone else until eventually she had three days plus eight hours time-back and Fourth of July, which she'd never taken, starting at seven-thirty Christmas morning. From there to Continental Airlines nonstop Newark to Chattanooga, Tennessee, with five minutes left over between the night shift and the cab to say good-bye to Sam.

He was there in the morning taking calls for H.B. and covering emergencies. It had all been arranged to everyone's liking, the department's and Connie's. He got the whole of Christmas Eve off, to assemble, wrap, hide, unwrap and reassemble presents with Tricia, Joel, Andrew, Connie and her parents. She did a goose for dinner, they always ate goose on Christmas Eve, he had said, with Baked Alaska for dessert. They walked around the neighborhood to check out the decorations and to deliver a few small packages, and then they went home to open their presents over spritz cookies and mulled cider. Same thing every year for twelve years, wherever they were living, same thing. Christmas Eve had been left intact, this year too.

Lydia finished reporting off and lost a minute and a half before she tracked Sam down and found him in the E.R. He was sitting at the main desk writing a note, with a clerk to his left, an orthopedic surgeon to his right, and a silver Happy Hanukah banner hanging over his head.

"Excuse me," she said to him. She tapped his shoulder, just another somebody tapping him, no intimacy in her fingertips, she made sure of that. "Excuse me, Dr. Wheeler."

He finished a sentence, he looked up. He smiled and nodded, as casual as her fingertips.

"Got a minute or three?" she asked.

The orthopod looked at her, the clerk looked. A cardiology fellow walked in. The place really wasn't very busy at all.

"Something going on upstairs?" His voice was a little loud. Lydia nodded and they left the immediate area but stood in full view, very casual, miles between them. Her shoulder muscles tightened to hold her back, all her muscles tensed to be casual. She wanted only to touch him, a light touch, not anything big, but more than nothing.

"New tie?" A medium blue with tiny yellow and red saucer things on it.

"Yep."

"I don't like it." She looked at her watch. Two minutes. "Well, good-bye."

"Right, good-bye." He held up his clipboard for effect, and shook his head, wrote carefully over his already written words. She tilted her head toward his words as if to read them. "I'll miss you," he said.

"Yes," she said.

"When're you coming back?" The cardiology fellow passed them. "No," Sam continued. "That patient is too awake for us now. We should have done him yesterday."

"Thursday morning. I'm back at work Thursday morning."

"So I'll see you then, I guess." A nurse hurried by with a man holding onto his bleeding hand. Sam raised his voice. "We can't study anyone else until the compound is purified anyway." Now there were people all around, back and forth, civilians, doctors, patients, nurses, technicians, everywhere.

"Damn," Lydia said.

"That'll be at least two more weeks."

He extended his hand for a handshake. It wasn't the touch she wanted, but she took it. "Have a good time." A dry handshake, flat.

"Sure." She turned, left him and his clipboard in the hallway, "Merry Christmas," with forty-five seconds to spare.

She ran through the long hall to the outside, ran through a list of things she had to do to get from the hospital to the airport. She counted off the underpants she packed, she matched up which outfits she would wear on what days, which presents went to which niece or nephew and which one of them would hate his present, ticked off how many gas stations between Lovell Field and the church, filled her mind with anything until she reached the back seat of the cab, where she could cry anonymously.

"Port Authority," she said.

Stupid to cry, out of control some, and she kept thinking, Well, you asked for it, you asked for it, you knew from the start it would stink. But you went ahead anyway.

The streets were empty Christmas morning, the cabbie made it across to the bus station in ten minutes, on a day when Lydia felt like spending forever with tears on her miserable cheeks, staring out the window from the far right corner of a yellow cab. The driver ignored her, she was glad. She was glad he didn't try to cheer her up and that he didn't say Merry Christmas to her when she got out. She lugged her bags to the proper gate, the weight of the load kept her mind off Sam. And within an hour she was high in the sky.

She wondered who would be picking her up at the airport. Maybe the whole lot of them would come, or else just Dinah, Dinah always did the pick-ups. Or maybe one of the nephews was old enough to drive. But maybe they would all come. That would be nice.

When the plane landed, Lydia was disappointed that no one was waiting for her at the gate. She scanned all the people on her way to the luggage carousels, but she didn't recognize anyone. Suppose they forgot it was today, with everything else going on? She waited for her luggage, waited, grabbed it when it rolled by, looked around again, no one. She headed for the phone booths. *What happened? You forgot or something?*

It was the Pastor there, searching all the faces, all the walks. She spotted him first, hanging back from the crowds, surveying each cluster and line methodically. He had grown a fat white mustache since last time. He glanced across her and she smiled, but his eyes went past her. She moved closer to him and he glanced at her again, with a two-beat delay before recognizing his own straight nose, his own gray eyes, his own daughter.

"Am I so different?" she asked. She hugged him, and realized she was so different. "You looked right at me a minute ago. Did you know that?"

"I did not."

"Really, you did."

"Well, you've got new glasses, don't you? And you look taller." He picked up the biggest suitcase. "Car's out this way."

They walked without talking to the green level, row L. Chattanooga smelled the same, like car exhaust, at least at Lovell Field. The Pastor gestured her along with his free arm and his head. They had never been good at making talk, especially not with each other. He cruised out of the garage to the access road, turned on the radio, Percy Faith's *Music of Christmas*, "Hark, the Herald Angels Sing," heavy on the chimes.

He pulled out onto Airport Road. "Good flight?"

"Bumpy landing, otherwise it was fine. Feels warm down here."

"Fifty-six degrees. Cooling off tonight though, forties tomorrow."

"Is everybody home?"

"Just about. Everyone but Walter when I left. Dinah said he had to deliver a few shut-in baskets. Finished by now, I imagine. Your mother's tending the turkey and Marie and Dinah were arguing about how fine to chop the fruit for the cranberry salad when I left them."

Nothing much had changed, then. She watched shopping malls go by, the bunches of cars near movie theaters, International House of Pancakes on the hill, full from the looks of it, people with no place else to go. Lydia was glad she was going somewhere, so glad she was on her way home.

There was more of East Ridge than before, spread out and filled in. It went all the way to Hamilton Memorial now, and the hospital had a new three-story parking garage. They got to the church and Pastor pointed out the new educational wing. Concordia Lutheran had caused a big stir when it was new, ten years ago, because it had been unconventional, its lines like the hull of a ship. Some of the members had left and joined Walter's church on the other side of the ridge, a brick New England style with white trim and clear glass windows. They claimed they just felt more comfortable in a regular building. Walter's church looked like the Ramada Inn, and Lydia thought Concordia resembled a Big Boy restaurant, although she never said so.

They pulled into the driveway between the church and the parsonage. Lydia could see her Mama through the picture window, folding napkins at each place on the dining-room table. The sight of her was a comfort, the sameness of the scene compared to times before, even if everything from the curtains to the Christmas tree ornaments to Mama herself had faded some in the two or so years since Lydia had seen her.

Turned out Dinah had gone short and straight and colored the gray, and Marie had a curly perm this time. Lydia could barely recognize David, or Mark for that matter, and Kristin was wearing stockings all of a sudden and playing records nonstop with Michael and Erin. Erin and Kristin kept smiling at her and giggling and whispering, and once on her way to the bathroom, Lydia overheard Kristin saying, "Don't you think Aunt Lydia is gorgeous? Don't you wish we could live with Aunt Lydia? She's so thin."

For Christmas the girls gave her a coffee mug with rainbows all over it. Everyone was polite and jovial and chatty that day, full of compliments back and forth, and good-humored teasing. They didn't say to Lydia who was she dating now, and if she mentioned a man's name, they were careful not to ask any specific questions. After all, she didn't ask her sisters what size they'd got up to, or what in the world they did with all the hours in the day, you can only vacuum a rug so many times.

Erin started in on her after dessert was served, cranberry-apple pie or else pumpkin if you wanted it.

"Aunt Lydia, you got a boyfriend?"

Dinah shrugged. "Shush, Erin. That's none of your business."

"I don't mind, Dinah."

"Well, do you? Have a boyfriend?"

"Not right now." Sam wasn't exactly what they would call a boyfriend.

"Shush now. Your Aunt Lydia had plenty boyfriends, more than her share."

"Well, why doesn't she have one now?"

No answer. Unless, over Christmas dinner, she wanted to explain that she had a married lover she spent one evening and sometimes one afternoon a week in bed with. Let's be brutally frank. And by the way, what does Walter do with his Saturday mornings anyway? "I don't know why. I just don't, I guess."

"Erin, stop now. Aunt Lydia has too many things to do already. She doesn't need a boyfriend. She's busy enough."

"That true?"

"Not exactly." Lydia pushed her fork under a cranberry, let it roll off, pressed it down until the juice bubbled up through the prongs of the fork.

"But you don't want a boyfriend? You don't want to get married or anything?"

The scrape and clank of silver on china, teeth into pie. The whole family chewed and waited and avoided looking up. Embarrassed for Lydia, still single and all. Poor Aunt Lydia. Marie's husband, Carl, swallowed the last bite of his dessert and said, "Sounds like Lydia's got plenty of boyfriends. She's just not talking."

Since Christmas fell on a Saturday, they had church the next day too. Way back when, Lydia hated Christmases that fell on Saturdays or Tuesdays. It meant having to be in church three days in a row. She never let on, she always acted like it felt fine to be in church for three days in a row, plus three days in a row New Year's weekend too. She didn't let on and she always felt pretty guilty about it: God takes care of me every day of my life and I don't even want to give Him back three days in a row for two weeks in a row, once in a blue moon. She felt guilty so she always stayed late to help Pastor straighten up and collect bulletins out of the hymn books, to make up for it.

It was years before she found out that everyone else felt the same way except the Pastor, who truly enjoyed composing sermons, and loved every word, every note, every swell in the liturgy.

He wasn't one for telling jokes in his sermons, but he had a collection of believe-it-or-not stories he liked to use. That first Sunday after Christmas he preached on the Resurrection. He talked about the small awakenings each and every one of us experience day by day, all leading to the final resurrection of our souls after death. He talked about blind faith and doubt, and he used one of Lydia's favorite stories to illustrate his text.

About a hundred years ago, there was this German baroness, from the province of Hanover, which is also the general area where Pastor's people came from, and this baroness was a famous unbeliever. In particular, she doubted the doctrine of the resurrection of the dead and the life everlasting. She died at about age thirty, having left strict instructions about her grave: it was to be lined with stone, its corners fastened with heavy iron clamps, and covered by a granite slab with the inscription THIS BURIAL PLACE PURCHASED TO ALL ETERNITY WILL NEVER BE OPENED. And she had arranged maintenance for her grave, to prevent any tampering or change. For years and years that stone vault stayed there, sunk in the earth, until one day, eight or nine years later, the loveliest thing occurred: a tiny sprig or leaf popped out from between the side stone and the granite slab.

"Slowly, surely," the Pastor intoned, "it grew through the joint until the iron hinges were rent asunder, and the granite lid was raised up from the grave. People came from near and far to wonder at God's power, and what they saw was the birch tree and the granite lid and the coffin split open and filled with roots."

Pastor always allowed a long pause before the punch line. He was a ham and had in fact once been given the chance to tour with an acting company out of Kansas City but had chosen the ministry instead. The last part came after a dramatic silence throughout the congregation. Most of the members had heard this story many times before, but something about Pastor's delivery made it new at each telling, and the people sat on the edge of their pews as if waiting for a surprise ending. It was a comfort that it came out the same each time—God triumphed over sinful man, His tree over granite and iron.

"The granite slab now rests risen upon the trunk of the birch tree, which is large and growing to this day." Pause. "We stand for the singing of hymn two eighty-one."

Lydia stayed after as she always had, going from pew to pew, picking up bulletins and putting hymnals in the racks, right side up. She started in the back rows and worked her way up to the front. As soon as everyone was out the door, Pastor returned to tend to the altar and the communion set.

Lydia was ten rows short of the front. Every so often she would catch a whiff of something—the hymn book smell or dust on the organ stops, candle wax, polished wood—she would catch a whiff of something and stop a moment, remembering everlastingly long services, fanning herself with the bulletin, keeping quiet and solemn and looking up at the Pastor in the pulpit, preaching the Gospel.

"I'm partial to that illustration, sir," she said. "About the tree."

"Oh?" He was carefully lining up the host in plastic trays like the trays Hydrox cookies come in. "One of my favorites too."

"I know it."

Someone had left a new pair of black leather gloves in the hymnal rack in row four. She put them in her pocket to tack to the cork board in the assembly hall later.

"Whenever you used to tell that story, I'd try to picture it in my mind, but all I'd see was Bugs Bunny with a tree growing out of his little toe. 'Big oaks from aching corns grow,' he used to say, and that's what I always saw when you told that story."

"That's why you liked it?"

"Oh no. I liked it because it was fantastic, and because our side always won. God always showed her. He came through and really gave it to that woman."

"Revenge then?"

"Sort of, I guess so."

Lydia finished with the hymnals and pews. She moved up to the chancel. The air thickened up there, full of burned beeswax from eons of worship, and moisture. Right next to the altar, the air was so heavy she had to mouth-breathe a little to pull it in. The candles were down to stumps after burning through three Christmas services in a row. Lydia took down the stumps and Pastor secured new tapers in the candelabra.

"The only thing," she said, "is that I'd like for that woman to find out that God won. I guess there's no way to know if she did."

"If you believe in the eternity of the soul, then she found out. Besides, isn't it enough that you found out? You can learn from her mistake, she could only regret it."

"Is that tree really still standing? And marked off?"

Pastor unscrewed one of the candleholders from the base to scrape out the leftover caked-up wax. "I'm told it still stands."

"And marked off?"

He screwed the holder back onto the base and pressed a candle into it. He checked the bowl of the next holder and started to unscrew that one. "With a small plaque."

She was getting used to the air now and even enjoying it. Along with the essence of smoke and beeswax came the scent of the heavy brocade paraments and the closets they were stored in, and red communion wine, and over it all, the pine of the Christmas tree set up behind the left-hand lectern. She inhaled through her nose, a slow, deep breath, then covered the communion chalice, stacked the entire set on the tray, to take it home for Mama to wash. It had always been a family business, everyone took part.

Two colored balls had fallen off the tree. Lydia hooked them both back on, and she thought about Sam. Was he home this afternoon or at work?

Mama had lunch just about ready, leftovers from the day before. Pastor held the door open for Lydia carrying the communion service. She set it on the dirty dish counter, and her Mama gave her a hug.

"So nice to have you here for Christmas," she said, only that. She meant so nice to have you in church again, so nice to see you at the Lord's table. And since it made them both so happy, Lydia was glad she had done it too: come home, gone to church, taken communion.

She had debated with herself about the last part. What happens to you if you take communion without regretting a sin? She was sorry to be sinning, she knew that loving Sam was adultery and that adultery is a sin and she was sorry for committing adultery but not for loving Sam. She could not ask to be forgiven for adultery if she didn't regret it, knowing she would make love with him again. So she asked for forgiveness for not asking for forgiveness, and for going to communion without a contrite heart. She did it for her folks, and it had made them happy, and she hoped God would understand, although she had a split-second vision of an oak tree growing out of the foot end of her grave.

Christmas dinner tasted better the second day and she liked having her parents to herself. They ate for a long time without speaking. Lydia kept thinking back to Sam, wishing she could talk to him, tell him everything, about the ancient air up around the altar, about the corpse wrapped up in tree roots. The stiff good-bye and all the hiding didn't matter. She just missed telling him things and joking around and wandering into his eyes. She just missed him period.

Sometimes in the past year, talking to Mama on the phone or now, for instance, she wanted to tell about him, to share him with Mama, maybe even with Pastor. Sam filled up her life, and she couldn't even talk about him to the two that gave her life to start with.

Pastor sopped up the last of the gravy with the last of the turkey dressing. "How's your work now?" he asked.

"It's all right. I may quit the research, though." Maybe sometime she'd tell them about Sam, but not now.

"How come? I thought that was the best part."

"In a way, but in a way it's the worst part."

"You want pumpkin pie or cranberry-apple?"

"Pumpkin, please," Lydia answered.

"I'll have pumpkin. Any whipped cream left over?"

Mama brought the pie to the table, pan and all, and dished it out right there. She set the bowl of whipped cream in front of the Pastor, for him to help himself.

"What part is the worst part?" he asked.

"You have whipped cream all over your mustache, honey."

Lydia handed him an extra napkin. "Hard to explain."

"Try us. We might, just might, understand some of it." He was always a little defensive about medicine, embarrassed about what he didn't understand and suspicious enough to match the scientist's suspicion of faith.

"I don't mean it like that. You might probably understand it better than I do. Well. Okay. I'm beginning to feel like we're tampering, and I don't much like some of it. See, first we started out just looking at patients, to see which ones got better and which ones didn't. Then pretty soon we got so we could predict which patients would do what. With our tests we could predict this. I'm pretty good at it myself. So what happens now is that someone may look bad on the outside, but maybe the brain waves and electrical connections on the inside are going along fine. So if we say this guy has a good shot at recovery or something, everyone starts working on him a lot harder."

"That sounds all right." Pastor helped himself to another half piece of pie.

"But what about the ones looking bad on the outside and on the inside?" Mama asked.

"I think you already know. It's not like anybody really quits or anything, but the energy isn't there so much, most everybody loses hope. Well, no one wants a person to turn into a vegetable and go on forever like that, I don't want it either. But I'm afraid pretty soon, when a person flunks all our tests, they'll start stopping things, pulling the plug and all."

"That's what I want. You hear, honey? I don't want to be a vegetable or paralyzed, if it comes to that. Pull the plug on me."

"Well, that's fine, Mama," Lydia said. "You've told us what you want, but what about me, for instance? Or what about old Mr. Schiefelbein next door? You want to decide for us? When our time's up? Sure, you pull my plug and then you wonder whether I was really ready to die or not."

Her mother's eyes dropped to her lap. "I didn't mean . . ."

"I'm sorry. I know you didn't. But we—I mean doctors and nurses—put ourselves in the position to decide things like that. And sometimes we don't know what death is anymore." Or life, she thought.

Pastor finished off the last bite of his second piece of pie. He carefully wiped his mustache. "So, you're for going back forty, fifty years, to a time when people just died and that was the end of it. Before artificial respiration and electrocardiograms and neurosurgeons. So you won't be faced with the responsibility."

"You know I don't mean that." Lydia got up to find an ashtray, handed the Pastor his cigarettes. He tamped out one for her and one for himself, lit them.

"Trouble is, I don't know. I'm looking for reasons to feel one way or the other. We get a lot of patients in who die and get resurrected on the street or in the emergency room before anyone has a chance to wonder what kind of life they're saving. Of course, you have to do that if you're there and you know how. But once a person's on a respirator, he's committed, and we're committed. I spend a lot of time taking care of young mindless bodies that can only gurgle.

"I don't like it. I don't like that John Smith the law professor gets his life saved so he can belly-laugh at cartoons all day long and get fed poached eggs and puréed spinach and have to wait until somebody comes along to wipe his nose for him. But I also don't know about pulling anybody's plug. Maybe John Smith really enjoys having the time to watch cartoons. Maybe he's developed a taste for puréed foods. Maybe, underneath everything, his soul is making itself fit to pass on and that's why he's got this second chance."

Mama started stacking dishes, clearing the table.

"If you wait a minute, Mama, I'll help."

"You sit. We'll load the dishwasher together later on."

Pastor sat with his head cocked back. He blew smoke out in a straight stream aimed at the wrought-iron chandelier over the kitchen table.

"Once we've saved a life, even part of a life, I feel like we're obligated to it. Not to save it necessarily if it starts to die again, but also not to kill it if we think the quality of the life is less than we'd want. You see what I mean? By saving a life, we seem to think it belongs to us, and we can decide what to do with it. I can't understand removing respirators and life support just because we're embarrassed to look at the damaged goods we helped to create."

Their two breaths shot alternately and sometimes simultaneously, combining in a blue cloud that surrounded the light and then drifting off and away until only the odor was left.

"I don't have an answer," Pastor said. "Were you hoping I'd have an answer for you? I don't even have a personal one like your Mama does. You have to be that confident to decide ahead of time. You have to have no regrets. You have to be ready, far in advance." A tired face all of a sudden, pulled, his cheeks draped down to his chin, sagging, tired.

He stubbed out his cigarette with great care, mashing all the ashes, like an old man with plenty of time. "I used to have answers. I had all the answers when I was young. Now I have only questions, more and more questions. Truth is, that's all I ever had, I can see that. If I had answers, I'd be God Almighty Himself, that's one thing I've learned in all this time."

He got up from the table, took his coffee cup and saucer to the sink, returned for the ashtray and emptied it into the trash. Every step and motion seemed deliberate, not bent or feeble, but slowed. Lydia tried to remember him from fifteen years back, or five, but couldn't recall looking at him except in a vague, nonchalant way, or when he was preaching from the pulpit and glorified by height and white robes.

He turned to her, saw her watching him. "I don't have answers, I said."

It stayed warmer than normal the whole time she was home. She walked all over the place, jogged around the schoolyard, and drove out to the church camp and Moccasin Bend to have a look. She stopped by the hospital to see if she still knew anyone there, but most of her old friends had finally all left, the unit was rebuilt and remodeled and divided in two, and Lydia felt like an outsider, which she was. Sam lived on the edge of her consciousness, she thought about him all the time.

Probably when she got back he would call everything off. Christmas could be a very guilty time, maybe he and Connie had fallen in love again. One look at the world's most perfect children being happy and, poof, all problems resolved. Lydia believed it could happen.

She also believed that she lived on the edge of Sam's consciousness too. And while there was a certain dread at the thought of seeing him in those first moments of not knowing if everything had changed, there was also the anticipation of having that dread dispelled and of tasting him and holding him for the first time all over again.

Marie had everyone up to Cleveland, Tennessee, for ham and sweet potatoes on Monday night. She and Carl and the boys lived several miles from Carl's church, in a split-level they were buying themselves.

The feast went around the table clockwise, with Marie up and down to the kitchen to bring in odds and ends she remembered as the food went along, salt and pepper, corn relish, napkins, butter. She finally settled down and everything had to be passed around again for her to fill up her plate.

"It's real good," Lydia said.

"Just simple food," Marie answered. "Nothing like what you're used to, I'm sure."

"What do you think I'm used to?"

"Fancier stuff, I imagine."

"Or practically nothing, if you ask me," Dinah added. "You look like you never eat."

"Leave her alone," Carl said. "She looks fine."

"Just what is that supposed to mean?" Marie glared at him. "I guess I don't look fine?"

"I didn't say that, now, did I? Sure you do. You look fine. But so does your sister. Let her be, that's all I meant."

They ate for a while without conversation. Lydia looked up once and caught Marie and Carl exchanging a smile and a nod, making up after the little irritation before. Carl went to the kitchen for the wine and when he poured it into Marie's glass he ruffled his hand through her hair. The gesture caught Lydia off guard, the intimacy in it.

Marie looked happy. Content, comfortable, going along without drama. Plump and pink, Dinah too. All the things Lydia had secretly mocked, the ordinariness, the dependencies, all those things could be desirable, not a bit foolish. That unique comfort they took with their husbands, the knowing, from years of knowing, very provocative.

"Of course I'll never have a figure like yours again," Marie said. She washed, Lydia and Dinah dried, and Mama put away.

Lydia handed a plate over to Mama to stack in the cabinet. "You could if you wanted to. It's just not important to you."

"Maybe not. I wouldn't mind it, though. Carl either, I'm sure."

"More likely I'll never have a figure like yours."

"Count your blessings."

"No, I mean, you're softer than I am, rounded and—I don't know—your body's more pliant than mine, warmer, made to take care. From being a mother. I wouldn't mind a little of that sometime."

"I'll just give you some."

Mama picked up a pile of teaspoons to load into the silver chest. "Nobody's ever satisfied."

Dinah had her hands full of forks, drying each one down in a straight, efficient swipe, prongs to handle, and fanning them out side by side on the kitchen table. "Must seem pretty dull down here to you. Not much goes on besides church or school functions." Dinah always introduced Lydia to people by saying, "She works at the Good Samaritan Hospital, you know. Where the former President had his gallbladder removed."

"I grew up here too, remember?" Lydia said. "It feels good. I'm not bored at all."

"Only boring people get bored," Marie said.

"Thank you, Dr. Joyce Brothers," Dinah answered. "But Lydia, honey, I know life down here doesn't appeal to you. Not in the long run. You never did especially like it."

"That's true." Mama grabbed up the fan of forks in one fist. She separated out the everydays from the good silver. "You were always looking for something different. You never wanted what the other girls wanted."

The whole lab was dark.

The door to Sam's office was closed, but some light came

through underneath it. He always got there before anyone else, beating the traffic, catching the worm.

She knocked. Went on in.

"Hi." What if everything had changed?

His desk looked the same, several piles of papers, the stapler, a roll of tape in a plastic dispenser, his two hands pushing himself up from the desk, dumping some papers onto the floor in his rush to get around to her. He took two long steps and grabbed her to him, held on tight. "Your cheeks are freezing," he finally said.

She took off her coat and he pulled her close again, kissed her now, kissed her holding her head firmly as if he thought he might drop it, kissed her again. "Oh, I missed you."

"Me too."

"It's been forever since Christmas." He pressed his forehead against hers, his nose on her nose, eyelashes flattened on her glasses, he looked intensely cross-eyed. "I wanted to be with you so many times, all the time. I wondered what you were doing, if you were thinking about me, all the time I wondered about you. Five wasted days. I was up at three-thirty this morning."

"When I got back yesterday was when I missed you the most," she said. She reached into her coat pocket and handed him a wad of purple tissue paper, heavy with something inside it. A prism, a pyramid with somehow a smaller pyramid within it, and within that a tiny carving of the Tennessee River twisting in on itself at Moccasin Bend.

"It's a paperweight, from Rock City. See Seven States and all that?"

He held it up to his desk lamp, studied it angle by angle, looking into each facet, and through the whole. "I'll keep it in the window for the sun."

"You'll get rainbows, everywhere."

"Rainbows."

He set it in the middle of the window ledge. It was too early for sunlight but the prism cast two distinct arcs of color from its base. The outer arc swung out and reflected onto a picture of Tricia cradling a soccer ball.

Lydia rang in the New Year at work, with Dick Clark in the background on the bedside TVs, rockin' out the old year and rockin' in the new, and celebrities from New York to L.A. rockin' along with him. Most of the patients slept right on through the festivities, and that was just fine.

New Year's Day came up bright blue, it hurt her eyes to look out into it. The city was deserted, everything slower, mellowed for a time. Lydia walked home, and the few people who were out smiled at her, an elderly man said, "Happy New Year."

Sam phoned at ten a.m.

"Happy New Year." She could hear cars, trucks in the background.

"Where are you? I can hardly hear you. You out on a highway or something?"

"Just about," he yelled. "I had to hear your voice."

"*Can* you hear my voice?"

He laughed.

"You snuck out? Just to hear my voice?"

"Sort of." A lot of traffic behind him. Surprising, so many cars on the road on New Year's Day. "I'm out near the parkway. Supposed to be getting gas."

"On New Year's Day?"

"Just wanted to talk to you."

That crazy Sam. To go out for gas so he could call her. Crazy wonderful man. Connie was probably fixing some kind of big breakfast, French toast or crepes or something, bacon, sausage, a fluffy omelet, something special for New Year's, and here he was, out on the highway talking to her. If she were Connie she'd be mad as anything.

The telephone belched. "Time's almost up," he said. "I'm out of change. Happy New Year."

Lydia got ready for bed. Lay down and was nearly asleep when the thought hit her. She shoved it back. Tried to sleep. There it was again. Sudden realization. They used to call it an ah ha (!) in nursing school, in a course they had sophomore year. Ah ha (!), as in, Chiggers Will Be Here Long After Civilization Has Destroyed Itself (!), or The Handprint Will Stay On The Wall Unless I Remove It (!). Small insights with larger implications if you thought them through. They walked around for three solid months exclaiming on everything. Windowsills Need Dusting (!), Mary Beth Will Never Be A Virgin Again (!), The John Is Backed Up (!).

Lydia's ah ha (!) on New Year's Day as she drifted off to sleep was Sam Will Never Leave Connie (!). She had been floating along in a half sleep, smiling to herself about him out in a phone booth somewhere calling her to say Happy New Year when it popped up, Sam Will Never Leave Connie (!). It didn't make sense but there it was with all the feel of a truth. She rolled over. She rolled back. She got up and smoked a cigarette. Drank a cup of tea with milk and honey and smoked another cigarette. Sam Will Never Leave Connie. There it was. Ah ha (!).

The phone call was proof. Sneaking out, not around the corner but obviously clear across town to the parkway. He had gone to a great deal of trouble to call her. That it was a deception was proof enough. Sam Will Never Leave Connie. The lie confirmed his fidelity to the illusion. The nuclear family preserved. Sam no doubt left the phone booth, filled his tank and returned home with orange marmalade for the waffles. Straight out of *Father Knows Best.*

It wasn't as if she had planned all along for Sam to leave them and join her. She hadn't thought about it much, not really, but somehow she had assumed it would happen. And now she knew it wouldn't.

Lydia shoved the thought back again, she would never get to sleep at this rate. Anyone else would have positively delighted in the phone call and left it at that, anyone else wouldn't have had to analyze the whole thing right side up and upside down. Anyone else would be asleep by now. Sam loved her, wasn't that enough?

She cried hard loud tears.

Harry Bristol faced the blackboard, his back to the room. He examined a time line charted by Bartlett to illustrate the exact course of a specific patient's illness, a woman who had insulted everyone by defying diagnosis and getting steadily worse.

Bristol had not put on his white coat. Without it, Lydia thought, he seemed diminished. The seat of his trousers sagged and his shoulders were narrower than his waist. Mitch said he had been an athlete in college, had trained for an Olympic track team and even broken some two-mile record, unofficially, during a practice run.

But now his stomach poked upward, making him look like a grandmother with an overused womb.

He turned around to face the meeting and was restored, his eyes glinting assurance and some scorn. It didn't matter what he looked like from the back.

"You're sure you've included everything?" he snapped. "No drug abuse? No venereal diseases?"

"Not according to her son."

"Of course a son wouldn't know about that. We would hope not." Bristol narrowed his eyes, looking from one doctor to another to another. He swung back to Bartlett. "No trips to the tropics? You're sure?"

"Yes sir."

The Chief paced in front of the time line, from one end of the illness to the other and back again. "Wheeler! Ideas!"

Sam leaned back. Was he smirking, or was it a nervous smile? Lydia saw a gold filling in a side tooth that she had never noticed before.

"Slow virus is the most obvious consideration," he answered. "Anything to biopsy?" It was a smirk, not a smile. Self-satisfied. Bristol always called on him.

"We only see atrophy on CAT scan," Bartlett answered. "Same with the NMR."

"You guys do exploratory craniotomies?" Sam asked Casper. Laughter around the room.

"It may come to that," Bristol said. "Don't laugh prematurely." He strode back to his chair, standing next to Sam for a moment, grabbing the younger man's shoulder. "My vote's with Wheeler. Slow virus. Unfortunately, we may have to wait until she comes to autopsy for our answer." He lowered his head, shaking it with great, public compassion.

Sam, in echo of Bristol, also shook his head, but his gesture was more believable, more private. Lydia thought Sam did feel some real sadness for this doomed, undiagnosed woman. Without knowing what was wrong, they had nothing to offer, although there would hardly be a guarantee if they had known what was wrong.

"Next case!" Bristol barked.

The woman was not yet in coma, but Sam was considering her for their studies.

"We'll just have a look," he had suggested. "See what we can see."

"But what's the point?" Lydia had asked. "We'll see, probably, diffuse disorganization. Interference, not potential. It won't tell us anything we don't already know. She's too nonfocal, and too awake."

"And you're too smart for your own good," Sam teased. "Okay. You're right. But suppose we studied her, gave her the cocktail, and studied her again? We might find some answers then."

"Use an unknown compound on an unknown illness? Are you crazy?"

Sam turned his back on her, he stiffened. With the slightest change in posture, she thought, leaning millimeters one way or another, his back might snap.

"We aren't even sure how this chemical compound works," Lydia argued. "I can't believe *I'm* the one explaining this to *you*. I can't believe it. Suppose if by speeding up brain transmission, you inadvertently speed up the disease process, and the woman's demise? What's gotten into you?"

"I'm thinking of that poor woman." His back to her still, rigid. "She's profoundly demented. Look at her. She doesn't know to lift a spoon to her mouth anymore, she barely remembers how to walk. I might be able to make her better. Don't you see?"

"Or put her out of her misery, more likely. She's not a horse, Sam."

"No. She's worse." He turned around. He didn't snap. She saw that he didn't understand why she didn't understand.

"This is horrible. You're horrible. All of a sudden. What's wrong with you?"

"What's wrong with you? It's not merciful to make a human being live like that."

"It's not up to you."

They stared each other down. Sam's jaw jutted forward, ready to take a punch. Lydia wanted to laugh, to break up the tension, to blink and let him win the contest. She saw he was dead serious. He blinked but didn't falter.

"If I study her, you'll help me." No question about it.

"Not if you're using the drugs." Lydia looked away, breaking the spell.

Sam walked out on her then, stalked away angry, disappeared, returned five minutes later, apologetic. "Felt like you were deserting me," he said, sober-faced. His eyes were in mild pain, pain of expected loss remembered. Lydia had expected the same loss, in the five minutes he had been gone. The look in his eyes now was laced with a confidence that she wasn't deserting him and had never meant to.

"I am. Sort of," she answered. She fiddled with her watch, unfastened and refastened the band. She looked up at him. "It's too risky, giving those drugs. I won't go along with it."

He made clicking noises with his tongue. He sniffed. "Okay. Probably wouldn't have proved anything anyway. I just was thinking maybe it would tell us something, but, okay, the compound probably wouldn't do anything for her. All right?"

Lydia wound her wristwatch, not paying particular attention. "Not just this time, Sam. I'm quitting altogether." She centered the watch on her wrist, rubbed the face with her right index finger.

He smiled at her. "Come on. I was kidding before. I wasn't mad at you."

"Doesn't have to do with that. Has to do with risk. And philosophical differences."

He forced a stage frown. "Oh, serious business now, I see." He pursed his entire face into mock gravity. For that moment, Lydia hated him.

"I am serious," she said.

With deliberation he hid a smile.

"I won't be part of that drug protocol anymore. It takes too many risks."

"Such earnestness. Really, Lydia, sometimes you are so tiresomely earnest." He reached for her hand, a twinkle in his eyes. He didn't believe her. "So boring." He imprisoned her hand in his grip. She tried to pull it out, but he clamped down more, a power play. This Sam was someone unknown. She relaxed her fingers, slid them out, and he let her.

"I'm not kidding," she said.

"I know. You mean it, I can see that. Fine, for now." He took her hand again, holding it lightly, massaging her thumb with his thumb. "You can always change your mind."

He still wouldn't believe she was serious. She felt some annoyance, and then gratitude, this was easier. An easier way to do it. Options open. No real break. An alteration in focus was all. She would concentrate on physiology and he would concentrate on treatment. Eventually he would see she was right. She lifted his hand to her cheek.

* * *

"Two carrots walking down the street," Mitch said. A cloud of cigar smoke obscured his face briefly, then dissipated into the medicine room air. "Two carrots, one gets wiped out by this delivery truck on Second Avenue. Got it?"

"Two carrots," Lydia repeated. "One gets hit."

"Bad head injury. They bring him to the Samaritan." He stood with his pelvis forward like a gunslinger, sucking his cigar.

"Yeah?"

"Bristol takes him to the O.R., long surgery. He comes out, finds the carrot's friend."

"Yeah?"

"Says, I've got some good news and some bad news."

Lydia smiled, waiting. She heard her name called down the hall somewhere, sounded like Sam but she waited for the joke.

"The good news is that leafy stalk went back on, no problem. You'll never know it fell off."

"Okay."

"Lydia," Sam interrupted. He stopped in the doorway. "I've been looking everywhere for you."

She held up her right hand for him to wait. "Give me a second. Okay," she said to Mitch. "They got his top back on, no problem."

"The bad news is—"

"Did the neck trauma get up here yet? McKnight, I think his name is."

Lydia ignored Sam. "The bad news is?"

"The bad news is he'll be a vegetable for the rest of his life."

"You lowlife." But she giggled. "Just goes to show you, everything's relative." She turned to Sam, who was staring into space and drumming his fingers on the wall. "Who're you looking for? McKnight?"

"I knew you'd appreciate it, Legs," Mitch interrrupted. "Say the word and all my jokes are yours." Another cloud of cigar smoke ascended into the air.

"I'll keep it in mind."

"Cervical trauma. Older man, seventies, I think, coming in from the Island, fell off his roof. Billed as quadriplegic."

"On his roof? In January?"

"Patching a leak or something. I don't know, that's what I was told."

"Hasn't come as far as I know. But check inside the unit. I've been out here all day."

Sam left them, turning to go to the unit and calling, "Eileen! Regina!"

Mitch touched a fresh flame to his cigar. "That guy has no sense of humor these days. Busy. Important research at hand. No time for jokes." He scowled, pumped his cheeks furiously to save the fire. Lydia thought kissing Mitch would be like kissing a full ashtray. "How's the project?"

"Your guess is as good as mine." Lydia propped the medication Kardex on the counter next to the sink, turning through it carefully, checking orders.

Mitch rested his elbow on the narcotics box next to her. "Sworn to secrecy?"

"Not involved anymore. I quit. I'm doing the Index but not the drugs. I think it's been slow, though. Hardly any comas lately, and the ones who did come in died pretty soon after they arrived."

"Why'd you quit? No time?" He sucked hard on his cigar, twirling it in his mouth.

"I just disagreed. I think it's too risky for patients."

"I bet Bristol was tickled to hear you say that."

"He didn't really hear me say that. As far as he's concerned, they left me behind, not vice versa."

"Is it too risky?"

"Depends on your point of view, I suppose." She urged him out of her way to reach for syringes and potassium on the shelf behind him.

"There has been some rumor to that effect," he prodded. "Up in the O.R. they love to gossip. They say Wheeler's been up there sniffing around looking for operative complications, anesthesia accidents. Like he can't stand missing an opportunity to play God."

A reflex, she leaped to Sam's defense. "Come off it, he's not that bad. Anyway, Sam's extremely ethical. He wouldn't do it if he didn't think he had something to offer. He wants to help people."

"Sure. And help himself at the same time."

"That's all the dirt you get from me. Take your cigar and go home, or go back to the O.R. where they appreciate a man with a quick draw and a lot of smoke."

Mitch blew another cloud over her head. "Okay, I'm going."

Lydia picked three thousand-cc half-strength saline bottles off the supply cart. She lined them up on the countertop. "Okay, goodbye."

Sam came back whistling. "Sorry to be so antisocial." All smiles.

Mitch grinned back. "You're a busy man. I understand. Just telling Legs my carrot joke."

"The man's in the scanner but he should be done soon."

"You wanna hear my carrot joke?"

"What's he got?" Lydia was drawing up multivitamins and injecting them into the IVs.

"All I know is quadriplegia."

"Okay. So long, kids."

"So long, Mitch. Cord transection?" She shot potassium into each IV in turn.

"Not sure. Maybe a contusion."

"Okay, if you need me, you know where to find me." Leaving a trail of smoke, backing out the door.

"See you, Mitch." Sam moved closer to Lydia, he watched her fill out labels for the bottles. "Hi."

"Hi."

"Long time since we've talked." Now Sam propped his elbow on the narcotics box, so close she could smell him.

"Yesterday."

"Is that all?"

She smoothed the red labels onto each IV. "Why are you so excited about a cord injury?"

"If it's contused, we're giving the cocktail a try."

"On a cord?" She sidestepped to the Kardex, and rechecked the IV orders.

"Looks that way. If we can wake up a brain, we sure as hell should be able to get through to a cord."

"You woke up a brain once. Maybe. Period. Don't get carried away."

"You are such a doubter. But anyway, what all this means is—"

"You're not coming over tonight."

"No. I'm going to work on this man, if he's a good candidate. I'd like your help."

Lydia punched clean drip chambers and tubing into the bottles, running the fluid through the tubes slowly, running all the air bubbles out. "Are you kidding?"

"Absolutely not." He touched the top of her quiet hand with his fingertips.

"Thanks, but no thanks." She pulled away from him. Walked to the cart for a fourth IV bottle, and began to prepare a heparin drip.

"Chance to be together."

"I said no." She flicked bubbles to the top of the heparin syringe. "How old did you say he was? Seventy?" She jabbed the needle into the rubber stopper of the IV bottle.

"I don't need another conscience. Mine works fine. The man's in good shape."

The medicine squirted slowly through the small needle, a vacuum sucked it in, the plunger jerked automatically behind the solution. They watched the process together, continuing to watch after it was complete, with nothing to say.

Lydia heard Bristol yelling, "Wheeler!" from way down the hall, maybe from the scanner with his head stretched out the door, and again, "Wheeler!" and again. The phone rang. A nurse's aide walked in, followed by Regina, who picked up the phone on the fly, breathless.

"Wheeler!"

"Maybe I'll see you later," Sam said, leaving to answer the master's call.

Regina cupped her hand over the telephone mouthpiece. "Sophie Glass," she said. "On her way up from the E.R." She paused, listened on the phone. "Uh-huh. Uh-huh. We'll put her into four-twenty-six. Uh-huh. 'Bye. Lydia, help me get the bed ready?"

"I'll meet you there. Let me deliver these bottles. Another stroke?"

"Probably. Found unresponsive on the kitchen floor, holding a peeled, hard-boiled egg in her hand. Woman's got nine lives."

"She'll do okay then. Last count, she was only on five or six."

Broken record. Instant replay. They had played this scene before. Always mixed feelings about having Sophie come back in. The delight of having her around again, the regret that she had suffered another illness, the fear that this might be the big one for her, the knowledge that it wouldn't be, the irritation of dealing with Sylvia again.

Sylvia arrived first, the green eyeshadow and strawberry-blond hair reassuringly unchanged. Sophie was having her head scanned.

Regina put an arm around Sylvia. She helped her to a chair that Sylvia didn't want to sit in, but sat in anyway then bobbed up from.

"Where's Dr. Wheeler? I want that treatment for her. Where is he?" She paced at the foot of Sophie's waiting bed, to the window, to the bed, to the chair. "Get him for me."

"That treatment didn't help her get better, Sylvia," Lydia reminded her. "She reacted badly to it. We had to stop it last time, remember? It didn't change anything."

"I believe it helped her." She walked to the window. "I believe you're wrong. Get Wheeler." To the bed, to the chair. "He'll help her again." Mascaraed tears streamed down her miserable face. "You should have seen her," she cried. "Terrible. I thought she was dead. Please call Wheeler."

"I will."

Lydia and Sylvia embraced and were embracing when Bartlett wheeled Sophie through the door on a stretcher.

"My favorite patient," he announced.

Sylvia wept, now embracing Dr. Bartlett.

Sophie was snoring. She looked gray and horrible. Her lips were chalky. Her eyes were open but pushed hard to the left and she didn't blink.

"A hemorrhage," Bartlett said. "On the left this time." He lowered his voice, speaking to Sylvia. "Very large, ma'am."

Sylvia collapsed into the chair. She sat with her eyes closed and her nose running while Regina, Lydia and Bart slid Sophie from the stretcher to the bed. Sophie showed no awareness of the jostling. She snored, dead weight, her flesh settled into the mattress.

Sylvia wailed. Regina shushed her and apologized to the other patient in the room, but Sylvia only wailed louder.

"She's going to die," she cried. "You said you'd call Dr. Wheeler."

"The prognosis is grave, Mrs. Goldfarb. Regardless of what we do or don't do for your mother." Sam had come immediately. He had reviewed the brain scan and examined Sophie carefully. Now he tolled the bell.

"But your treatment," Sylvia pleaded, painful hope on her face. She held on to Sam's coat sleeve.

"Won't work. Too much damage." Sam lowered his head to look more directly into Sylvia's eyes. "Let me go over this with you again. There is already extensive damage to both sides of the brain. This last insult is enormous. If she lives—I said *if*—she will be totally dependent."

"They say that every time. And every time she gets better. You should know by now."

Sam's sleeve was permanently pressed into bunched-up wrinkles where Sylvia had grasped it.

"Not this time," he said gently. "It's extensive. I'll be surprised if she lives."

"Your treatment?"

"Won't help. Not this time. Too much damaged brain."

His attitude surprised Lydia. He had always wanted patients no matter what. Maybe he was coming around, or maybe it was because Sophie was someone he knew. He spoke so patiently to Sylvia.

"You were good with her," Lydia complimented him later. "Thank you for being so open."

"I always try to be honest. You know that."

"But this time you didn't twist it. You didn't give her any false hope with the drugs."

"Didn't last time either. She latched on to that herself." He shrugged. "Sure you won't reconsider and help me tonight?"

Lydia shook her head. He wasn't coming around. Sophie was just too far gone.

"See you tomorrow then?" He leaned close. "I'm not angry," he whispered. "Are you?"

A hesitation, barely noticed by either one of them. "No," she answered.

Sam held her as if holding something precious, a fragile prize, a crystal ball. Lydia wished she could have seen them in a mirror. Bittersweet. He studied her face.

"You look different," he said.

"I'm not." But she pulled away. She felt an edge to her, impatience, she didn't appreciate him so much. "I'm just tired. You want me to make some coffee?"

"I want you to make love with me."

"I'd rather sit down and talk a while."

"If that's what you want. About what?"

She did love him and he did love her. So what good would changing the pattern do? Probably none. Probably if she would just let herself relax, just let him go on and kiss her, the edge would round off.

She took coffee beans out of the freezer. She fine-ground them. Sam stood in the doorway of the tiny kitchen, talking and talking. She couldn't turn in any direction without finding him there, crowding her.

"You're never going to leave them," she blurted. "So what are you doing here?"

He stopped talking. He moved one step into the kitchen. "Please."

She regretted saying it. She hadn't meant to, not today. Today was supposed to prove to her that she was wrong. But she saw she was right.

His eyes looked straight at hers, the way a liar's eyes looked. Shrewd innocence. "I don't know what I'm going to do. How can you?" He took another step toward her, he reached for her face again.

Lydia was taken by the sweetness of the gesture. She believed him, he really didn't know.

Later, they simply lay together for many luxurious minutes, not saying anything but just being there naked. Sam ran his fingers over the slopes of her face and shoulder, her arms, breasts and belly, and thighs. Lydia hooked her leg between his legs and fitted her cheek precisely in the hollow of his shoulder and chest. She skimmed the palm of her hand over his chest hair and traced designs on his thighs.

He massaged her back, straddling her rump; he kneaded the edge out of her, his hands knew exactly how. He stretched out over her, belly to back, covering every bit of flesh, pressing her into the mattress. She rolled over under him, moving to savor the feel of his skin, and its aroma.

"My Lydia," he whispered. "Don't leave me alone."

She looked at his eyes studying her, his hands massaging, reaching, probing most gently. A delicate touch, as if she were cherished and they had all the time in the world.

They stayed interlocked until Sam had to leave.

Perfect together, she kept thinking. Why have we been cursed with that?

"Don't think about anything," he said as he was leaving. "Don't say anything. I'm so happy now, don't make me sad. I love you."

She didn't say a word.

She waved to him from her window when he got into his car across the street. She smiled at him and waved, waved at his taillights.

Indoor soccer that afternoon. Andrew played forward, Joel at goal, Sam on the sidelines. Lydia had always imagined Sam there by himself, but Connie seemed like the kind of mother who would show up at the games too and cheer and clap as a proud mother should, sincerely. She would wear a blue plaid kilt with a navy shetland sweater and loafers, Weejuns. And Lydia would be forgotten except for the lilt in Sam's mood. She saw them jumping up to yell together for their sons, laughing and glancing at each other with Tricia between them.

Lydia slammed the open window down to block the cold. After the game they would all go out for pizza or Chinese.

On Monday Sam winked at her and squeezed her left forearm on his way through the ward.

On Tuesday he said, "See you later?" on his way through the ward, but when she saw him later they were interrupted by Bristol, who led Sam away to discuss a new protocol. Bristol didn't look at her and neither then did Sam, except to turn back and smile as he walked down the hall.

On Wednesday he came to her, squeezed her left forearm and said, "I've got to see you. We haven't even talked." She was gratified by that and gratified to see his face drop when she said, "Not tonight."

"Tomorrow then?"

"Maybe."

"There's a game Friday night."

"Maybe tomorrow then," she said.

He seemed to have successfully split himself into three different men: the husband/father, even-tempered, morally upright, good in math; the scientist, balanced, curious, logical; and the lover, hungry, pressed for time.

On Thursday there was an unexpected meeting called to discuss major complications with the resident staff. It ran long and Sam got out late, so he only had time to stop by and apologize, and to kiss her briefly, with passion, on his way home.

Jane hunched over the bowl of cake batter and stirred intently, counting underneath her breath, increasing the spoon's momentum for the last ten or so beats. "So this guy thinks he's got me over a barrel, because he claims he didn't know his daughter's therapy was so unorthodox. Says he's not going to pay." She handed Lydia the spoon. "Taste this."

"Mmmmm."

"So I say, 'Look, the bottom line is it worked. Your daughter got some benefit from it. Who cares if it's unorthodox as long as it worked?' You think this needs more nutmeg?"

Lydia tasted again. "It's fine. Nutmeg gets stronger in the cooking."

"Oh yeah?" Jane took the spoon and licked off the back. "Live and learn. I never heard that."

"So did the guy eventually pay?"

"More or less. I told him, 'Your daughter's working again, supporting herself. I think you'll agree that means something.' He agreed it meant something. So I said, 'Pay me whatever you think it's worth.' So the bastard paid half my fee and walked out smiling."

Jane rummaged through cabinets, looking for cake pans. Lydia stuck her finger into the batter for another taste. Jane pulled out three tins.

"It's always the sky's the limit, until it comes time to pay for it. Grease these for me." She flopped into a kitchen chair and began breaking up walnuts and throwing them into the batter. "Regina same as always? She ever ask about me?"

"On rare occasions. She sort of sits back and talks to the air, 'Remember Jane?' like it was twenty years ago. Then she acts really surprised that I know how you're doing. 'You mean you still talk to her?' she says. She wonders why you never call her."

"Right. Just to chat. I always enjoyed chatting with Regina. We were on the same wavelength."

Lydia laughed.

"And Mitchell? That old lecher still hanging around you?"

"Of course. He doesn't sleep well unless I reject him at least once a day."

"I never figured out why you do reject him. He's available, he's fun, he's interested."

"You could pass for one of my sisters. I don't mean it as a compliment."

"They're not far off the mark. You're not getting any younger, you know."

"You either. What about you?"

"I'll never settle down. Not the type."

Lydia carefully buttered the cake pans, buttered them twice, sprinkled flour in the first pan and shook it to dust the entire surface. Jane meanwhile built up a mountain of walnut pieces on top of the cake batter.

"And Sam?" Jane asked. Now she dropped the walnut pieces with great care, not to upset the mound. She didn't just throw them on but dropped them cautiously. Some kind of game with herself.

"Sam's fine. Same as always. Did your Pop request carrot cake for his birthday? Or was it your idea?"

"Mine. Remind me next year how I hate to grate carrots. Henny likes pies. Banana cream, coconut custard, fruit pies. Wet desserts, he calls them. Claims cake is too dry. So I thought, introduce him to a wet cake. My luck, he'll love it."

Lydia tapped the excess flour from the first pan into the second pan and worked it over the surface, shifting, patting the pan, rotating it. She tapped the excess into the third pan.

"I'm not going to see him anymore. Sam."

"I had a feeling. How did I know that?"

"Except at work."

"Something about you today." She threw the last of the nuts into the bowl, starting a slight landslide. She cut the spoon through the middle of the sliding mountain, blended batter and nuts.

Lydia shook flour over the third pan. There seemed to be many ungreased spots. She wiped out the whole pan with a paper towel and started over, smearing a thick, even layer of butter on the bottom.

"Butter's too thick," Jane said.

"Go on," Lydia snapped. "Go on and say it. You knew it wouldn't last and I'd be hurt. Go on, don't hold back. Say whatever you want."

Lydia examined the pan, tired of it, shut her eyes.

"I wasn't going to say anything."

"You wanted to."

"No."

"Yes. You already said it last summer. I'd get hurt, it wouldn't last. Might as well say it again. Go ahead."

Jane worked the batter and the nuts together, the stirring took effort. And Lydia wiped butter off the surface of the third pan again. Around and around the surface of the pan.

"I wasn't thinking 'I told you so.' I was thinking you deserve to be happy," Jane said quietly.

"Great. Now make me feel bad for blowing up."

"Sudden decision? You been thinking about it a long time?"

Lydia shrugged. "Probably been thinking about it since the first day. I don't know. Too much time alone. Too much hidden stuff. He seems very deceptive to me now. I know, we're both deceivers in this, but he seems like it comes easier to him. He's always covering his back, and it's like he's used to it. But I can't take it."

She talked to the cake pan, held it up pretending to check it for unevenness and she talked directly to it. Her nose burned unbearably, it made her eyes water, and then she just cried and didn't care. She had never cried in front of Jane.

Jane had stopped mixing batter and set the bowl aside. "What did Sam say about it when you told him?"

"I didn't tell him yet." Lydia's nose was so full she had to mouth-breathe. "Got a handkerchief?"

Jane handed her a Kleenex box. She picked up the bowl and spoon and started stirring again. "Haven't told him yet. Guess I'll believe it when I see it, then." She eased some of the thick batter into the first layer pan.

"I will do it."

"Sure you will. Eventually." Easing batter into the second pan. "I've seen this before. I hate to sound like a know-it-all—"

"You? Know-it-all? Never."

"Look, I mean it." Scraping the bowl to fill the third pan. "I know you resented my pessimism from the start of this thing. I think I was being realistic. Was I wrong? No."

"I didn't say I expected him to leave his family. I never expected that."

"Sure you did. Somewhere inside you, you had to be imagining a future together. You're not the type to expect less."

"I didn't."

"Whatever. Anyway, you resented my honesty. You said so."

"Insensitivity."

"Okay. So I'm doing it again." Jane crouched to examine the three cake layers on a plane parallel to them. She scooped batter from one and lopped it into another. "So what I'm saying is, save your tears for now. You're not ready. You won't do it yet. You'll go along a while longer, you'll start to do it another time, you'll retreat again. These breakups take ages. Especially since you still love the guy. Now we have to wait forever because there's only room in my oven for one pan at a time."

"You're wrong. I'm really going to do it. Soon. I've already done the back-and-forth business. I've made up my mind."

"Sure. Okay." Jane placed one layer in the oven. "I believe you." She set the timer for thirty minutes. She sat down at the table. "Don't get mad, okay? Because if you do break it off, it won't last. Believe me. The first breakup never lasts. You love each other. You work together. How's it going to last? Here, lick this." She gave Lydia the spoon and took the bowl for herself.

"I'm too unhappy this way." Nevertheless, Lydia stopped crying. What Jane had said gave her some hope in the continuity of things. In the perverse possibility of breaking up but maintaining ties. The possibility of making up.

"If you're really serious, I think you should quit at the Samaritan. You can always come in with me. Open invitation."

Not that she wanted to make up, but the possibility was a comfort.

Once again, Sophie didn't die. She didn't do anything, she remained status quo. Sylvia took this as a positive sign.

"You heard him yourself. That Wheeler. He said she'll probably die in a couple days, right? He said that. A couple days. So now it's a week and look at her. She's got color back in her cheeks."

Sophie did have color in her cheeks. She was flushed with fever. But her eyes weren't forced to always look left anymore, and she blinked and closed them to sleep. She had a feeding tube in her nose, an oxygen mask, an IV for antibiotics, a Foley catheter to drain her urine, and fat foam-rubber booties to prevent bedsores on her feet. All the trappings of improvement.

Lydia spent a lot of time with Sophie, five minutes here and there. She tried to be the one to bathe her, she talked to her or turned on the television to daytime game shows, hoping stimulation might give her a boost. She exercised the limp arms and legs, gossiping the whole time, complaining about dust on the windowsills and closet shelves in Sophie's very room. Lydia wanted an argument from the woman. She watched for awareness of any sort, a sneeze or a burp or a roving eye, but Sophie remained stingy with her favors.

If Sophie's roommate was out, Lydia would shut the door and talk about Sam, going through the whole thing in detail.

"I know what you're thinking, Sophie," in response to herself. "You're thinking I'm not a nice girl." Or, "You're thinking he's got it made," or, "You're thinking I'm an idiot and I deserve what I got."

Sam and Lydia worked together on the Wheeler Scale same as always all night Sunday, and then in the morning when they were going over everything, she said it, it just came out. Into her head and out through her mouth, "I don't want to see you anymore." She believed it. She braced herself.

He acted as if he didn't hear her, he kept unrolling the monitor tape and measuring squiggles with his calipers. So she told him again, "I'm not going to see you anymore."

He measured carefully the height of each slope, its length, the distance between each one. He kept his head down, intent on brain waves. "Not today," he said. As if it were a whim.

"When, then?"

"Never?"

"I'm tired of being unhappy. I won't be."

His office door stood open, a protective device, serving several purposes. It was open so everyone would know there was nothing between them, so they could be stopped every few minutes with people in and out asking questions, favors, telling about interesting cases, telling jokes. It also kept Lydia at a distance for that period of time, she realized. Kept their conversation from being too serious, too hot, kept it to fragments and phrases trailing off, never-finished fragments, interrupted.

Casper wanted a reprint of an article he couldn't find in his own files, H.B. wanted an update on the studies, Bart just wanted to chat. Lydia counted rainbows cast around the base of the Rock City prism, she wondered if he would keep it or throw it out, she distinguished three colors from each reflected plane, and she concentrated on them. Sam was jovial, stalling.

She stood to leave.

"No, don't," Sam said. "Don't go."

"I think I might as well. Anyway, I'm tired."

Bart, in his regulation blue oxford-cloth button-down shirt, finally caught on, cleared his throat, excused himself. Lydia still stood, holding her coat by the collar, the hem dragging on the floor. Sam stared at a spot on his desk between the phone and a black ballpoint.

"Take a walk?" he asked.

Because of the cold, hardly anyone was on the East River walk except for runners, and only a few of them. Lydia and Sam headed uptown for a change, up to the stairs and toward Gracie Mansion. They walked watching the river and not talking for a long time, struck sideways by a cold wind.

"I'll die," Sam finally said.

"No you won't."

"Yes. I'll die if you stop looking at me. If I can't talk to you. I'll die."

"We haven't talked all week, and here you are." He could just start talking to someone else, Connie. Lydia wouldn't say that out loud, she wouldn't give him the idea. "You'll be fine." The thought knotted up her stomach—Sam talking to Connie.

"I won't." The wind froze his cheeks rosy, alive. "I need you."

He looked good. She wanted to take his arm, to kiss him. "Me too." Talking had been a mistake. Talking would just make them reasonable, get them together again, prolong the agony. "I need you, but I never have you. Not even when we're together. You're always on your way to someplace else. Can't blame you. I guess suburbia is just too wonderful." Gaining momentum. Anger dried up her tears. "Wholesome. All-American, all that blond hair. It's so sweet it must almost make you sick. All that honesty and openness. All the support you get in your nuclear home."

"Lydia, don't."

"Nuclear family. Ha. Nuclear weapons. Nuclear freeze. What an ideal world it's turned out to be. Is it like the storybooks? Except you don't have a Spot, right? Because Connie and Tricia would die, right?"

"Lydia."

Tired of being reasonable, tired of understanding. Borderline psychotic, about to cross the line. She took two gulps of cold air and walked ahead. "Anyway, you won't leave them, that's number one, and even if you did and we lived happily ever after, you'd always be miserable. And I'd always have one ear to the ground, listening for the war party coming through the pass. Anyway, you won't ever leave them. Period." She felt real wise now, strong, cold, inside and out, but her eyes kept tearing.

They stopped opposite the old stone lighthouse on the north tip of Roosevelt Island. Lydia stared into the painfully bright morning.

"This isn't a trick or anything," she said. "I really mean it that I don't want to see you anymore. I'm not trying to make you leave them." What was she trying to do, then?

"I know it." He picked up bits of loose gravel from the promenade and let the fragments fall to the water rushing south. They didn't even make a splash, invisible by the time they hit.

"You don't believe me."

"I do believe you."

"Well, you're sure calm about the whole thing. Are you relieved? Or something? I mean, not so long ago you told me you'd leave them like that"—she tried to snap her fingers, but it didn't work with gloves on—"if I just practically looked at you cross-eyed, and now you're acting perfectly reasonable about ending everything. Was it all a lie? You lied?"

"I just told you I'd die if you left me and you said no I wouldn't and now you're mad because I'm not dying? I have a splitting headache and chest pain, okay? Satisfied?"

They stood back from the barrier wall, faces away from each other and clenched like their fists, their separate bodies tensing and their separate breaths forming quick dense clouds. Lydia laughed. Then Sam. But their faces were still turned away from each other.

"You'll never leave them. I know that," she said. "You're a company man. But you did fool me, when you get right down to it. You did."

"Fuck you." Sam stepped up to the wall that kept him from falling into the river, he leaned on it and first he looked out toward the Triboro Bridge and then he looked at Lydia. "Fuck you, I know what you're going to say. It's all my fault, you think. I tricked you, right? I used you and it was never any good for you and I knew it and I just kept stringing you along. Well, fuck. I didn't fool you. I fooled myself." His eyes were drowning eyes, sinking fast. He rubbed them until his whole face was red, he pulled at his nose, nodded his head, and nodded. "I have loved you, I really do love you. I didn't try to trick you. I will sometime though, I promise I will."

He put his arm around her as they started back to the Samaritan. It looked like an ice palace, gleaming white in the winter sun and catching reflections from the river, it loomed in the near distance. Oz, up ahead.

"You can't do this," he said. "I'll die."

She almost gave in, almost changed her mind on the way back, but she couldn't forget how needy she felt when she had him, and that memory saved her. There was a picture in her mind from a Sunday-school book, a crawling hungry picture of the beggar Lazarus holding onto one leg of the rich man's table, his own legs dangling over a void, legs not strong enough to support him upright, with hollow eyes that were her eyes. That's how she felt loving Sam, and the picture kept her strong.

They stopped at the footbridge that crossed over the FDR Drive, the Samaritan directly behind them. Sam dropped his arm and faced her.

"What about the Index? You'll go on with that?" Now he was the one looking like Lazarus, reaching, grasping, slipping off the ledge. It gave her some satisfaction, to be perfectly honest, seeing that losing her really did affect him. Over the satisfaction was the old urge to reassure him, to hold him, to make him feel better.

"No. I won't. If I did, we'd still be the same, maybe worse. Like just before we finally started up. Obsessive. You know. I have to move on ahead, so do you." Still, she wanted to hug him, to lay her cheek on his chest.

For a few weeks she waited for him to trick her the way he promised. To make her believe they had a future, to make her believe she was the only important thing. He didn't though, and sometimes she knew he didn't because he really loved her and wasn't willing to leave her lonely again, and sometimes she believed he didn't because he had gotten over her very well. She heard him talking on the telephone once, congenial, laughing, sharing something funny, she guessed with Connie. Well, good for him.

She felt lightweight, airy and energetic. She had space in her life. She marveled excessively at her airiness and the space. She read books, she saw movies, she caught up on her sleep, and she watched for some sign, negative or positive, either one, that she had done the right thing. A small sign is all.

She stayed away from Sam. They both attended the morning conference still, but she kept her eyes off him except in a critical way. She noticed that his ears were uneven, the left one stuck out, he sneered sometimes when he laughed, and he had little of value to add to the meetings. When he did have something to say, she looked away and studied the other men in the room.

She glanced over the field but shied away from it. She considered the impending annihilation of the world as we know it, and death by random violence, she gave quarters to homeless men on the street, she shopped for sweaters and wool pants on sale, she renewed her passport, she watched for signs to tell her that she and Sam belonged together or that they belonged apart.

Sophie nested in 426. She occasionally made noises, grunts, when moved side to side. The staff dietician was concerned about adequate calories for optimal brain function, so they increased the tube feedings to every four hours and invariably gave them on time.

Sylvia pestered everyone to come watch her mother perform.

"She opens her eyes when I ask her, I swear it. Come and see. Ma! Open your eyes! Ma! She just did it, I swear, and she looked at me. Ma! Maybe she just doesn't like having you in here watching. She's a stubborn lady, you know."

When Carlisle Simms returned to the hospital, Lydia thought he might be the sign. Sam came looking for her to tell her he was back. She made a show of hesitation and then they went to see him together. Simms was balking at having another arteriogram.

"They done the exact same X rays twice before. Exact same, both in the last year. Now tell me, how much can a man change in such a short time? No sirree. That test was bad enough the first time, and then they went and did it again, but I won't have it another time."

Lydia and Sam together took him down to the X-ray suite to show him the films from both times before. The right touch, because it made Simms finally feel like he had some real say. He could see for himself that the arteries had changed from one time to the next, that a few months could show a difference. They looked worse, rattier.

Lydia watched from several feet back, the two collaborators. Sam traced the path of disease with his thumb and Simms leaned his face in toward the film. He grinned.

"That's my neck, right?"

They compared the two sides, the left open, cleaned out from the last time, the right one closing up.

"It might not be worth it to operate if it's much worse," Sam said. "Honestly. If this one's completely blocked, you might need a different kind of operation. It's why they have to take X rays again." His hand held the film to the view box and patted it absently with the longest fingers in the world.

Simms agreed to the X rays, had them done, read them with Sam, but then refused surgery, after all that. Sam came looking for Lydia again.

Simms stood, studying his arteries, shaking his head. "I see they bad, I see that, but I'm not ready for any more operations." The light from the view box turned him into a gray ghost. "No."

Even Sam ran out of patience. "Okay, Simms. It's your prerogative. But why did you come to the hospital anyway?"

"I had symptoms."

"Okay."

"Lost the use of my left hand for an hour. I need both hands to drive a train, so I put in a call to Dr. Culpepper."

"Yes?"

"And he says, 'I think you better come into the hospital where we can keep an eye on you.' Says nothing about cutting, just says 'we want to keep an eye on you,' so I came in to get watched. Pure and simple. Not to get cut."

"Okay. Okay, forget it. If you're not fully convinced, then you shouldn't have it. Fine. We'll keep you on the drugs and we'll pray they do the trick." Then Sam turned his back and left.

"He's mad at me?" Simms asked Lydia.

"Nah. Frustrated. Surgery's not necessarily the answer, you know that already, but it's all they've got to offer you now."

"The medicine."

"Your hand went bad anyway, right?"

"They can double it."

"Aspirin doesn't work that way. They've already juggled the dose. Changing it again won't help."

The two looked at each other for a few full seconds. Simms's eyes had started to dull in the last year, with a pink rim along the iris, wearing out. He and Lydia headed back to his room.

"You still thinking about working on the river?" she asked.

"Oooh yeah. Forgot all about that. Haven't even considered the river since the last time I came in here. Yeah, I'd like to work on that river, I still would."

His room had a view looking north at the powerhouse, with a patch of sky visible if you stretched your neck sideways and pressed your cheek to the window. He couldn't see the river, didn't know if it was sunny or not, snowing, polluted, winter or summer. He didn't bother to try finding out, just sat down on his bed, one of four, and stared into his folded hands.

He looked up. "You ever had surgery?"

Lydia sat down next to him, said no.

"I been two times now, the first when I was a little boy. I thought they was going to kill me, or cut off my balls or something awful like that. Must be I heard stories about the Germans and some cousins in Georgia who actually did have they balls cut off, and so anyway I put it together and that's what I figured would happen to me.

"I can still feel that mask closing in on my face, if I think about it. Felt like a damn fool when I did wake up, had to pee. Had to pee so bad but I didn't think I could do it, still thought they'd cut everything.

"Felt like a damneder fool when I found it all still there, every piece. Had a pain in my belly from appendix, but nothing else was gone. I was all together." When he laughed his gums showed above his teeth, kind of a pitiful nervous laugh at himself, mortified all over again with the memory.

"You can laugh," he told Lydia. "Go ahead, you can laugh because it is funny, now."

She didn't laugh, and so he told her the rest.

"The second time I had surgery was that time right in here, you remember. Same thing happened all over again. Now I'm grown and I know in my head that nobody's about to kill me or cut my balls, they don't even use that gas anymore."

"Not the same one, anyway, and not right off."

"No, first they give you shots to make you feel relaxed. That was fine. I felt good. So I'm all woozy and they wheel me on up to the operating room and there's that same machine as before, or near enough the same, and that rubber, operating smell. I might just as well have been a child again. It terrified me. Terrified."

He shrugged, staring into his big hands, rubbing and twisting them, squeezing the white of his palm over the ash-brown fingers and cracking his knuckles so she could barely hear the pop.

"You believe that? Carlisle Simms ascared of some kids' story."

"I believe it," Lydia answered. "I used to be scared of the voice on a record we had, I don't know why. A woman's voice telling fairy tales. I dreamed once that it started up on its own, the voice without the record. I have that same dream sometimes now and I wake up, afraid to go back to sleep." She hadn't dreamed the dream in years, hadn't remembered the voice, but even so felt a thrill of fear at the base of her skull. "I guess you never forget some things."

They left it at that. But that night Carlisle finally agreed to go through with the surgery, all smiles and putting in an order for a river view and a medium-rare T-bone, first thing when he came down from recovery.

He had his surgery on Valentine's Day. They all felt very upbeat about it.

At some time around two or two-thirty, Casper came down from the O.R. "Very smooth," he said to Lydia. "Simms looks fine. A little slow waking up, but he's a big man, took a lot of anesthesia."

Around three, Casper phoned her from recovery asking for an ICU bed for Carlisle. "Not a big deal," he said. "Relax yourself. He's just not waking up like we want, and his gases aren't great, so we'll keep him tubed for tonight and watch him in the unit. Big-time smoker, probably just needs extra attention to his lungs."

"You're sure?"

"Absolutely. He'll be a star by tomorrow a.m."

Simms came back intubated and being breathed by Casper squeezing a black rubber ambu bag. They pushed him down the hall, a whole group of them from recovery, pushed him right past Lydia and into the unit. He was disguised under layers of heavy adhesive strips, so all she could make out were his eyes, and they were closed and slightly caked over.

At least he had a window this time, at least when he did wake up he could look out at the river. Lydia took the ambu bag away and replaced it with a respirator, turned the thing on and listened to the click-click, click-click and hiss when it inhaled and exhaled for him.

"The joke's on all of us, Carlisle," she said softly. She pulled open his eyelids and stared into staring back eyes, no recognition in the stare, no thought, no surprise. "Time to wake up, Simms."

"Some of it may still be anesthesia." Optimistic. Casper half smiled, the corner of his mouth twitched. He leaned on the bed rail next to Lydia and pinched the soft underside of Simms's upper arm without effect. "Not a lot of it, but some."

"He didn't want to go. Look at him. Just look. I talked to him this morning, we talked."

"It could have happened anyway, you know. I mean he could have just stroked out anyway today. Done the same thing, only done it down here instead of up there in the O.R. Rotten luck." Casper scratched dandruff out of his scalp. "We took him back, when it was clear he was stroking. His artery reoccluded, sometimes they do, we took him back and opened it up again. He could still wake up and do okay. We reoperated right away. Right away."

Not soon enough. She had a feeling Simms would never wake up, never talk or tell fairy stories, never snap his fingers or drive a train or collect buried treasure from the East River, never. If he was lucky, he would die. She adjusted the arm of the respirator so it wouldn't stretch his mouth so much. She wiped the sleep from his eyes. She helped turn him to the side facing the window and fading daylight.

By the time Sam got there, Lydia was on her way out.

"Simms?" He walked toward the face behind cross tracks of tape, toward the equipment surrounding the head of the bed, set up like a shrine. Lydia waited for him.

"He went because of me, didn't he?" Sam said. "I made him feel like a schmuck. He went to surgery because of that, I know it. What did he say beforehand, he say anything about it? God, look at him."

They watched the gentle lift of his chest filling with air, deflating, filling again, deflating. His left arm lay passive behind him, limp and forgotten and already swelling from lack of use.

So they both thought it was their fault and Casper probably thought it was his. They had to take the credit or the blame, one way or another, it came with the profession. Maybe that was why they either couldn't ever give up on saving at least some of a life, or were ready to trash it if it was flawed, get it away, out of sight, out of mind. Polish them until they're presentable or else dump them. If you couldn't forget the failures, you would never take a chance and succeed.

Sam picked up the dead arm, let it go, let it flop, flaccid on the bed, nothing there. "Will you help me study him?" he asked. He expected her to say yes. She could tell by the way he looked right at her when he asked, no blinking. Was this finally a trick? The one he promised?

She almost said, Of course I will. She looked at Simms instead. "He hated our machines. He thought they were like a death knell. He'd see us studying someone and a few days later that person would be dead."

"Not all our patients die. Most of them don't."

"But the ones he saw did. They were all pretty badly off when we saw them."

"Help me, please?"

"Suppose he knows what we're doing. Even minimal awareness. He'd heave one big sigh and give up."

"Please. We'll talk to him while we work. Tell him how well he's doing."

She looked at the limp left hand, the drool sliding down Simms's chin. His forehead was already shiny with bed sweat. "Right," she said. "Tell him how well he's doing."

"I'm going to study him. He may be better than he looks. If he is, maybe we have something to offer him."

"Not that compound."

"I'll be here at four tomorrow morning, I'd appreciate your help."

"You're not going to try that cocktail. Not on Simms."

"I don't know. Lydia, I'm not the bad guy. Did you forget? So soon?"

There were five people on life supports that morning, and, except for minor differences in respirators—the size of the bellows or the color of the hoses, for example—you couldn't tell them apart. Comatose patients bore a striking resemblance to one another until you really got to know them.

Lydia stood at the door to the unit and listened to the rhythms of artificial animation. It was whispers and honks, beeps, occasional bells, it was desperately loud life compared to, say, herself, alive on the threshold, soundlessly watching. She could imagine the relief when the switch was flipped off, the startling silence after white noise, the peace.

She waved to Diana and headed toward Carlisle Simms's bedside. Sam already had almost everything set up. He smiled.

"Thanks for coming." But he had known she would come.

Diana strolled over to them and grinned a wide warm grin. "I thought you told me you retired from all this." Her eyes barely showed through the smile.

"Special guest appearance," Lydia said. "One time only."

"If you say so, but I'll believe it when I see it." She looked at the man in the bed. "We had a long talk last night. He was going to be fine. Girl, you just never know. You don't." And she went along to the next bed.

Simms looked pretty much the same as twelve hours before, maybe more settled, used to his role. Lydia wet a washcloth and wiped his face, wiped especially his eyes again. Sam had put him flat on his back, with his head tilted up about thirty degrees.

"He's unresponsive, flaccid left hemiplegia," Sam said, "Right side moves slightly but without purpose to noxious stimulation." All business. "Respirations increase to pain. Eyes deviated right at rest, no spontaneous eye movements, but full doll's across the midline. Pupils react, depressed left corneal, otherwise I don't know because of the ET tube and all the tape." He kept his head in the record sheets, checked off boxes as he spoke.

It was like picking up where they left off, as if no time had passed between then and now, like riding a bicycle, swimming a crawl, the rhythms of research, their own ritual. They each murmured reassurance to Simms, taking turns between him and his waves, patting him, whispering, studying the scopes silently.

Lydia explained it all at least once, leaning close to the man's ear, "Listen, Carlisle, it's me again, Lydia. Okay, I know, you don't want to hear from me, I understand, truly. But listen anyway." *They can almost always hear, isn't that right? Isn't that the last thing to go? Well, we don't know exactly what's preserved. I'm sure he senses you're nearby.* It comforted her to talk to him.

"The machines, remember our machines? Dr. Wheeler's and mine? Don't get scared now. We're just checking, just checking. I know there's a lot more going on inside your head than you're letting on. I know it. That's all we're checking for, that's all, that's all."

She was thinking that if anything would get a rise out of his brain waves it would be their machines coming within hearing distance. Another would be the click of the stimulus.

"There'll be two things. There'll be a buzzing, a tickling sensation, in your right calf. And sometimes some clicks in your ear. We'll be measuring how fast you pick up on them." If he did understand what she told him, he'd sure have something to say about that. And if he didn't understand, it didn't matter. How would a laughing brain show up? How about one running for its life? Or giving up?

She pressed the earpiece into Simms's ear, Sam strapped the probe onto his calf, and they began. Neither of them said anything much through most of the tests. "Ready?" Sam would ask, or "Enough?" or "Okay," he'd say, and Lydia would nod her head or shake it No, making gestures with her hands.

She was thinking about diamond tiaras floating through the East River, old sinks and dead bodies, and about Carlisle Simms picking up on the electricity between Sam and her, without benefit of machines, with just his instincts, way back before they even felt it, or admitted it. She thought of rotted-out tree trunks, about vacant houses and ghost towns, and about how Sam kept watching her think while she worked.

His face receded into shadow when he watched her, his eyes went from plain brown to dark brown and his whole complexion deepened, not symbolically but really, it did. His left hand moved to touch her arm but he checked the act and the thought and she saw it.

"Anything going on?" she asked him.

He didn't take his eyes off her.

"The somatosensories, I mean." She moved down to look at the scope for herself.

"Not really," he said. "No surprises, anyway."

Behind Sam's head was the window, and the river going along as usual, as if Simms weren't up here dwindling but were instead watching too, as usual. The streetlights of Roosevelt Island sent sequins clear across the black water, almost to touch the hospital, almost.

"Looks like a big stroke." Sam's Adam's apple bobbed, or lobbed, up and down in his neck when he talked to her. She had forgotten how prominent it was and how she loved to feel it sliding sometimes when he spoke or hummed or swallowed. How she used to kiss it.

"Right hemisphere," he was saying. "If he recovers, it's not the worst anyway. He'll still be able to talk."

"But maybe not walk or steer or tie his shoe," she said. "He can probably find someone to cut his meat for him."

"Right. I know."

"Sorry. I feel as guilty as you do. I was whipping us both. Simms too, he knew what he was doing." Smooth rolling waves on the screen, babbling brooks and foothills lacking firm definition, sometimes rolling into each other.

"Too soon to tell anything for sure. Could be a lot of swelling, could be that's in the way of the impulses. Could be." Dark gray fans under his eyes, she hadn't noticed them ever before. Not even night after night studying all last fall.

"You look tired."

"I'm all right." He looked to his instrument panel, a short shelf of knobs and levers, dials in several sizes. "I must have gotten used to being awake nights. I wake up about this time, three or four, almost every morning. I lie there and think." He sat facing two separate screens and the printer squeaking out graphs of electrical movements and impulses, the impulse to breathe, to beat a heart, perhaps to dream. "I don't sleep."

He was suffering. She was glad he was suffering. Sometimes she wondered if he was just relieved it was over, the hiding and the arranging, the fitting in, the juggling, the lies. She thought he had successfully substituted the children, she thought he had taken another look at Connie and seen that Connie was good.

His suffering made it easier for Lydia, for her self-esteem. And then it made it harder too because she knew they could go back in an instant. A snap of her fingers, one word—six, *Let's go to my house now*—and poof, they would collect their paraphernalia, put it away and be off, and she would be back, alone with Sam. That was the only thing to keep her strong. Alone with Sam. If she were devious, she would make anonymous phone calls, write notes, confront Connie outright, "He loves me, can you live with that?"

"Hell," he was saying. "I wake up and I think about you. I slug down three drinks so I can sleep and I think about you, then I wake up at three o'clock thinking about you." *I'll never have anything like this again.*

"Don't. Stop it, or I'll leave. You want me to look at his neck?"

"Absolutely."

They disconnected the probes and electrodes, wiped off the various contact goos, and touched occasionally, Sam with a lingering finger on her skin.

"Stop it," she finally said again.

Now there was the responsibility of holding up her end of the deal. If she truly wanted to go along without him, if she truly meant it, then she couldn't tease him with her ambivalence, with her desire. He wouldn't understand it, he would get confused. She would get confused. So she said Stop it and started to scan Simms's neck.

"Almost done, Carlisle. Just this one more thing, you've had it before, remember? Left common carotid . . ."

Sam stood with his back to the river, near the head of the bed, where Lydia sat and worked the ultrasound, where he could see firsthand the arteries throbbing onscreen. His hands rested holding Simms's dead arm. Sometimes he patted Simms's shoulder, sometimes he reassured the forearm. When Lydia started loving him it was from those small delicate touches with his clumsy hands, sending comfort to patients from his uncomfortable fingers, transformed. She remembered watching them become confident, strong healer's hands.

If Connie would just disappear. Zap. Instant. Painless. Gone. If only. PLANE CRASHES INTO MT. KISCO KITCHEN—HOUSEWIFE KILLED INSTANTLY. Or maybe she could get sucked into a rapture, boom, gone without a trace, gone to heaven to be with Jesus.

Another thing Lydia had done to make herself strong was to scan the literature on eternal triangles, an enormous amount of it from all angles. She unsympathetically weeded out first of all the wronged-wife stories and then, after very little more reading, put aside the so-called faithless-husband versions. It was herself she cared about, the wronged mistress, and there were books, short stories, essays, self-help, unbelievable numbers of words about herself. Scenarios, fiction and nonfiction, and most of them fit. She was not as original as she had thought.

One major fantasy of mistresses and also husbands the world over was the case of the disappearing wife, in varying degrees of violence. She did not feel so guilty anymore.

> Dear Connie,
> I have often wished you dead, or simply
> gone from the face of the earth. Does

this make you uneasy? Angry? I don't wish you pain, only nonexistence.

Sincerely,
Lydia Weber

Lydia moved from the left side to the right, ducking under the aqua hoses reaching from the respirator to connect with Simms's endotracheal tube. She accidentally knocked the connection loose and the respirator honked, irritated, disturbed from its rhythm. It buzzed a long complaint until Sam reconnected the ends.

"Right common carotid," Lydia said. "Frontal approach, head's at the bottom of the screen now, foot's at the top." And the respirator hissed an uninspired background tune. She ran the imager in front of the sutures as much as possible, the wound was already inflamed from being opened up twice.

"Looks pretty clean," Sam said. "At least what we see of it."

"Well, that's a good sign, right?"

"Depends on the timing."

It looked open and sounded open with blood whooshing up to heal the brain. Lydia tried hard to catch sight of the arteries going up past the neck behind the jawbone. She angled the probe awkwardly, pressed hard under the chin. The respirator honked. She removed the probe and turned off the ultrasound. "Sorry," she said, but the respirator honked again anyway. "What's wrong with that machine?" And it honked. "Cool it." She checked the hose, the adapter, the tube, finally the patient. "Sam, it's Carlisle."

The machine honked again.

"Sam, he's coughing. Carlisle! Carlisle, open your eyes!"

Not a flicker.

She shook him hard, oh, the hope in that shaking. "Come on, Carlisle! Wake up and breathe!"

He coughed once more but not enough to buck the breath coming at him, then he stopped altogether and passively took the oxygen pumping in.

His face was relaxed into a mask with the grimace taped on around a gaping hole that emitted all that plastic apparatus, a Gorgon's mouth. Lydia stepped back away from him. "What's the point?"

She cleaned off Carlisle's neck, leaned close enough to smell the decay starting in him, sweet decay. She scraped dried-up leftover

EEG paste off the hair on the back of his head, drained water from the corrugated respirator tubes and placed them to rest on the pillow by his face, but he didn't care.

"No point," she mumbled. "The answer is, no point, none."

She collected the lead wires and wound them into a ball, took the leads themselves and lined them up neatly in the drawer, put the headset in its place, covered Carlisle with a fresh sheet and tucked it under his arms and over his feet so he looked like a window display.

"Ready?" She looked up to Sam, she couldn't see any sadness in him. She looked for it in his eyes, his posture, in the set of his fingers holding the printout, but nothing. Nothing gave. "Don't let this get you down. There'll be other patients, you know. There always are. More interesting ones, more compliant."

"Don't," he said. He took hold of her hand.

"Don't what? I'm okay. Don't you." She jerked her hand away and started toward the door with the electroencephalograph. "Bound to get to me sometime, so it's just got to me now, that's all. Too much dying." Her muscles ached as if she was getting a cold.

They finished packing their gadgets into the storage closet and he did it again, took hold of her hand, only this time she didn't have the energy to pull back. Her arm tensed but that just made it easier for him to snap her body against him in one pull, and, hidden behind the door in the six-a.m. half light, he held her to him to press out the aches.

"Oh no," she said, "oh shoot," and gave up, it felt good.

"So long," he whispered. "I've wanted this, it's been so long."

She leaned against him, her cheek on his breastbone, his chest as firm and warm as her own bed, his arms the down quilt she curled underneath. She lifted her head and now saw the sadness there in his face, sadness, why now?

He kissed her, his taste familiar, craved. "So much time, wasted time."

She kissed him again, craving the taste of him again, the taste of someone living, herself alive.

"We could have been together all this time," he said.

"Together."

It wasn't so, they couldn't have been, and she knew it very well now. She remembered what being together with him meant, how meager it was, and she knew she didn't want it. Still, she couldn't keep from kissing him, the fit of their lips and the movement was so well remembered and longed for.

"I'll call you tonight?" He was smiling. "I can leave work early."

Tell him, Lydia thought. Tell him you're sorry you kissed him.

"I may be busy," she said. Why couldn't she tell him? Get it over and done with. *The first breakup never lasts*, Jane mocked. "Don't call," she said.

"Some big foreign job coming down now," she babbled. "Orange on the bottom, spanking clean white on top, it's a beauty, real big. Oil company, I bet." Continuous chatter while she cleaned up Simms's face and changed the tape around his endotracheal tube. Mindless talk, a reverse travelogue in her own style, to pass the time, alleviate the boredom of changing the tape, to keep Carlisle posted just in case.

Two days without a bit of change. She had thought when he coughed it might be a good sign and not only a reflex, and that by today when she came in he would have waked up, surprise! If he ever did wake up, his bed was actually facing the wrong way to get a decent view of the river traffic, but she could handle all that when the time came, if it came. Meanwhile, she reported. "Lots of traffic out there today. Here comes a blue tugboat, coming up like sixty from the Sound, I guess." Life on parade, passing them both by, there it goes.

She cut long even strips of adhesive and hung them over the bed rail, lined up for easy access. Equal widths, equal lengths. Creative Nursing I, making the patient look good in spite of how he looks. "Now a barge. Empty. What do you suppose they put on all those barges that go by? Where do they all go?"

Not a sign of improvement in two days, he got washed and wiped and breathed and drained, fed and changed, and he took it all without one single word, not a wink, or even one movement all his own.

"You seem to have an inordinate amount of time for staring out of windows." Dr. Bristol had snuck up behind her.

She smiled, friendly as she could be. "Just keeping Mr. Simms up to date."

"I see." He frowned.

He studied Simms's chart, shook his head several times studying it. He got to Sam's note apparently, because he said, "Totally inconclusive, totally inconclusive study," which is what Sam had said when they did it.

Lydia concentrated on loosening the old tape from around the neck of the ET tube. She used a surgical clamp and held the tube steady with her free hand.

"Has Wheeler been around yet?" Bristol asked.

She shook her head. "You're not planning to try the cocktail on Simms, are you?"

"I don't know yet. I need Wheeler." He flipped through the lab sheets, the medication notebook. "What's this man's status? I suppose you can tell me that much."

"Same as yesterday, same as postop. Some slight movement of the right arm to noxious stimulation, nothing on the left. No eye opening, no spontaneous respirations, but we haven't tried him off the machine. Blood pressure's okay, stable, one-forty to one-fifty over eighty to eighty-five. Don't you need permission from someone?"

He only stared at her, over her, through her. "Where's Wheeler?"

On Lydia's own island, the smokers and nonsmokers got along fine together, and nothing was hazardous to your health. Harry Bristol was obsolete, they kept him around to come up with obscure answers to obscure questions, or they didn't keep him at all. Maybe he and Connie could be flashed out to heaven together.

She wrapped the first long adhesive strip from Carlisle's right cheek, once around the tube and back to his right cheek again. Same on the left, winding the tape under and around the hoses and various plastic connections, and then she heard the whistling, "It's All in the Game," and Sam was there. Smiling, open, ready. Her chest tightened up, her stomach growled, her heart took up beating against her throat a few beats.

"No change?"

"Not yet."

"Would you please examine the patient," Bristol commanded Sam, "so we can be sure of what we've got?"

Sam winked at Lydia behind H.B.'s back. Friends again, conspirators, but he was a double agent.

"What've we got?" Sam asked her, and then, "I'm sure Lydia's done a thorough exam already, sir," grinning some more.

"Please examine the patient yourself, Dr. Wheeler. I don't want any doubts. And stick your head in my office when you're finished." Already halfway out the door.

"Pleasant this morning."

"It's because of me and the cocktail. I think he knows deep down that I'm right and it's made him even angrier than when I pulled out of the project."

"Don't kid yourself. He doesn't think you're right."

"At least he looked at me today, said a few words, hostile or not. I was invisible there for a while. Psychological warfare, I suppose. He can't really get my job since he has no jurisdiction over nursing so he's been trying to make it uncomfortable around here, hurt my feelings, needle me." She pressed the last strip of tape in place, to anchor the mouthpiece. "Simms hasn't changed, you can see for yourself."

"I believe you." But he poked and prodded in a few crucial spots, and he took the man's blood pressure himself. "I tried to call you yesterday. You were out?"

"I guess I was. You think you're using the compound on him? Don't you need permission?"

"A cousin in Virginia." They had really checked it all out. "Can I see you later?"

"Don't use that drug. This is unbelievable. How can you do that to Simms?" She thought Sam was a convert when he winked at her back there. "Please, you can't, please. Not on Carlisle."

"One more time, Lydia. I'm not the enemy. Bristol is not the enemy. This drug works. You saw it work yourself."

"Once."

"Many times."

"With complications."

"Okay, with complications. So we work on it, manipulate the doses, purify it, change things around. So that it will work with fewer complications. And then we go through the whole process again. And again if we have to. We wouldn't get anywhere if we didn't take risks."

"Look who's talking about risks. You aren't risking yourself. You wouldn't. You're risking other people."

"Most of the time, I'm risking a long vegetative life, at best a profoundly disabled one, against virtually no change, or death with dignity."

"It sounds completely reasonable. Put that way. Who passes judgment on the worthless lives that are better off dead? That's what I want to know. Who rejects them as beyond hope?"

"And you make it sound so monstrous."

"Maybe because it is."

"It's movement. We are moving."

"Back or forth? Or both?"

"This is insoluble. For a while, a good while, I wasn't so sure either. Because of you, things you said. But I've spent a lot of time on this issue. And I've looked around at these people, the ones with walnut brain, with drool slobbering onto the front of every shirt they wear, with mindless, empty laughter at mindless, empty stimuli. We can improve on that, Lyd. Sometime in the future, soon, we won't have these half-living, half-dead people. We can improve on the quality of the life, make it whole, soon."

"What about the ones who die of the treatment in the meantime, while you're adjusting dosages?"

He shrugged his shoulders. "Would you want to live like"—he looked around the room and settled, after all, on Simms—"that?"

"No. Neither would I want to laugh mindlessly at the least provocation or muss the front of every blouse I own, not to mention chafing my chin with the constant dribble, if I had a choice and I had to choose this minute. But who knows what I'd choose if I were Carlisle? Sometimes your priorities change. He may be having profound thoughts in there, out of your reach."

"I disagree with you completely, completely. But I love you." He lowered his voice to a hoarse stage whisper, looked around. "I love you that much more for the strength of your believing."

Disarmed. She had nothing to answer back to that. She stooped down to empty the hourly urine output from Simms's drainage bag. She watched his urine drizzle down the clear soft tube.

Sam leaned over the bed and looked down at her. He got a chummy kind of look on his face. "I'll be back. Don't leave until I come back."

"Before four, then." Lydia bent further, to close the nozzle on the drainage bag. She heard his whistle crescendo out the door.

* * *

After lunch she transferred one patient out to make room for another, at least there was time to make room. The man going out had lost his brain tumor yesterday and was doing fine without it. The woman coming in was Chloe Caldwell, soon to be minus her aneurysm.

One round on Carlisle, blood pressure, temp, level of consciousness, pupils, output, intake, and a turn, and then Lydia covered for the other nurse so she could go to lunch, dealt with the details of the transfers, waited for a clean bed, meanwhile cutting Mr. Ryan's beef tips and helping Matilda Marotta with her tea. She mixed the two o'clock antibiotics, let visitors in and finally returned to Carlisle, goodness knows why because she could have predicted every number, every size, every amount he produced, he was that unchanged.

She wiped off his face with a cold washcloth, she seemed to do that for him more than anything else. She wiped off his eyelids, rubbed crud from the lashes again and again, stopped looking for flickers of improvement and cursed herself for knowing too much. She wanted to keep hoping for him, she wanted that so. But the worse he was, the worse he would be, a fact backed up by piles of data, and the odds got longer each day, each hour.

She sucked saliva out of his mouth and wiped his face again, his eyes. "Open those brown eyes," she said, "and I'll show you a huge sailboat blowing up along the East River with the tides." She watched it by herself, all the way to the Triboro Bridge, wishing she could be on it out in the wind.

Mitchell came by to talk about Mrs. Caldwell. Stable through surgery and so far so good in the recovery room. "A rose," he said, "a peach. No problem. She'll be down in, say, an hour, hour and a half." He had a cigar shielded in the cup of his hand, ready to be relit as soon as he walked out the door. Its odor stayed behind, refreshing, a bit of warmth floating through the sealed blue atmosphere.

It was almost four when Sam breezed in, also smelling of cigars. Lydia sat on the far window ledge, charting the successful return of Chloe Caldwell from recovery.

"You've been with Mitch," she said, with Sam still nearly ten feet away.

"Clever girl."

"Unmistakable aroma. What is it about men and cigars?"

"Got me. Something latent, I'm sure." He stood to the side but pressed his elbow on her one knee, safe behind his lab coat and the chart. "I'm happy. I felt like a cigar. What about tonight?"

Lydia jumped down from the ledge, took a couple of steps back. "What about tonight what?"

"Can I come over?"

She shook her head no, looked at him, looked away from him, returned the chart to its rack at the foot of the bed. "You haven't asked about Carlisle. He hasn't changed, he's the same as before. When're you shooting him up?" Stalling.

"We're not. You're busy tonight? Tired? I thought—"

"How come you're not using him?"

"Couldn't get permission. How about tomorrow?"

"I don't believe you. Couldn't get permission, my foot. You two? Tell me the truth."

"We couldn't reach the cousin."

"Come on."

"And . . . he's too risky. Too many complicating factors, too dangerous. It could kill him."

"Sudden humanitarianism from Harry Bristol and his boy? What's going on?"

"Lydia. Give me a break."

He was lying to her, daring her to call his bluff. "He's a poor candidate," he said finally. "We're rejecting him as unstable."

"He's stable as stable can be. At least as stable as the others before him. You're stacking the deck. Weeding out the potential failures. Admit it."

"We'd just have to abort the trial. You know that yourself. I thought you'd be pleased about it anyway."

"I am. I am pleased about it. I just hate the way you keep with it. And now it's not even honest research."

He turned away from her to face the river. He stood with his arms rigid and holding onto the sill. "I'm trying to restructure the whole thing. More responsibly, okay? With less impatience."

"Ah, well, what's an extra year when you're dealing with Nobel-sized ideas?" It stung her to say it, ice-pick pain, the memory shot through her of lazy happy afternoons laughing about it, about power and control, winning. She didn't know nearly what she thought she did then, not nearly.

"I'm redesigning the project." He turned around, away from the window. "I want to try to make it safer, I hope safe enough for you to consider coming in with it again sometime."

"Probably I wouldn't. Don't consider me."

Through the unit doors, Lydia saw crowds of people out in the hall, maybe the entire population of 4 East plus friends and relatives. It was Main Street before dinner, people strolled and laughed, exchanged good luck, stood around in bathrobes and foam-rubber hospital slippers, mingling with the civilians, who wore furs and boots and three-piece suits, watching beautiful women make their ways with wheelchairs or four-legged aluminum canes, great hunks of hair shaved to leave skewed bald spots with gashes sewn through the middle. A few newcomers looked horrified but only for an instant before they found a polite face to put on. They were all being civilized and tolerant, pleasant to everyone, nodding introductions.

Lydia waved to Sylvia Goldfarb, she saw Mrs. Cass working her way to the bathroom, hugging the wall. It was a great place for all of them. Protective. Monstrosities were mostly overlooked. A fair share of patients appeared to rival Frankenstein's handiwork, but who noticed? A stiff-legged walk, a major limp, the left arm drawn up into a claw and speech bordering on a low wail. No one cared about such things here. What would they do when they were forced to cope with an impatient world, the world of the *un*deformed?

Regina was scurrying past the clumps of funny-looking people, coming toward the unit, her eyebrows raised into a point.

Lydia smiled as the head nurse rushed through the ICU doors, coming straight at her, breathing hard. Must be something really big, Lydia thought. A celebrity with a brain tumor?

"Come," Regina said. "Come. I have something to tell you." She looked at Sam. "Privately." She had lipstick on her teeth.

"So what is it?" Lydia asked. Perhaps a prominent public official.

"Not here." Regina guided them through the hallway with her hand grabbing Lydia's elbow as if to support her. Lydia only just realized then that whatever Regina had to say, it was probably something awful and it had to do with her. She thought that Bristol had issued a formal complaint and that she had lost her job. Then she thought that she or someone had made a huge medication error and caused anaphylactic shock or something, or that her apartment was burning down. And then, she thought, knowing Regina, it probably had to do with her not scheduling enough people to work the first weekend in March.

It seemed as if everyone stopped talking and turned to watch them leave the unit and head for the medicine room. She felt in a way like a bride going down the aisle. Sam followed them out, Regina directed him away. Lydia briefly thought to say that Sam could come, they had no secrets, but it was more for him than for her, so he wouldn't feel left out. She thought, That's what you get, Sambo, when you have adulterous relationships. You get left out, so there. She was feeling kind of punchy and nervous by now.

Regina closed the medicine room door and locked it. "It's your friend Jane." She pulled a chair out from the table for Lydia to sit on, she sat down herself. "Jane Clarke?"

"I know her name, Regina. What's wrong?" Irritated now. "For Pete's sake, just tell me. Say what you want to say."

Regina pulled up a wad of tissues and handed them to Lydia. "Jane's in the emergency room. I didn't want to talk in front of Wheeler because she's your friend. They didn't tell me anything, but I bet it's an O.D." She sat back waiting, pleased.

"Bull. Not Jane."

"Look, she's in the E.R. and she's half conscious. I know you're her friend, but you can never be sure about people like that."

"People like what?"

"You know what I mean."

"Boy, you can't be even a little bit different around this place without everyone—"

"Got any other ideas?"

"Unfortunately, yes. Her mother had some kind of cerebral hemorrhage."

Lydia wore a path between the medicine room and the CAT scanners around the corner and down the hall. The technicians were too busy to stop and talk, Lydia imagined they were deliberately avoiding her. She hated being in the dark. At one point she stormed the door to the room where Jane was being X-rayed but it was locked against her. She was mad at Jane for getting sick in the first place. She didn't have the time or the energy for it, she had too much to struggle with as it was.

Though they were both off-duty now, Regina found busywork for herself and Lydia. She planted herself at the desk, making schedules and checking off evaluations of new orientees. She set Lydia to straightening the medicine room. Lydia inventoried narcotics and sedatives, stocked the crash cart, and updated each and every Kardex on each and every patient on 4 East, in between terrorizing the X-ray department, waiting for Jane's brain scan to finish, waiting to see for herself what was wrong.

She helped with six-o'clock turns and gave Sophie her feeding, two hundred-fifty ccs of formula, plus crushed-up pills that clogged the tube.

"Do you see how she turns her head toward you?" Sylvia pointed out enthusiastically. "I think she knows it's you, she knows, it's her friend Lydia. Right, Ma?" With all the conviction in the world. "She doesn't turn her head for everyone, you know. She does it for me sometimes, and for you. You can't tell me she isn't aware. She knows her friends, believe me."

Lydia watched Sophie's head lob hesitantly to the direction Lydia was holding the feeding tube. Sophie's head made one last effort toward the tube before slumping back to the left against the pillow.

"What can you expect?" Sylvia insisted. "She's tired. It's six o'clock." In response, Sophie yawned and belched appreciation of her dinner.

Jane was awake at least. She was conscious and holding her head between her hands and rolling back and forth and back with her face pinched inward. Regina wheeled her from the scanner.

"Okay, Janey. Can you roll over onto the bed?"

"I've got hold of the bed," Lydia said. "Come on over. Grab my arm."

Jane opened her eyes enough to see Lydia. She smiled, or anyway the frown on her face smoothed out for a spare moment before she grabbed her head again.

"She got codeine in the E.R. I can't give you anything else right now, you got codeine in the E.R. Take deep breaths and give it a chance to work." Regina, offensive as ever. "Good. Good girl."

"You haven't changed one iota, R.B.," Jane mumbled, and Regina beamed at her.

Lydia patted Jane's arm, rubbed up and down her forearm,

rubbed and patted. "What happened?" She didn't know what else to do for her.

"Aneurysm. I knew right away. This headache. The worst." Her right heel pounded the mattress. She curled up, she straightened out, she twisted side to side.

"They scanned you."

Jane nodded. She had her eyes shut but still she shielded them with her hands.

Regina shook her head violently at the mention of the scan. "They didn't read it yet," she said. "We have to wait for them to read it."

"Okay, I'm going to take a look at it, then," Lydia said. "See what they know."

Jane opened her left eye. She looked as if she was winking. "They told me already. You know Jimmy, I made him, he told me everything. It's an aneurysm. A big one. Basilar. Ow! Shit, it hurts so much."

Lydia stayed close by her, not talking at all, she just stood there. Regina brought in another phenobarb injection and someone started another IV. Jane opened her eyes to Lydia about twenty minutes into the phenobarb. "Hold your fingertips along my temples, don't press, only touch me." She seemed more calm, less pained than before.

Lydia felt the pulse in Jane's forehead and held steady, setting up a ring, with her heart at one side, Jane's head at the other, and her arms connecting the two.

"Good. That's good," Jane said.

Lydia stood just that way for she didn't know how long. It was dark by the time Jane spoke again.

"Blue. Blue heals."

Lydia thought blue. Atlantic Ocean, Tennessee River, Lake Chicamauga, Jane's blue eyes, East River running into New York Bay, blue skies smiling at me, nothing but blue skies do I see.

"Somebody call Pop?"

"Regina called him. He's coming." Her thumbs buzzed slightly, and her forearms ached. "Should be here any minute."

Blue birds, blue books, blue movies, blue oxford-cloth button-down shirts, Wedgwood china, Spanish eyes, Mediterranean pools, the Jersey shore, the Blue Ridge Mountains, Moccasin Bend flowing straight through into Jane's head, washing out the headache, leaving her cool and sweet and clean. She wasn't really any good at this, she was sure, but it gave her something to do.

Lydia's fingers trembled. She leaned her elbows on the bed. She watched the monitor. A ship on the river sounded its foghorn.

Jane smacked her lips, yawned. "I think I'm okay. I mean I think it's enough, I'm better, you can relax." She opened her eyes, shaded them with her hand. They were puffy slits. "You can go home, I'm okay, really. Just get them to bring me some more codeine and I'll sleep. Go on and I'll see you in the morning. I just want to sleep now, that all right?"

"I'll get you the codeine myself."

"Thanks. For holding my head, I mean. Somebody called Pop?"

"He's on his way."

"I said this already, right?"

Lydia stopped at Sam's office on her way out. She knew what she was doing, she had no strength to fight it, needing him and his knowledge, his data, his percentages, the comfort of his arms. She wanted to give in. An instinct of self-preservation, she wasn't inclined to resist him right now.

His room was dark. Lydia rattled the doorknob. The silent hallway took up the empty sound, enlarging it. She felt like a thief at midnight, tripping the burglar alarm. A door at the far end of the hall opened, the light startled Lydia and froze her, blinded, with her hand on Sam's doorknob. Bristol peered out.

"Oh, it's you," he said. "Wheeler left for the day." He waited. With the light behind him, he was difficult to see, his expression was undecipherable. He had the advantage. He watched Lydia compose herself, exposed in bright light, watched her give up and leave.

Halfway home it started snowing. By morning there were eight inches on the ground and the whole city slowed down. Lydia called in to Diana, to make sure about Jane, who was status quo, sleeping off and on, and then she tucked her white uniform pants inside rubber boots and walked crosstown to work.

She didn't run into anyone on her way, not even a dog walker that early and out in the snow, no other footprints, no squirrel tracks, just uninterrupted white. Except for a few clusters of evergreens, the trees were all bare branches gnarled into webs of black lace against the sky, the snow mostly blown off them. She walked across the Great Lawn, with big deep steps leaving a path of holes diagonally, northwest to southeast. She came out at Seventy-ninth and Fifth. Traffic had already turned the snow a beige color and packed it down like piecrust on the street.

"You're not working in the unit today," was the first thing Regina had to say to her when she got to 4 East.

"I figured that."

"Okay. As long as you understand. I don't think you should be taking care of Jane if it can be avoided."

Lydia went in anyway, to say good morning, and to say she'd be around now. Jane's headache had eased up, but her eyes were still puffy.

"It's calmed down a little," Jane said. "I'm dopey as hell, but my head's not split in two." She opened her eyes cautiously, shut them fast, down tight. "Damn."

Lydia lay a cold wet washcloth across her forehead. She watched Jane's blood pressure roll up and down the oscilloscope, she took comfort in the sweep of it, and she watched Jane's eyelids relax and her breathing deepen into sleep. Lydia smoothed the sheet for something to do, and then started to leave.

"Lyd?"

"I'm here."

"Could you bring sunglasses when you come back from lunch?"

Morning conference was the hardest for some reason. They all sat in their usual places and they all acted like their usual selves, as if Jane were just another anybody come to seek their help. When the case was first presented, Lydia didn't even realize it was Jane they were talking about.

"Thirty-three-year-old white female . . ."

She hated when they presented young people. They were usually the most devastated.

". . . former neurology nurse with acute onset severe burning headache and brief loss of consciousness, brought by ambulance within half an hour of onset. No prior medical history, no history of headache, but her mother died of cerebral hemorrhage. Her scan is the first one on the left."

Bristol squinted and leaned forward toward the X ray. "Big aneurysm. What was her name again?"

"Jane Clarke. She left here a year or so ago."

"Jane Clarke?" He squinted at the ceiling, calling forth memory.

Sam turned around, his eyebrows raised, puzzled. "Jane?" he mouthed silently.

Well-nourished, well-developed female with no prior medical history. A piece of livestock. Her Jane. Delightful, multi-faceted, talented, beautiful woman who could have made a mint in shampoo commercials with all that hair, and incidentally never sick a day in her life until now. You remember Jane.

Bristol stood, stretched, and walked to the scan. He studied it, obliterated the aneurysm with his forefinger, returned to his chair. "Clarke, you say? Maybe when I see her. In any case, bad place for an aneurysm. What do you think, Casper?"

"Give her a few days to stabilize, then ask me." Casper shook his head. "Terrible location. Huge sucker, too. Terrible. Would you operate, H.B.?"

"I'll follow your lead. Wait for it to cool down, arteriogram her, see how she is, then think about it again." He squinted at the view box once more, grunted. "Who's next?"

So, the sum total of Jane, as far as they were concerned. A scan, a squint, a grunt. A case. A tough case. Not at all a person anymore.

At lunchtime, Lydia pulled her boots back on and walked up to the Lamston's on First Avenue. The streets were only wet now, cleared by traffic, but the sidewalks and especially the gutters were covered in brown slush.

"Sunglasses," the cashier said. "Sunglasses?" He glanced outside.

She walked down to Woolworth's. She tried a couple of drugstores. Well, where did people taking winter vacations in the sun buy their sunglasses? Where did the junkies buy them, and the movie stars? She finally found a pair in a toy store on Second. Pink plastic with red roses clustered along the top outer corners. Good enough to keep the light out. Jane would get a kick out of the roses.

She went straight into the unit without taking off her coat or her boots. She opened the package and took the sunglasses out, ready to slip them on, and she concocted a story to go with them: You will see beneath the surfaces, through all façades, into the Twilight Zone. Jane would laugh if it didn't hurt too much. Lydia put them on, exchanging them for her own glasses, and stepped through the automatic doors. Everything looked green, and Lydia's nearsightedness made the room appear soft, like an old movie, as if through gauze.

Regina stood at the desk, the phone at her ear, tapping her foot and letting out loud sighs. She turned her back to Lydia when she saw her.

Lydia went over to the bedside, pushing the sunglasses up on the bridge of her nose.

"Jane."

A nurse was taking Jane's blood pressure. Mary glanced at Lydia, rolled her eyes.

"It's a joke," Lydia explained, thinking it was the sunglasses. But Mary ignored her, concentrating on the blood pressure.

Jane slept. Snored. Lydia never knew Jane snored, she would tease her about it sometime later. I know you won't believe me but you snore like an old geezer. Really. "Jane," she repeated. "Wake up a minute. I brought you a treat."

Mary rolled her eyes and rechecked the blood pressure, pumping up the cuff, watching the mercury fall, pumping it up. Regina sighed and tapped her foot. Lydia took off the sunglasses, put her hornrims back on, and finally took a good look at her friend.

Jane's skin had gone pale, with a fine bluish mottle underlying it. Her whole face was like that, lips, nostrils, earlobes, everything pale and flat, no blush. She snored. Snorted. Occasionally stopped breathing altogether.

Regina hung up the phone and twirled around to face them. "I can't get anyone. They're all in rounds."

Lydia thought everything seemed so leisurely, there couldn't be anything wrong. Lined up on the windowsill were eight syringes full of clear liquid something, big fifty-cc jobs lined up neatly side by side, with empty Mannitol bottles lying around, and finally Lydia figured it out.

"I'll page them overhead, STAT," Regina decided.

Lydia ran to the supply shelves and grabbed a medium airway. She pulled open Jane's mouth and shoved the hard plastic in over her tongue to open her throat. "Bag her!" she ordered Mary. "Hyperventilate her!" Lydia took up the first syringe and started pushing the Mannitol IV.

Regina flew back to the bedside, suddenly, rapidly active. "I paged them STAT," she explained. She took over the bagging from Mary. "Get the crash cart. We shouldn't be doing this, you know. It could be big trouble."

Lydia had the third syringe in her hand by now, pushing the drug as fast as she could. She grabbed for the fourth, to have it ready. "How long would you have waited?"

"We were right on top of things. We had it all set up for them." She tossed her dark hair back from her face and bagged about forty a minute. "I hope no one hears about this. It's my neck if they do."

"It's Jane's neck. We know what's wrong, we know what to do, so why not do it? It wastes time not to go ahead."

"I just hope nobody finds out."

Regina jumped at the sound of the automatic doors. She stopped squeezing the bag and was busily adjusting the mask over Jane's face when Bartlett reached the bedside.

"Rebleed," she said. She sounded apologetic.

"Don't stop," Lydia commanded.

Bart looked around at all they were doing and all they were prepared to do. "Well, geez. Keep it up, ladies." He took out his penlight to check Jane's pupils. "That's probably enough with the bag. Give seventy-five of Mannitol, total, to start. I'll arrange for a scan." He walked to the desk. "What happened?"

"Her pressure shot sky-high about fifteen minutes ago," Mary said. "I gave her the hydralazine that was ordered, came back a few minutes later and she was snoring, with the left pupil blown."

Lydia finished pushing the last of the Mannitol. Jane was still fast asleep but her breathing was even and quiet, her pupils normal sized. Lydia stepped back and pressed her eyes shut but not before she caught a glimpse of Simms across the room, him and his life supports hissing at her, mocking her.

She returned to the unit after the brain scan. Sam was standing there, with Bristol pinching Jane like produce, tapping her joints to check for ripeness.

"The scan?" Lydia asked.

"New blood. Lots of it. With a rupture into the third ventricle."

Bristol stared at her, ungiving. He deserted the bedside for the central desk, picked up Jane's chart, without any great interest.

Sam took Jane's hand, rubbing her limp fingers. "She's pretty bad." He turned the fingers over, over and over, warming them, caressing them, caressing Lydia by comforting her friend's fingers. His eyes locked Lydia tight to him, Hold onto me I'll hold onto you. "She's got some brainstem left. No cortex. That's all."

"At least she's breathing on her own," Lydia offered.

Bristol glanced back and forth between snoring Jane and her vital signs stepping lively over the monitor screen. He slammed the chart shut and stalked to the foot of the bed. "How well do you know her family?" He stroked his beard and looked clear-eyed and innocent, even compassionate.

"Keep away from her," Lydia said. "Don't you dare come near her with your drugs."

Sam cleared his throat.

"Approach the family, Wheeler. She's perfect for us. Send them to me if you have to." Bristol slapped his hand on the side rail and left the unit.

A lot of bustle then, beds being straightened and monitors running three separate patterns apiece, Mary hung a new IV bottle, some X-ray technician set up for a portable chest at the next bed, there was so much bustle all around behind Sam, who stood clearly in front of her.

"Please don't?" she asked. "You won't, will you? Don't persuade her father."

Sam fingered the monitor cable. He jiggled it so that the heartbeat on the scope became a jagged fibrillating imitation. "I don't know." He beat on the side rail with his fingertips and risked looking at Lydia.

"Please," she pleaded.

She studied Jane's face, all smooth, practically unlined it was so slack. Looked as if wiping out the lines and shades had wiped out her personality. And her silky Breck-girl hair clashed awfully with that thick, dull complexion. Jane drew in a long snort and chewed at something in her mouth.

Lydia took one more look at her friend. "Just please don't use her," she said to Sam. She left the sunglasses on the cart next to Jane's bed.

She dragged through a million mindless details and irritations. She dealt with nineteen patients, forty-three loved ones, hundreds of pills and thousands of ccs going in and coming out, moving from point to point with no memory of the transit, only thoughts of Jane.

Regina finally reached Mr. Clarke, who wanted no stone left unturned for his daughter, but all Regina had told him was that Jane had taken a turn for the worse, not the worst.

Lydia had met Jane's father twice before. He was only just his daughter's height, stocky, with a smooth bald head. "We always joke about the milkman and the mailman," he had said. "The milkman was tall but the mailman had a full head of hair." He was the one who had given his daughter the mix of common sense and curiosity that made her distinctively Jane. He was a telephone repairman who faithfully read the *Daily News* and Thomas Mann.

She saw him hurrying into the unit, a thousand keys jangling from a ring hooked to his waistband. She followed him in, watched him slow down and stop several feet from Jane's bed. He held his hat in front of him, his head hung forward, taking everything in.

"They didn't say—" he started. "I didn't know it was this bad."

Lydia put her arm around his shoulders and led him closer to the bed. They stood silently, and then in a few minutes she told him what had happened. She was surprised at how separated she sounded when she explained everything. Caring but composed, the perfect nurse, protected from feeling. Her voice came out low, reasonable, automatic. She couldn't stop it.

Mr. Clarke said, "Wait, she's all I've got," interrupting her. "You don't understand, she's all I've got. She has to pull through."

"I feel the same way, sir. I want Jane back too."

He smoothed his daughter's hair, combed it with his fingers, and simply gazed at her distorted face, adoring it.

"I'll leave you with her?" Lydia asked.

"Thank you."

"I'll find a chair. You can sit."

The pink-rimmed sunglasses sat on the cart exactly where she had left them. They looked playful, childish. Lydia tossed them into the trash on her way out.

She walked the long hall to the solarium and then returned, dragging a bent bamboo easy chair with her. Sam was approaching Mr. Clarke. Lydia cursed herself for leaving him there undefended.

"Sam Wheeler." He extended his hand the same way his wife did. "I worked with your daughter."

Lydia scooted the chair through the space between beds and sat it near Jane's head. The two men stood on the opposite side of the bed.

"Would you like to sit?" she asked Mr. Clarke. "Over here?"

Sam was opening and closing a safety pin. "Mr. Clarke," he started, interrupting her. "Everything possible is being done for Jane. Did you want to sit down? We're doing all we can. There's just one other thing that could possibly be done."

Lydia's mouth opened to say, "No," then it closed, then it opened, "Could I have a word with you first, Dr. Wheeler?"

"Later." Closed. "We're currently using a new drug that may do the trick for her. It's experimental, but we've used it with relative safety on a total of seventeen patients in the last six months or so." He fastened the pin to a belt loop on his trousers, freeing his hands to drum or fold, to touch Jane or not. "We believe that it improves the efficiency of the brain, thus diminishing the area of permanent damage left by an insult such as this." The speech was smooth, confident, unstoppable.

"You want to experiment on Jane?" Lydia emphasized the word "experiment" and hoped it offended Mr. Clarke.

Sam turned it to his advantage. "It's experimental, yes, in the sense that it is a revolutionary idea. As you well know, Lydia. Lydia has actually been assisting me in this work. She knows how careful we all are." Transparent gold eyes, cool, glazed. "We have had several mediocre results with the protocol, meaning no overall change in the patient's clinical status. There have been a few complications, in certain risk-prone individuals, all elderly and somewhat debilitated to start with. And finally, we have had one spectacular success, with a young woman close to your daughter's age, otherwise healthy, as is Jane."

"She was an electrocution victim, Sam," Lydia intruded. "It's not the same thing, Mr. Clarke."

"That's correct. It's not the same thing. I don't want you to misunderstand me. I'm not promising the same kind of results with Jane." He patted the sheet covering her thigh, he rested his hand there, a tender touch. "In fact, I wouldn't count on any change at all. But there is that chance. I'm offering you that one chance."

"Back to normal?" the father asked. "Back to her old self?"

"No guarantees. Realistically, I have to say probably not entirely her old self. But perhaps very close to it, very close."

"How dangerous is it?"

"Well, yes, there are several uncomfortable side effects, gastrointestinal irritation, increased sweating, occasional rapid rise in blood pressure, a headache in awake individuals, and," he paused, glanced at Lydia, "I feel bound to warn you that of course, at the most extreme, death could result. We have had no deaths so far in direct association with the protocol." He removed the safety pin from his belt loop, closed it, opened it. "There was one hopeless patient who died, several hours—six or so hours, wasn't it, Lydia?—after we had completed our studies. An inevitable death, though. A hopeless case."

It was all the truth, spun brand-new, with evident compassion and clarity, and with calculation. She started to speak, but how could she go up against this amazing persuasion? Oh God, don't let him be fooled, she thought.

The older man turned away from all three of them, the doctor, the nurse and the patient. He confronted the window and through it a gray dusk, snow, and the river flowing north. He tracked a bus on the FDR Drive until it disappeared into the tunnel at Eighty-first, then he turned back to them.

"I'd do anything to save my daughter's life. I would give my consent to anything that gives her even the smallest chance to get better. But she'd kill me if I did." He smiled at his joke and said, "Be worth it, yeah?"

Neither Sam nor Lydia answered.

"Look, doc," he continued. "It's not you. You seem to care about Jane. If it were up to me, I'd say go with it. You seem like a man I could trust. But it's not up to me, it's up to her. She told me last night not to go overboard—her words. She says, 'Pop, believe me. Nothing works, no matter what they tell you. If it busts, let me go,' she says. 'Believe me,' she says." Wet eyes, red nose. He blew his nose. "I believe her. If she comes back, she comes back. If not," he swallowed on dry words, "then not."

The snow fell wetter, heavier than the night before. It clung to Lydia's glasses like drifts on windowpanes until she finally had to take them off to see in front of her.

At home, she looked for all her gifts from Jane, a tarot deck, a copper bracelet, a book of spells, the wool cap and scarf, a blue ceramic teapot from Mexico. She cleared off her desk and made a pile of the gifts.

She took down the macramé hanging. They had spent their first summer of days off checking out beaches from Rockaway to Jones, to all the way out to Montauk Point. They rented a car or they took the train, but every week that summer there had been a different beach. Jane collected shells from each one, hundreds of shells and odds and ends washed up from the ocean. She was into Transcendental Meditation, and she nearly drove Lydia crazy talking about her center, her core, all the time. She wove the seashells into a wall hanging and gave it to Lydia for her birthday. "Summer of Seventy-five," it was called, and there were bottle caps and bottle necks woven in with the shells. Lydia had hung it high in her front window so the sun shining through it made patterns on the floor, liquid patterns if the wind caught the fringe and set it to fluttering. She took it down and draped it over the entire desk, and then she tried to sleep.

She would start to doze off but think about Jane. See her picking up shells off the beach, or diving into the coldest morning waves, see her frowning over the tarot cards, digging into raw oatmeal cookie dough, then she saw her snorting and chewing and smacking like some dumb animal. And her hair didn't even match her skin anymore.

Lydia got up. She poured herself some sherry and turned on the television to all-night news. She walked from one room to the other and back to the first room again, she went through Jane's gifts. She put the teapot away, she decided to wear the wool cap and the copper bracelet tomorrow, she left the book of spells right where it was, shuffled the tarot deck, and figured out a new place for the macramé hanging, over her bedroom window. She hammered her own thumb twice in the process and it hurt like crazy.

Jane kept on the same way for another day, day and a half, and then she made a slight rally. She started opening her eyes from time to time and making the noises people make when they dream and turn over in their sleep. She looked straight at Lydia once or twice and seemed about to say something—something sarcastic, by the cast of her eyes—but then she fell back asleep. She had stopped snoring.

Lydia knew the basic physiology of all this and she tried to keep reminding herself that it didn't mean much in the long run, but she couldn't help but hope. Jane's eyes seemed intelligent again. Her complexion didn't clash with her hair and she slept with a look of peace about her, not so much like a house pet or an old man.

As a favor to Lydia, Sam ran electrical studies on her at forty-eight hours after the second bleed. Lydia was convinced they would find more on the inside than they saw on the outside, but they didn't. All the cortical waves were delayed, some were so late they didn't even show up on the screen, and the ones that did come were stunted and they trembled, retreating.

It meant Jane could breathe forever and keep a blood pressure pumping, and chew and smack and snort off and on. She would have time enough for her skin to get that cheesy smell and to flake off from bed sweats, time enough to be fed from a blender directly into her stomach, to be propped up in a stretcher chair and flopped back and forth into old age, to keep her bottom clean and dry.

After the shock, after the first days of sorrow and some regret, Regina responded to Jane in a way similar to the way Sam did. To her, Jane became anyone, not a person known and remembered fondly, just another vegetative patient. When Regina passed her bed sometimes she would pause, take a deep brave breath and then proceed as usual. She hesitated profoundly before she asked Lydia to work nights in the unit over the weekend. She claimed her back was to the wall, an old story. Something about needing someone with experience to break in the new nurses. Regina said Lydia could just supervise and let the others do the actual work, she wouldn't have to get involved at all, if she didn't want to, and it would give her some extra time to be with Jane.

The rest of the unit was quiet that Saturday night.

Mrs. Caldwell had recovered steadily since surgery, but on her second postop day, her ulcer had flared so they kept her in to stabilize her. Carlisle festered quietly by the window, sometimes better, sometimes worse, but always essentially the same. He had passed his critical period, but still he hadn't waked up. Lydia sent the two new nurses for a coffee break while she finished up the three o'clock chores. Then she went over to look at her friend, to stand watch.

Amazing how Jane just kept on. She woke or slept with no rhyme or reason to it, right then she was awake with her eyes roaming back and forth like a slow tennis lob. Sometimes she sighed and yawned so big you could see her palate, shaking way in the back.

Lydia took a gauze four-by-four and wiped sweat beads off Jane's forehead. They'd have to change her bed, she had sweated so much. She looked directly at Lydia, she really seemed to look straight at her, about to speak, but then her eyes went bored. They blinked, slow and lazy, and went back to their roving, left to right to left to right, Lydia wiped the sweat off again.

She had taught Jane how to play backgammon once, then they played for weeks. They were always going to walk across the Brooklyn Bridge but they never had, they were always going to go to Vermont. Jane had spent one evening making fun of Lydia's accent, claiming that she, Jane, had no accent, none. She was offended when Lydia insisted that she sounded like Archie Bunker when she talked, so then they spent months comparing words. Say *orange*.

Say *sure.* Say *New Yahk.* Isn't that how you're supposed to say it? They had always planned to make a tape and settle the issue once and for all.

Say *ruin. Rune. Rew in. Rooone. Battery Park. Pahk, pawk, pok?*

Lydia leaned on the bed rail thinking of words to say, and while she stood there, Jane's breathing changed. It went uneven, loud. Her pulse sped up briefly, and then it went down way down while her blood pressure climbed up way up. Lydia watched the bouncing balls and lines streak across the scope, fast and jagged, and sometimes slower, worn out. She lifted her friend's eyelids and looked into massive, unmoving pupils, and her whole body leaped on the inside, Lydia's whole inside, the reflex of an intensive care nurse. She automatically ran to the emergency medicines and automatically grabbed some Mannitol and syringes, she rushed to draw the solution out of the bottle, to push it into Jane, but she stopped. With the injection site in one hand and a syringeful in the other, she stopped dead.

So. Jane had bled again. She was dying by halves, just as her mother had.

Every thought came clear in Lydia's mind, clear and whole, but quick, filling up only a short pause. The unit brightened, all of it defined and clean and sharp, especially Jane.

Lydia weighed the pros and cons and held the syringe of medicine back in her hand. She scolded herself for weighing pros and cons. Pompous. And Jane was her friend. And Jane was snoring and choking up air right there in front of her while Lydia got stuck in the pause. By what right did she wonder what to do?

She looked at her friend.

Jane's breathing was hard as a piglet's, her face distorted into two nostrils and a wide gaping mouth struggling with effort.

Only God could decide, right? Lydia should work to save life, right? As an instrument of God's will, she should preserve Jane. Lydia picked up the gauze pads and wiped Jane's forehead, nothing quick about it now. She wiped her chest and sopped up the pool of sweat forming in the notch of her neck. Lydia touched the gauze to her own nose.

When her grandfather died, she had claimed one of his old black berets for herself. First she thought she would wear it, but it turned out his head had been smaller than hers. So she lay it in her top drawer, between her baby bonnet and some rhinestone jewelry she had saved from high school. Something like six months later she reorganized her chest of drawers and there were the jewelry, the bonnet, and the beret, back to the left, still sitting there. She tried the beret again, it was still too small, and then she smelled it, for no reason. She just happened to hold it up to her nose, and she could have sworn Pop-pop was right there in front of her. She smelled his hair and his Old Spice and some of his sweat, she smelled him. Lydia had cried, it smelled so real and so false.

The damp gauze from Jane put her in mind of nothing, living or dead. It was respirator sweat, plus three-days-of-lying-in-bed-immobile sweat. Musty, offensive, dishonest. Not from hard work or a fever, but from a foul-up of the nervous system. Not even Jane. Not even close.

Lydia put the Mannitol aside. She maneuvered a plastic airway into Jane's mouth, over her tongue, down her throat. She secured it with adhesive tape. It quieted some of the gasping. She double-checked the blood pressure, falling now along with the pulse. She checked everything at least once more, and then, after all that was done, she called the intern and waited.

Lydia was wired for days after Jane died. It was either work or go crazy looking for things to do at home, so she worked nonstop, long hours. The despised routine brought some peace. The repetitions, the tasks, the automatic observations and responses, the exhausting boredom of cycles and circles, they were a comfort, the sameness of them. Even the unchanging status of Carlisle Simms, rhythmically breathed, continuously fed by measured drop after drop to the hum of his infusion pump, the artificial cadences lulled her. Progress would have asked something of Lydia. The stagnance required nothing.

At some point she realized she hadn't seen Sam, even in passing or at a distance, since before Jane died. At some point it didn't matter. She wondered briefly what had happened to him, and wondered how she could have taken so long to notice. She didn't feel the emptiness without him anymore, there was only the memory of emptiness.

She took blood pressures, calibrated monitors, checked pupils, had patients make fists and push and pull, she turned them and cleaned them, she measured urine outputs, changed sheets, fluffed pillows, yes, fluffed pillows, she mixed IVs, injected antibiotics, antihypertensives, anti-arrhythmics, analgesics, she counted narcotics with Regina.

She had to pull out an entire roll of codeine 30 and count them one by one because the numbers were off by two pills and Regina was going crazy. Federal regulations. Lydia found the two loose pills at the bottom of the box. She had to do it again with the Demerol 50s because they came up one pill over. Shoved underneath the Demerol pack was a small manila envelope stamped JANE CLARKE F6095381. Lydia picked up the envelope and shook it. Felt like a ring and a necklace. F6095381. JANE CLARKE.

Regina said, "Oh yeah. Her father's coming over this morning to pick those up."

"I could take them to the funeral. He wouldn't have to make the trip."

"No funeral. He cremated her yesterday."

Cremated.

Regina went back to counting the lines on the Demerol signout sheet. She shrugged. "She wanted to be cremated, he said. No funeral. You didn't know that?"

It made sense, but no, she hadn't known. "We never really talked much about funerals, Regina. I can't even think of one time that we discussed them. Do you talk about your funeral with your friends? Would you maybe like to tell me what you want, Regina?"

"You don't have to be so hostile. I didn't mean anything. The count is actually right. I signed out one pill across two spaces yesterday. I'll just renumber the lines."

"When's Mr. Clarke coming up?"

He wasn't coming up. He wouldn't. He had first said to just mail them, but it was against hospital policy, so he agreed to come for Jane's things, only so far as the lobby.

Lydia saw him before he saw her. He was standing by the great marbled west wall, the GO AND DO THOU LIKEWISE wall, with the Good Samaritan chiseled into it. He stood completely still, leaned slightly forward to scan the main hall. He didn't recognize Lydia when she passed through his stare, maybe he was expecting Regina.

"Mr. Clarke," she said.

His eyes were dry, so dry the rims burned red. "You have Jane's things?" His skin looked dull, used up.

"I have them. Regina, the head nurse, Regina Baker, told me about the cremation."

"It's what my Jane wanted. No funeral, just the cremation, she said so when her mother passed away." He spoke in a monotone, nothing would faze him. "She told me a few days ago too. I was planning to call you. I thought to myself that I should call you but it slipped my mind. We didn't have a real service or anything. It was me and a great aunt and we just had it done."

"I understand. I just wanted, well, Jane and I were very close." She meant to comfort him.

"Could I just have her things? I hate these hospitals."

"We were very close and I know, well, we talked about it once, about dying and about living and everything, and I know she wouldn't have wanted . . . Well, you know all that." To give him some small comfort.

He shifted his weight from one foot to the other, and back and forth. He worked his keys in his right hand. "Just give me the things."

"Ah, what I'm trying to say is she wasn't herself anymore. For a couple of days before she died, she wasn't Jane. You could see that yourself. I know she wouldn't have wanted to live that way, you wouldn't have wanted her like that. She was always one to do things for herself, her way, to just go ahead and do them and not depend on anyone else. She was brand-new every day. But not anymore, sir, not just before she died. She was a shell, she wasn't Jane anymore."

He reached for the envelope, he pulled it from her and backed off to leave, then he stopped. "You think she's better off? You trying to say we're better off this way?"

Then he left her. Lydia watched him leaving, she watched his back through the revolving door and up the walk until it was lost in the shadows of the street.

When she got upstairs, she first went to Sophie. She stopped at the foot of the bed and looked at the old woman staying alive. Sophie mouth-breathed under an oxygen mask. The mask had left a permanent imprint over her nose and cheeks, all around her mouth, a red outline etched into her skin.

"She's so strong, my mother," Sylvia had been boasting. "No one ever thought she'd make it this far." She beamed with pride at Sophie's strength. Sometimes she would sneak a spoonful of rice pudding into her mother's mouth and watch for her to swallow. The pudding would mostly sit on Sophie's tongue for hours, melting, dripping down her chin with the drool until someone came by to suction it out, and scold Sylvia for feeding her mother.

"Do you think she's comfortable like that?" Sylvia would ask, pointing attention away from her own crime. "She hasn't been turned for hours. I would, of course, turn her myself, but I thought you girls wouldn't like that. I know you have your routines."

Sophie usually looked uncomfortable. Some part of her body always seemed skewed, tilted too far or not far enough, twisted unnaturally.

Lydia silently rolled her to her back, straightened her arms and legs over the spread. She combed her hair away from her face and padded the oxygen mask with cotton where it cut into Sophie's nose. Lydia stood back. Sophie's head gradually, steadily, drew left, pressing into the pillow.

By the time Lydia returned to the unit, they were preparing for an emergency admission, encephalitis, a man. There were two beds empty in the unit.

"I'll take him," Lydia said. "Put him next to Mrs. Caldwell's bed."

"I don't know, that's not a good bed." One of the new nurses. She chewed bubble gum. "We had the head trauma and the basilar aneurysm in that bed. Both very quick."

"I'm not superstitious. Give him to me."

"Okay." A very loud pop, she chewed with her mouth open. "But if I get sick or something?"

"Yes?"

"Don't put me in that bed."

"I'll keep it in mind."

On Thursday morning, Carlisle Simms started smacking his lips and in the afternoon someone said he opened his eyes. Lydia wasn't even there to see it.

They mentioned it to her first thing Friday, and all she thought was, Oh sure, he's smacking his lips, so what? So now he can smack his lips. That's what she thought.

She took her time about going in to see him and starting her shift. She had Chloe Caldwell to take care of, and Carlisle, and the noisy man with an encephalitis, Michael.

It didn't mean anything, the lip smacking, a primitive pleasure so why get your hopes up, not even the primitive pleasure itself but a vestige of it and a lip-smacking response. His eyes were probably passive, nothing left to do but let the lids go slack, too much trouble keeping them closed and so they opened a slit and everyone got excited. So what? Did they blink? Did they tear? Could they hide true feelings like other people's eyes?

The three patients formed a corner, with Chloe as the centerpiece. She sat upright in her bed, the tray table in place in front of her, covered with liners and blushers, mascara, three eyeshadows, foundation, pressed powder, after-bath powder, cologne and perfume.

"Miss Weber!" she called. "Lydia, thank God." She smoothed back invisible hair from over her shaved right temple. She rolled her eyes toward the young man next to her, who slept now, on his side with his bare ass facing Chloe. "I mean, really, this is too much. They can't keep clothes on the boy, believe me they tried all night long, but really. At least cover him up." Which Lydia was doing just then. Michael kicked off the sheets and then stretched flat out, uncovered, smiling in his sleep.

Carlisle lay passive, unchanged on his end of the triangle. His eyes were closed and he wasn't smacking his lips. They must have imagined it.

"It's not that I haven't seen my share," Mrs. Caldwell was saying "I just prefer to choose whose I see. I don't suppose you could pull the curtain."

"Sorry. I have to be able to keep an eye on him." Lydia tried once more with the sheet but Michael flung it off, opened his eyes and smiled at her. He kissed the air in her direction and rolled again to his original side. Pleasant guy. Not a bad encephalitis to have, all things considered. But she knew this was only one crest of one wave, and he had just had his phenobarb half an hour before.

"Drugs?" Chloe whispered. "Bad trip?" Her suture line formed an inverted question mark that ended at her right ear.

Lydia laughed, shook her head. "What do you know about trips, good or bad? Nothing, I bet."

"You're right. But I imagine that's what they're like. He shrieks occasionally. Screams. And sometimes he giggles."

"Encephalitis. Noninfectious." Lydia picked up the midnight

purple eyeshadow stick and smudged some on her finger. "Getting ready to move out?"

"To the East Tower. I'm stable, they say, Dr. Mitchell says. Out of danger." Some movement from Carlisle's directon. No, probably not. Just the hope of movement.

"I'll have someone around the clock for the first few days. A private duty nurse. At least there's a view of the city up there. . . ."

Was he breathing sometimes on his own? Yes. The orange light kicked on, he was triggering the respirator himself.

". . . and I'll have my own room. Of course, I will have to give up the scenic attractions of Four East, but I'll do my best." Chloe Caldwell smiled at Michael's umblemished bottom smiling at her. "I'll be okay up there, won't I?"

"Sure." She was sure he was breathing a little on his own, she was sure he had opened his eyes. "Excuse me, Mrs. Caldwell." But really, opened his eyes.

"Carlisle Simms," she said, not yelling or excited, just conversationally.

He opened his eyes again and looked at her, conversationally. He smiled, big and wide, which made him cough several times. The respirator joined in honking and Lydia just laughed. "Carlisle Simms. You old cheater. You understand me?"

He nodded, careful not to set the respirator off again.

"I'm Lydia?"

He nodded.

"I'm Dr. Culpepper?"

He frowned and shook his head.

"Hey, Mrs. Caldwell! Look at Mr. Simms! He's awake! Hey, Eileen, come here."

Chloe picked up her magnifying mirror and the liquid foundation. She carefully applied dots of beige to her forehead, nose, cheekbones, eyelids and chin. "Well, of course he's awake." She spread the dots out with light strokes of her fingertips. "He woke up last night. Oh, s-h-i-t." She took a wet washcloth and wiped over her entire face, then dotted her skin again. "I explained everything to him, where we were, what day it was, who I am. Well, everyone else was busy with that young man over there, and I certainly couldn't sleep." She held up the eyeshadow sticks. "Which one?"

"I think the brown," Lydia said. "For daytime. So she explained it all to you, did she, Mr. Simms?" He nodded, he smiled. He smiled!

"That was wonderful of you, Mrs. Caldwell."

"Nonsense. Anyone would have done the same. Brown? Are you sure? My dressing gown is lavender."

"Brown. Unless you want to look bizarre."

"You're sure?"

"I'm sure," Lydia said. "Can we try a few things, Carlisle? Just a few. Close your eyes. Okay, you can open them. Now pick your right arm up off the bed." He raised his arm and then he laughed, it sounded like choking, he laughed so hard. His belly shook and the respirator honked and beeped and buzzed and even Chloe Caldwell had to stop in the middle of her face to smile at the man who woke up last night.

He could move his right side and maybe his left leg but not his left arm, not so far. He breathed on his own about two-thirds of the time, with the respirator there for backup the other third. It seemed as if his mind was okay. In the afternoon, after she had transferred Mrs. Caldwell to the tower, Lydia gave Simms a pad and pencil. He wrote out his name, FOOD and WHERE'S DOC? and he winked with his right eye.

"I'll call for him to come see you. But he may be kind of busy this afternoon."

Simms frowned. It took him five minutes and three separate sheets of paper to write YOU TWO OK? but Lydia went to page Sam without answering.

Michael's temperature started going up and he began to rattle his side rails and wail just before visiting hours. Lydia gave him his phenobarb and some Tylenol and sponged him off with alcohol, more to calm him than to bring his fever down, so by the time Sam arrived Michael was sitting at the foot of his bed, his legs dangling through the railings. He was serving an invisible tea all around.

"Tare for, care for tea? Tare for chee?" He poured slowly. "Sugar? Scream? I mean, oh, scream?"

"No, thanks just the same," Lydia heard Sam say.

She was standing with her back to the room, leaning against the windowsill next to Simms's bed, watching the river flow downtown. It turned a royal blue where the shadow of the Samaritan hit it. It really could be the Nile, through that one window, she didn't care what Ali had said. The Nile, or even Moccasin Bend, if you squinted.

Lydia turned to see Sam staring at her. He said, "How's Simms?" Looking right at her, not at Simms.

"See for yourself." She picked up her clipboard. "Well, look at him, talk to him. He's breathing practically all on his own."

"Simms!" and Simms looked at Sam and winked. "Wow. When did this all happen? Simms, close your eyes, good. Now open them. Now raise your right arm." Same paces, same steps.

"Now stand on your head and whistle 'Dixie,'" Lydia added.

"You look great, Simms. We're all very pleased." He spoke to Simms but looked at Lydia again. "Especially Miss Weber. Lydia never gave up on you. Not once. He does look great."

"He does."

"You just never know with these things, do you?" He clasped Carlisle's right hand in both of his hands and hugged it.

Lydia turned back to the river. She felt Sam come up behind her. His hand curled around her arm.

"A lot of things have been happening," he said. "Have a minute?" So close again.

A big white pleasure boat churned toward the bay. Three men and two women stood on the deck with the wind blowing their full faces pink. They must have been happy, they seemed to be free out there in the cold wind.

"You should just see this white boat, Carlisle. Out in the cold. Man, could we go someplace in that." Wide fans of water trailed the boat. "What do you think of when you think of the East River, Sam? Quick, what did you think?"

"It's not a river. It is partly estuary, and a canal of sorts, separating Manhattan from Queens and Brooklyn."

She watched the water fan out behind the boat, gentle waves gaining speed and size until they slapped and clapped hard against the stone walls on both sides and the foam sprayed six feet higher, at least six feet, before the next wave clapped in its turn. She thought of the bicycles and horseshoes and tires, corpses and diamond tiaras and all the stories under the waves, and she thought of Carlisle out there collecting them. That's what she thought.

She left Sam at the window and moved to the space where Chloe Caldwell's bed had been. She began preparing it for the next patient. Sam followed her. He leaned his arm up on the cardiac monitor and played with the knobs and dials, pretending an interest.

"I spent the last three whole days at home," he said. "Enforced togetherness. Connie's idea. But I thought about us. We're great together, you and I. I want us to be together again. I need you."

"No."

"What do you mean no? I know what I need. I'll work something out." He studied the way the monitor tape fit on the roller and wound around to the front. "What do you think?"

"Obviously it doesn't matter what I think."

He snapped the panel into its place, turned to her. "Of course it does, don't be ridiculous. What about us?"

She reached up and unsprung the roll of tape, then she threaded it slowly around again. The memory of Jane roared back at her, the image of Sam carefully holding her limp fingers, the image of him sad, comforting, guiding, persuasive, the image of him trying so sincerely to railroad Mr. Clarke into agreeing to the protocol. Liar.

"There is no us." She pressed the panel in until it clicked.

"That was true four days ago. Not anymore," he persisted. "I want us to be together."

"Won't work."

"It will. I love you. I want us to be together again."

"We weren't ever really together. That is the truth of it. And I don't even like you much now. That is also the truth."

"Just like that, you don't like me? I haven't changed. You're still upset about Jane."

"You bet I am, but that's not it. It's just something I realized, that's all."

"All? Shit."

"I don't know, but there it is." She walked back to the window.

"Just listen to me," he insisted.

"No. You listen to me. You really listen to me. You and Connie have exactly what each of you needs."

He smiled. "You're wrong."

"I'm not. Anyway, I would demand way too much of your time."

"But that's the beauty of us. If we worked together, there would be lots of time. Common goals. Sharing the work as we did." He touched her cheek, brushed a stray hair back away from her face. "You'll change your mind. We're good together." As if she didn't know her mind, when finally she did.

"I won't," she said. But nothing she was saying seemed to get through.

"Listen to me, okay? My turn?" He forced her to face him once more, Michael in the background conversing with the air, Simms sleeping, or resting his eyes, or listening carefully to every word, and Eileen tactfully keeping to her patients on her side of the room. What did she suppose was going on?

"We have a new plan," Sam continued. "I spent part of the last three days calculating it out and now I've spoken with Harry about it. I believe it's safer. Even safe enough for you."

She turned away but he swung her around. "Please pay attention?" he begged. "A fraction of the former amounts of naloxone and nitroglycerine by continuous drip for one hour before we try the Kay-oh-six-six-seven-one-eight-one. Sort of priming the brain. The compound will also be given more slowly, over half an hour's time."

"It doesn't matter."

"There's a patient on his way down now. Valve surgery yesterday. Hasn't waked up. Probably going right in there to that empty space." He walked to the space, turned around in it, a medium picking up psychic vibes, getting a feel for the territory. "Totally gorked. I may be his only chance." He strode back to Lydia, cupped his hands over her shoulders. "Are you with me?"

"No way."

He left her again, he stalked around the empty space, unable to keep still. "He's comatose, he's a goner, he's forty-three years old." He laughed at himself, "I'm really worked up, aren't I?" He couldn't stop moving.

Carlisle Simms coughed, struggling against a plug of mucus. Lydia turned on the suction and worked on unplugging him. She loosened the secretions with squirts of saline and sucked it all out right away, the whole while talking to him, he coughed and choked on the suction. Sam walked back and forth.

Michael had curled up bare-assed again, sleeping with his hand covering his nose, thumb in his mouth. He looked sweet, he would most likely recover as soon as all the infection cleared out.

Sam followed Lydia from chore to chore, watching her, smiling, repeating, "See? Don't you see?" He was at her elbow watching her mix antibiotics when Bristol's voice charged through the automatic door. "Wheeler!" and then Bristol himself.

"Ah, Wheeler, here you are."

Sam turned around but stayed at Lydia's side. Bristol hesitated, then came forward.

"They're sending him down within the hour," he said. "He'll have his CAT scan on the way."

The two men beamed at each other, then at Lydia. "So you'll work on him this evening?" Bristol asked. "Shall I call Culpepper?"

Sam said, "I've asked Lydia."

She rolled a vial of ampicillin between her two hands. "Call Casper," she said. "I'm not working on this project anymore, did you forget?"

Bristol pulled at his beard, massaged it. "Miss Weber, ah, Lydia, we'd be happy to have you back. That's not a problem."

"Yes it is, because I don't want to work on it."

Sam shook his head, Bristol pursed his lips.

"Most people," Bristol said, "considered it an honor for you, a nurse, to participate in these studies. You obviously didn't." He turned to Sam. "I'll call Casper."

"I did consider it an honor," Lydia interrupted. She rolled the small bottle ever faster between her hands. "I was honored to work with Sam on the predictive index. It's the cocktail I can't go along with. The way you pick subjects, the subjects you use, the ways you justify it all."

"I don't need or want a lecture on ethics, young lady. I have taught whole semesters of medical ethics and I don't need a lecture from you."

Lydia was conscious of the air moving in and out through her nostrils. Her heart beat in her gullet and her voice came out a rasp, she barely heard herself. "You two think you can pick human beings to receive the bounty of your great goodness. Your expertise. You think you have a right to decide who is better off better, or better off dead, and who doesn't matter one way or the other. For one success, you'd sacrifice ten failures and you would consider yourselves merciful for easing the failures out." Her hands shook, her arms, the antibiotic fell to the floor, bounced twice and rolled under a cabinet.

"I should have known better than to let you in on this. I should have known you'd be too"—Bristol paused—"too emotional. Emotion has no role in science, except as the subject of control. I'll call Casper. Sam, you speak with the man's wife." Then he was gone, halfway down the hall before either Lydia or Sam moved.

"Lydia my Lydia," Sam sighed. "You'd cut off your nose to spite your face."

"I'm not your Lydia." She stooped to retrieve the ampicillin. "It's not the same thing, anyway. I believe every word I just said." Her legs were trembling now.

"Self-destructive, then. Did you have to say it to Bristol?"

"I don't believe in what you're doing. I think it might be dangerous in a lot of ways. I had to say it, to both of you."

"The cocktail is not demonstrably harmful in any major way. Every patient is closely monitored. You know that."

"And they're all half dead anyway, so who cares?"

"Lydia."

She backed away to return to her chores.

Lydia aspirated medication from the vial with a ten-cc syringe, then injected it into a small, hundred-cc IV bottle. She hung the bottle next to Michael's main IV, connecting it with a needle to the line that entered his vein.

Sam waited in the empty space, while Lydia adjusted the drip of the ampicillin. He watched her discard the empty vial, the cellophane wrappings, the needle and syringe.

"Wheeler!" Bristol's voice mobilized Sam. He approached Lydia.

"That's not the end of it." He stood an arm's length away from her, yet spoke very quietly.

"Yes, it is. I say it is."

"I won't stop trying. You can count on it."

Michael slept with his thumb in his mouth, Carlisle stared at the wall clock. Two patients had visitors feeding lunch to them, and Eileen was just that minute squirting yellow vitamins into an IV bottle already hanging at her third patient's bedside.

Lydia returned to the river. A barge loaded with dirt and fragments of concrete and brick lumbered slowly downstream. Bits of glass gleamed like jewels in the sunlight. Carlisle should see this one.

She saw Sam huddling with Bristol and Casper Culpepper near the central monitor. Bristol slapped Casper on the shoulder and he blushed with pleasure. They all chuckled exclusively with each other in their small ring of privilege.

Lydia pointed a thumbs-up to Carlisle. She rolled his bed up to forty-five degrees, took his blood pressure, rearranged the paraphernalia.

"It's a long haul ahead, Simms. I believe you'll make it. We both will."

With some maneuvering and an extra length of corrugated aqua hose, she got him set up and turned his bed around so he could watch the river for the rest of the afternoon.